THE RAVEN

DANI LAMIA

WITH GWENDOLYN KRESS

This book is printed on acid-free paper.

Published by:
Level 4 Press, Inc.
14702 Haven Way
Jamul, CA 91935
www.level4press.com

Library of Congress Control Number: 2019943916

ISBN: 9781646305131

Printed in the United States of America.

Large print edition.

Other books by
DANI LAMIA

Scavenger Hunt
666 Gable Way

DEDICATION

To my teachers, who encourage me; my friends, who cheer me on; and my parents, whose unconditional love inspires me.

PROLOGUE

The manor loomed empty but for eight-year-old Beka and the Raven.

The creature called the Raven made no sound at all, save for the faint rustling of fabric. Few sounds filtered into the aged wood-paneled hall: distant crowing calls, intermittent scratches against the exterior walls, and the skittering of insects as they fled from the pittering claps of Beka's bare feet on the cold marble floor.

She slipped through the gathered dust, slid into an ornate foyer, and caught herself on the pillar of a rattling banister. The wood broke with a dry *crack*, raining twisted splinters into her black curls. Beka glanced back, face hot, glimpsing the hazy form of the Raven—like a shadow racing toward her, sweeping silently closer with each pounding heartbeat.

A hairline crack in the wall beside her revealed a secret door, and she tore it open, slipped into the dark passageway beyond, lungs burning from her held breath as she pulled it shut behind her, then peered out through a tiny eye in the wood.

The shadow skimmed past her hiding place, darkness blotting out the spare light from the dusty windows, then vanished.

Beka covered her mouth but failed to keep her giggles from escaping.

The passage was too narrow for her to spread out her arms, and the short walls didn't allow for any light. Blindly she bumped into grimy corners and stumbled over the shredded, threadbare rug, the alien pull of the spiderweb tugging at the edges of her skin and straining against her leaf-patterned nightgown.

She careened around a corner and pushed through the half-eaten drapes covering the next doorway. A hole in the wall revealed a reptilian face, ghastly green in the dying moonlight, mouth open in a fanged hiss.

Terror froze her to the spot until she realized it was a stuffed serpent. Harmless.

Beka ducked around the creature and stumbled deeper into what had once been some macabre office, the scent of decay and rotting upholstery heavy in the air. Glassy eyes of decapitated animals followed her every move from their mounts on the peeling walls. She tripped over the shifting folds of the bearskin rug and spilled into a cavernous fireplace, narrowly missing the spearpoint legs of the iron basket protruding from the ash.

Crrreeaaakkk.

Another doorway opened, different from the one she'd entered, hidden behind mottling cloth and set beneath the gaping maw of a moose. Beka recognized the silhouette of the Raven and scrambled to conceal herself in the recesses of the wide fireplace.

Her back hit the rough stone, and several bricks came loose. Eager to escape, to keep their game of hide and seek going, she shoved against them until they gave way, opening a tiny crawlspace barely big enough for her. Beka pulled herself into the strange little tunnel, glancing back long enough to see her pursuer framed by a room of sharp teeth and open jaws. The Raven belonged there, a human-shaped shadow but for two pinpricks of enduring light reflecting from its eyes. The dreams were always like that: part video game adventure, part horror show.

Beka stuck her tongue out at it and scurried away with another giggle.

Based on the Raven's size, it couldn't fit in her crawlspace, but she spied it between the cracks in the wall, looming in the rooms and corridors surrounding her, waiting, watching, whether as a passing shadow or as a still shape peering back at her. As she wriggled through the tight, winding space, her nose itched from the musky scent of ash on her clothes and hair, but she couldn't stop to scratch it.

Finally, Beka found a room without the shadow's looming figure and broke the rotting planks to crawl out from between their claw-like edges. She climbed to her feet, bedraggled and covered with spots of ash and dust, and stared at the empty library surrounding her.

A glass dome crouched distantly above, slicing a beam of moonlight into ironwork cross-hatches that fell through tall rows of empty, cobwebbed bookshelves. A decrepit painting hung over a bone-cold fireplace, three mismatched armchairs faced a wide foggy window, and dark corners collected spiderwebs and triangular shadows.

Against one wooden wall, curtained by streams of hanging dust, sat a dark wooden desk. Thickly built, with cloven feet and floral designs at each corner, only one item rested on its surface—a heavy leather-bound tome untouched by age.

A blood-red silhouette embossed the black cover along with the book's title.

The Complete Works of Edgar Allan Poe.

Beka picked it up and then stumbled back under its weight. A signature scrawled across the inside front cover and a handwritten note slipped from between the pages to flutter to the ground, landing open for her to read: *Compliments of the Raven.*

A sound of a door closing somewhere behind her echoed in the empty room, startling her. She shut the book and hugged it to her chest, searching for the shadow.

No sign of the Raven, but that didn't mean

it wasn't close. Pulse racing with gleeful excitement, Beka grinned and sprinted away with the book, ducking beneath a fallen ladder crossways along an arch and past a massive hall.

Her bare feet clapped on the disused tile of a cold kitchen, and she slipped around a corner—running headlong into cool folding cloth that shrouded a warm body. Two firm hands gripped her shoulders; the dark-hooded Raven stood over her, two reflecting moons of light instead of eyes and . . .

Beka shot awake in bed, legs tangled in the blankets, arms embracing herself.

Dark and familiar, her bedroom seemed eerie in the moonlit night. She took a deep breath, grateful for the smells of soap and laundry and books, not dust or cobwebs or the sour scent of rotting flesh. Her dolls and stuffed animals were the only terrors strewn along the floor. Like every time she dreamed of the Raven,

Beka relaxed into her pillow once she got her bearings, both grateful and dismayed that the dream was over.

She loosened her grip on the black book in her arms.

The Complete Works of Edgar Allan Poe.

Beka yelped, and the book landed heavily on her bed.

The same black tome, the same embossed raven. Real. That part was new. She'd never brought anything back from her dream before. Fingers trembling, she poked it. Yep. Still there. Opened the cover and saw the signature scrawled there like an incantation.

She yanked her hand away and glanced around the room for the creature itself: her pursuer, her playmate, her angry shadow. But the Raven was nowhere in sight.

She was in the real world, with real, still shadows.

A cool breeze swept in from the open window, shivering through her.

And then the book was real, too. A gift from her dream world. A gift from the Raven.

Carefully, as if it might disappear, Beka opened to the first page.

1

Rebekah snagged her backpack from its spot on top of an old pair of jeans and stepped over a pile of comics to grab her clothbound sketchbook from the overcrowded desk. She threw it and a collection of spare pencils into the misshapen canvas bag, snatched her homework folder, and tossed that in for good measure.

"Beka!" her mom called for the third time.

"Yeah!" She zipped up the backpack and pulled her bedroom door shut behind her.

"I fed the cat. We're officially running late!"

Rebekah raced down the hall of their worn-in

house—memories stacked up on top of one another like a pile of old magazines—past off-white walls decorated with off-center photos and dodged around Dupaw, a black cat that tried to trip her before she could reach the great room at the end of the hall.

"Bek—"

She stopped by the black-tile kitchen counter, cutting off Nora's fourth call. Her mother stood by the front door, half a step away from Rebekah's spot by the kitchen and a side step away from the dining room, which was little more than a round table shoved between the front window and the couch.

It was called a "great room," but it was small, the dining-slash-living-room denoted by flattened carpet. The kitchen was tiny, the black countertops seeming to shrink it further, but at least it was sort of open to the dining and living room, and the hallway led off between them to the two bedrooms. Dark and dingy in a way that the sunlight couldn't pierce, like a cave, but familiar.

"I'm here," said Rebekah, shrugging into the straps of her backpack.

They shared the same curls, but Rebekah's hair was black and loose rather than dark brown and taut in a bun, and she stood at least a half foot taller than Nora. At the moment, they wore the same expression, too—identical in emotion as well as the eyes, green and vibrant, remnants of a forgotten lineage—each of them waiting for the other to break first, their game of chicken when it came to being tardy in the morning an old one.

It'd been eighteen years of no one in the house but them and the cat. They knew each other pretty well; or, at least, they knew how to act around one another, what habits to curtail, what reactions to expect. Nora's word was law—an authority she didn't exercise very often—but Rebekah was rarely the one to lose that fight.

True to form, her mother winced and cradled her latest hangover. "Got everything? Your sketchbook?"

"Yep. All ready to go."

Nora shrugged her well-worn shoulder bag and said, "I should have your skirt fixed by the end of the day."

"Thanks." Rebekah had tried to tell Nora there was no need to mend her clothes during the workday but had long lost that fight.

Nora led the way out to the car.

Grant High had been designed by someone who thought highly of him or herself. Expertly bricked, with window brackets and rooflines that curled and filigreed for no reason at all, its slender spires rose as if to consecrate the venerable grounds of the gum-pocked high school. The interiors paneled with rich mahogany, automatic doors gleaming with a fresh coat of overpriced glass-cleaner spoke of the kind of conceit only absurd amounts of money could purchase.

After they parked, Rebekah's mom left her with a "See you later" and headed toward the school, wearing a jacket that bore the same dull crest as on the front of Rebekah's black shirt. They'd arrived early enough for Nora to set up the nurse's office, which meant they'd arrived before the bulk of the students.

The school's manicured front entrance opened from the drop-off lot, a small park filled with brick planters and tall leafless trees, a concrete trail leading to the front doors. A wintry grazing area for teenagers. The overcast sky lent everything a misty haze, a widow's veil draping between the empty branches.

Students weren't allowed inside until twenty

minutes before the bell, so most of them timed their arrival to make a beeline from their fancy cars directly into the heated building. Which meant that if Rebekah found a seat outside, relatively hidden from the direct path, she could avoid pretty much all of them.

She'd long claimed the perfect place: where one of the planters met the cold brick wall of the school, where she could lean back and put her feet up on the benchlike rim. The shrubs playing tenant to the planter acted as a shield, so its power was strongest in the summer when it was vibrant with full leaves.

Slouching behind the dark screen of the empty branches, she could only barely make out the pompous roofline over her, and she could almost pretend she was somewhere else entirely. She pulled out her sketchbook, rubbed her thumb along its grass-green fabric cover, and continued work on her comic.

Rebekah had been working on the same

story about an adventurous cat since she'd first picked up a pencil; at that point, Pluto's long history of tough scrapes and near misses had become second nature to her. Writing about him was as close as she could get to catching up with an old friend. Drawing him was like visiting a different dimension.

Somewhere other than Grant High, with its teens in black-gray uniforms trickling in, tossing balls or posing for selfies. Somewhere the parking lot didn't growl with convertibles and brand-new electric cars, sparkling four-wheelers, and low-to-the-ground sports cars. Somewhere Rebekah wasn't found wanting.

Because there, she was inescapably different from everyone. Even her uniform was wrong, somehow, like there was a secret sort of fashion to wearing a black shirt and gray pants she'd never figured out. She watched them, a slow-growing crowd of similar colors crowned by fancy hairstyles and careful contouring meant to slide under the feeble no-makeup rule. They shouted and laughed and filmed each other, hiding in the heat of their cars, a tiny society from which she'd been barred entry.

When Rebekah was little, being different had never been a problem. She'd worn it like a badge of honor. What had happened to that?

In her sketchbook, she shaded the surface of the moon, the stark light glinting off her one-eyed cat's fur. All four of Pluto's legs pumped as he ran, sprinting—not away from, but toward the people who'd caused misery to himself and his friends, the concrete path of a dark moon-lit otherworld whizzing by beneath him in the action shot.

Rebekah could only dream about having such righteous confidence, such power. The curl of Pluto's cat-smile, the determination in his eye, claws partly extended. Not courage, because he had no fear to overcome. His life was once again in his control.

A hand reached in and snatched the sketchbook.

Rebekah yelped, which earned a laugh. Coralie Rennell, of course. Tall and slender, and daughter of the man the building Rebekah currently leaned against was named after. Coralie had perfect blond hair, perfect makeup, perfect symmetry in her perfect face. She looked like an adult, like an actress, with her thick lashes and pencil-thin nose.

Rebekah's chest constricted with thick darkness, a haunting reminder of sharp words and regrets. A blanket of worn-in dread.

She pushed through the feeling, tried to remember that Coralie was just like everyone else, and so were volleyball-star Andrea and perfect-auburn-hair Veronica, both of whom posed and smirked behind Coralie like backup dancers. Coralie was just another person, a regular human.

A person who liked to thumb through

someone else's sketchbook with a bemused expression, like the drawings were a child's scratchings written in some other language. A sharp pain pulsed deep inside Rebekah for each page turned, each picture besmirched by Coralie's fingertips.

Pluto wasn't something to be shared. He was a creepy comic book hero, not a stupid little kid's story, and he deserved a lot better than having Coralie's contoured sneer cast down on him without warning. Rebekah wanted to rip the book out of Coralie's pale hands, but she couldn't move. Too many instances of being shoved back into the dirt overlapped in her memory.

"Beka's a furry," Coralie announced to her gaggle of long-limbed friends.

Rebekah's face burned. "Don't call me that."

"What, now you hate furries?" Her blue eyes found Rebekah's, aghast in mock surprise. "I thought artists were supposed to be accepting or whatever."

Rebekah snapped her mouth shut. No sense giving them more material. If Coralie knew she hated being called Beka, it would only ensure it happened more often.

"Okay, this guy's cute." Coralie stopped somewhere in the middle and showed the page to her friends. Then she tore the page out, carelessly, watching Rebekah wince. She stuffed the drawing into one crinkling pant pocket and snapped the book closed with her other hand. "The rest sucks."

The bell rang for the first class, and Coralie tossed the remainder of the sketchbook over the planter. It landed in the middle of the concrete path next to the glass-paneled doors, where a mass of students was already headed, where the highest number of feet were guaranteed to trample it before Rebekah could reach it.

Scotty, a tall boy who always had a football

in one hand, called out from farther down the path. "Hey, nice throw!"

"Thanks," Coralie answered with a little wave. To Rebekah, she said, "Oops. I dropped it. You can just get another one, right? Didn't your dad leave you money when he died or whatever?"

Rebekah clenched her tongue between her teeth again to keep from correcting her. At the silence, Coralie rolled her eyes and led her friends away. Taking, of course, extra care to tread on the green sketchbook on her way into the building.

When they were gone, Rebekah raced from the planter and dove for the sketchbook. With it safe in her hands, she knelt on the grass and flipped through to find the page Coralie had stolen, the haphazardly torn edges jutting from the spine like a knife between two ribs: it was the scene where Pluto had been captured by an underworld version of Animal Control.

Yes, it was just a stupid comic. Yes, Rebekah was upset.

Tom Schultz, a B-level bully from her stats class with his blond hair cut into an odd and unattractive fashion, who mostly left her alone, came up behind her, his school uniform too big on his scrawny frame. "Oh, so we got ourselves an artist. Not a very good one. But an artist." He guffawed and went with the flow into the school.

Alice Bedloe stopped beside Rebekah, strawberry hair done up in that day's fresh braids from some online tutorial. The dark uniform made her skin look pasty; slight freckles turned into splotches of color. Despite having parents who could afford to send her there, Alice was generally kind, if sometimes a bit thoughtless. A breath of fresh air among the cloying perfume of Grant High. She wasn't unpretty but she wasn't beautiful either, and, being shy, she kept herself separate from the shallow kids, pre-ferring her own company. And Rebekah's.

"You should report them," she said, in that soft voice she always used when she thought she was right. "Your mom's the nurse, right? You could tell her, and she'll tell someone else."

Rebekah slipped the injured sketchbook into her backpack. "Who, the principal? He's Veronica's dad. Nora would get fired and I'd get expelled. It's fine. That wasn't an important page anyway."

"Are you sure?"

"Yeah, it's fine."

Alice frowned, uncertainty in her eyes, but she didn't argue the point. The two of them crossed through the doors into a blast of warmth and walked to class together, more or less silent.

Despite the "equalizing" uniforms, everyone at Grant High was classist, whether Coralie's outright hatred or Alice's misplaced concern. It wasn't being poor that caused most of Rebekah's problems. It was all the rich people around her who thought it should.

Anyway, it really didn't matter. She could redraw the page if she wanted to; it wasn't like she'd forget what happened on it. Everyone always said to ignore people like Coralie, anyway.

If only things worked out the way those people always said they should.

The school day itself always found both new and old ways to be irritating. Rebekah was okay when it came to the lessons themselves, particularly art, though Mr. Ellison seemed to be tougher on her than everyone else for no reason. But for each class she had alone—or, blessedly, with Alice—there was another with Coralie, or Andrea, or Coralie's not-boyfriend Scotty.

Although Ms. Armen wore a severe bun and a gray blazer made of sharp angles, her English classroom felt like a dark library. Cloud-filtered sunlight from tall windows lost its battle against wood paneling, and a wall of books at the back of the room gave an austere weight to the subject taught there. Rebekah loved books and tended to finish the ones assigned in class before they were due, but the best book in the world couldn't make up for the fact that Coralie sat immediately behind her.

"Do you smell that?" Coralie whispered to Andrea beside her, unerringly just beneath the threshold of Ms. Armen's hearing loss. "Is that alcohol?"

True to her part, Andrea shot back, "I didn't know you could smell the school nurse from here."

Rebekah burned. Posture stiff, she pretended she couldn't hear them. Ms. Armen maintained her lecture, oblivious, jagged handwriting on the whiteboard.

"It's Beka." Coralie's voice held an explicit sneer. "She drags it around with her."

"You know, they say addiction is genetic."

Ms. Armen turned toward the class to emphasize some point about the various definitions of art, something Rebekah would normally have been interested in, but she couldn't hear any of the words over the hot pulse of blood in her ears, the dark, hollow, prickly feeling, like coarse static, that came from being around Coralie.

It was the only class of the day where even raising hands was out of the question. Forget about bathroom breaks. Rebekah already had two demerits for "speaking out of turn" in English; getting three Armen demerits in one semester was one of the easiest ways to land yourself in after-school detention. Rebekah had gone twice last semester and wasn't keen to go again.

The worst part of the entire detention

experience was when the willowy principal, Mr. Bransby, made a point of showing up for the sole purpose of looking over the top of his glasses and tutting at the ne'er-do-wells imprisoned there.

She couldn't draw, or they would laugh. She couldn't complain, or she'd get detention. All she could do was listen to their words and ignore the heavy feeling of dread, like pressure from all sides, immobilizing her.

The class bell rang. Rebekah stuffed her notes into her backpack with a speed honed from three years of practice, stood, and slammed—directly into Coralie.

She stumbled away from the clear disgust on the other girl's perfect face, landing hard on her seat again.

"At least sober up before you get to class." It was practically an announcement, the opposite of the just-quiet-enough whispers from earlier. A series of chuckles from the rest of the class

pummeled into Rebekah, and she sat motionless until the bulk of them were gone.

She should have thought of something to
say, some comeback—but she wasn't aware of
a single problem with Coralie's life.

Payback wasn't in the stars for Rebekah.
That's just how it worked.

2

The outdoor cafeteria, a massive court-yard with a series of heavy mosaic tables and leafless gray-brown trees, salvaged its purpose with the employ of a series of free-standing heaters and umbrellas. The effect was more like a hotel restaurant than a high school cafeteria, but knowing Grant High, that's probably what they'd been going for. At least it didn't really snow.

Alice and Rebekah tended to eat their lunch on the damp cobblestone floor against the outside wall of the art classroom. The ground was cold but not any worse than the seats of the cement tables, and it offered them a view of the tree-pocked courtyard where students sat or tossed a football. Like Rebekah's morning spot, there were enough shrubby planters between them and the student body to provide plausible privacy but not so many to prevent people-watching.

When it was overcast and on-off drizzly like it was that day, the art classroom behind them kept its window shut. On sunny days, even in winter, Mr. Ellison propped the window open, suffusing their hideaway with the sharp scent of paint and primer. It was one of the reasons Rebekah was thankful for the threat of rain.

They and the rest of the students were encouraged to eat at the tables, which were shielded from the rain and the cold and technically had enough space for the modest student body, but Alice and Rebekah had quickly learned they weren't welcome at any table. So they ate their food in peace, at the cost of their sandwiches sometimes tasting like paint.

"Okay," blurted Alice, breaking their quasi-comfortable silence. Energy sparked the blush that spread so easily on her round cheeks. "I have an idea."

"A lot of people have ideas. You're not special."

Alice snorted and smacked Rebekah lightly on the shoulder. "I found out Hector's throwing a party."

Hector was on the track team. More importantly, he was one of Scotty's friends, which made him one of Coralie's friends. Rebekah picked him out, a lean but well-built shape among the mosaic-topped lunch tables.

He had short fluffy hair, and the same black-and-gray jacket as everyone else. He sat back against one of the tables, legs stretched out side-by-side in front of him, as he chatted with two boys who tossed a football back and forth.

Scotty was the tallest of the trio and Eddie the shortest, but Eddie's laugh was the only one loud enough to pierce through the crowd's noise to Rebekah. Eddie's lopsided smile made it seem like he knew a secret, and his uniform was always messy and wrinkled. Like it never got washed.

Scotty was the one in charge. Built like a Dorito—big, broad shoulders and tiny hips—he was on the football team, though Rebekah didn't know or care what position. And the only reason she knew he wasn't dating Coralie was because they would be disgustingly public about it if he was.

They'd be perfect together. Two assholes, creating a little parade of baby assholes.

Hector smacked the football from its trajectory, eliciting laughter and some punches from Scotty and Eddie. Harder but no less friendly than the one Alice had given Rebekah.

"So?" Rebekah focused on the sandwich again. When it was Nora's turn to make lunch, she always prepared the same PB&J; as the only one with access to a microwave at school, Nora was the one who got dinner leftovers, if there were any. Logical but annoying.

Alice tilted her head speculatively. "So . . . I think maybe if we go—"

"No way. If Coralie sees me at one of her parties—"

"No, listen to me." Alice leaned in. "I think maybe if we go, and we like, drink and hang out, they'll see a cooler side of us."

"It won't work."

"Well—then we can take the opportunity to get back at them." She nudged Rebekah, a grin on her face. "Right? There'll be something there we can break. Some drama we can get on camera. It'll be fun!"

It'd be better if the party was at Coralie's place. Rebekah could find something there of hers, something in her room to tear apart. "How'd you find out about it?"

Alice's eyes sparkled. "I have my ways. So? What do you think?"

Rebekah found Coralie at her own table, chatting with Andrea and Veronica, gesturing, a piece of salad waiting on the end of her fork, like nothing was wrong with the world. Beautiful, skinny, perfect, and obscenely wealthy. Everything everyone should want.

Andrea laughed, throwing her head back, her long, athletic torso curving away from the table, and Coralie's grin was practically a leer, but Veronica preened, fixing her immaculate locks. She was probably the one who'd told the funny story.

"How about we hang out that day instead? Like, just you and me."

Alice didn't answer. She didn't look outright hurt but maybe a little disappointed. "My dads wouldn't let us drink."

"Nora wouldn't, either. But I don't care. We can do a puzzle or something."

"Tea and a puzzle. Diametrically opposite from Hector's party."

"Like an ironic protest."

They laughed together, but it felt a little forced.

Rebekah lived about twenty minutes by car from Grant High; she knew the way, but it was a long bike ride, part of it either along a windy road or a shortcut through the forest. On one hand, driving with Nora to and from school saved her the trek and the possibility of running into anyone on the walk or bike ride she might want to avoid. On the other hand, it was pretty hard to conceal the spectacle of waiting around beside the cheapest car in the staff lot for the school nurse to drive her home.

When she finally approached, Nora just asked, "Hey, how was your day?" with a gentle tone that Rebekah wasn't sure was sincere.

"Fine."

"I fixed your skirt," she said, loud enough to

be heard by the students around them. "It's like the tear never happened."

Rebekah flushed. It was bad enough that her mom was the school nurse; it was bad enough they knew she drank. They didn't have to know they couldn't afford to replace a simple uniform skirt. Tom from her stats class with the stupid hair gave a braying laugh and called over, "Starving artists are only romantic if they're dying of consumption, Beka!"

Keeping her eyes down, Rebekah rushed into the backseat of the dingy off-black sedan. Settled in, buckled up, she dug her nails into the aging blue upholstery.

The car smelled like memories, like dust and fabric cleaner. Rebekah saw Coralie through the window, in the distance, walking with Andrea and Veronica toward a bright red convertible worth more than Rebekah's house. Had they heard what Nora said? They were laughing, and Andrea—who had taken off her jacket to reveal colorful ribbons pinning her sleeves up on her toned shoulders, which had to be a dress code violation—stole a glance back at Rebekah. Like they were talking about her.

Rebekah found her eyes drawn to Coralie's pocket. Had she done anything to the page yet? Burned it? Thrown it out? Did she still have it? Had she actually liked the drawing, or had that just been some stupid joke?

She forced herself to look away, out the other window toward the edge of the parking lot, where manicured trees gave way to a forest. Nora commented on the cloud cover, which had come in the morning and refused to leave, but the car fell into silence when Rebekah didn't respond.

The "porch" of their small house was a narrow stoop leading up to the front door, once-black faded to gray. Taking up a quarter or so of the front yard was instead a meager garden, a collection of half-grown tomatoes to be sold or traded with a few other growers in the town. The rest was a messy lawn that did its best to reach out into the unwelcome floor of the narrow street, trying and failing to make up for a lack of sidewalk.

It was Rebekah's responsibility to tend to the garden, which was why the garden hadn't been doing very well. She was generally supposed to do it right before school or, barring that, right after; she'd gotten into the habit of sitting outside with her sketchbook instead, then walking back in later and pretending she'd done it. She doubted her mom didn't notice, but she'd long given up caring. It was winter, anyway. There was nothing in there but spinach and onions.

She sat where she usually did, against the low wall, comprised of whatever bricks or cement blocks Nora managed to pick up for free, which kept the meager crops partitioned from the near-wild growth of the lawn. Once, when she was little, Rebekah had tried to free the garden from its enclosure, to let the plants grow rampant. She'd spent all her strength to move just one of the planter bricks, spilling a handful of soil, and had decided it wasn't fair to fight so hard for so little progress.

She opened the sketchbook and lingered on the missing page, straightening out the tears and crinkles the students had trampled and scraped into the paper. It wasn't a great deal of damage, but, still, tears burned her eyes. She only ever cried when she was alone; she wouldn't let herself shed any tears while she sat outside. It had to wait until she could lock herself in her room.

Some of the houses along her winding street were outlined with chain-link fences, some with hedges; Rebekah's had a wooden fence blocking off the backyard but was open in the front on either side. Their neighbors on the left chose to punctuate the difference between their two yards with tall, leafy trees, but little to no distinction sat between Rebekah's seat among the dry planters and the driveway of the house to their right.

That's why she used to know the family who lived there. She wasn't exactly friends with the boy, well, now he was a man, but she'd been out front enough times to see him and his father coming and going. The father, Bill, was a teacher at the local community college. She'd played with his son, Mike, when they were little, but he was three? four? years older than she was; worlds apart in kid time. He was a cop, wasn't he?

Mike drove up in his unremarkable compact car, and Rebekah watched him get out and carry bags to the front door of his home. Like every other day, he cast her a little wave, grinning under the brim of his bright-blue uniform cap. Black hair curled out from under it, lending him a sort of boyish charm.

She waved back, and he disappeared inside. A wide bay window beside the door looked into their home library; someone sat in one of its armchairs, a shadowy shape out of reach of the sunlight. Probably Mike's father, Bill. Rebekah wondered if he could see her from there.

How would it have looked, a girl sitting on a sagging porch next to a couple of dying plants, crying in the cold over some book? What would Mike and his father think of her?

"Mom," Rebekah said when she came in, tucking her ruined sketchbook under one arm. She knew it was a long shot, but she needed to ask. Needed to hope Nora might understand.

"Yeah?" Nora turned away from the kitchen sink, drying her hands on a towel. She hadn't changed out of her work clothes and had gotten a few droplets of grease on her blouse without noticing. A half-empty bottle of wine sat on the counter. Rebekah didn't know if it was freshly opened or if Nora was polishing off last night's booze.

Stacks of envelopes lined the wall on the kitchen counter. The dishes usually got done, but a few stragglers haunted the rest of the house: a dusty wineglass on the coffee table, a plate smeared with dried jelly keeping a collection of crumbs in the dining room. The carpet smelled freshly vacuumed, but stubborn stains outlined paths from the hallway to the couch, to the TV, to the front door.

It was a house. Just a house, in the regular definition of the term, walls and a roof and food and such. A house Nora spent most of her energy keeping intact.

Rebekah's question suddenly felt stupid. She should either leave it for some other time or drop it altogether.

What would Hector's house look like?

Nora frowned. "What is it, honey?"

Rebekah cleared her throat, glancing at the sketchbook. "I was just . . . wondering . . ."

Chicken sizzled behind Nora on the stove next to a half-empty glass of wine. Rebekah was interrupting. But she'd already started, so she might as well finish.

"I was wondering if I could get a new sketch-book. This one got . . . messed up."

Nora's concern seemed genuine. "Oh, honey, let me see."

The curl of the black counter allowed for only one or two people to cook at a time; not usually an issue in that house, except for moments such as that one when Dupaw decided to launch rocket fast between Nora's legs and race into the living room. Nora caught herself on one of the counters to keep from tripping over the feline health hazard.

Rebekah had been in charge of naming the cat. Her first thought had been Pluto, after the cartoon character she'd modeled from the Poe story, but, in her ten-year-old wisdom, she had been afraid that calling a live cat Pluto might tempt fate to bring an early death. So she'd picked Dupaw instead, like Dupin, rationalizing that he was a very smart little kitty, just like Poe's amateur detective.

Having regained her footing, Nora held the book delicately, like an injured arm, inspecting the binding and the pages. She found the spot where the drawing had been torn out but didn't seem to think anything particularly special about it. With a thoughtful look, she said, "The spine is still good, and only a few pages and one of the covers were damaged. It looks like you can keep using it without much trouble."

Rebekah grew hot. Nora was right, of course. Pragmatic. "Yeah, but—I mean, it's—it looks like I got it out of the trash."

"Honey, it's not that bad. We can clean off the dirt from the cover and maybe tape the inside. You can barely tell—" she glanced back and cut herself off. "Shit, the chicken's burning. Hold on." She shoved the sketchbook into Rebekah's hands and dove to rescue the smoking pan.

"Thanks, Mom." Chest hollow, Rebekah left, heading down the narrow hall.

Of course, it was irresponsible to want to replace a sketchbook that still had plenty of empty pages left. Of course, it would be better—for the wallet and the environment—to just repair what she had instead of getting something new.

But why did Rebekah have to be so responsible every single day? Why did she have to shut her mouth and not give Coralie any ammo or any tears, tape up the sketchbook and water the onions? Coralie was allowed to be irresponsible, say whatever she wanted, spend her time however she wanted. Why did Rebekah have to be perfect all the time while Coralie was given attention and power just for consistently fucking off?

Money, that's why. Having a rich dad who

bought entire school buildings. Having a dad who decided to give a shit rather than walking out on his family before his daughter could even stand.

"Did Dad have another family?" Rebekah had asked once, crossing the unspoken barrier on a day when Nora had been particularly drunk. It might have been an anniversary. "Did he leave us for someone else?"

"I have no idea," Nora had answered darkly, looking off somewhere in her memories, cradling an empty wineglass that reflected the empty bottle beside it. "Never told me a thing, he just up and left one day while you were still crawling. You and me, Beka, we're better without him. Everyone would be better without him."

Rebekah always hated to see Nora that drunk, that deep in a sadness she rarely exposed. But those kinds of days were the closest thing she had to a memory of her father. Those were the days when she felt courageous enough to ask what he looked like, what his job was, if he'd said anything when he left, what he liked to do when he was home. She always got the same answer: We're better off without him. Don't go barking up that tree, Beka.

Then Nora would pour another glass of wine.

Rebekah and her mom weren't poor, exactly—they could eat without struggling, they went out to restaurants on special occasions and bought something fun for the house once a month or so—but all they had was the income of a school nurse and the vague memory of a nobody.

They didn't make enough to afford condescension.

Rebekah composed a text to Alice from her bed. Her window was closed, and her bedroom door muffled the stove's sizzling, so the only sounds in the room were her breath and the inconsistent tapping of her finger on the phone's screen.

I want to go to the party.

She chewed on her lip, rereading those seven words where they sat patiently in the message field. She deleted them, erasing each letter with a tap of the backspace button, and their previous conversation glared into her face: a shared meme and a laugh react. Then she typed out the words again, but they felt insufficient and too complex at the same time, so she deleted them and tried something else.

Let's do it.

Rebekah hit send, and her heart fluttered.

3

The police precinct was a squat, one-story building made of wood and mottled signage, a big space with thin carpet that smelled like a community multi-purpose room—sweat, must, and cheap solvent. Between the intake, the chief's office, and the holding cell in the back, there was barely room for the detective's desk and the conference table. A counter alongside the conference table hosted a coffee machine and a small fridge, making the table inherently a break room and the only workable space left for uniformed officers.

Mike, Rebekah's neighbor, came in for his break, sci-fi novel in hand, and saw a clump of his fellow uniforms around one end of the table, howling with laughter, some eating snacks or sipping from bland white mugs. He recognized a couple of them from the academy, but the rest were older, and yet they all functioned as a clique together.

Centered in the lot of them with his feet up on the table sat Dempsey—short and muscular like he'd been at the academy. A rookie, like Mike, but still, somehow, he had managed to command their attention, urging them all to laugh at some story he'd told.

They'd been working for the precinct for the same length of time, but only Dempsey had earned their respect.

Mike pretended he didn't hear them, didn't see them, or at least didn't think it was anything remarkable. Instead, he hid his novel behind his body and poured himself a cup of coffee, trying to puzzle out where he'd gone wrong.

A simple answer sprung up: Maybe he just hadn't tried enough.

It was possible. He could forget about people and get lost in his work. It'd happened more than once. He knew that about himself. The simplest things could be the easiest to miss; maybe it wasn't as complicated as he'd made it out to be. So maybe he needed to try again, or harder.

By the time he had his own unmarked mug of watery coffee, a different officer had started telling her own story. Mike walked over, found an empty spot, and listened.

Her eye caught on him, and she stopped. The others glanced his way, too, or pulled out their phones, pretending they hadn't seen him at all.

He felt those gazes in the pit of his stomach.

Dempsey snorted. "Go read your book, Officer Mike. You don't have to stoop to our level if you don't want to."

Oh. They thought he was pretentious be-cause he liked to read. It was so much worse than he had expected. His hand tightened on the novel he'd apparently failed to hide un-der his arm.

"My name is Wilson," he said, arguing against what was probably the least important part of what Dempsey had said, and then he left be-cause he didn't see any other option.

Lesson learned.

Rebekah waited for Alice on her front porch on Friday. She had a purse with her—big enough to hold her green sketchbook and a change of clothes—a faux-velvet bag she'd gotten as a present during middle school. It looked . . . all right. It'd probably be fine to take to the party.

Anyway, she could get Alice's opinion on it.

With a bit of time to kill, she thought about taking out the sketchbook, but instead she found herself hugging her jacket around her while staring through the front windows next door. Mike wasn't home yet, but she thought she saw someone in the front room: a vague shape through the window, sitting quietly in an armchair. She couldn't see who it was well enough to be certain they weren't staring right back at her or reading or playing on their phone.

It was likely Bill, Mike's father. Rebekah remembered him mostly in the backdrop, standing apart while she and Mike played street racer or whatever they'd gotten up to.

She hoped Mike realized what he had. She didn't know if his parents were perfect, but she had a feeling they wouldn't wave off his departure from the house while refilling a glass of wine.

A little hatchback named Apollo turned into Rebekah's driveway. Alice waved brightly from the driver's seat.

Apollo was messy, the backseat crowded with papers and forgotten notebooks, but otherwise well cared for. Her parents had gotten the car for Alice, a nice, safe choice, brand-new, as a reward for getting her license and having decent grades.

Rebekah tried to imagine getting an entire car as a reward for something other than a game show or lottery. If she hadn't already been inundated with the shit that went on at Grant High, she would have thought it ridiculous.

Rebekah and Nora's house squatted on one of the many suburban roads littering the crevices of the town's valley, but Alice lived farther up the mountain. Not quite enough to get regular snowfall, but enough for a view, since the house occupied the crest of a hill with jaw-dropping views on every side.

It was, despite the way that it made her feel small and useless, one of Rebekah's favorite places. When the sun set and painted the sky in pinks and oranges, Alice's house stood out against the trees like the subject of a painting.

Rebekah had tried to capture it a few times from the yard, but Alice didn't seem to understand her fascination, so she avoided bringing it up in conversation.

They finally pulled up a long, winding driveway to the two-story house with white wooden paneling. Alice left the car out front because the three-car garage only had room for her dads' cars and a pottery workspace, and—like every other time Rebekah had been here—she led the way to the front door without glancing up once to the sights around her.

One of Alice's fathers, a muscular middle-aged man with round eyes, waved at them from a brightly lit kitchen as they passed. Alice led Rebekah too quickly past to be sure, but it looked like he was trying to figure out how to bake bread, up to his elbows in off-white dough. If Alice hadn't told him Rebekah was coming, then at least he didn't seem very concerned.

She thought of Mike's parents again and got

that same sharp sensation, a dry soreness in her chest.

Alice's bedroom was twice the size of Rebekah's, with a window that faced out along the valley. Wispy-thin branches cast skittery shadows in the tall grass of her stewarded backyard while beams of sunlight swept inside and illuminated the browns and pinks of the room's decor. Alice bustled directly to her closet and pulled out handfuls of clothes, laying pieces out across the soft pink duvet of her queen-sized bed.

"Okay," she sighed, surveying her choices. "I was thinking about this blue one." She picked up an odd-shaped shirt with misplaced frills, and it took Rebekah a moment to realize it was specifically off-the-shoulder rather than an unusual collar. "And my black skinny jeans. But do you think that's too plain?"

She paired the items, covering up a number of other tops and bottoms.

Rebekah shrugged, feeling out of her depth. She knew almost nothing about fashion; it was one of the few reasons she felt grateful about attending a school that required uniforms. She'd brought the only dress she owned but started to wonder if she should have Alice pick something out for her instead. She hadn't been to a real party since middle school, and she doubted the experience would be at all comparable.

"I think it looks cute," Rebekah tried.

"You know what?" Alice turned and grabbed a black jacket from her closet. Was that leather or faux leather? She placed it around the side of the shirt and said, "Yeah. I like that."

"It covers up the shoulder."

"Yeah, but then if I take it off, I think the effect would be cooler." She set the items aside, then clapped her palms together and faced Rebekah. "Okay! Your turn!"

Suddenly Rebekah didn't want Alice to see the year-old dress Nora had made her wear to her grandmother's funeral. It was plain: black silky fabric, probably not real silk, that went down to Rebekah's knees. At the time, she'd liked the fishnet-like lace it had instead of sleeves, but now she couldn't stand the idea of wearing it to one of Coralie's parties.

"Um." She dropped her faux-velvet purse to the floor next to the bed. Maybe she shouldn't take that, either. "Can I borrow something of yours?"

"Of course!" Alice swept her arm across the selection on her bed. "What do you think?"

There was a storefront's array of choices. Shirts in various styles and colors, a couple of pairs of jeans, and several skirts. It wasn't the kind of ludicrous wardrobe some rich people kept—the kind Rebekah assumed Coralie had on display in a bedroom-sized walk-in closet—but, still, it was more than she'd expected.

"What do you think?" Rebekah asked, trying to sound unconcerned.

"Well, I don't know. I haven't been to a lot of high school parties." Alice pulled out a red shirt with an unfamiliar logo. "What about this one?"

Rebekah owned a jacket in the same rocket-red color. She'd considered bringing it and wished she could have had the courage to wear it but had chickened out and left it behind. It was too bright, too attention-grabbing, too certain. If it weren't for Nora's hard-ingrained frugality, she probably would have thrown it out or given it away a long time ago.

She said, "Isn't red kind of eye-grabby?"

"Well, if you want to impress them, then eye-grabby is good, isn't it? No big deal, though. This one's nice."

Alice replaced the red shirt with a long-sleeved gray one, where the uneven bottom hem slanted from the hip to mid-thigh. There was no pattern or logo but a slight sheen that came from the interweaving of some metallic thread.

Rebekah considered it. "Yeah. Yeah, I like that."

"This should go with jeans. I think that hem would look weird with a skirt." Alice put it aside and pulled out two pairs: a loose, dark-blue set and a smaller, faded pair with fashionable holes in the thigh. Rebekah hadn't known Alice to wear anything like that, but honestly, she hadn't really hung out with her too often outside of school uniform or pajamas.

Rebekah said, "Let me see if the faded pair fits."

"I was just thinking that." Alice pushed the shirt and jeans into Rebekah's arms. "I'm going to hunt around for a jacket."

The bathroom was attached directly to Alice's bedroom. It was tiny, but it was dolled up like Alice herself, all brown-pink with painted stencil patterns on the wall after some online fashion.

The clothes were a touch big but still a pretty

good outfit as far as Rebekah could tell. She turned in the mirror, frizzy black curls and a gray shirt that stuck in some places and fell loose in others, denim fitting oddly on her hips; she looked as inadequate as she felt.

They shouldn't crash Coralie's party. It was a terrible idea.

"I found this black scarf!" Alice called through the door. "It looks warm enough to function as a jacket. How's it looking?"

"Fine." Rebekah opened the door. Alice had taken the opportunity to change and looked cute in the shirt and dark jeans; a lot more like she was headed to a party. But she looked Rebekah over, grinned, and handed her the scarf. "Try that."

The only thing Rebekah could do was put on the scarf, tying it at her chest to trap the heat. Alice beamed like a child playing with dolls, proud of her creation.

Rebekah said, "Alice, I'm not sure—"

"You have to try this new makeup palette I got." She pushed Rebekah back into the bathroom and helped her take off the scarf again before fishing out a thin box, bright gold-yellow with silver highlights. Alice opened it to reveal rows of eyeshadow in a wildly colorful array, each with stranger names than the last. "Isn't it cool? It's Georgia Sun's latest collection. It was only on sale for, like, a second before it sold out. Come on."

They started on the long business of applying makeup, if "they" meant Alice doing her own while pushing foundations and blushes at Rebekah that were worth more than what she ate in a week. She kept up with Alice as best she could; she hadn't put makeup on in a month or more, and most of her experiences came from middle-school sleepovers. And she'd only done one or two of those.

Her attempts weren't complete failures, judging by the scant amount of times Alice corrected her or offered advice. By the end of the adventure, Rebekah had more money on her face than Nora kept in her wallet, and she found herself standing awkwardly while Alice put her own hair up in a different but equally complicated set of braids as earlier in the day.

"Do you think I should do my hair?" Rebekah asked, for lack of anything else to say.

"No, I think yours looks really good down." Alice glanced over as she worked. "It's full and curly."

They fell into silence again. If Rebekah wanted to call off Operation: Attend a Grant High Party As If It Sounded Fun Rather Than a Special Sort of Hell, she had to do it right then.

Instead, she stood silently while Alice put up her hair. She pulled the scarf on again, then tied it back over her chest.

It wasn't like Coralie or her friends could think any less of her than they already did. Or maybe she could avoid them completely and just have fun at the party. There would be a lot of people there, and everyone knew each other, but some people at Grant High didn't care about Rebekah at all. Maybe she could hide behind them until it was over.

Maybe she could try getting drunk. Everyone else seemed to like it.

"All right," Alice sighed, checking her phone for the time. "Are you ready?"

No, Rebekah tried to say. Instead, she nodded, fiddling with the end of the scarf.

"If we leave now, we'll be late. Perfect. Let's go."

Alice led the way out of her room, nearly skipping with anticipation. Rebekah grabbed her phone and followed, leaving her purse on the floor behind her.

4

—

Hector's house made Alice's look like Rebekah's.

Two tall stories, a Roman palace of right-angled confidence and long-pillared contempt, pressed into an unwilling spot on the mountainside. Its grand entry boasted a haughty arch that stood open, spilling dance music like a gas leak with a stuttering bass heartbeat. Flickering colors of light fought against the sunset, casting an array of undulating shadows from the open-top convertibles and lifted trucks that filled the circular driveway. Teenagers crawled amongst them, laughing in the beds of the trucks and chatting from the doors of the convertibles. More of them littered the lawn, and Tom from Stats class had his ass stuck in a piece of topiary. However he'd gotten there, he didn't seem to mind, wiggling his butt then holding up a plastic cup to clack against a friend's.

Then he caught sight of Rebekah and Alice and smirked. "Hey, it's the starving artist and her benefactor. You wanna paint me? You know you never seen an ass this pretty!"

His friends laughed and they all clacked their cups again.

Rebekah wasn't supposed to be there. She could feel it in the cold wind that wicked through the heat that radiated from the entry, she could smell it in the wafting mixture of alcohol and e-cig vapor. Rebekahs weren't allowed in that place, and weren't invited or welcomed. A gazelle strolling toward a lion's den.

She turned toward Alice but stopped the words in her throat; the light that glinted coldly from the hoods of cars seemed to sparkle in Alice's hazel eyes. She lit up with some new energy Rebekah had never seen before, something that glowed from beneath her skin. Something like hope.

"Yeah?" Alice asked, red with the flush that came so easily to her round cheeks.

"Yeah. Let's go have fun."

The house's grand entry opened into a mess of bodies, disjointed lights decorating a field of skin and cloth and laughter. Guests stood in pairs and clumped along the grand staircase. Grant High rarely afforded the opportunity to dress up, and by the short skirts, heels, and bold logos spiked and curled around folds of cloth, it was clear everyone had taken the chance to show off. Feeling underdressed, Rebekah followed Alice between them, flitting in her wake like a bug hiding in a shadow.

They passed between the weight of two tied-back curtains and found the center of the party:

a mincemeat dance floor that pulsed with the music's oppressive beat, hair and cloth flowing back and forth in rhythmic echoes of one another. Rebekah pressed back against the wall to avoid contact with a couch-table overflowing with filled and empty cups. She and Alice edged into the open-concept kitchen, a mob dominating the space.

The wraparound kitchen was a bigger, flashier, better version of Rebekah's: a circle of white marble instead of black tile, wide enough for ten or fifteen occupants rather than just two and a cat. Taking up the middle was a vast island, big enough to provide prep space for a feast—and all accounted for by bottles of alcohol, mixes, chips and snacks, stacks of paper plates and cups. There was an entire plastic tub, identical to the wide one Nora used to store every single scrap of fabric she owned, three-quarters full of some half-ice, half-bright-green concoction spotted with chunks of fruit. Written in old Sharpie on the side of the tub were the words "AT YOUR OWN RISK."

With an odd, goofy grin on her gentle face, Alice took up the long handle of the ladle waiting in the tub and poured out a scoop or two into a Solo cup, certain to get a few chunks of passionfruit. She handed the cup to Rebekah before serving herself.

It smelled like alcohol and sugar. Rebekah was willing to bet there were few other ingredients. She couldn't hear Alice's words over the music that blanketed the space, pressing up against their ears, thrumming on the white-paneled walls; but they tapped their cups together with a hearty thump that vibrated into her hand, and they drank at the same time, daring one another to be the first to lower the cup.

Rebekah had tried alcohol before but only sips of Nora's red wine. The toxic-looking punch was sharper, somehow, and the sugar seemed to make it worse, like an acid pretending to be syrup.

A sparkle drew Rebekah's attention to the dancing crowd across the towers of snacks, and there was Coralie, glittering in silver, casting her gaze over the room like a prison searchlight.

Vibrant green At Your Own Risk Punch spat out of Rebekah's mouth, making Alice yelp. A miracle kept her from spilling any of the drink on Alice's clothes, and she laughed until Rebekah dragged her down to hide behind the counter.

"What?" she whispered, protecting her own drink from sloshing over the plastic rim.

"Coralie's here."

"Yeah, I know. Isn't that half the point? Come on."

She started to stand, but Rebekah dragged her down again. "I don't know about this. What if she does something?"

"What if she doesn't even notice us? There are, like, a million people here. Anyway, come on. We can't let them control us, right?"

There wasn't a way to argue against that. Rebekah let Alice drag her to her feet, hesitating at the crest of the sleek marble countertop to search out Coralie again. There she was: tall, graceful, sparkling. She danced next to Andrea, who wore an elaborate braid to rival one of Alice's, and whose booty shorts and crop top made Coralie's clubbing dress look mature and elegant. Coralie seemed, thankfully, to have locked her searchlight gaze on one spot across the room: the place where Scotty stood talking to Hector, both of them in jeans and brand-name tees.

Veronica appeared between Coralie and Andrea, pulling them both into a selfie, her vibrant hair an enviable backdrop. She hadn't done anything to it; voluminous, wavy, and a lovely auburn color that shone in any type of light, it was already perfect. They fell into a comfortable three-part pose, duck lips and pleading eyes, then Coralie flicked her hair as she located Scotty again.

She hadn't seen Rebekah.

"Okay." Rebekah determinedly sipped at the acrid cocktail then raised her cup toward Alice in a slight salute. "Following your lead."

"Let's go check this place out. Come on." Alice grabbed Rebekah's hand and pulled her out of the kitchen.

Hector's house was a maze of grandiose rooms. The leather couches and armchairs had long since been claimed, and the coffee tables and end tables teemed with red plastic cups. A weak evening breeze from a tiled hallway in the back tried vainly to counteract the rising heat of the dancing bodies, but there were too many of them, a cloud of laughter underlined by techno beats. The ceilings were higher than usual as if to accommodate not only the house's family but their egos as well; and Hector was the only one who seemed to fill the space properly, a track star with legs like stilts and a demeanor that puffed out the space around him. He was easy to find because he was ubiquitous, refilling the alcohol in the kitchen, micromanaging the music, encouraging the dancers, and wrapping his arm around Scotty to nod meaningfully toward Coralie.

Not only was he the host of the party, but he was actually trying to *host* the party.

What if he saw Rebekah?

Alice, reading into her worried gaze, pulled her into a side room—no, an entire second living room for some ungodly reason, which had the same music but slightly fewer people. She found a spare spot on a marble-topped coffee table, iron feet curled into decorative florals, and set down her drink so she could start dancing.

Rebekah had never seen her dance. They'd messed around before, dancing together beside a Bluetooth speaker when a particularly good song started on Alice's hangout playlist, but that was always filled with giggles and lackluster gyrations, ending in more embarrassed laughter.

Her round face was beet-red, maybe with embarrassment or just with the courage it'd taken them to walk in there, but when Alice let go and started to dance, she transformed into a completely different person. Someone who didn't care about everyone else. Someone who was just happy to exist, happy in her body, enjoying the moment.

Oppressive envy curled cold in Rebekah's chest, but when Alice motioned for her to join in the dancing, hope shot through it like a spear of light.

Was it possible for her to be like that, too? There was only one way to find out.

Rebekah took a determined gulp of the At Your Own Risk punch, set it down on the coffee table beside Alice's, and tried to dance.

Rebekah's heart sped up, thumping anxiously to the beats of the music. She laughed, half nerves and half disbelief, and Alice grinned at her, and they danced together. After a few moments, something unlocked, and Rebekah started to move more unselfconsciously. A new warmth spread from her chest out through her limbs. There was no one else around except Alice, no sounds except for the electronic beats of the music.

And it was fun.

She spun in place, moved her hips and shoulders to the rhythm of the song, snapped to the beat. Alice laughed, maybe at herself, or at both of them, or at the whole situation at once, and Rebekah joined her; and just for a second, everything made sense.

"Oh, my God," Alice laughed. "What is Eddie doing?"

Andrea had migrated into that second dance room, free from Coralie or Veronica, apparently so she could dance with her eyes closed. Shifting lights and smartphone camera flashes shone from the bare skin of her thighs and stomach, and Eddie stood leaning against the fireplace behind her, his elbow almost knocking over one of the plastic cups resting there.

He had his phone out, apparently recording her dance, and let out a loud whistling catcall. She turned, no longer oblivious to his gaze. Rebekah would have burned up or melted away, but Andrea posed for the video before performing some hyper-athletic dance move. When Eddie tucked away his phone, he put his finger and thumb to his mouth like he smoked a phantom joint, then gestured away down the hall. She followed him without a single word exchanged.

Alice snorted and they laughed together again.

Rebekah felt bizarre. That was the only word for it. She'd stepped into an alternate world, somewhere she knew she wasn't allowed access, and could see what regular Grant High kids did. Could see what it was like to be born into that rarefied space.

One song ended and another started, staccato high notes off-beat from the bass, and Rebekah spotted a free loveseat beside the doorway to the kitchen. She pointed it out to Alice and they settled into it together, taking a break from the music. Rebekah relaxed, really relaxed, for the first time since she'd agreed to the party.

"Hey, are you going to dance?" asked Coralie's voice.

Rebekah froze, but Coralie wasn't in the room with them. Belatedly, she realized the words had come from the kitchen behind them, talking to someone else.

"Not tonight," said Scotty.

"Come on. One dance, with me. You must have seen me call you over."

"Yeah, I saw you."

The silence after that line was palpable. Rebekah met eyes with Alice to see that she'd heard the same thing.

"We've known each other since kindergarten." The tone was icy-sharp as if she were talking to Rebekah. "You know me. If you have some kind of problem with me, tell me what it is."

"It's nothing. I just don't want to dance."

"You don't want to dance *with me*. Say it."

"I'm not going to lie—"

"So you do want to dance with me?"

"Cory, chill out."

"You've been avoiding me all night. I've been waiting for you to ask me out for two years, I finally bring the heat to make it happen, and you're avoiding me."

"Did you even think about asking me what I wanted?"

"We're *supposed* to be—"

"We're not supposed to be anything!"

Rebekah covered her mouth. Other people

had started to notice the fight, glancing over from their spots in the spare-living-room dance room to try and get a glimpse.

Scotty continued, "You have this whole thing built up in your head, but you never once talked to me about it. We grew up together. You should know me better than that."

"There's someone else, isn't there?" Coralie asked, voice low but not low enough to avoid being overheard. "Tell me who she is. I want to know who you think is better for you than me."

"God—not everything is about you!"

Something slammed and footsteps retreated into the distance toward the big dance room. There was a chorus of *oooohh*, a crowd admitting its guilt in eavesdropping, and then a clicking of heels as Coralie took her exit from the kitchen.

Toward Rebekah.

She turned to put her back to the kitchen doorway and bowed her head, trying her best to look unremarkable. But that put Alice's face in perfect view to anyone behind her, and seeing one made the other perfectly identifiable, and the heels stopped with an astonished, "Beka?"

Rebekah turned around. Coralie's makeup was somehow both extravagant and perfect. Only she could put sequins along her eyes and pull it off as a mature look. She'd even placed sequins on her bare shoulders, perfectly patterned to trail off at identical points along her arm.

Rebekah tried to tell her not to call her Beka. She opened her mouth and tried to demand it, but no noise came out.

Coralie took the cup out of her hand and smelled it, raising her eyebrows to somewhere between impressed and disbelieving. Then she leaned closer, and Rebekah froze, expecting some remark, something that would shoot through to her soul.

Maintaining eye contact, Coralie poured the cup of At Your Own Risk directly onto

Rebekah's crotch. Rebekah jumped from the shock of the sudden cold, but Coralie didn't cease, emptying the entire the drink, ruining both Alice's jeans and Hector's loveseat. With no regret whatsoever she said, "Oops." She dropped the empty cup to the ground and pronounced loudly, "Oh, my God, Beka. Did you piss yourself?"

Everyone saw it. Drawn to Coralie's fight, they'd been watching. But they acted along or somehow fell for it, gasping and pointing. Rebekah froze, muscles locked in place like their gazes were iron pikes skewering her to the spot.

Coralie's smile was pure malice as she slipped away.

Alice tried to clarify the truth, the hopeless optimism of using a pebble to dam a roaring river current. Laughter drowned out her voice, and the rectangular glare of phone cameras glimmered from every direction in mockery of her attempt.

Rebekah felt like liquid. Like her body was made of something other than her, speared through from all directions, an effigy of the monumentally stupid. Rebekah's chest constricted and, for a moment, the other party guests seemed to disappear, the glare of their phones gone. In their place was the desolate cold of midnight, a wash of unnatural air that prickled the skin.

Rebekah mumbled to Alice that she'd be right back. Then she got up and pushed past bodies with their leering mechanical eyes.

She'd known it was a bad idea from the beginning. She'd let Alice talk her into it, even though her friend couldn't have predicted how bad it could go, how low Coralie would stoop to make Rebekah's life hell.

Rebekah ran until she found a door that didn't have people near it. It was a spartan bedroom with an attached bathroom, the suite reeking of carpet cleaner and Febreze; Rebekah locked the door behind her, grabbed a wash-cloth, and tried to dry her pants.

It was hopeless, of course. Even if she could get the dark splotch to fade—unlikely—the damage had already been done. In the solace of the restroom, Rebekah started to cry, her efforts shrouded by dancing blotchy smears, the hot pressure in her face as if everything Coralie had ever done was trying to squeeze out through Rebekah's eyes and nose at the same time.

She gave up on the pants and splashed water on her face before she remembered her make-up. She cursed and grabbed the At-Your-Own-Risk-scented hand towel to dab at her face, inspecting the damage in the mirror.

Not too bad. The mascara didn't even run. Maybe Georgia Sun had experience of her own with crying in the bathroom. Whatever. Feeling drained, Rebekah rinsed the towel in the sink and pressed it against her cheeks, welcoming the chill; she was probably removing the blush, but it wasn't like she needed it. Her entire face had turned red.

It would be fine. It was bad, yes, but it wasn't too much worse than any other day. Rebekah had already been relegated to the floor under the art classroom window. Everyone already ignored her. This wasn't any different from that. All she had to do was leave and go home and hug her cat and disappear under the covers of her bed forever.

She should never have come. She should have trusted her instincts.

Rebekah had opened the door, ready to duck out and head for the exit, when a voice stopped her. "Oh, uh, I didn't know—"

Scotty stood in the bedroom, startled at the sight of her. Without Hector and Eddie at his side, he looked smaller, more like a person and less like some Hollywood jock. His dark brown hair stuck out in all directions like he'd been running his hands through it.

"Beka. You all right?"

She froze. He knew who she was, didn't he? They all did. She was Beka, the weird girl, the nurse's daughter. He hadn't seen what Coralie had done, but the splotch was still on her pants. Her face burned and she couldn't find any words.

"You look like shit. What happened?"

What was he doing? Why wasn't he laughing?

She forced some words out, gesturing at her pants. "I, um, spilled my drink."

"I can see that—"

The door burst open again to reveal Eddie, phone in one hand and a drink in the other, a dark stain on the shoulder of his fancy-branded shirt. She should have known he'd be nearby. She should have realized members of the pack rarely traveled separately.

"There she is! Check it out. Beka pissed herself!"

She had to leave. There were people behind him, shapes in the doorway, but it was the only exit. Panicked, she shoved through them, heading for where she'd left Alice.

"Watch it, piss bitch!" Eddie called after her.

Lovely. A nickname.

"Piss bitch! Where are you going?"

Because everyone hated her and because they were drunk high schoolers, the jeers caught the nearest half of the party, and soon the entire multitude had joined in. "Piss bitch!" "Where you going, piss bitch?" "Yo, piss bitch!"

Rebekah couldn't physically feel anything. Her body had turned numb, awash in its own heat. She marched into the crowd, grabbed Alice where she stood beside the loveseat, and pulled her toward the exit, moving like a puppet on strings. Someone with voluminous red hair recorded her as she left. Laughing behind the screen of her phone.

The shouting devolved behind them into whoops and laughter.

5

By Monday, the videos had made the rounds on campus. The resulting attitude toward Rebekah was startlingly unchanged, except for the boys' new propensity to shout "Piss bitch!" whenever she walked by.

Despite that, she what she'd been through wasn't really that bad. There were stories online of bullies shaving people's heads, shoving them upside-down into garbage cans, calling them slurs or throwing things at them, making sexual gestures—or more than gestures. What Coralie and the rest did to Rebekah, comparatively, wasn't a big deal.

So she ignored the calls, ducked her head, and walked past.

"We could sabotage her senior project," Alice suggested, leaning back against the cold brick wall of the art classroom. The day was overcast again. Chilly and damp, with paint-free sandwiches.

Rebekah snorted. "Like that would do anything to her. Anyway, it isn't just her. It's everyone."

"Everyone didn't pour a drink on your pants."

"No, but they laughed at it."

It wasn't just incidents like that, though. It was the way they looked at her, like they knew she didn't belong. The way they'd trampled thoughtlessly on her sketchbook. No one paid any attention at all to Alice, so she remained oblivious to most things. Their malice they saved for Rebekah.

If some of the students at Grant High hadn't noticed Rebekah before the party, they definitely noticed her after it. At their individual tables they felt more hostile than usual, crouching over the mosaics, casting furtive glances. One of them, a girl with a button nose and messy hair, covered her mouth when she accidentally caught eyes with Rebekah. She was from English class, one of the ones who'd snickered at Coralie's joke about Rebekah being an alcoholic.

But . . . then there was Scotty. He hung out where he usually did, sitting backward against the tabletop, chatting with Eddie and Hector under the heat of a lamp. But he hadn't laughed at the party. He had actually looked concerned. He hadn't joined in the taunting.

She watched him, talking and laughing like normal, and felt something almost like hope.

"Any plans this weekend?" Alice asked, trying vainly to pretend it all wasn't a big deal.

Rebekah looked at her food again. "No. Maybe a bunch of reading. Or help Nora with the housework."

"We should hang out, like we were going to. You could come over, maybe do a puzzle? Really low-key."

Rebekah's first reaction was to turn Alice down. She just wasn't in the mood to sit in someone else's house and pretend she felt all right, not after what'd happened on Friday. But when she glanced over, she saw kindness in Alice's eyes. Sure, she was oblivious and accidentally classist sometimes, but she was genuinely a nice person. And like she'd said, it would be low stakes. A puzzle. She could do that.

"Yeah," Rebekah made herself answer. "Yeah, that sounds like a good idea."

After lunch, Rebekah stalked alone through the narrow hallways toward her locker. Everyone noticed her, but no one saw her, tracking her progress through the school like some kind of natural disaster.

When she reached her locker, she saw that someone had broken the lock. Great. Had they stolen her backpack? Why? There was nothing remotely valuable in it.

She pulled the door open and a sharp, acrid smell billowed out from within.

Urine. The smell was urine.

Her books and backpack were discolored, pages wrinkled, a sticky pool congealing around the crumpled papers at the bottom. It dripped along the back wall of the locker and was scattered throughout, soiling everything.

Someone had pissed in her locker.

Rebekah stumbled away from the creeping stench, heart pounding in horror, but it reached toward her anyway, grasped at her. She felt it settle onto her arms, her clothes, her hair, tagging her, mocking her for what she'd attempted to be.

Someone said, "Oh, my God, is that piss?" and before Rebekah could process Veronica's voluminous hair behind a smartphone's camera, she had the attention of the entire hall.

Laughter crept in around her. Rebekah felt herself grow hot. The crowd had appeared from nowhere, shrouding out the dark walls, the long windows. Everyone knew what had happened; they were laughing at it. At her. Had they planned it? How many of them had been at the party? The noise echoed from the crowded metal lockers, piercing through the smell and pounding into her head. Urine was on her books, seeping through the thick fabric of her backpack and wrinkling the pages of her sketchbook. Why hadn't she taken it to lunch?

Tears stung her eyes. She started to shake. She couldn't cry there, in front of everyone; she was stripped bare enough already, their surrounding stares prickling her skin, closing in on all sides.

Rebekah turned and ran, ducking through a gap in the gathering crowd and dodging around the lanky figure of the school principal, Veronica's father. She panicked that someone would clutch at her—she saw Coralie and instinctively leapt past to avoid being tripped—and hurtled into one of the heavy crash doors and down the hall.

Resounding laughter followed her, hunted her, chased her long after the sound had faded away.

Rebekah headed by instinct toward the nurse's office but realized that she didn't want to face her mom any more than she wanted to face Alice or anyone else from Grant High. She didn't break pace, running right past the office, down the grandiose entrance hall, out the automatic double doors, past her planter and the wide lawn, and off campus.

Echoes of laughter snapped at her heels as she ran, the cloud of stench that'd wrapped around her, the pool of urine that'd soaked through her sketchbook. Everything Pluto had done since she'd started at Grant—gone, ruined. The page Coralie had ripped out would be the sole survivor, if it even still existed.

She'd biked to school only a few spare instances in her time at Grant, days when her mother had been too sick to go in to work. She knew the way, but it was just far enough to make it frustrating and difficult, with tall hills and isolated paths through the gray husks of late-winter woods.

She hadn't biked that day, so she sprinted as long as she could then slowed to a jog, bursting into another sprint whenever her mind turned—which was every new moment—to the smug, pointed laughter of the students in the hall, the glare of phone cameras at the party. The cold didn't touch her; she steamed in the wild air, leaving a path of heat in her wake, leafless branches stretching overhead.

Why couldn't they leave her alone? Why did they hate her so much? What had she done to them? Why did they get to laugh and take photos, videos? Rebekah lost in panic as she watched everything she cared about get fucked by some anonymous dickbag. Why did they get to do all that? Nora was going to come home with armloads of piss-soaked books and a plan for cleaning them, and Rebekah would have to finish out the year with home-cleaned piss books and the glittering, mocking smiles of everyone else in the class.

Who had thought of doing that? Why did they actually carry it through? How could they hate her that much?

When she got near home, her own street felt eerie in the middle of the school day. Quiet.

She didn't notice that Mike had parked his car and was heading toward her instead of his front door until he stood in the street in front of her with concerned eyes and a crisp police uniform.

She tripped to a stop in front of him, panting heavily, too aware of the tears on her face, as she tried to reorient herself.

"Hey," he said softly. He was taller than she was, with thick black stubble, his kind eyes blue-green in the even light. He reached for her. "You all right? What happened?"

She had a flash of him grabbing her arm and smelling some stranger's urine, so she jerked away on instinct. The front windows of his house. His parents could see her if they were in there, and they usually were, when they were home. What would they see?

Mike backed off, showing his hands. "I just want—"

She did what she should have done to begin with: completely ignore him and run for the spare key hiding on the porch. The longer she waited to shower, the worse it would be. The worse everything would be.

"Beka?" Mike called after her, but she slammed the fading black door behind her.

Panting, she dodged Dupaw, who tried to get between her legs, stormed into the bathroom across the hall from her bedroom, and turned the shower as hot as she could. She threw her uniform into the garbage, stepped under the spray, and leaned heavily against the wall, glaring at the white tiles, listening to the water spatter against the shower curtain.

She had run away from school. Nora wasn't going to like that, even given the reason. A stranger could piss in her locker, but Rebekah couldn't ditch school.

There, alone in the scalding water, she allowed herself to cry.

She sank to the floor, giving in to her exhaustion as steaming droplets pelted her with a calming heat. She became a puddle, melting in the corner between tiled walls and folding into herself.

The laughter had followed her even there, echoing in the narrow space.

She ducked her head to drown out the memory, but it dogged her, mocking her. Everyone had been delighted by the spectacle, everything of Rebekah's drowned in someone else's urine. Had they been gathered around to start with, knowing what would happen? How many of them had been in on it?

All of them. All of them had been in on it. The sea of faces and phone cameras, bright eyes and vicious expressions, that shrouding, viscous stench pervading the hall. Even if they hadn't known about it ahead of time, they were all in on it.

Rebekah tried to dissolve into the corner of the shower, but she couldn't get away from the memory of that smell.

* * *

When her arms were raw from the heat and the scrubbing, Rebekah had to assume she'd gotten the stink off. In all likelihood, none of the actual urine had physically touched her—but she could still detect it. She had the feeling she'd be smelling it for a while, no matter how long she spent washing it.

She turned off the shower and found a towel—a dim gray one, thin as a T-shirt, and her least favorite—but at the moment, she couldn't bring up the energy to care. Numbly, she wrapped it around herself and found a spot on the floor in her bedroom where she could curl up and feel sufficiently small.

There was nothing she could do to make them back off. Coralie, her friends, the rest of the students; torturing Rebekah was a game to them. Even if her father sauntered back into her life with bushels of cash, and she could suddenly afford her own car and the best brands of makeup and those shoulder ribbons the girls all seemed to like, they would never let up. It was its own game, Who Can Torment Rebekah the Most, and so far, the asshole who'd come up with the dastardly plan to piss in her locker was winning.

Now that they knew they could get a dramatic rise out of her, their games were only going to get worse. Wasn't that what people always said? Maybe not. There was so much advice out there about getting bullied, all of it mixed up in Rebekah's head. Besides, whatever the kids at Grant High had against her wasn't just bullying. It couldn't be. It was way too personal, too vindictive. They were repulsed by who she was; it had nothing to do with their own internalized whatever.

She didn't want to face them again. Ever. She

barely wanted to move. She didn't want to face her mother, much less Alice, who would never get it, or Mike, who didn't even know her. Who else was there?

No one was actually Rebekah's friend on purpose. She and Alice had come together because neither of them had other friends on campus. But Alice didn't really care about her; she never texted unprompted, asking how Rebekah was doing, not even so much as a "What's up?"

No one would notice or care if Rebekah disappeared. Not even Coralie, who'd find some other game to play without batting an eye.

Rebekah ducked her forehead against her knees, coiling herself as small as she could, like she could just wink out of existence. She wished it could be that simple. To just not have to deal. She wanted more than anything to not have to think anymore, to not have to go back to school ever again. She braced herself tighter, gripping her legs, tense, but she'd cried all her tears already, so all she did was sit there in a pounding silence.

Dupaw meowed. Beka lifted her head, blurry-eyed, to see the black cat climb into the space between her thighs and stomach. She choked a laugh and gripped him in a hug. He headbutted her and ran back into the hall, leaving her cold.

Exhausted, Rebekah surveyed her small room, the trampled carpet, the empty walls. She'd absentmindedly stepped over piles of comic books and dirty laundry strewn on the floor and sat on a shirt without noticing. She wished she'd closed the door, at least—there was no telling when her mom would find out what had happened, and Rebekah needed to know she wouldn't suddenly be staring at her from across the hall.

Her door had a lock. Her windows faced Mike's house, but they were already closed and the blinds drawn. If she shut and locked the door—and jammed a chair under it for good measure—then she'd be completely alone, completely free to lie face-down in her pillow and suffocate.

She stood up, pain spiking into her over-worked legs. Her towel fell off because she hadn't bothered to tie it, but she was alone, so nothing mattered anyway, and she stumbled across the short distance to close and lock the door.

The feet of the desk chair scraped a path along the floor when she dragged it over and wedged it under the knob. Didn't feel like enough. Maybe she could shove some heavy books in front of the door or something for extra protection. She reached over and grabbed the biggest book on her shelf, nearly stumbled under the weight, and bent down to drop . . .

The Complete Works of Edgar Allan Poe.

A chill rolled through her. Distant memories

of an imaginary friend she'd forgotten. She'd lost that book forever ago. How had it found its way back? Had it always been hiding on her shelf, a blind spot in a sea of mess?

Rebekah drifted her fingers across the embossed red raven on the cover. Carefully opened the first few pages.

There it was. Poe's signature, just where she remembered.

She'd loved the book. Had read it cover to cover, even though she didn't really comprehend a few of the more verbose stories; she'd loved those even more because reading them was like dreaming.

Suddenly Rebekah needed that feeling. Needed to remember what it was like to love that book, to bury herself in the strange words and stranger feelings, to dive into an unapologetically dark world.

Delicately, she rested the night-black tome

on her bed, then took the time to towel off properly and change into pajamas.

When she was dry, she tucked herself under the covers, hefted the book, and opened the cover.

That night, Rebekah had a nightmare.

6

Deathly still air, the numb silence of a held breath. Sharp branches of twisted trees grasped for the starless sky, like corpses straining for the faintly remembered glimmer of life.

Rebekah walked along a dusty path. Her bare feet sank into the plush earth as she wound quietly between twisted bark and gnarled root, releasing a miasmic aroma of rot and soil with every disturbed step.

The mansion at the end of the path struck her with a cold familiarity. She knew the overlapping boards, the spires piercing the darkness, the air like a mouthful of dust, but at the same time, it felt like she'd never seen it before. The narrow windows squinted down at her. The crawling carvings of animals with stone and wooden heads regarded her from their perches. The entrance stood partly open, a long shadow leaking from between the high doors.

Every detail of the house watched her approach, waiting, like a great cat crouching in the weeds.

She stopped, unable to force herself any closer to the shadow that loomed in the doorway. The still air pressed in around her, as if the darkness itself spied on her from every direction. She felt exposed, vulnerable to the straining branches and whatever creatures lurked beyond their broken silhouettes.

A long time ago, that had been a play place of hers. A hideaway, an invisible clubhouse, nothing more. Had the place changed, or had she?

A flicker in one of the windows, a shape passing out of sight. Someone was there, someone who had seen her. Her breath caught when she saw it again in a different window. It was too far to have moved so quickly—but she knew it was the same thing, the same creature. She blinked, and it disappeared.

A steady groaning churned from the interior of the house, rhythmic, like steps on sagging wood, moving steadily toward her. The groans grew progressively louder, a series of explosive sounds in the dead quiet.

A shadowed form shot out from the door—a pair of glowing white eyes like cold stars looming over her.

Rebekah shot up from her bed.

She panted, heart thundering, the echoes of a shout ringing in her ears as her bedroom faded in around her. Stark moonlight cast her floor into a mess of alien figures, illuminating one side of books and comics and forgotten dishes only to stretch out their silhouettes into misshapen shadows on the other. She felt a frigid chill and realized her window was ajar, letting in the cold night breeze.

Rebekah swung her legs off the bed, intending to close it, but her hand landed on the Poe book. Thick, heavy, bound in black leather, the stylized embossing of a raven on the front cover. She picked it up and ran her fingers over it, the silhouette of the bird with its closed beak and bowed head.

The feel of it calmed her. The weight of it. She studied it, and her fear subsided; but it wasn't quite the same feeling as coming off from a nightmare, the comfort of realizing it'd only been a dream.

Instead, it was a hazy collage of memories: the mansion, the creature, running over cracked floors and through overgrown hallways, beneath the crisscrossing boughs of dead trees. In those memories, the mansion was . . . it was her escape. It was of her, and for her, and it was creepy, but in a fun way. Like an inside joke. Like playing the part of a ghost inside a haunted maze. It was a dangerous place, rings of knives all pointed inward, like an eel's mouth; but it would never swallow her.

Rebekah flipped again through the pages, eyes lingering on distantly familiar couplets, and a wave of relief washed away the last of her apprehension. That book, that mansion . . . they were dark, and sad, sometimes overwhelmingly grievous or frightening, but they were hers. They belonged to her heart.

Holding the tome close, exactly as she had when she was little, Rebekah laid back on the bed and lost herself in the words until she fell asleep again.

The next morning, Rebekah dug through her closet, a graveyard of toys and stuffed animals, until she unearthed a pink corduroy backpack from elementary school. Determinedly, she cut the cartoon character off its pencil pouch and repaired it with duct tape.

The kids at Grant already thought she was shit-poor and worthless, so looking the part wouldn't make the situation any worse, and using a duct-taped backpack would be better than using the pissed-on one that probably still sat in a gross puddle at school. Her textbooks had been ruined, but her grades weren't great anyway, and Alice shared most of the same subjects; she might be able to lend a couple of books. Rebekah salvaged some notebooks and folders from her half-used collection of middle- and elementary-school materials and crammed them into the pack with a pair of cleaning gloves and a folded-up trash bag.

After a moment's hesitation, she put the Poe book in there, too. It more than doubled the weight of the small pack, but something felt wrong about leaving it behind.

Nora tried to talk about the incident—of

course she would have heard about it, she worked there—but her shallow words of concern or commiseration meant nothing when, in the end, she was only really thinking about the cost of the ruined textbooks. Rebekah ignored her and pushed open the front door. She wanted to get to school as soon as possible.

Dupaw appeared from nowhere and launched into the lawn; he ran nearly to the edge of the property then laid down abruptly, rolling in the damp grass. Nora cursed and pushed past Rebekah, but her approach startled the cat farther away. He jogged toward Mike's car, confident in his freedom—until Mike stepped out from behind it and swept the cat into his arms.

"Who's a cute little kitty?" Mike asked the cat as he walked back toward Nora. Dupaw tried to escape, claws digging into Mike's shoulder, but Mike blocked his progress with an expertise that could only come from years of cat ownership. It bothered Rebekah that she couldn't remember him having a cat at all.

"Thank you, Mike," Nora sighed as she pulled Dupaw off his shoulder. "Oh, your uniform! I can fix that for you tonight."

Mike checked the small hole in his jacket shoulder and waved her off. "No, it's no big deal. I promise. What's the little guy's name?"

"Dupaw," Nora answered.

Rebekah added, "It's the name of a detective. Dupin. It's a pun because cats are smart."

When Mike met her eyes, Rebekah blushed, feeling stupid. She shouldn't have said anything—well, she should have named the cat something normal, but it was too late for that.

"I insist," Nora continued. "Come on by with that jacket whenever you want. I can fix it in just a few minutes. If you hadn't been here, Beka and I would have been worried sick over Dupaw all day."

Dupaw meowed again, trying to escape,

but Nora clung onto him and braved a kiss on his head.

Rebekah chewed on her lip. She didn't miss the distinction. They would have been worried sick over Dupaw because they would have gone to school anyway. Heaven forbid they skip a day to ensure that a member of their tiny family didn't get run over by a car.

Nora nodded toward the door. "I'll put him inside. Thanks again, Mike."

"No problem," he said as she disappeared into the house.

For a moment—only a spare moment—Rebekah and Mike stood alone together on the lawn, the threat of rain looming above them. His expression filtered into a concerned look, and Rebekah froze because she knew he was thinking about yesterday. Had he been able to smell it? Could he guess what had happened—or did it matter because the story would soon be spread throughout the entire town, if it hadn't already? She glanced toward his front window but couldn't see anyone sitting in the armchairs on the other side of the glass.

He smiled again. "I'm glad you're all right."

A sharp wave of relief caught Rebekah by surprise. She couldn't think of anything to say. Then her mom was there, waving toward the car.

"We're going to be late," said Nora, which wasn't exactly true, but it was close enough. "See you later, Mike."

"Yeah." He looked only at Rebekah.

Rebekah flushed again, waved like an idiot, and followed Nora into the car. She slouched in the passenger seat until they'd pulled out of the driveway, face burning.

Why did she always do the wrong thing? Why couldn't she have said bye?

Whatever. Okay. She thought through her game plan: She was going to have a good day. She was going to be seen around school, totally unconcerned, having the time of her life.

If anyone mentioned yesterday, she'd wave it off or ignore them. The fuckers at Grant High were going to have to go without the satisfaction of witnessing her emotional breakdown.

She just needed to clean out her locker before anyone else got there.

Grant High's front doors were monitored for students coming in more than twenty minutes early, and Rebekah didn't want to co-opt Nora's side door; so, keeping an eye out for the meager security staff, she snuck around to the opposite end of school.

The theater was as ostentatious as the rest of the school, all gleaming facades and ornate front doors, its brick walls coated with awards, donor plaques, and posters for upcoming and past performances. It was also, by necessity, open directly to its own parking lot. The front doors were always locked, but the drama kids tended to leave the side door ajar for their own purposes. Rebekah let out a breath when she saw the abused rubber flip-flop serving its sentence at the doorjamb in question.

When she pulled the door open, she hesitated, listening to the school at large. No alarms, no mutterings of students collecting early. She slipped inside and let the door close again on the shoe, navigated the racks of costumes and randomly assorted furniture that had accrued in the small room, and used the theater to get directly into the school proper.

Why couldn't students go inside early, anyway? What if they didn't have a choice but to get dropped off before the doors opened? Why force them to sit outside in the cold?

Rebekah beelined for the hallway that hosted her locker, moving as silently as she could, waiting at corners for instructors to pass. She had no idea how many—if any—security officers might be pacing the halls in the early morning, but she hated the thought of being seen there at all, let alone getting sent to detention.

The last thing she needed was Principal Bransby's pretentious disapproval. It was bad enough he'd seen her humiliation firsthand.

There it was. Her locker, innocently nestled between all the others. Someone had closed it.

Rebekah raced to its side and fished out the gloves and trash bag from her childhood back-pack. The books had disappeared overnight, but she'd been planning to throw everything out anyway, so it wasn't a loss. Everything with even a splash of urine on it—which was every-thing left in the locker, pencils, pages, notes, trash—went into the garbage bag, including her whole backpack, which she threw in with-out opening.

Including her sketchbook. *Good luck salvag-ing that, Nora.*

Rebekah rinsed the inside and outside of the locker with a massive collection of wet paper towels from the nearest bathroom, washed it thoroughly with hand soap from the dispenser, and rinsed it again.

The squeak of a sneaker on polished wood. Rebekah glanced up and froze at the sight of a security officer she didn't recognize—some woman with thick arms and a sturdy build, chin-length brown hair. Her uniform was a knockoff of the one Mike wore every morning.

The security officer saw Rebekah at the same time, and her hand went to her radio; Rebekah could only sit and watch, waiting for a report of her failure, waiting for yet another fucking thing to go wrong.

But the security officer's eyes flicked to the locker, then down the hall, and there was a stroke of recognition. With a sad little smile, she let her arm drop and said, "Get outside as soon as you're done, all right?"

Rebekah nodded silently and the security officer turned to leave. What was that expression, that strange smile? It was coldly familiar.

Pity. The security guard had pitied Rebekah.

Her face burned with shame as she went back to work.

The locker was as good as new before the twenty-minute mark. Good. Great. Rebekah threw away the gloves and spent a few extra minutes scrubbing her hands and arms raw again, then went outside before she had any chance of being caught by early-arriving students.

Through the front doors, brazenly, because they were closer, and she just didn't care anymore.

Her sketchbook was gone—completely gone, far beyond anything Coralie had condescended to do to it—so Rebekah pulled out the Poe book to read instead once she'd ensconced herself in her usual spot. At that point it wasn't important that she continue the saga of Pluto the One-Eyed Cat, and it was paramount she be seen minding her own business as though nothing at all had happened.

7

Rebekah wound up doodling all day, aggressively not paying attention in class. She didn't have any of the books, anyway. Without her old sketchbook, she made do with the margins of a black middle-school notebook, starting with sketches of Pluto, because he was easy and familiar to draw, but it felt wrong then. Pluto was dead. She'd buried him with the other piss-soaked garbage in one of the bigger trash bins in the courtyard.

Instead, she found herself sketching out some of the scenes from her dream from the night before. The way the trees had twisted around themselves, the shadow with glaring white eyes flicking out at her from the front door of the house. It gave her chills, but she welcomed them. It was something she could focus on, something that wasn't the stares of all the Grant High kids.

And it truly was all of them. They stared and laughed, giggling while glancing up from their phones. Of course. News of what had happened—and at least one video—had made it all through campus. Probably all through town by then, or at least the other schools in the area. Everyone knew exactly what had happened, and if anyone had any doubts, those could be assuaged by the propensity of shit-stain Grant High boys to point at her in the hall and call out, "Piss bitch!"

People online said teenage boys were like elementary school kids, but it was another thing to see it firsthand.

"Hey," Alice said near the end of lunch, her

voice gentle like Nora's had been earlier. "I saw the video."

"You and everyone else in the school. Can we talk about something else?"

"Yeah, but—I heard some people talking. They know who did it. Scotty Trucco."

Scotty. She remembered standing alone in a bedroom with him, the pure concern on his features. Cold speared through her. No. No, that couldn't be true. Scotty was supposed to be different. He'd . . .

He'd what? Looked at her once? Had a fight with Coralie? That wasn't exactly hard to do.

Alice continued, unabated, "We should do something about this. Talk to the principal—"

"He won't go after Scotty Trucco without proof." It wouldn't surprise Rebekah if Principal Bransby regularly played golf with Scotty's dad. She recited an applicable line from her morning's reading. "But see, amid the mimic rout, a crawling shape intrude: a blood-red thing that writhes from out the scenic solitude."

"Um." Alice regarded her for a second, then lit up as if Rebekah hadn't spoken. "Let's do something to him ourselves, right? Let's take the door off his locker. We just need some pliers—"

"No." Rebekah sighed, thinking of the gore that ended the same poem that'd come to mind. "Just drop it. I'm trying to. By the way, can I borrow your English and history books?"

"Oh! Sure, of course. Um, but I need them for homework . . . maybe we can trade them back and forth."

"That works." She regretted bringing it up.

Alice focused on Rebekah's drawing. "Oh, a Pluto Halloween special?"

Rebekah stood, stowing the notebook and replacing it in her arms with the Poe tome. She got up and left without another word.

Alice meant well, but she never seemed to do well.

A clump of boys had the video playing loudly on one of their phones by the automatic door to the hall, hitting one another on the shoulder and whispering details of the story when they noticed her. She recognized one of them from one of her classes: Tom, from stats, his hair cropped in that weird fashion she didn't understand. "Poor starving artist can't even afford a toilet!" he barked, then gave a honking laugh and his friends joined in.

How proud was Scotty of what he'd done? He was certainly getting acclaim for it, if that's all he'd wanted. Everyone had already known his name—Grant was the sort of place where it was impossible not to know everyone by name—but he had gained even further admiration as The Boy Who'd Made Rebekah His Piss Bitch. Was that everything Scotty had dreamed it would be? Had he accomplished what he'd set out to do?

Had he realized he'd come across like a

human being at the party and wanted to make sure she knew he hadn't meant it?

Rebekah paused when she entered the hall. Scotty stood at the opposite end, framed by Hector and Eddie, a triad of idiots silhouetted in black against the dark-paneled walls, all of them laughing as he rummaged through his locker.

She pictured him tearing open her locker, pissing against the walls, broad shoulders pressed in. Why had he done it? Why, if he'd thought enough of her to notice she wasn't okay at the party? If he hadn't joined in the taunting?

How could he do that to her?

Scotty had a pretty face and fetching dimples, so everyone let him get away with shit. He happened to meet Rebekah's eye, and there was something in his expression, something almost like regret, but he looked away before she could make sense of it.

The end-of-lunch bell rang and students

flooded the corridor. Coralie, Andrea, and Veronica walked past the boys, allowing Coralie the time to mutter something Rebekah couldn't hear. A catcall whistle followed and someone jostled Scotty; Veronica made a little wave at Hector, then the three girls were gone. The boys erupted into laughter again. Whatever look had been in Scotty's eyes was gone, replaced by an awkward mirth, a preoccupation with something more important.

Rebekah's grip tightened around the Poe book. Why did he get to laugh and mess around while she had to wear a duct-taped backpack and borrow textbooks from the only person at school who'd give her the time of day? Why did she have to be so responsible when no one else did?

Scotty shouldn't be allowed to get away with that.

* * *

"Want to watch a movie tonight?" Nora asked, colorless trees blending into gray mush through the car windows. "It's been a while. We should do something."

"No, it's fine." Rebekah wasn't in the mood to talk, and, regardless of her intention, she knew for a fact that Nora would wind up trying to talk about what had happened. In fact, since Rebekah turned down the movie, she'd probably cut to the chase and bring it up right then.

Right on cue, Nora glanced into the rearview. "I can help, Beka. I know how insular the staff looks at Grant High, but I can find the right person to talk to."

And what, tell them what happened? Everybody already knew what happened. Even if you could find someone who didn't know, bringing more people into the fold was hardly an answer.

Rebekah tried to shrug it off; she tried to say the words *It's not a big deal,* but they refused to come out of her mouth. So she just said, "No. Thanks."

"Well, I'm here if you need me."

Her heart thumped with a painful jolt of gratitude. Nora was a lot of things, but unkind wasn't one of them. It wasn't her fault there was nothing she could do.

When they arrived at home, Nora headed purposefully for the door like she usually did, ready to carry out her list of tasks for the evening. Rebekah took her time, grabbing her backpack and pulling her hood up to ward off the gentle rain that'd finally decided to fall. Then she saw the clump of cars in the driveway next door and paused halfway to the door.

Both Mike's parents were home? That was unusual.

Rebekah hesitated long enough to peer

through the bay window, and she saw them all sitting in that front room reading their books.

Why did it make her feel so sour? Just because she didn't have it didn't mean Mike wasn't allowed to. He should take every scrap of happiness he could find.

Rebekah went inside, closed herself in her room, and buried her nose in the Poe book again.

The stories there were messy, dark, and unapologetic. They were complicated even when they were simple, metaphorical even when they were prosaic, and even though they had nothing to do with her, Rebekah felt like nothing understood her better.

The manor stood over her the same way it had last night. Like it'd been waiting for her, hungry for her attention, aging in its own dust until she dreamed again.

The woodgrain of the heavy front door

fluttered beneath Rebekah's fingertips. The hinges produced an unearthly groan when she pressed forward, a scream of sound echoing through the long, empty hall within. She tensed, waiting for something to scamper toward her out of the darkness, hesitating between the too-still forest watching behind her and the chambers yawning before her, exhaling a warm breeze.

She stepped inside and the door moaned shut. Its iron lock thudded into place, reverberating down the long corridor, which was covered in burnished wood paneling with narrow crosshatched windows letting moonlight in from either side—a physical impossibility—slanting both ways along the hall, illuminating the hanging dust, outlining mismatched stark rectangles on an otherwise black rug.

Rebekah walked slowly through it, hyper-aware of herself. The squares of moonlight slipped over her skin as she passed. Up ahead, the windows stopped and sheer darkness began, but she couldn't seem to get any closer to it. When she glanced back, however, she saw no moonlight at all, only a long corridor dim with shadow and shrouded as though in fog. The house had closed itself around her.

When she turned forward again, she saw two reflective eyes glistening in the indirect moon-light. As Rebekah stared, the rest of the crea-ture's shape settled around it: a dark hood, a cloak hugging its form and twinkling dimly, like the oily sheen of black feathers. It stood tall over her—and yet it seemed to wait on her somehow, watching her, leering with an animal intelligence.

One hand emerged from the darkness be-neath its cloak and beckoned her closer, the curling finger of a leather glove. Something shone on the back, a filigree of red embroidery, before the hand disappeared again.

The creature turned its back to her and all

but vanished against the shadows of the enduring hall—only its footsteps padded softly against the aged rug. The windows' shutters clattered together in unison, swallowing Rebekah in pitch.

She woke with a start, her heart in her ears, her blanket twisted around one fist. Her eyes hunted her bedroom for a confused moment, then landed on the Poe tome that rested on the nightstand, where she'd placed it after hours of reading. The embossed red bird seemed to glimmer on its cover, illuminated by the real moon.

The Raven. Rebekah couldn't believe she'd forgotten about her imaginary friend. It was a creepy thing, invented by a creepy little girl, but it wouldn't hurt her. It was her creature, and it lived in her dreams. She remembered playing with it. She wouldn't let herself fear it.

Rebekah took a long, deep breath and forced herself to release the tension in her shoulders. The sinister place she'd dreamed up around the

Poe book had once brought her nothing but adventurous joy, and she resolved to discover that feeling again.

She picked up the book and opened it to the title page to admire the signature. She'd read a few more pages before going back to sleep.

The panel of unblinking statues guarding the foyer broke only for a descending staircase carpeted by plush red cloth. The steps were uneven, and as they wound steadily down—increasingly canting to one side to create a disquieting twisting sensation—the carpet thinned eventually to tatters, coming apart in pieces and betraying the cold brick of mortared stone.

When the stairs relented their downward spiral, Rebekah stepped into a low-ceilinged dungeon, suffused with the dampness of moss and earth, a choking stickiness to the thick air. The walls and floor were made of the same thick stone, but their lines seemed to pulsate in her vision.

The Raven awaited her in the middle of an empty room, blocking the exit behind it. Patient. It took stock of her, flicking its bright eyes up and down her body before it stepped smoothly aside and gestured with a wave of its cloak to the dark stone archway beyond.

Rebekah paused as she walked past, close enough to examine the creature she had once called a friend. It was silent—as always—and bore no visage beyond the shape of its body and the reflective glint in its eyes. Still, it exuded patience to her. After all those years, it continued to be her friend.

The Raven cast her a nod, a slight, sharp movement that was nonetheless familiar. Acknowledging her just as thoroughly as she acknowledged it.

She crossed through the archway.

A massive cistern lay beyond, the walls and

roof stretching into a smooth, high-ceilinged dome. A narrow bridge led out to a wide circular platform surrounded by a pool of still, stale water of such a depth that the green of its slimy algae gave way to a vast darkness beneath.

Wooden racks of tools outlined the platform, surrounding old, stained tables and chairs. Chains hung from the distant vaulted ceiling, some bearing hammers and wicked blades, others unadorned but still thick and heavy. Sickly yellow light filtered through the grated circle at the very top of the dome, the indirect glare of some dying bulb; there was no indication any heavenly eye could so much as glimpse the depths of that dungeon.

In the perfect center of the room was the largest of the tables, long and broad and thickly built, with tough leather straps nailed to its surface at intervals. The straps had been secured tightly around the body of the table's occupant: a broad-shouldered teenage boy with dark brown hair, a bare chest, and old red sweatpants. His eyes were wide and wild with fear, muffling panicked breaths against the strap secured firmly over his mouth, and he struggled anew against his restraints—but they were secure enough that he could hardly shift his weight.

Rebekah stopped at the edge of the platform. "Scotty."

Scotty Trucco's eyes flicked over to her as well as they could, straining against the brace that held his head still. He released another *Mmf* against his gag, and his skin puffed pink where he pulled vainly on his tightly bound straps.

The Raven drifted in behind Rebekah, a silent hooded wraith moving as comfortably on that torture platform as she did in her own bedroom. It strolled along the racks of tools, inspecting them: a clawed hammer, a selection of wrenches in order from large to small, several handsaws of various lengths. It selected, with all the delicacy of a chef procuring the correct knife, a set of rusted hand pliers.

It then turned toward her and bowed slightly over Scotty's head, eyes on her, proffering the pliers—not to her, just showing her where they rested in its black-gloved hand.

It was asking her for permission.

Rebekah approached the table, slowly, voice caught in her throat.

There were no parents or teachers, no cadre of laughing friends. There was no gulf of clout or money separating them. There were no free passes. Scotty was a boy strapped to a table—leather straps groaning in protest of his struggles, countless words muffled against his gag—a boy who'd lied to her, let her think he was different, let her think he was human, before he literally pissed all over her life.

The Raven cocked its head, its eyes fixed on her. It wanted to do that for her. It wanted to do it because it wanted to help her.

Rebekah nodded.

Scotty struggled anew, and when the Raven unhooked the strap that acted as the gag, he begged, "Please, make it let me—"

The Raven gripped his mouth open with the firm fingers of one gloved hand, pinning his tongue against his jaw, and Scotty's plea twisted into a garbled yelp. The Raven carefully braced the corroded pliers around one of Scotty's canines.

Scotty started screaming, desperately, high-pitched in terror, his echoes multiplying against the cavernous walls. Suspended in the moment, half-turned in the pale light from above, Rebekah was able to make out the dim slope of a nose buried under the Raven's shrouding hood.

With a forceful, wrenching motion, the tooth tore free. Scotty's screams sputtered as blood leaked into his mouth, spitting reflexively into dark clots on his chin, the clumps congealing on the table's surface. The Raven stepped back, slipping its arms back under its shiny cloak, and the only life in the room was the carnal agony of Scotty's writhing body, the hiccoughing, garbled inconsistency of his panicked breaths.

The Raven offered Rebekah a deep nod, then disappeared into the shadows.

8

___

Rebekah sat up in bed, cold in the breeze of the window she'd accidentally left open, surrounded by a nest of thrown-off blankets. It had felt so real, like a lucid dream. The textures, sounds and smells, had all been so vibrant. Like life inside a painting.

It had felt good, too, in a visceral way. Like she'd finally found a way to stoop to Scotty's level and get away with it. It hadn't been real, but . . . a small part of her wished it had. She pulled the Poe book into her lap again and thought of the end of that poem from earlier: *The seraphs sob at vermin fangs in human gore imbued.* But maybe they wouldn't if the humans had been the ones to turn on the vermin.

She was ready for school and had Dupaw's food in the bowl by the front door before her mother woke, and even found time to put some toast in the oven for both of them. Nora paused in the entrance to the hall, blinking, as though waiting for the apparition to melt away.

"Good morning." Rebekah scratched Dupaw behind his ear. He purred loudly, even as he wolfed down his tuna-flavored food.

"Morning," Nora echoed, watching uncertainly from where she leaned against the counter. "How are you feeling?"

"Well enough," said Rebekah in all honesty, and took the two steps back into the kitchen to check on the toast. "I'll be fine. They'll move on to something else soon enough."

Nora frowned. "Okay. As long as you're all right."

Rebekah hesitated, watching Nora's eyes.

Red in the corners. Had she drunk more than usual last night? There wasn't enough time to make coffee for her.

Rebekah removed the toast, opened the peanut butter, and didn't correct her mother's implication. She wasn't sure she was "all right," or anywhere close to it, but she felt a lot better. In its own way, the Raven had certainly helped.

In the long quiet stretch before school began, Rebekah settled into her nook at the base of the ostentatious walls of Grant High and drew in the lined middle-school notebook that had become her new sketchbook. She turned the page from her patchwork of Pluto doodles and instead started drawing the Raven, its reflective eyes, and the glossy featherlike surface of its cloak. It was tough to draw—the strange quality to its shape and movements had such a dreamlike tint to them that it didn't translate well to paper—but it was comforting to try. As though the Raven itself might be able to leap off the page to her defense if she needed.

"Hey." Alice was bundled up in her school-issue jacket. She'd arrived weirdly early; she was usually in the habit of sprinting out of her car directly into the classroom, but today she'd come in enough time to chat. And, apparently, she'd decided to do it awkwardly, watching Rebekah like Nora had that morning. Like she was some unpredictable animal or something.

Rebekah scooted over, dropping her feet to the side of the planter to make room. Alice accepted the seat, dropped her backpack to the grass at their feet, and pulled out her English textbook.

"Here," she said. "We can trade tomorrow morning. How's that?"

Rebekah accepted it and slid it under her notebook. "Thanks. Really. I just don't want to ask Nora to buy more books. She's . . . you know, busy."

"It's so weird you call your mom by her name." Alice nodded to the notebook. "That's spooky," she remarked, clearly trying to avoid talking about something else.

"I had a cool dream last night. What's up?"

"Nothing. I mean—" She chewed on her cheek like she always did when she thought she might hurt Rebekah's feelings. "I just decided to come early today."

Being pitied was an understandable consequence of getting pissed on.

Rebekah stowed the textbook next to the Poe tome in her backpack to buy herself a bit of time. It was a nice thought, but being alone in the morning was one of her favorite times of the day—

A set of hand pliers, lightly rusted with red rubber handles, rested snug against the Poe book, as casual as an errant pencil, stark against the malleable folds of the bag.

Stomach dropping to her toes, Rebekah pulled them out to make sure they were real. The handles were comfortable in her grip. Familiar. For a moment, all the world's sound grew buzzy and indistinct, numb against her skin except for the slight pressure of the tool in her palm.

"Yes!" Alice leaned in, touching her shoulder. "Let's break into Scotty's locker and steal all his homework."

Rebekah jumped at the contact. Alice had . . . suggested something like that yesterday, hadn't she? Had Rebekah put the pliers in her backpack last night to take her up on that offer, then forgotten about it? No, that made no sense. She couldn't have done something and then forgotten.

She chewed on her lip, shook her head. "Maybe, but not today."

Alice sighed. "Yeah, fair."

Rebekah held the pliers for a moment longer, feeling a chill crawl up her spine that had nothing to do with the cold morning. Then she stuffed them into her backpack and zipped it shut.

By keeping her head down and her ears open, Rebekah learned that Scotty had stayed home from school. A rumor was that he'd ditched, but another simply reported he'd stayed home sick—apparently each of the sources claimed to have texted him about it directly, which either meant he was giving different stories for the hell of it or the gossips were lying to try to look cooler by having some sort of direct access to him. Rebekah wasn't sure how anyone thought they could pull that off in a school as small and intertwined as Grant High.

"I bet his parents grounded him," said Alice at lunch, where the clouds had parted to allow the sharp smell of paint to mix with the petrichor. "We could do his locker tomorrow morning."

"No." Rebekah tightened her grip on the Poe book. "It's . . . no. It doesn't matter. There's no way to fight back at those people in a way that actually does anything. Let's drop it."

She buried her nose in the book again, and Alice shrugged. "Your call, I guess."

The volume rose in whispers and hushed voices, students looking up from tables. Rebekah and Alice followed suit, raising their heads from the spot of cold concrete they called their own.

Scotty sauntered through the sea of tables, between the red flames of the heat lamps, laughing with his friends like he did any other day—but looking ridiculous with his mouth stuffed with gauze.

Rebekah went half-numb, prickles on her skin.

"I'm going to go see what's up." Alice didn't wait for Rebekah's answer before climbing to her feet and making her way to the nearest clump of students. She didn't join them, a group of sophomore girls with their hair in matching braids, but she hovered near them without making it look like she was eavesdropping.

Rebekah couldn't hear anything over the thump of blood in her ears and the overlapping echoes of chatter that filled the cafeteria courtyard. Her gaze latched onto Scotty's face, searching it for . . . she wasn't certain what for, exactly. Proof, maybe, one way or another. But he seemed the same as always, laughing, bragging, sending calls over the table to Eddie with his curly hair and shit-eating grin. Eddie made a feint at him with a football, and the entire table laughed. Coralie sat at the next table over, sharing something on her phone with Veronica and Andrea, seemingly ambivalent about the commotion.

Alice came back, eyebrows raised and a flash of pink blushing her cheeks. She sat down and reported, "One of his teeth came out last night while he was playing football with Hector."

"His tooth came out?" Rebekah couldn't look away from the carefree group.

"Yeah. Apparently, the corner hit him in the wrong place, and his canine just ripped out. All they could really do at the dentist was bandage him up for now."

Rebekah remembered the wild fear in his eyes, his panicked, uneven screams. The dark, clotting blood spurting out of his mouth. Her memories of the Raven were tinted with dream logic, but her memory of that moment felt so clear.

Was Scotty lying? Had she caused his accident somehow? Or was it all just a massive coincidence?

Alice grew a sly smile. "Isn't this great? It's like karma."

Dizzy and chest tight, Rebekah reminded herself to breathe. "You believe in karma?"

"Maybe I do now. Or maybe I believe in the curative powers of football."

The bell rang, and students filed out of the courtyard and back through various sliding-glass doors, gossip flitting eagerly between them. Rebekah watched Scotty even as she stood and shouldered her backpack.

He walked alongside his friends, between mosaic-topped tables, toward the clean glass doors near the side of the school's brick walls. His lips puffed out around the gauze, and most of his friends' laughter seemed centered around his inability to enunciate. He glanced around as the group lost it to another joke and happened to meet eyes with Rebekah.

Scotty stopped in his tracks, breaking the cadence of his group's stride. His gaze betrayed a dark shadow of the same wild, frenzied panic from last night when the Raven had reached toward him with the pliers. He looked away fast, but not before Eddie had followed his gaze and shouted, "Yo, piss bitch!" Then they all passed through the door.

"Did you see that?" Alice asked.

Rebekah's muscles tightened with adrenaline. She tried to play it off as best she could. "What? They were just making fun of me again."

"No, I mean Scotty. I don't know. I think he believes in karma, too."

They watched where Scotty had disappeared into the school. That look in his eyes, the shot of panic edged with guilt. He knew he deserved what'd happened. He was afraid of her—no, he was terrified of her.

The knowledge sent a weird frisson of strange pleasure through her, an electrifying sensation that shot through her own confused guilt. It crawled out to her fingertips. Flooded her with energy.

She'd never been *feared* before.

* * *

Rebekah doodled the Raven in her stats class, leaning in her seat against a wall that smelled of dust and Pine-Sol, thinking circles around herself. Could Alice be right? Or had Scotty had the same dream as Rebekah? Was that even possible?

Could it happen again? Was there anything real about it, or was it a huge, weird coincidence? How could she know for certain?

When class ended, Rebekah piled the class handouts into a pink holographic folder that used to house her lists of subtraction problems, but before she had the chance to stuff the lot of it into her backpack, a hand came down and levered it off the desk to scatter on the varnished floor. The flurry of paper elicited suppressed laughter, especially from the boys, like Tom with his weird haircut, who smirked at her and whispered something to a friend, which she assumed had the words "starving" and "artist" as the punchline. When Mrs. Morell glanced over from the other end of the room, as usual looking like she had something much more important on her mind, it was only to chuckle and ask Rebekah to pick up after herself.

Eddie, with his rumpled uniform and smug expression. The inventor of the nickname. He was short for one of Scotty's friends but still taller than Rebekah, especially while she sat at her desk. He leaned in closer and whispered, "Piss bitch" with a wink on his way out into the hall. Like it was an inside joke between them.

Why did that feel even worse?

Face hot, Rebekah did her best to snatch her handouts back before they could get trampled, but she still wound up alone for a moment as she stuffed them all into her backpack, the last student to leave.

Mrs. Morell, a tall, pale woman with messy curls of blond hair, spoke while watching out her window, even as her hands continued to organize her papers. "I understand you've been having some trouble, Beka, but that's no reason to get distracted in class."

"Please don't call me that," Rebekah muttered on her way out the door where she nearly collided with Principal Bransby on his way in to talk to Mrs. Morell. She tossed an apology to him without looking.

It only took one moment of someone's shitty behavior to tear down the positive attitude she'd worked so hard to scrounge up all day. Eddie got to be mean without consequence because he was friends with the principal's daughter, and she wasn't. That was one of the core rules at Grant High: Kids with rich or important parents got to do whatever they wanted and fuck the rest.

But maybe—just maybe—she'd found her own way around those rules.

Nora had been in a weird mood on the way home, trying to talk again, so Rebekah grabbed her warmest jacket and went outside to pretend to water the plants a little earlier than normal. She hoped to hide out there, cradling the Poe book in perfect silence all the way until dinner. She loved her mom but talking about anything remotely serious never ended well for them, especially once Nora started drinking, which was a given after a certain time in the evening. They hadn't said anything substantial yet about the locker incident, and if Rebekah had her way, they never would.

However, by the way Mike looked at her through his car window before pulling into his driveway and how quickly he made his way along the short span of grass between their two houses, she'd only traded one awkward conversation for another. She closed the book on her finger, marking her spot.

"Beka," he said once they were in earshot. "I wanted to get you, um, alone and make sure you're all right. What happened the other day? You were really upset. You had me worried."

He knew next to nothing about her. She saw it in his eyes: He really had no idea what had happened. That . . . that felt kind of nice. They'd been almost friends when she was little, back when everyone was weird and no one was. He only knew her from playing street racer and hopscotch and from seeing her not water the onions. He hadn't even gone to Grant High at the same time. He graduated the year before she entered freshman year. But she was the oldest in her class—something she was glad her classmates didn't know because that would only make her stand out more—so she and Mike were really only a couple of years apart in age, as she had just turned eighteen. She smiled, and it didn't feel forced. Someone was showing true concern for her welfare. "I'm fine. Thanks. It was just a bad day."

"Oh." His shoulders relaxed, and he blushed slightly. "Good. I mean, not really—I mean, I'm glad you're all right. I'm still glad. From yesterday."

"Yeah. Thanks, I'm fine."

"No problem. I mean, yeah, good. That's . . ." He clapped his hands. "See you around, then."

"See you."

"See you."

He caught his repetition, and with a deepening of his blush, he turned back toward his own property.

Rebekah peered into his front window and thought she saw Bill. She couldn't help wondering what he made of her. Whether he'd found out what had happened. If he was wait-ing for Mike to come home, if he would greet his son with a hug or just continue reading in his armchair.

She chewed on her lip, wishing Mike hadn't left so quickly. She didn't know what they would have talked about, but . . . it was nice to talk to someone who had no idea what was going on.

9

Mike shut the door behind him and leaned against it, settling his nerves. *Idiot.* Of course Beka wouldn't trust him with her problems; she barely knew him. They hadn't spoken at all since they were kids because Mike kept avoiding her, because actually walking up and talking to a girl he'd liked since elementary school was apparently so deeply unreasonable.

Because it was better, in the long run, to keep an eye out for her when he drove home and try to analyze her mental space from the two seconds in which she grinned back at him instead of, for instance, talking to her. Their age difference wasn't *that* bad, but coupled with the hyperawareness he had of her comings and goings, *creepy* was not too much further down the road. He had to either do something about it soon or, specifically, not do anything.

"Mike?" his dad called, his lanky frame leaning out of the reading room. His expression was concerned, but the way he peered over his reading glasses always made him look like a disappointed professor. Then again, Bill was often disappointed, and he was a professor, so maybe there was a reason for the look.

Mike took off his hat, hanging it with his fleece-lined jacket on the rack by the door. "Hey, Dad."

"How was work?" His father took off his glasses as if to promise he wouldn't ditch the conversation in favor of a book.

It was nice of him to make an effort. Neither he nor Mike's mom understood their son's drive to join the police force. In the short few years since he'd graduated high school, they'd told him innumerable stories of police brutality, corrupt bureaucracy, the ethics of a surveillance state, and statistics about policed versus non-policed cities and towns around the world. The way they talked made Mike think they were trying to convince him to change careers, which would probably make it the one thing his parents agreed on, but they never out-and-out said it, so he ignored the subtext. Instead, he dismissed their points with the air of someone who wanted to change the system from the inside.

To be honest, Mike wasn't sure he did want to spearhead those changes, at least not in the brutal way that was probably necessary. It was tough to do that sort of thing without backup, anyway, which meant having friends on the force. And Mike had . . . zero.

"Fine . . ." Mike stopped himself from saying more. He didn't want to tell him about Rebekah;

didn't want to hear what he already knew. That he should just go talk to her. Instead, he said, "It's fine. It's really no big deal."

"Once they see your drive and dedication, they'll change their tune." His father liked to speak with an absolute confidence, no matter how unwarranted; he knew nothing about the guys at work whose goal in life seemed to be to make Mike's miserable. His dad didn't know a single cop personally, except for his son. And on the whole, police officers didn't behave at all similarly to college staff.

All Mike had done was try to be one of them. Why was that so terrible? What, exactly, had he misread? Why had they stopped their conversation, awkwardly waiting for him to leave?

Shouldn't have tried in the first place. At least he'd gotten some reading done.

"Thanks, Dad. I'm just going to change and I'll be back in a sec."

His father disappeared back into the reading

room. Despite being a professor who spent most of his time either pacing a lecture hall or sitting in an armchair, his motions were always smooth and careful. Like he was trying to be as quiet as possible.

Mike ran upstairs, took a quick shower, and changed into his sweats, what his parents would antiquatedly call "loungewear" before launching into a discussion about the etymology of the term, which would evolve into a debate, then an argument, then eventually the subject would be dropped in favor of their most recent talking points, and ultimately, his mom would get fed up and walk out.

At least, that's how it usually went.

The reading room was the picture of some old-fashioned study with wall-to-wall book-shelves and a big fireplace that rarely got used. The most eye-grabbing part of the room was the fake head of a coyote baring its jaws above the fireplace. Mike used to be terrified of the thing when he was little but had gotten over the fear by developing the habit of blowing the creature a kiss.

The front wall featured a wide bay window that let in the rare sunlight, a clear view of the grass and street. Mike often found himself wishing they lived somewhere where it snowed more than once a year, so they could have that view blanketed in sparkling white. Rebekah's house was visible from certain angles, most-ly only where his father sat in the corner and mostly only the tomato garden that curled for-ward out of its confinement.

But while the coyote and the window drew the eye, the reading room was devoted to books. Old books, new books, complete and incom-plete sets; poetry, literary, non-fiction, novels by genre; first edition hardbacks and used-copy paperbacks. The wall-to-wall shelves were full to bursting.

There were three armchairs total—Mike had

fond memories of the day they'd taken him to pick one out for himself—and a desk that shrouded the shelves opposite the fireplace that hadn't been used in years. His father fit so perfectly into his own armchair, such a staple of the reading room himself, it was easy to overlook him entirely.

"Hey." Mike went automatically to the bookshelf, although the end table next to his armchair was already overflowing. He grabbed another one anyway: an old favorite, familiar and easy to read. He knew his dad noticed the pulpy selection, one eyebrow raised contemplatively, but, thank God, he didn't ask him to try a new one instead. After that hellish lunch break last week and then the conversation with Beka, Mike wasn't in the—

"Have I told you that author has a new release soon?"

Mike paused before sitting in his chair; they usually spent those hours reading in silence together, nothing but the sound of nature through the front window. When Mike elected to join his dad instead of watching TV in his room, anyway. His dad chuckled and gestured fluidly for him to finish settling in.

"A new series?" Mike asked, encouraging the complete change of topic.

"Yes—well, no, a standalone, from what I understand."

He went over some of the details, and they decided to preorder it, and that was the end of the conversation. Mike buried his nose in the book, staring at the pages without actually reading the familiar words.

Something had definitely happened to Beka, something worse than a "bad day." Mike kept seeing her panicked expression, the tearstains on her cheeks, the way she'd jerked away from him. He wished he could hold her and let her confide in him.

But he couldn't help her if she wouldn't talk

to him. The way she'd shrugged him off just then—it reminded him of the awkward break room interaction, the other officers staring at him until he wandered away. Rebekah didn't know him that well anymore. It had been years since they'd spent real time together, and even then, they had been children. Simply being a couple of years older was enough to separate them. She didn't think he'd be able to help her.

But he could. If she trusted him—if the officers at the station just got to know him, came to respect him—he knew he could help.

That's what it came down to, wasn't it? He had to prove himself. He had to do his job well. Be reliable. But damn it, it didn't seem like any of the other officers had gone through that. Mike had graduated along with some of them; knew them from high school, from the police academy. But he'd been so focused on doing well in the actual lessons he'd never gotten around to making friends.

Turned out that part was actually important.

It was too late then, anyway. If he did his job well, protected his town, made the right calls, did the right things, stayed *reliable* . . . well, maybe that could be the same thing as helping Beka. And maybe it would help prove to the other officers that he wasn't a complete waste of space and resources.

Maybe it would help prove to Beka he was worthy of her time. Worthy of her trust. Worthy of helping her tackle whatever she was going through.

The architecture of the decrepit home of the Raven was, in a word, unreliable. So much as trying to recall which rooms had once been explored proved elusive. Simply existing there was such a strangeness in itself that putting mind to it as any other state, whether once past or hypothetical future, bent the imagination as sharply as did attempting to navigate it as it was in the moment.

Rebekah walked through a hall from and toward nowhere, pacing along one of many thick tapestry rugs, soft beneath her bare toes. All was quiet except for the patter of rain and a distant hollow wind, as if the house itself were calling out to her. Rodents squeaked and scuttled along the corners and walls, but Rebekah couldn't bring herself to fear them any more than she did the Raven itself.

At the end of the hall appeared a wood-paneled study lined with empty dust-buried shelves. A faceless stone bust sat cold and dark in a recess in one wall, and on either side of the room, narrow, high-vaulted windows let in the frigid night air and ice-cold rain.

In the very center of the room, illuminated only by indirect moonlight, was a heavy wooden chair; every bit as securely bound as Scotty had been, Eddie sat there, his gaze darting fearfully between her and the Raven—which stood beside Rebekah, smooth and silent as any shadow. When it approached the chair and offered her a friendly nod, Eddie flinched in his restraints.

The chair pointed upward at its top with three decorative peaks, and Eddie's curly hair caught in the corners of the aged wood. His jaw had been secured shut with a tight leather muzzle, but unlike Scotty, his head hadn't been locked in place. His black shirt was as rumpled as his uniform, boxer shorts revealing pale legs restrained by leather straps.

Rebekah approached slowly across the groaning wood, closer to the chair and the Raven, a chill of nervous excitement rolling through her. She couldn't help but remember Scotty's glance at lunch, the terror in his eyes. Scotty was afraid of her. He actually respected her. And after that night, if that was real, Eddie might, too.

The Raven turned silently to collect a tool

from the dusty shelves, and Rebekah paced closer to Eddie, filled with electric energy. He'd pointed and laughed and shouted "piss bitch." He'd smirked and laughed and winked, standing over her desk, papers spilled across the floor, but then, right then, she was the one towering over him.

They watched one another, Eddie bound and gagged, Rebekah standing free, looking into one another's eyes—he tried to say something, but his muzzle was too thick and secure—and what she saw on his face was bald fear and an unhidden guilt. Merely by seeing her, he knew exactly why he found himself bound to a chair in a nightmare manor, and just like Scotty, he knew he deserved it. He was Scotty's friend. He'd been complicit in the plan; he'd been at the party; he'd come up with the nickname.

Maybe Alice was right, and the Raven was karma.

The ink-black cloak rustled softly as the

creature turned, hefting a sledgehammer she'd have sworn hadn't existed a moment before. Rebekah stepped back, giving the Raven space to navigate around Eddie's chair, and it floated soundlessly across the wooden boards that groaned under her weight.

With a flick of its wrist, one arm section of the dining chair came away, leaving Eddie tied by the wrist and elbow to unconnected pillars of wood. His forearm was completely exposed.

Eddie's eyes grew wide, staring at the sledgehammer, and he let out panicked whimpers that grew quickly into muffled shouts. He struggled to free himself, pulling desperately at the restraints along his threatened arm. When he realized he had no chance of escape, he looked up, searching for any sign of humanity in the Raven. The Raven, however, only turned to face Rebekah. Patient. Its starlike eyes empty and kind. Eddie followed its gaze, breathing hard, tears in his eyes, begging her with muffled pleas.

She hesitated.

Would Eddie do it? If that study was some secret place of his own, if the Raven were his friends, if Rebekah was the one in the chair?

If he knew he could get away with it, he'd do it without a thought. For a laugh. And Rebekah hadn't even done anything to deserve it.

With that energy, the feeling of raw power in her arms, in her chest, Rebekah nodded.

Eddie's eyes filled with that same terror as Scotty's had in the school courtyard, and his begs evolved back into shouts, incoherent against his muzzle. He pulled on his arm again, shaking, struggling, tears streaming down his face.

The Raven hefted the sledgehammer, raised it overhead, swung down, and broke the forearm with an echoing *snap*.

Eddie screamed, the noise shoving through his leather straps with a fresh ferocity. Blood poured around exposed bone and leaked onto the wooden floor, flowing out in rivulets to drip down into the cracks between the planks, a steady stream of thick red ichor.

His money and his grades and his parents couldn't protect him there. There, he was merely human, like anyone else—and, like anyone else, he could bleed.

10

The next day was a Saturday, and Rebekah spent what felt like half of it pacing in her room as much as that was possible. Had it worked? Would she know on Monday, or would all evidence have been swept under the rug by then? No—a broken arm couldn't heal in two days. She'd know on Monday, if not earlier. Even if he didn't show up to school, someone would have found out by then, and Rebekah would know for certain.

Whether it was, somehow, real or whether Scotty's tooth had been a fluke.

A text from Alice, however, jolted her out of her worrying. *When did you want to come over?*

Hanging out at Alice's. Rebekah had completely forgotten about that. She hadn't even remembered to ask her mom about it.

For a long moment, sitting in her bedroom with a cozy black kitty on her lap, Rebekah considered canceling. Really considered it, staring at her phone, an attempt at silence broken by her mother's CD player as it started blasting one of her '90s albums. But sitting alone in her undecorated room wasn't going to bring her any answers, and Alice didn't deserve punishment.

Besides, what if she found out about Eddie's arm?

Rebekah gave Dupaw a kiss and carefully deposited him onto the floor, changed into actual clothes, and tossed her pajamas toward her closet with the rest of her laundry. Finding Nora was as easy as following the pop drumbeat back along the hall into the master bedroom, which also doubled as the workroom where she repaired clothing, blankets, bedsheets, some kitchen utensils, and a few of the simpler household machines.

Rebekah poked her head through the door. The room wasn't much more than a bed, a dresser acting as a nightstand, and the wide desk where Nora accomplished the bulk of her work. At that moment, it seemed like she was lost in one of her foul moods, sitting at the desk and working on mending a tear in one of her jackets, a dark shadow having settled over her eyes.

Nora had a lot of things to complain about when she got like that, but the topic that really started the foul mood tended to be Rebekah's father. And when it was Rebekah's father, there was usually . . .

Yep. Rebekah found the glass of wine on a mismatched dark-stained side table, where it wouldn't spill on the jacket. Nora even got drunk responsibly. So, that's a no on driving Rebekah there, but probably a yes to going if Alice could come pick her up.

"Mom?"

"Hmm?" Nora glanced up for barely a second, raising one tired eyebrow.

"Mind if I go to Alice's?"

She paused, looking over at the wine on her side table. Rebekah doubted it was her first one; it was full, and Nora was already buzzed. Sure enough, she said, "I wish you'd brought it up earlier, honey. Can she pick you up?"

"Yeah, I think so."

A sigh of relief and Nora went back to work. "Then of course. Have fun, Beka."

Rebekah hesitated. Nora sounded only about half present. If she kept drinking—and Rebekah knew she would—she'd wind up in tears.

On the one hand, Rebekah hated seeing her mom like that and wished she could figure out how to distract her from it. On the other hand, those were the moments when Rebekah came the closest to wheedling out information about her father.

Nora didn't look up from her sewing again. "I love you. Come back safe."

Regret pushed needle-sharp into Rebekah's heart that she'd even consider taking advantage of her mom's emotional state. She chewed on her lip and thought of the few times she'd done it, both crying over the callousness of a man Rebekah had never even known.

She forced a smile and said, "I love you, too. Sew safe."

Nora laughed, and Rebekah left to text Alice.

Rebekah had brought her faux-velvet purse with her, but only because it felt wrong to leave the Poe book behind, unguarded, at home. She didn't really think anything would happen to it, not really, but she'd brought it anyway. The purse hardly zippered shut around both it and the sketch notebook.

"He's in the A/V club," Alice continued.

Rebekah had missed the beginning of the topic, but it wasn't hard to catch up. "Thinks he's going to be the next Tarantino or something. But the man has hair like you wouldn't believe, Rebekah. It defies gravity."

It felt nice to let her talk and not have to worry about . . . well, about anything.

About whether Eddie would come to school on Monday. If he'd have a broken arm, and what Rebekah would do if he did.

Alice kept chatting, filling the air, sparing Rebekah the need to figure out what to say in response. The overcast morning lent a completely new cast to the landscape of Alice's house, but she dragged Rebekah inside, up the stairs to the loft, without a second glance.

Alice generally preferred the loft to her bedroom because it had a wide coffee table perfect for puzzles—of which she'd already set out a selection. But Rebekah loved it for the huge, slanted window with the best view on the property.

The meadow behind the house framed the distant view of a full-forested valley. Some other houses dotted the landscape, marked by pockets in the forest, but the town itself lay in the other direction. From the second-story loft, Rebekah saw a rippling sea of tapered evergreen treetops poking out from a field of leafless branches, gray clouds like the underside of the ocean, the border of a national park on the far side where the mountains began; and when it rained, like that day, the water tapped on the glass in a comforting rhythm.

"Tea?" Alice offered, revealing an electric kettle she'd set up on an end table by the out-let. Rebekah snorted at the sight of it, the two handmade ceramic mugs she'd already prepped.

"The loft, puzzles, and tea? You're really pull-ing out all the stops."

Alice blushed as she poured. "I know a lot

of stuff's been going on. I guess I just want to hang out, you know? Like we used to."

It felt too much like hiding. Like trying to ignore what was happening, to Rebekah, maybe to Scotty and Eddie. She braced one hand on the purse with the Poe book inside.

Rebekah smiled anyway. "Yeah, that sounds nice."

Alice delivered a warm mug of tea and opened a puzzle. They settled onto cushioned seats on either side of the coffee table and leaned over the pile of colorful pieces.

Rebekah did actually manage to relax, for maybe the first time since Scotty had pissed in her locker. Hanging out with Alice didn't help in any real way—Rebekah didn't tell her what had really happened, didn't tell her about the Raven, and Alice didn't ask any direct questions—but for a little while, it was like Rebekah got to live in a world where none of it had happened at all. It was just the two of them fitting little chipboard pieces together, talking about boys and memes and TV shows, updates on their lives. Things that didn't really matter.

"It's seriously wild, what happened to Scotty."

Rebekah's burgeoning peace fled through the tilted window, but Alice didn't notice, scouring the surface of the claw-footed table for the place where her piece belonged. Had she found out about Eddie? What had she learned?

She continued, "It's weird and creepy, like karma, but with a sort of *Monkey's Paw* flavor. Isn't that cool?"

Alice was just making conversation. Rebekah needed to play along. Anyway, maybe it wasn't real. Rebekah couldn't know if it was real until she found out about Eddie, either through social media or at school on Monday. And there was no way to ask about it without sounding insane. She tried instead to study the puzzle piece she held between two fingers: uneven blue lines tracing across darkness. The puzzle photo was of a cat outlined in neon. She probably had part of the whiskers.

"Rebekah?" Alice asked.

Rebekah nodded robotically. "Yeah. It's pretty cool."

She placed the piece where the whiskers probably went; that part of the board hadn't been built out well enough yet.

"Papa's been saying that's why the pulp mill shut down. Karma. Apparently, the owner cheated on something like three people at once."

"Did those people shut it down?"

"No, it was completely unrelated. Karma. Anyway, the place is dead empty now. Oh! You and I should check it out!"

Rebekah stiffened. "You mean break in? Why?"

"Isn't that the kind of thing teenagers are supposed to get up to?"

Yeah, that and going to a party. "It sounds like a bad idea."

Alice shrugged. "I mean, it is, so that's fair. I wouldn't force you to do it, anyway."

"Sorry."

"Hey, no worries." Alice placed the piece she'd been holding and picked up her phone.

Rebekah fiddled with a puzzle piece, chewing on her lip. It couldn't be karma if she'd directed it. The Raven wasn't just some agent of a cosmic force; it was a creature that had done what she'd asked. Sure, Eddie had picked the stupid nickname, but Coralie had poured the drink. Karma would have gone for her first.

"Whoa!" Alice exclaimed. "Speaking of karma!"

She showed Rebekah her phone: An Instagram picture of Eddie's arm in a cast.

Rebekah dropped the piece she was holding.

"He was bucked off his horse," Alice told her. "No surprise. He was probably mistreating it."

Rebekah hadn't even known Eddie's family

had horses. She hadn't known anyone in that town owned a horse.

But Eddie had *broken his arm.*

The Raven was real.

Eddie's forearm had been busted in an early-morning ride; the horse had gotten spooked by some animal and he'd been thrown off. His parents made for a spectacle, talking to the straight-backed demeanor of Principal Bransby under umbrellas from the middle of the parking lot, so Eddie had ducked away from them as quickly as possible.

Rebekah searched his face whenever she could throughout the day, his free arm, the way he walked, but he otherwise seemed completely intact: no bruises, black eyes, cuts, or scrapes. Either he'd been really lucky during his accident, or falling off a horse wasn't as dangerous as she'd thought. Or he was lying.

Maybe her dreams caused the accidents somehow. Maybe Eddie and Scotty were too scared to admit they'd been tortured by a cloaked creature in a nightmare, and they'd made up the accidents instead.

Eddie never looked at her that day. His eyes skipped over her when they passed in the hall; he avoided her glance in class. He didn't make fun of her or talk about her either. From what she could tell, he just pretended she wasn't there.

It was wonderful.

"Nice backpack," a voice broke in from beside her. "Very DIY. I always wondered what they did with homeless tents after confiscating them."

Coralie passed her in the hazy sunlight of the high-windowed hall, all flawless hair and expensive makeup, meeting Rebekah's gaze for the shortest moment before rolling her eyes. Andrea followed like a pompous ghost, the shoulders of her shirt tied up in ribbons and her nose buried in her phone, pointedly contributing nothing more than a scoff.

A different voice, from directly behind Rebekah, said, "Oh, you've got something here—let me get it for you."

Before Rebekah could turn, a sharp tug on her backpack jerked against her shoulders, and there was the harsh ripping of duct tape from fabric. Clatters of wood and plastic against the floor meant they'd ripped off the tape covering the hole she'd cut from the pencil pouch, and writing implements and erasers and sharpeners rained behind her with tinkles and *thunks*.

Rebekah turned, flushing hot, as Veronica Bransby laughed into one hand, still holding the piece of duct tape in her other. "Oh, my God, there's actually a hole there," she said between her fingers, eyebrows raised. "Don't poor people at least have sewing kits and stuff?"

Veronica scoffed and broke into giggles as she turned to catch up to Coralie and Andrea, the perfect curls of her famous auburn hair bouncing on her shoulders.

Rebekah stared after the small troupe through the between-class crowd until they turned a corner, disappearing between wood-paneled walls. Then, when her muscles loosened enough for her to move, she numbly dropped her backpack to the floor and crouched to collect her fallen things.

Under her breath, Rebekah paraphrased, "I am monarch, and here rule with undivided empire under the title of 'Queen Pest the First.'"

Even after what she'd done with the Raven, Rebekah couldn't face those girls. Knowing how she'd made Scotty and Eddie feel, the power she'd leveraged over them, she'd still completely frozen when faced with Coralie, Veronica, and Andrea.

With the Raven . . . Rebekah didn't have to be afraid of them anymore. She didn't need to drink the foul drink they offered. She had the power to fight back. That's what all that meant. That's why Eddie couldn't look at her. It's how she'd commanded the respect of a couple of the most popular kids at Grant.

Could she put Coralie in front of the Raven? Could she do it that night?

Dread rushed in, the thick, dark fear, heat on the back of her neck, as she moved all her pencils into one of the pouches without a giant hole. But what if Coralie managed to get power in the dream? What if she won over the Raven? Was that possible? What would happen then?

No. No one could possibly win over the Raven. It was a creature designed by Rebekah, a nightmare thing that loved only her. But she needed time to prepare for Coralie's night with the Raven; she needed to know what she was doing and how, needed to figure out how to use whatever it was to its full power. Then she could decide on the perfect torture for Coralie. The perfect payback.

In the meantime, Veronica's famously perfect auburn hair would make a superb guinea pig. What expression would she make when she realized she was completely at Rebekah's mercy? Would she regret how she'd acted? Would she leave Coralie?

Maybe Rebekah couldn't fight back in person. Maybe Veronica's father made her untouchable. But everyone was vulnerable while they slept.

Veronica's restraint wasn't a chair or table like Eddie's or Scotty's. She knelt among the dry weeds of the garden with her hands chained behind her, head held firmly in place by the Raven's gloved hand, in the center of circles of dead plants, framed by the still branches of bare trees, the pure darkness of the starless sky.

She wore the same muzzle Eddie had and a dirt-stained set of pink silk pajamas, streaks of improperly removed mascara along her cheeks.

She'd scrunched her eyes shut, and the only sounds between the dark forest and the crumbling manor wall were her muffled sobs.

The Raven wound its fingers through a hefty chunk of Veronica's thick, wavy hair. It pulled back on her head, eliciting a strained whine, and when her eyes rolled open they focused on Rebekah. She struggled anew, straining against her chains and muzzle to get some message across.

Her heart thrumming, Rebekah stepped closer, finding soft footing among the weeds. Veronica's eyes lit up with hope, but when she tried to duck forward, the Raven yanked back again, and she let out a whimper of pain.

She tried to speak, muffled words against the leather muzzle, desperate pleading in her eyes, sobs wracking her throat.

Rebekah knelt to eye level and watched fresh tears roll down the tarnished tracks on Veronica's cheeks. Then she looked up and met the Raven's reflective gaze, two circles of light from the shroud of its hood, one of its hands wound in Veronica's hair and the other gripping her head for leverage.

Even despite its violent stance, despite its inhuman gaze, Rebekah always felt a kindness radiating from the Raven. An unwavering, silent loyalty. It was a wraith, but it protected her. It broke physics for her. She could pour her trust into that shadowed face, like a leap into the abyss, and know it would catch her.

She looked at Veronica again, and nodded.

With a burst of smooth movement, the Raven ripped its fistful of hair from her scalp. A terrific tearing sounded, louder than Rebekah had expected, and Veronica screamed through her leather muzzle, her eyes clenched shut, pulling on her chains with heavy clinks that muffled against the musty earth. Droplets of blood flecked in a halo around her.

The Raven tossed the clump of hair and skin

aside and stepped back from Veronica. With her arms chained to her feet behind her, she didn't have much additional leeway, but she used all of it to collapse to the ground and sob as violently as her restraints would allow.

Rebekah wanted to say something, but nothing came to mind, nothing that would get across how she felt. What she felt. That new, unparalleled energy.

She rose, standing tall with Veronica curled up at her feet. The discarded hair formed a dull heap in the dirt.

Rebekah had done that to her.

She felt like Delilah.

11

Scotty and Eddie had stopped calling Rebekah "piss bitch," at least in front of her. Whenever Coralie or her friends passed by, Veronica ducked her head, touched the gray school-brand beanie she'd gotten permission to wear over her bandages, and neglected to participate in the collective scoffs and snickers. Whatever Rebekah and the Raven actually were, they were making a real impact on Grant High.

On her way through the crowd between biology and U.S. history, she saw Mike in his vibrant blue uniform following the principal, whose lips were stretched in an uncomfortable line, along the narrow hall. Rebekah stopped in her tracks, openly watching the encounter, forcing people to walk around her, jostling her shoulder.

What was Mike doing there? Had he followed her for some reason? What could he have to talk about with the principal?

They disappeared into an office at the end of a short hall. The frosted glass of the door's window shook slightly as it closed behind them.

Rebekah pulled over into the little hallway, dropped her backpack as close to the door as she dared, and knelt as if to fish something out of it, straining to listen in on their conversation.

"I don't want to cause any panic, officer."

"Neither do I, sir, but this is worth looking into. The department has been asked by two different families to investigate, and it's my job to help determine how the school might connect these incidents."

Rebekah's breath stilled in her chest. She

glanced up but couldn't make out anything more than a shifting shape behind the frosted glass.

When she looked back down, her eyes caught on an unfamiliar piece of maroon tucked in the corner of her bag. She dug it out with trembling fingers, breath held.

Veronica's hair. Long, wavy, and lusciously red-brown, there was no mistaking it. Rebekah stared at the thick lock in her palm, held together on one end by a rubber band.

"Of course, I won't get in your way," said Principal Bransby, a strained tone to his voice. "I only ask that you try not to upset the students."

Bransby. She shoved the hair back into her pack, heart pounding. If he saw it, everything would be over.

"I'll do what I can, sir, but these things can't be controlled. You should be prepared for anything."

"Yes, thank you," said the principal with curt discomfort as footsteps approached the door.

It swung open then, and Rebekah wrenched out the Poe book and zipped the bag shut.

Principal Bransby closed the door with a clatter, and Mike stopped abruptly. "Beka?"

She looked up, tucking her hair behind her ear, and finished zipping up her bag. "Mike, hey. Um. Please don't call me that. Rebekah is fine."

"Of course, no problem. Sorry."

He offered her a hand to help her up, and she accepted it, coming to her feet. She glanced into the frosted glass but saw no Bransby-sized shape through it.

"Strange meeting you here," Mike added with an awkward laugh.

Had he seen the lock of Veronica's hair? *Could* he have seen it? What would he do if he had? Would he know what it meant?

Her heartbeat rushing in her ears, Rebekah blurted, "Well, this is my school." Had that come across bitchy?

He turned away, then back again, stammering

some sounds she couldn't make out as words, and Rebekah realized he was nervous talking to her. Why? Did he suspect her? Did that mean he'd seen the hair in her bag? He'd say something if he suspected her, right?

"Yeah," he said, finally.

"Um. I have to get to class."

"Of course. Um—want me to walk you?"

Rebekah hesitated. "To . . . my class?"

"Sure."

That wasn't the kind of thing a police officer would do at a high school, was it? Was he trying to separate her from everyone else? No, that didn't make any sense. He wanted to walk her to class, not a back alley.

"No, that's weird, huh?" He gave a derisive chuckle. "No big deal, I can—"

"No, it's fine," Rebekah said quickly. "I mean, yeah. Sure."

Mike blinked. "Oh. Sure. I mean, great. Let me get your bag for you."

She realized she'd left her backpack on the ground, in all its duct-taped glory. Before Mike could grab it, she snatched it up and slung it across her shoulders, holding the Poe book tightly under her arm, and the two of them set off through the thinning crowd, their footsteps creaking on the pretentious wood.

Why had she agreed to the walk with Mike? He'd always been nice before, but what if she was wrong?

"I'm looking into some incidents that may or may not be related," said Mike, like he was trying to fill the silence. "It's nothing to worry about. There's almost nothing connecting them to the school."

Some incidents. Rebekah knew he was talking about Scotty, Eddie, and Veronica. He had to be. Nothing else of any interest had happened in town, much less the school.

She chewed on her lip as her thoughts went to the clump of hair in her backpack. Why had she put it there? There was a hole in that pocket. If the duct tape came off again, it could fall right out—and the color marked it clearly as Veronica's.

Mike clearly mistook her silence for concern because he added, "I didn't mean to worry you."

"Oh, no. You didn't. You aren't. Um. Not really. Can you tell me more about what's going on?"

"I'm sure you know already." He shrugged. "A couple students had some pretty bad accidents. Their families suspect there was something weird and choreographed about the incidents themselves, but the students haven't said much, so the families asked my department to investigate a possible connection. I don't think it's enough to warrant investigation, but you know how it is with these rich families." His eyes went wide. "Oh, wait, I didn't mean anything—you're probably friends with them. I didn't mean to imply—"

"I'm not friends with them." Rebekah gave him a sour look. "And it doesn't surprise me their families have pull with the police."

"That's . . . not exactly how it works." Mike's tone heavily implied that it was. "Either way, I shouldn't have said that. I shouldn't have told you anything at all since the investigation is ongoing. Please don't mention it to anyone."

"My lips are sealed."

They stopped in front of the propped-open door of her history classroom. Mike gave Rebekah a half-smile. "See you later, then."

"Later."

She watched him retreat down the hall, clutching the book like a shield.

If Mike didn't suspect her, why had he walked her to class? Why did he always act weird around her? Wasn't he supposed to be a cop?

What if he found out about the Raven?

She entered the classroom, ducking her head out of habit to avoid eye contact with anyone.

There was no way Mike could find out about her. There was nothing tangible to find out in the first place. Or at least there wouldn't be once she got rid of the hair.

"You're still on hiatus from Pluto?"

Rebekah shut the notebook and glanced at Alice, who peered over her shoulder at her sketch of the Raven. She had a half-eaten turkey sandwich in one hand, almost forgotten as she inspected the drawing.

"What?" Alice took a bite of her sandwich. It was raining, so they sheltered together underneath Alice's bright pink golfing umbrella. It was a pain in the neck, and Rebekah shouldn't be drawing, but at least their lunch wouldn't taste like paint.

Rebekah shook her head, rolling her shoulders to release some tension. "Nothing. Sorry. It's private."

"No problem." Alice lowered her voice. "Did you hear about that cop?"

"Mike?"

Alice blinked. "You know him?"

Should she have admitted that? Was that a mistake?

"He's my neighbor," she said finally, figuring the damage had already been done and it was best to play it casual. "My cat ruined his jacket, so Nora gave him an open invitation to stop by and get it repaired. I saw him here this morning."

"Wild. Apparently, he's looking into what happened to Scotty and Eddie and Veronica. I didn't even realize something had happened to Veronica—did you hear? She lost like a quarter of her hair in some freak accident!"

"Yeah, I guess."

"You wouldn't even know it. Her hat game is on point." Alice ducked her head to gaze at her subject under the lip of the umbrella, through the lunching students and the lamp heaters. "Or maybe she got a really good wig. Or both."

"Yeah."

Alice nudged Rebekah. "Hey, are you all right?"

"Yeah, sorry, it's just been a lot recently."

"You're not wrong. It's only been, what, a week since Scotty peed in your locker? They normally would've fed off that for a month, but they've got so much more already. It's a veritable gossip buffet."

Alice was right. Since Eddie, she'd borne a lot less piss bitch-related teasing. It hadn't completely vanished, of course, and everyone still lined up to remind her she was less welcome at Grant High than an industrious worm, but they weren't nearly as vicious as they would have been if the rumor pool hadn't been diluted by the "unfortunate accidents" haunting the worst of the student body.

"Anyway." Alice shrugged, watching one

group of students that had, for some reason, decided to sit on their table in a ring, facing outward. "If it really isn't just a set of timely accidents, let's hope they figure out what it actually is. I don't want to come in one day to find out you've lost two fingers or something."

Rebekah opened her mouth to promise that nothing could ever happen to either of them, but as far as Alice knew, there was no way she could guarantee that. Instead, she unzipped her backpack and stowed the sketchbook, taking a moment to run her fingers over the embossed raven on the cover of the Poe book.

"I'm not at all ready for the history test," she said instead, changing the subject.

Rebekah shared her art class with Hector, at whose unnecessarily huge house all her trouble had started. They normally ignored each other in class, even since the party: a welcome respite from the way he and his friends liked to act in public. She kept up her side of the bargain, head down, working on her project. The paint-stained floor of the art classroom had been cleared of desks in order to allow for canvas work, and the heady musk of charcoal filled the room. The cadence of Mr. Ellison's footsteps marked a steady beat as he examined each student's progress.

It was normally Rebekah's favorite class, but she could hardly focus.

According to the whispers Alice managed to overhear, Mike had set up shop in one of the theater green rooms, apparently in order to call students out of class and interview them.

Rebekah was sure Scotty, Eddie, and Veronica remembered what she'd done to them. Maybe they wouldn't tell anyone because it sounded so impossible, but she didn't want to stake her future on a "maybe." What if Mike figured out how all the "accidents" had her in common?

Would he arrest her? Would he arrest her mom? How did that work? Then Nora would get fired, wouldn't she? They'd lose everything.

Rebekah drew the Raven, trying to keep it more vague than usual, but the prompt had been "dreams," so she couldn't help thinking of her nightmare creature. The Raven looked particularly good in charcoal, as indistinct as it was clear, vibrant in shades of gray. Even with little to no detail, it looked more like itself than when Rebekah used a pencil or pen.

She hesitated, hovering over her work. Should she draw it so openly? Shouldn't she keep a lower profile? What if Scotty or Eddie had described the Raven, and someone recognized it?

The insanity of the nightmare manor should have been enough to protect her, but Eddie wouldn't have to describe being tortured in a chair in an impossible mansion to describe the Raven or to point out Rebekah had been there.

She needed to protect herself in a way that also protected what she was doing. That was the first time in her life she'd finally managed to scramble together the amount of power everyone around her seemed to wield without a moment's thought, and she couldn't give it up.

Not then, not ever.

"Rebekah," Mr. Ellison said softly from beside her. With curly red hair, a kind face, and hands that were always held behind him like a respected art critic instead of a high school teacher, he at least was usually decent to her. "Is that an art thought or a distracted thought?"

"Um. Distracted. Sorry."

"Don't apologize to me, apologize to your piece."

"Sorry," she said to the charcoal rendition of the Raven because Mr. Ellison was weirdly literal about those things. He nodded and kept moving.

Rebekah hesitated, though, focusing on her

painting. If she did get caught, what would happen to the Raven? Would it disappear? Would it keep going through Rebekah's dreams, even if she was expelled or locked up? In other words, if she handled it wrong, would she need to apologize to it?

When the bell rang, the students handed in their semi-complete projects to work on again tomorrow. When Mr. Ellison lined them all up on the counter along one wall—the one with the window—Rebekah grimaced, knowing that every art student would have the opportunity to see the Raven. As if she'd left her sketchbook sitting out on a table.

Well, everyone who actually knew the Raven already knew Rebekah was involved. It wasn't them she needed to worry about.

It was Mike.

After class, Hector lingered in the doorway. Waiting for Rebekah while pretending not to. Breaking their unspoken truce. She couldn't stay in there without drawing attention, so she stood tall and tried to ignore him on the way out. Of course, that didn't work.

"I'm not scared of you," he said, stopping her in the hall out of Mr. Ellison's line of sight. He loomed, emphasizing his height, his arms stiff at his sides. "I don't know what you said to Scotty and Eddie, but you won't get me like that, piss bitch. Lay the fuck off, or you'll find out why I was kicked out of my last school."

He left, disappearing around the corner. And Rebekah felt . . . surprised. In a good way. Because already, she knew in her gut that his threat was empty. At least, emptier than hers. She was bigger than he was. More powerful than he was. And there was nothing he could really do to her anymore.

Rebekah was going to introduce Hector to the Raven, and he'd eat his words. The knowledge brought with it a feeling of security she'd never known.

She needed that. Needed to be able to keep doing it and to protect herself as well as the Raven.

But first, she needed to know what Mike knew.

At the end of the day, Rebekah ran into Mike on her way out of the school.

It had taken several tries; he'd remained in his little green room-cum-office longer than she'd expected, and she didn't want to linger, so she wound up doing three laps in the misty rain around the modernized brick theater before she finally saw him emerging from a side door, bundled up in the jacket Dupaw had scratched. She slowed next to him with her nose in the Poe book, walking along a concrete path, pretending not to notice he was there until he exclaimed awkwardly, "Oh—Rebekah! Hi!"

She hoped she looked as surprised as he did

as she tucked the book under her arm. "Oh, hi! Um. How are you?"

"Since this morning? Good. Sorry, I hope I'm not interrupting."

"No, I've read it already. It's fine."

"You read it already? The whole book?" He lit up, impressed. "I've read a few of Poe's short stories but not a lot of his poems. Getting through a copy of his complete works has been on my to-do list for a while."

Rebekah held the book a little tighter. "Yeah, I love his perspective." That was not where the conversation was supposed to be going. "You're heading out?"

"School's over, isn't it? I've been interviewing students all day, and now my interviewees are leaving." He laughed, so she did, too, trying not to sound nervous.

They went quiet, crossing through the building and toward the parking lot, passing plenty of students who cast them odd looks. Then again, they gave Rebekah odd glances all the time, so she couldn't be sure if there was a difference.

Principal Bransby stopped in his stroll along a crossing hallway and openly watched them pass. His disapproving frown gave Rebekah chills.

"Um," she said, ignoring Bransby. "It was . . . nice to talk to you this morning. I don't think we've really spoken in years."

"No, not since . . . you were in elementary school, right?"

"Yeah, third or fourth grade, I think." It was around the time she'd discovered that drawing meant she could exist in her own little world for a while. She'd lost a couple of distant friends that way.

Would it be weird if she asked outright about his investigation? Would it be obvious?

Mike said, "I was wondering—"

"How was—Oh, you go."

"I was wondering if you'd let me drive you home. Since we're both here, and I already know where you live." He held his hands up. "Wait, no—I just meant because we're neighbors. I didn't mean—You know what I mean."

Was that some way to arrest her without making a scene?

The grass and benches and walls were peppered with students waiting to head home. They chattered in clumps, took pictures together, jumped in and out of one another's videos. Coralie and her friends leaned against her rocket-red convertible in the parking lot while Scotty and Hector exchanged a football on Scotty's favorite part of the lawn.

Nearby, the students eyed Rebekah and Mike, who was dressed in his bright-blue uniform. Did it look like he was arresting her? No, how could he? They were walking side-by-side. They probably looked like friends, and the students of Grant High were unaccustomed to her having any friends other than Alice—who stood near their usual planter with a similar surprised look on her face.

Rebekah realized the silence had drawn out when Mike started backpedaling. "Or not, it isn't a big deal. You usually ride with your mom, right? I get not wanting to worry her, and we haven't spoken much at all, so it's fine if you feel you don't know me that well—"

"No, that sounds great," she answered. "I'll just text Nora. I mean, yeah, we're going to the same place anyway, right?"

"Right." He sounded as shocked as she felt by her answer. "Well, wait—we're not technically going to the same place. I have to head back into the precinct. But I can drop you off on the way."

"Oh. Um. Okay."

His expression was kind and grateful. He waited until she sent a text to her mother then gestured toward his personal vehicle. "This way, then."

He hadn't driven a squad car to Grant High but rather his personal sedan. A dark navy blue, well-cared-for-but-not-exactly-expensive model. It straddled the line in quality between a typical Grant High car and what Nora drove every day. Average, in other words.

He opened the passenger door for her, and she caught a glimpse of Coralie's startled expression as she slid inside. It was only then that she realized Mike's presence on campus would've been noticed by everyone in such a small school. What was Coralie thinking, staring at her from beside her fancy convertible? Was it just that surprising to see Rebekah with a boy?

She was, technically, "with a boy," wasn't she? It hadn't occurred to her like that. Not exactly.

Veronica refused to turn around, touching her hair self-consciously. Andrea fiddled with a series of green and blue ribbons, tying them into knots like some kind of friendship bracelet.

She didn't even glance down, but her fingers moved confidently.

As Coralie's surprise evolved into a soundless discussion with Andrea, Rebekah's uncertainty resolved into pride. It was the same sort of all-over rush she'd gotten from Scotty's terrified glance and from Eddie's and Veronica's whimpering. Coralie thought Rebekah wasn't capable of meeting anyone. She thought Rebekah was worse than useless, a stain on the pavement of Grant High. She was wrong.

It was still too early to go for her. Rebekah needed to think of something perfect, something Coralie deserved. But she'd get her soon enough. That night, Rebekah had to show up Hector.

Mike started the car, oblivious of either Coralie or the disbelieving look she'd cast through the windshield, and they put Grant High behind them.

12

"I see you drawing in your book all the time," Mike said, as they drove home, the evergreens lining the country road blurring past the windows. His car was sort of clean, organized but with forgotten dust in the cupholders. It smelled of old coffee and pine freshener. The faux leather seats squeaked with every movement, so Rebekah sat still, watching his face as he glanced between her and the winding road. "What do you draw?"

"All kinds of things." It was a stupid answer, but she wasn't sure what else to say. "I was sort of working on a kids' comic."

His eyebrows rose. "Really? That's cool!"

She shrank a little, producing a whine along the back of the seat. "Sort of. I mean, it isn't really much good."

"I'm sure it is. Can I read it?"

He looked genuine, the short whiskers of stubble shifting back along his cheek. No one aside from Alice had asked to read Pluto in years, and even she hadn't seemed all that interested. And honestly, Rebekah preferred it that way. No one looking at her work meant no one making fun of it, or her.

"Um." She floundered. "I don't know. Maybe. Wait, no. I mean— It's just that I lost my most recent sketchbook, and the old ones aren't any good."

"Oh, man, that's a shame. Do you have any idea where it is?"

The memory rose in her mind's eye, the way the stench had crept up on her, suffusing out from her locker, permeating the books and her bag. The laughter of the crowd that'd surrounded her, closing in like coyotes around a kill.

She felt the need to shower again.

Mike glanced over. "You okay?"

Rebekah forced herself to smile. "Yeah. Yeah, sorry. It just sucks that I lost it."

"Oh, yeah, I can't imagine. All that work?"

She nodded, then changed subjects, hoping she sounded natural, though she was pretty sure she'd forgotten how natural sounded. "Um. I was wondering, how's it going with your thing?"

"Well, it's nothing," he answered with a sigh. "We knew it would be, anyway. That's probably why they gave it to me, of all people. Everyone so far either saw everything or knows nothing. Usually both. It's just a couple random, unconnected events, anyway, and the only reason I'm looking into the school is because they're all students there, and the chief thinks—" He stopped himself and gave her a side glance.

"Um, please don't repeat any of this to anyone, okay? I'm not supposed to talk about it."

"Oh, no problem. I don't even have anyone I would tell." She meant it as a joke, but it didn't sound like one once it was out of her mouth. "Well, there's Alice, but she— I mean, I promise I won't."

He didn't say anything for a while, and Rebekah inwardly cursed herself for killing the conversation. Still, she'd gotten what she wanted. Mike said the investigation hadn't gone anywhere. So far.

What was she protecting anyway? What was she actually doing with the Raven at night?

"Do you want to go out sometime?" Mike asked, a jumble of words all at once.

Rebekah froze, turning to him. Where had that come from?

He glanced over, uncertain. "I mean, unless you . . ."

"No, that sounds great," she said, hardly

aware of herself as she said it. "Yeah. I mean, yes. That sounds nice."

"Cool." He looked as astonished as Rebekah felt at her answer, but a tiny bit of the tight tension in her shoulders melted. "I'll call you then."

"Yeah. Um. Do you have my number?"

"I don't think so."

Mike pulled up in front of her house, and Rebekah gave him her contact info then got out. After an awkward sort of wave, she pulled up her hood and darted through the rain to the onion garden.

Had Mike just asked her out? Had she accepted? She hadn't thought at all, it just sort of happened.

He *was* cute, in a geeky sort of way. And he'd only been a cop for a little while. And he'd been nothing but nice to her, even after they'd stopped playing together. He always gave her a kind look when he saw her across the uneven grass between their houses. He'd even stopped her that day after she'd run home from school following the urine incident. He'd run out to meet her and make sure she was all right.

She'd been asked out. On a date. By a cute guy who seemed to care she existed.

By the cop who might figure out what she'd done to the kids at Grant High.

Mike sat in his car, grinning like an idiot, until Rebekah unlocked her front door and disappeared inside.

She'd said yes.

He needed to figure out how to relate better to Rebekah as she was versus the kids they'd been once upon a time. Back then, things had been easy. They could just hang out and exist together. They'd understood each other. And despite Mike being a little older than she, they'd had much in common. But years had gone by since then, and things had changed.

He couldn't remember the last time they'd had a real, long conversation. That day was the most time they'd spent together in recent memory. He pictured the Poe book she'd had with her. Maybe that was a starting point. He hadn't lied about wanting to brush up on the author. They could talk about Poe's works and go from there.

He left his car idling in the driveway and ran into his house, not bothering to take off his rain-spattered jacket as he ducked into the reading room.

The fake coyote head over the fireplace drew his attention, as always, jaws open, either in laughter or agony, he wasn't sure. He gave it a friendly wave and blew it a kiss, then turned toward the shelves. He knew there was at least one Poe volume in his family's collection. They had a copy of what seemed like everything, and no self-respecting reading room could claim the name without boasting a selection of the most famous poets. If he remembered right, it had been in the same spot for years.

Right in front of the bookshelf in question, however, was his father's high-backed armchair—currently occupied by his father. He was so quiet Mike had almost written him off as a part of the furniture.

"Hey, Dad. Um. Excuse me." He pointed toward the poetry shelf.

His father closed his own work of literature to set it on his armrest. "Michael, aren't you at work right now?"

"Oh, uh." He checked his watch. "I took a break to come home and get our Poe book."

His father's thick eyebrows rose with genuine interest. "Why?"

Mike did his best not to fidget. He'd asked a girl out. Not a big deal, even though it was. That was exactly why he never talked to his parents about girls.

Unfortunately, his dad zeroed in on that immediately. He took off his glasses. "Who are you trying to impress?"

Mike cleared his throat and looked away. "No one. It's not like that."

His father didn't buy that at all. "Let me hazard a guess, Michael. You're smitten with someone—"

"Don't say 'smitten'—"

"—and they're a Poe fan. And you think by reading Poe, you'll impress them."

Mike noticed the gender-neutral language. His parents had never made any assumptions about their son's sexuality. Mike had a sudden impulse to point out that it was specifically a girl, but that impulse was probably what his parents would call "internalized heteronormativity" or something. And besides, the less his dad knew about who Mike was interested in, the less likely that he'd be able to guess who it was.

So he shrugged. "Yeah. Basically."

His father stood with a gleam in his eye, setting his folded-up glasses on the surface of his book. "Ah, now, that might be how you impress the fan of a *novelist*, but Poe was, at heart, a poet."

Mike could recognize one of his father's lectures. He gesticulated as he spoke, paced without thinking as if words alone were insufficient to carry the passion of his thoughts.

"If this person really loves Poe's work—loves it because of its *Poe-ness*"—his hands clenched—"they'll want to experience the poetry with you. It's such an intimate thing; at the core of great art is something incomprehensible yet substantive, something real, a profundity that parries the mind and strikes deep in the heart. Poetry is this thing bared. Prose shrouds itself in fancies and fantasies that distract and soften the blow, but poetry is art at its most condensed. Poetry is distilled music, a knife taken to the soul, and like music, Michael, it absolutely must be experienced aloud."

Lectures like that were the reason Mike had never wanted to admit that he didn't really care for poetry.

His father continued, life in his eyes, "Why not ask them to read their favorite poem to you? Why not share that moment of abstrusity? There is nothing so loved by a lover of poetry than to provide this sharp depth of the mind, to experience it alongside someone they care about. I think it's no great leap to say that this potential would be ruined by your having studied the poetry beforehand in some mere effort to discuss it academically."

"You love discussing poems academically."

His grin was wide and genuine. "Yes, but that's not why I love poetry. Or *Poe*-etry!"

He seemed very impressed with his pun, so

Mike gave him a laugh. "Yeah, okay, that's a good idea. Thanks, Dad."

Mike's father winked and picked his book up again. "Now, don't you have people to save?"

"Don't you have papers to grade? Come to think of it, isn't Mom supposed to be home right now?"

His father gave a dismissive wave and settled back into his leather-cushioned seat, sliding on his reading glasses. "I've given up on predicting her schedule. Me, you've simply caught on a break."

"Sure. Bye, Dad."

Mike's dad said goodbye with raised eyebrows and a nod; he had already disappeared into his book again. He had the uncanny ability to go deep into any piece of literature at lightning speed, and sometimes, there was nothing that could be done about it.

Yeah. Okay. Ask Rebekah to read him her favorite poem. That could actually be pretty cool.

He made his way back to the car, an uneasy eagerness in his chest.

It didn't strike him until he'd almost arrived back at the station that because of the investigation into the strange incidents at Grant High, dating one of the students there—even just taking her out to dinner—would be a blatant conflict of interest.

Damn it.

If he wanted to do a good job and earn the respect of the other officers, he needed to stay away from her.

Mike pulled into a parking spot, checked his watch again, then grabbed the metal posse box he'd shoved all his notes into before battling a sudden gust of rain on his way to the station doors.

Mike sat at the conference table in the break room-slash-office to go through his paperwork, even though it made him feel oddly vulnerable. Anyone could creep up behind him and peer over his shoulder, but there weren't exactly any other options. Dempsey was there working, too, on his own papers, but otherwise it was mostly empty.

Mike settled at the far end of the table, away from Dempsey, and spread his notes out to go through for clarity. He wasn't a detective; his job was just to gather all the facts for the real detective to go through.

He could see Detective Ash from his seat. Her desk occupied the middle of the room, a sad attempt at a precinct bullpen, but she didn't seem to mind the odd placement. She had a sharp nose and a teardrop-shaped face, but Mike chiefly knew her as a frazzled brown ponytail puffing out over a crest of files.

Ash was the town's only career detective since the other had retired last month. As far as Mike knew, she was a force to be reckoned with. He doubted she even knew who he was, given her impossible workload and the fact he hadn't been there that long.

Officer Dempsey, however, was another story. Same age, same height, and same hair color as Mike, he worked through traffic tickets on the other end of the conference table, glancing over when he thought Mike wasn't looking. For whatever reason, Dempsey seemed to have it in for Mike. They'd gone through the academy together, and the guy had taken every opportunity to make Mike's life hell for no discernible reason. He'd even pushed for Mike to be the one covering the school . . . incidents. And meanwhile, Mike fell behind on his ticket quota. Dempsey had probably arranged it on purpose for just that reason.

Mike tried to focus on his paperwork. While someone had needed to do it, or the Trucco family would have pulled their biannual donations, the whole thing was little more than an exercise in futility. Both Scotty and Eddie had insisted their injuries had been purely accidental, and Veronica had been hesitant to talk about hers at all.

He was inclined to think that meant drugs rather than any kind of serial attacker. Then again, while that made sense for Eddie, how could Scotty have stripped out his own canine? But if he had, wouldn't that have warned the others off of it, at least for a while?

It didn't matter. It wasn't Mike's job to draw conclusions. He focused on his responsibility: he consolidated his notes for the day and made a list of questions for tomorrow, borrowing and adding to the ones Ash had half-interestedly given him already.

"Hey, Officer Mike." Dempsey finally acknowledged his presence. Mike couldn't figure out if the guy's voice was oddly low naturally or if he did it on purpose to try to be intimidating.

"It's Wilson," Mike corrected him, unfazed.

"Officer Mike," Dempsey said again, his tone provoking. "Did you figure it out? Is it ghosts?"

"I'm taking notes for Detective Ash. She'll decide whether or not it's ghosts."

"Kiss-ass." Dempsey chuckled under his breath and took off.

Mike pretended not to notice, the knot of frustration between his shoulder blades pulling tighter. Staying on Dempsey's bad side was a sure way to stay ostracized by the rest of the staff. Apparently, all Mike had to do to remain there, though, was do his job.

He thought about Rebekah, talking to her in his car, asking about her drawings, her hopeful look, her delicate fingers. He'd missed her. He wanted what they had back. The friendship, the easy connection.

There was something real there. Something he'd been looking for, for so long. Something that mattered.

Something way more important than getting on Dempsey's good side.

As he sat in the quiet station, the only sound the scribbling of Detective Ash's pen, Mike realized he didn't care anymore about being friends with and respected by the other officers. Letting that go felt . . . good. Like a weight lifted from his chest. The feeling of freedom.

He was going on a date with Rebekah. And he'd keep seeing her, too, if she let him. To avoid any problems, he'd leave her out of his notes and wouldn't talk about her around the office. Not like he had any friends there to discuss that stuff with, and there was no need to invite trouble anyway. But Mike deserved some modicum of happiness, and he wasn't going to let Dempsey, or the department, take it away from him.

* * *

By the time Rebekah caught up to the Raven, it had Hector's arms pulled behind him, clasped in its hands. They stood—well, the Raven stood, dragging Hector to his feet—at the center of the kaleidoscopic manor. The house's shifting shadows and cruel tapestries hardly registered with Rebekah anymore, but Hector's wide eyes darted around him in a wild panic.

Shirtless, wearing gray sweats, and restrained by the Raven's inhuman strength, Hector had never looked so vulnerable. She stepped silently toward him, and Hector's eyes latched onto her.

Unlike Eddie and Veronica, the Raven had decided not to muzzle Hector.

"You." His voice shook. "This is—this is what—how are you doing this?"

Rebekah didn't answer. He tried to stand up straight, to loom over her again, but the Raven held his hands too low behind him, and either way, the panic was clear in his face, in the way he shivered at every gust the manor exhaled over him.

"You're not going to scare me," he lied.

The Raven threw him to the floor and brandished a knife, long and gleaming in the intermittent light. The color drained from Hector's terrified face and he scrambled away from them, wild-eyed, scampering down a tilting hall, slipping on the dust on its floor.

The Raven pursued him with the knowing grace of a great cat, silently slinking with enough speed and dexterity to keep at Hector's heels. Rebekah watched with that all-over cognizance of a dream; she floated beside the Raven, observing the way it expertly mirrored Hector's movements—slowing when he slowed, speeding up when he ramped into another sprint, careening around corners and grasping twisted gargoyle statues, tripping and nearly impaling his hands on the jaws of rotting taxidermy. The

Raven didn't allow him to slow or his panic to subside, panting, running, bleeding, searching the impossible manor for an exit.

Cloak billowing behind it, the Raven slipped smoothly out of the way of the obstacles that caused Hector such grief, revealing a roughly human shape, still couched in shadow, the adept footfalls of its black boots making no noise against the aged wood.

Hector finally catapulted himself through a stained-glass window, landing in a pool of shards and earning himself myriad lacerations along his body. He got to his feet with a desperate spot of hope as he glimpsed the freedom of the night sky. But as he ran into the tangled trees encircling the mansion, getting lost among their dry trunks and grasping branches, ripping his clothes, scratching his skin anew, he only earned himself the choking damp air and moon-speckled darkness of the unearthly night.

The Raven kept unceasingly after him as Hector's stamina slowly dwindled. When he finally collapsed, gasping desperately, it was in the middle of a vast clearing that lay shrouded under cloud cover, a canvas of dark desert between the waving boughs of the dead forest. The Raven stood over him and Rebekah beside it, both looking down on the teen who couldn't speak for his exhausted, labored breaths.

Covered in bloody gashes—from the glass, the trees, the manor's sets of gnashing teeth—his eyes bloodshot, his lips red, Hector raised his trembling hands between himself and his pursuers.

But they said nothing. Only watched his whimpers until he collapsed from exhaustion.

Rebekah shot awake with a fast-beating heart and an ache in her legs. The dusty blinds lifted in the wind as they did on every night she dreamed about the Raven, letting the moonlight drape across the black tome on her nightstand. She picked the book up and hugged it to her chest, the way she had when she was little, and bathed in the frigid night air until the energy retreated from her limbs.

She felt like she'd chased Hector herself, although she couldn't have left the room. Even if she had, there was no way she could've done to Hector what the Raven had. Hector was on the track team. She'd never have been able to outpace him.

Then again, she couldn't have had the strength to rip out Veronica's hair, but she could almost remember how it felt, how she would have gripped the strands between her fingers, how she would have braced the pliers against Scotty's tooth. She couldn't have had the speed or stamina to chase Hector, but she felt the aftershocks of it all the same.

If she'd snuck out of her room to physically do those things, someone would have noticed, wouldn't they? Whatever was happening was stranger than all that. Less possible than all that. And whatever it was, it belonged to her.

13

Rebekah and Mike left school together again the next day. She hadn't said a word to her mom about Mike except to text that they were going to go hang out. All she'd received in response was a question about whether to have dinner waiting. No interrogation about who Mike was, what they were going to do, or when Rebekah would be home. She wasn't sure how to feel about that.

"Any place in mind?" She pocketed her phone as Mike started the car. Coralie's expression had upgraded from confusion to suspicion as she leaned against her bright red convertible, glancing over from between Andrea's ponytail and Veronica's Grant High beanie.

"Yeah, I know a spot." His expression might have worried her if it wasn't so genuine, with a glimmer of eagerness in his eyes like he'd been planning that moment for a while. Was it the date that he'd spent so long thinking about, or had he specifically planned something special for her?

Why would he? They barely knew one another.

As Mike pulled out of the parking lot, they managed to make conversation without it feeling forced. They discussed Rebekah's classes for a while, but she ran out of things to say that weren't related to the torture the kids at Grant High subjected her to—or the torture she gave back to them—so she pushed the topic instead onto his career.

"Oh, I have no idea," he said with a nervous laugh. "Everyone assumes I'm aiming for detective, but I'm not sure. I'm still new and getting a feel for how the precinct works."

"If you're so new, why did they put you on this thing at the school?"

He scoffed. "That's why they put me on it. There's no evidence anyone was with Eddie when he was bucked off his horse, and Veronica outright said she was alone, although if you ask me, she's just trying to protect her friends from some drug charges. I don't see these accidents having any connection at all, much less through the school. The chief just wants me to be seen around campus to make the parents happier."

"Do you know . . . what happened to Veronica?" Rebekah knew she shouldn't ask, but she hadn't been able to find out a thing, except for Alice's summary of a "freak accident." She hadn't heard anything about Hector yet either, but she couldn't bring him up first.

Mike hesitated, shooting her a look. "Everything I tell you about this case is strictly confidential, okay? Even the fact that I'm telling you anything."

"I swear, I won't say a word to Nora or Alice. I won't even tell my cat."

That earned her a snigger. "I'm not supposed to talk to anyone about any details in case something makes it out to the press. But the assignment they have me on is insane, and there's no one I can talk to at the precinct." He said it a little darkly but moved on before she could ask. "Veronica said she was out mountain biking, alone, middle of the night. She got her hair stuck in the chain of her bike somehow, and it fell down the hill without her." He shook his head in frustration. "There're too many implausible pieces to that story. Any mountain bike enthusiast would wear a helmet or at least tie her hair back. I doubt she'd go off alone in the middle of the night. I think she snuck out to hang with her friends, and they all got fucked up and had an accident. Maybe the part about her hair getting caught in the chain is even true." He winced. "God, if her family ever found out and thought I was implying something though . . . Man, this town is a social minefield."

"I know what you mean," Rebekah added quietly, frowning at her hands in her lap.

He flashed his eyes to her. "You all right?"

"Yeah. Yeah, no, I'm fine. You're just starting to get an idea of what it's like to go to school with these people."

He let out a sharp laugh. "Yeah, I guess you're right. Hadn't thought about that."

The drive was a bit longer than Rebekah expected, out past the edge of town, along a winding road that crumbled out to dirt. A hopeful line of tall, stringy grass separated two worn-in tire tracks, brushing the underside of the car. It occurred to her she ought to be nervous about a guy taking her someplace remote on a first date, but she couldn't be afraid of Mike. He was so genuine and naïve, things she wished she could mirror.

And aside from that, she found it difficult to be truly afraid of anyone since she had the Raven on her side.

The dirt road morphed into gravel: the long, overgrown driveway to an abandoned house perched near the edge of an oceanside cliff. A break in the evergreens allowed the endless horizon of water to paint a blue backdrop to the looming façade of the aging manor, all weeds and wood and faded peeling paint. It was a poor copy of the Raven's nightmare home, the way a photograph failed to encompass a sunset.

Rebekah's breath froze in her lungs. He knew. Somehow Mike knew about the Raven and wanted her to talk. That's why he'd taken her all the way out there, alone.

"What do you think?" he asked, and the grin on his face was so genuine that she doubted herself again.

"I—"

"Oh, I brought a picnic." He pointed to a cooler in the backseat.

Rebekah's thoughts whirled. Could that be a coincidence?

As if sensing her discomfort, his expression morphed into a frown. "You don't like it. I'm sorry. I should've asked."

"No! No, I do like it." The strange thing was, it wasn't a lie. If it weren't for the Raven— and everything else happening in her life—it would probably have been a great idea. "This was thoughtful. I just didn't expect you to . . . how did you find this place?"

"It's called the Lee house. Been coming here since I was a kid. I actually used to call it—" He stopped himself, watching her. "Look, it's no big deal if you want to go somewhere else. There's a nice park closer to the beach. I just—"

"No, let's stay here. I'm sorry for how I— I just had a dream about a place like this recently, so it threw me off. That's all I was thinking about. Come on."

Rebekah got out of the car, hesitating only long enough to wonder whether she should bring her backpack with the Poe book and the notebook sketchbook. She wasn't likely to need them, not if she and Mike talked the whole time, but she usually liked to keep them on hand.

In the end, she decided to leave her backpack on the floor of the passenger seat. If he wanted her to draw something for him, she could go back and get it. The book would be safe on its own, in a car in the middle of nowhere, and there weren't any drawings she wanted to show off.

She certainly didn't want him to see any pictures of the Raven. He'd said he was getting nowhere with his investigation, but it still felt too much like tempting fate.

He met her in front of the car with the cooler. It was easier to be around Mike than it was other people. He didn't seem to need anything from her first, any assurances or qualifications. He didn't seem to think she was some problem child he needed to tiptoe around or a weird girl he got saddled with.

He just thought she was a person. And that felt fantastic.

"I normally hang out inside when I want to be alone." He gestured toward the admittedly dangerous-looking entry, the wooden boards of the porch cracked and uneven. "But I was thinking we could picnic in the grass over here, with the view."

It was obvious he loved the place and actually cared about her and what she liked. It wasn't some convoluted way to draw her out and get her to confess.

"No," she said, bumping his shoulder with hers. "Let's eat inside. It's too chilly out here and I want to see the house anyway."

Happiness sparked in Mike's eyes, and a

bubble of hope rose in Rebekah's chest, frightening and lovely.

He led her past the rickety front porch and around the side of the house, along a sparse stone path between tall, thorny weeds and in through a back door that opened with a hauntingly familiar groan. She stepped into an earthy hall of aged wood and dust, the cool-moist air of stagnant life, and when Mike closed the door behind them, the birds and the distant ocean and the wind through the grass vanished behind the bracing arms of time. The walls were old and rotting, a danger to them with their warped planks, but the house itself gave Rebekah the impression of being embraced by a hollow tree, not warmed so much as sheltered from the wind.

"Quiet," she noticed, feeling the need to whisper.

Mike whispered back, "That's one of my favorite things about this place. It's weirdly good at keeping out sound, and you can pretend you're sort of nowhere."

One door had fallen from its hinges and stood off-kilter in its doorway, but the others had swollen shut. Mike led her past them all and into a tall foyer with a once-grand staircase.

The floor there had been swept clean, a broom leaning in the corner by the boarded-up front door, and a pile of carefully folded blankets at the side of the room looked considerably less old than the rest of the house. Mike shook out one of them and laid it on the floor, the pale plaid catching slits of sunlight slipping between the boards.

"I come here to be alone sometimes." A normal volume. But his tone was hesitant. "What do you think?"

"It's . . . really calming."

He visibly relaxed, letting out his held breath in the stale room. "I'm glad. Here, have a seat."

They sat on the soft fleece blanket, and he

served food from the cooler: an after-school selection of chips alongside turkey-and-tomato sandwiches. It wasn't a remarkable feast, all told, but it must have required a decent amount of foresight. Like he really had been planning their date.

"This place means a lot to you, doesn't it?" she asked, before she had a chance to think it through.

Mike shrugged. "Yeah. It's nice to be alone sometimes, and this place is the most alone I can get."

"Then that's . . . pretty brave of you. Showing it to me, I mean. We kind of hardly know each other anymore."

"That's true." He finished plating her food and set the meal in front of her. "But at the same time, it felt natural. This place has always reminded me of you somehow."

They'd once been as close as two kids in different age groups could get. Had she explained her imaginary friend to him back then, the trappings of her strange dreams? Maybe he remembered that story on some level and still thought of her sometimes because of it.

That would be kind of sweet, actually, if it was true. And it'd mean that he'd taken her there because she was Rebekah and not just because he thought it'd be a nice place to take a girl. Which would also mean he'd *asked her out* because she was Rebekah and not just because she'd smiled at him in the hallway and asked about his job.

"Thank you," she said, focusing on her sandwich. "I mean—I don't know if that's the right thing to say, but— I'm just glad you asked me here today."

He stopped mid-bite. "Really?"

"Yeah. Is that weird?"

"No! No, I don't think so. I hope not."

As they ate their meal, the bubble of hope inside her expanded to fill her whole chest.

* * *

After the sun set in a blaze of golden light, Mike turned on the flashlight on his phone, casting the room in stark white as he revealed two small pieces of cake he'd kept hidden in the cooler. The plastic wrap clung a little too firmly to the cake, and they laughed as they wrestled chocolate frosting away from it. The cake itself was store-bought, a touch stale, and a little too sweet for Rebekah's taste, but it was one of the nicest things anyone had done for her.

They'd sat there for hours, talking about anything and everything.

"It was terrible." Mike continued his story about the police academy.

"Then why'd you do it?"

"I don't mean the learning-how-to-be-a-cop part. The procedure stuff, emergency driving, firearm training, that's what I signed up for. But I guess I got off on the wrong foot with . . . well, everyone. At first, the other recruits ignored me, but then they started pulling stupid jokes. All the classics, you know? Throwing my stuff on the roof, getting me blamed for things, putting little rocks in my shoes to slow me down on the mile."

"That's terrible."

He finished his cake then balled up the cellophane. "The jokes cut off after we graduated. Now they just don't talk to me."

Rebekah watched him. He seemed unbothered by it—or was he just good at hiding it? Did it matter?

What he'd gone through was different from what Coralie and Scotty had done to Rebekah, but somehow, it made her feel safer around him. He knew, at least a little, what it was like. He knew how it felt to be looked down on by all your peers.

She hadn't thought much about Mike the last few years, and recently, when she'd seen him at school, only about his investigation into the Raven and the dreams. But that night she realized that their old connection was strong as ever . . . it was like a vacation in a different life, one where no one seemed to mind she was there, where she was allowed to just exist.

When the food was gone, they laid on their backs, staring up at the arching wooden ceiling as though they could see through it to the stars.

"I'm glad you said yes," Mike whispered after a breathless moment.

"I'm . . . glad you asked," she said, feeling like she was taking a risk. Exposing herself too much. Wishing she could trust him.

Mike propped himself up on one elbow to study her, his eyes calm and kind in the moonlight. Then he leaned down to kiss her, and she kissed him back.

It was Rebekah's first kiss. It was a bit awkward, and quiet, and warm with his breath, the soft pressure of his lips against hers. It was a strange feeling. Comforting, even as it sent buzzy energy through her limbs, a new warmth in her chest.

When he pulled away, all she wanted to do was kiss him again.

Mike gently tucked her hair behind her ear then said, "We should probably head home."

"Yeah." Then she kissed him again quick because she could.

He lingered a moment, then pulled back, taking her hand. "I wish we could stay longer, but I'm serious, I need to get home. But . . . Let's do this again."

"Definitely."

"Definitely."

When he stood to clean up their mess, Rebekah felt the sudden absence of his body heat. Cold in an abandoned house at night. She kept close to Mike as they walked back to the car.

* * *

The night had turned the ocean into an endless black void, the wild grasses whispering in the moonlight. Mike's car gleamed, sitting in the clearing where they'd left it—with the passenger door wide open. Rebekah ran over and looked inside, her heart in her throat. No. No, no, no. The backpack was gone. She raced back toward the house and found it, open and disheveled, discarded under the eaves of the house.

Rebekah knelt beside it and rapidly searched through the contents to make sure nothing was stolen. Poe book, check. Sketchbook, check. Homework folders, check. Her pencil pouch was still intact, corduroy patched with duct tape. Good. Nothing was . . .

The little bundle of Veronica's hair.

Rebekah's breath caught in the quiet evening. Why had she kept that? Was it on the ground somewhere? Had Mike seen it? Or had it been taken by whoever had attacked her bag?

If it had, then they knew. They knew, at the very least, that Rebekah was connected.

She zipped up the pockets, hands shaking. Someone knew. They'd come all the way out there searching for proof, and they'd found it. How had they known where to look?

"The hell?" Mike came up behind her, shining his phone flashlight on her. "Are you okay? When you ran off like that, you scared me."

Rebekah straightened, afraid her voice would waver. "I'm fine. Sorry. I just . . . I have all my homework in here and didn't want to lose it."

Mike scowled at her a moment, then swiveled back toward his car. "I wonder why my alarm didn't go off?"

As she started to shrug into her backpack's straps, Mike shouted, "Rebekah, wait!"

There was a tug and a scraping sound from above, and Rebekah looked up in time to see a plastic bucket upend over her from the sagging roof. Cold water splashed down on her before the bucket itself struck her in the head then rolled away.

Stunned, she stood there in shock as her senses slowly came back online.

No. Not water. The cold liquid in her hair, stinging her eyes, creeping down her shoulders, was not water.

She was getting way too familiar with that smell.

"Holy shit, Rebekah," Mike said, stepping closer. "Are you hurt?"

She put out a hand to stop him, trembling as the acrid fumes of someone's urine surrounded her. She found a dry spot on her shirt to wipe off her face, carefully cleaning her eyes.

A car turned on in the distance, revving its engine and grinding its wheels against the dirt road. Bright headlights illuminated the trees for a fraction of a moment before they turned out of sight, vanishing into the country dark, leaving only echoes of laughter. Rebekah glimpsed one of the luxurious brand-new convertibles that frequented Grant High.

Who else would it be?

"What is that?" Mike scrunched his nose from the stench. "Is that . . . ?"

Her eyes burned. She burned all over, hot and light and cold, and the sharp smell crowding her nose was enough to make it plausible that the tears were nothing more than a biological reflex.

Carefully, Rebekah removed her backpack and set it aside. The light was imperfect, but it seemed like a miracle had spared it and its contents from the worst of the piss-fall. No, that had been reserved squarely for her head.

A piece of string, thin enough to go unremarked in the uneven moonlight, connected the loop at the top of the backpack to the bucket's handle by way of a rusty hook in the wall.

Behind her, Mike walked to his car then returned with something. "Here."

He offered a fluffy towel, colorless in the moonlight. Its baked-in scent of dust was a welcome, if brief, respite from the stench of the urine. Rebekah avoided his gaze as she accepted it, mortified that Mike saw her that way.

Ever gallant, he never mentioned it. "Always carry a towel, right?"

She didn't want to dirty his towel with some stranger's piss—but she'd already soiled it by touching it, so she started to wipe off, her movements on autopilot.

Mike stayed beside her, despite the smell. "Sorry I don't have a change of clothes, or a robe, or anything. The closest I have is my windbreaker, I guess. You can change into that. I just feel like it would be uncomfortable for you."

At that point, she'd ride home naked just to get rid of the odor. "No, I—"

"I'll go grab it." He disappeared again, crunching over to his car, a hurried half-jog.

Rebekah shivered in the cold, the wet clothes sticking to her skin. She wondered if she should run down to the water and wash off. She didn't want to ruin his clothes, too.

When he came back, it was with a police-issue windbreaker over one arm.

She leaned away from him. "No, Mike, that's your uniform. I—"

"It's no big deal. Just wash it when you get home and give it back. It's not like I don't know where to find you if I need it."

He shoved the windbreaker into her hands, then turned away, pointedly staring in the other direction to give her privacy as she changed.

Rebekah hated crying, but tears of gratitude slipped down her cheeks anyway as she peeled off her urine-soaked clothes and patted herself as dry as she could. Then she picked up his windbreaker, finding the hole in the shoulder

Dupaw had made during his escape attempt. It felt like so long ago. She put it on and zipped it up, whispering, "I'm sorry."

"Sorry for what?" Mike asked over his shoulder.

"I'm getting . . . I'm getting it all over your towel and your jacket. I'll get it all over your car, too."

"That's not your fault, Rebekah. You have nothing to apologize for. What other options do you have? Walk home?"

The idea was like a spark of hope. "I could—"

"Are you decent?"

"Yes."

He turned around again and looked her directly in the eyes. "You are not walking home. It's the middle of the night."

"It's not that late, and I know the way."

"No way, Rebekah, I'm taking you home."

"You don't want to smell like—"

Before she could react, he pulled her into a hug.

Rebekah stiffened, but Mike held tight, his cheek against her piss-soaked hair, rocking her side to side as if to maximize contact.

She laughed, a disbelieving chuckle that forced its way out of her.

He brought them still again, just holding her. "Come on. Hug me back."

She hugged him back, fighting all her instincts to spare his clothes.

"Kids can be assholes sometimes."

"Yeah." She pushed away and winced at the damp spots on his shirt.

Mike didn't seem to mind at all. He gestured to his car. "Come on. I'll take you home."

She hesitated. "Mike?"

"Yeah?"

"Thanks. Really. Thank you."

Moonlight glittered in his eyes, and her heart pinched. "Anything."

Anything. Not anytime, but anything.

Rebekah picked up her things and followed him, head down.

He couldn't mean that, could he? He wouldn't if he knew the truth about her and the Raven. Even given his history with the police academy, could she trust that he would understand? He wanted to write off the rich bastards at Grant High with "kids can be assholes sometimes" and let them get away with their stunts, like everyone else did.

But they wouldn't get away with it that time. They weren't going to get away with any of it, not anymore.

A massive bell tolled, broad and heavy and brass. The clapper, like a cold teardrop, announced every new second with a bellowing strike that hit Andrea like a physical weight. Thrumming from all sides, rattling her bones. The ceiling was unreachable, shrouded in darkness, but the bottom of the bell—the considerable weight of the clapper, bigger than she was—bore down above her, driving her to the floor.

There were no chains, no ropes or pulleys. The room around her was perfectly square, a near-seamless stone broken only by one slit of light centered in each wall, reaching from floor to distant ceiling but not wide enough for escape; just wide enough to see out into the unearthly forest far below. Just wide enough to see a ghostly girl and a shadow creature watching her from some impossible lamplit hall, one of them sickly amused, the other dispassionate with flickering animal eyes. There was no door, only that slight gap of a window.

She pressed herself against the gap into the impossible hallway. That girl was Rebekah, wasn't it? She wasn't easy to recognize, standing tall, emblazoned with a creeping smile. The black clothes she wore reflected the creature beside her. The bell tolled again, echoing through Andrea's body.

The shadow thing had no signs of life, so Andrea begged Rebekah to let her out, or at least to stop the bell, but every new clang drowned out her thoughts, her screams, suffocating her like she was screaming into a pillow.

The vibrations rocketed through her body, pounded into her head, an unflinching assault against the inside of her skull: again and again and again, always, allowing less than a moment's respite between attacks.

Neither of the creatures at the door would help her. Andrea fell, braced herself on the floor, clutched her hands over her ears, but they might well have been made of tissue paper, ineffectual against the pounding, pounding, pounding. Tears flowed from her eyes, but through the endless rattling, she could hardly feel them.

There was no thought behind her anymore,

no conscious impulse that could be heard over the bell; as she curled there, digging her fingernails into her scalp, she recognized the strain on her lungs and throat that meant she must have been screaming, but she couldn't hear it over the relentless toll.

14

Rebekah sketched the Raven where she sat on her planter on Grant High's front lawn, legs stretched before her. She doodled, familiarizing herself with the creature's shape: a narrow build shrouded beneath a hood, two glistening eyes like a cat's reflecting the moon. Its hands were black leather gloves with red filigree, but they were usually hidden by the smooth folds of its cloak, which had an oily glimmer to it, like a raven's shining feathers. She'd seen it wearing black boots once, but usually its feet were simply hidden, or maybe didn't exist at all.

A nightmare thing, invented by an

imaginative child who'd read too much Poe. An imaginative child who . . . was magic?

The more she tried to figure out exactly what she was doing each night, the less Rebekah could be certain about any one option. It sometimes felt like she'd physically done something, like how her legs had been sore after chasing Hector, and sometimes she woke up with some physical object or reminder, like Veronica's hair or the rusty pliers. She usually found her window open the next morning, even when she'd made it a point to close and lock it the night before. But she knew she couldn't have physically done the things in her dreams, and if she had, then her tormentors would have been able to prove—or at least claim—it was her. It was their reactions more than anything else that made her think there must have been some kind of real magic bringing them into her dreams.

But if that was the case, then how had those "accidents" occurred? Had her victims all made up those stories to cover up their nightmares? Rebekah couldn't imagine Veronica busting her bike just to avoid explaining an impossible dream.

Rebekah drew Eddie while she thought about it, the look of anguish on his face as the sledgehammer had come down on him.

Alice appeared at her side, standing uncertain on the grass. Elaborate strawberry braids hung over her plain black-gray uniform. Rebekah snapped her sketchbook shut and sat up to make room for her to take a seat.

"What's up?" Alice asked, still standing. "Are you okay?"

"Yeah, why wouldn't I be?"

"I don't know. You've been weird lately. I mean, you don't even draw Pluto anymore, just that creepy guy from your nightmare."

Rebekah ignored the sour taste that Alice's words imparted. She wouldn't let it ruin her good mood. "I guess I outgrew him," she said, fishing Alice's English textbook out of her backpack.

"You loved that little cat."

"It's just a stupid kids' comic, Alice."

Alice raised her eyebrows. "All right, sorry."

She took the seat, and things got quiet between them. Rebekah handed over the textbook, and Alice studied it, her fingers lingering on the title. There wasn't much people-watching to do; Rebekah had picked the spot forever ago specifically because it didn't put too many students in her line of sight, nor was she in theirs. So they sat together in the cold, watching the walls, the length of grass leading to the parking lot, kicking their heels against the stone ledge.

"I just—" Alice paused, worrying at her upper lip. "Look, I don't mean anything by it, but . . ."

"But what?"

She glanced around, but there was no one else near them. She leaned in anyway. "It's just kind of weird that these accidents are all happening to people who've gone after you, specifically."

Rebekah stiffened.

Alice met her eyes. "Look, I'm just saying. You've been acting kind of weird. You went out with that cop guy? And the way you were just drawing Eddie—"

"What, I'm not allowed to feel happy he got what was coming to him?" Rebekah pushed her words out in front of a rising panic. "It's weird that I think it's cool Scotty lost a tooth after what he did to me? It's weird that a cute guy asked me out?"

"I'm not saying—"

"Then what are you saying?"

Alice shut her mouth. Rebekah felt numb all over. Alice had guessed it? How? Was Rebekah really that obvious? How could she keep anyone else from drawing the same conclusion?

Maybe if she targeted someone else, someone

random at the school. But that defeated the purpose, didn't it?

Did it? Almost everyone owned just as much blame as Coralie and Scotty. Everyone who'd watched and done nothing, everyone who'd stared and laughed, everyone who'd trampled on her sketchbook and taunted her at the party and taken a video of her opening her locker, everyone who'd whispered "piss bitch" as she passed. She didn't have to limit herself to Scotty's and Coralie's friends.

Everyone at Grant High deserved to meet the Raven.

"Nothing. Sorry." Alice stuffed the textbook into her backpack and stood. She didn't exchange the English textbook for her history one. She just took it. "The bell's about to go off," she said and headed into the school without a glance back.

Something had gone wrong. Rebekah had made a mistake, but she didn't know what it was or how to avoid it again. Except for Mike, Alice was her only friend, and she'd pushed her away.

Rebekah turned to hunt for Coralie's clump of followers. Sometimes they hung out by her bright-red convertible, and sometimes they jetted inside out of the cold. That day, they stood in the unseasonal sunlight at the edge of the parking lot, talking amongst themselves, light glinting off the plastic coating of their binders. Squinting, Rebekah made out Andrea's face among them. She had something in her hands, scribbling down notes.

The school bell rang, announcing the beginning of class. Andrea jumped at the sound, dropping her notebook and pen to clamp both hands over her ears.

Rebekah grinned at the panic in her eyes.

After a week of toting her collection of reused and repurposed notebooks and folders from class to class, Rebekah decided she needed somewhere to set it all down. Even if it was the pee locker. She'd cleaned it pretty thoroughly, anyway.

When she opened it that day, however, she found an envelope at the bottom. Unmarked. Worried it might be a glitter bomb, a note smeared with someone's shit, or something equally "hilarious"—she slowly picked it up and opened it carefully, trying to make it look like she was merely going through her backpack.

It was the lock of Veronica's hair, along with a note.

I know it's you.

Lightning shot up Rebekah's spine. She shoved the envelope and note into the big pouch of her backpack, cramming it to the bottom to make absolutely certain no one would see it, on purpose or by accident. Then she glanced around, searching the hall for anyone who was watching, anyone who might be too interested.

She had assumed it was Coralie, but she didn't recognize the handwriting. If it was someone else, she needed to find whomever it was. She needed to figure out who it was and bring them in front of the Raven.

But no one around seemed to be noticing her; they talked among themselves, slammed their lockers, scrolled through their phones. For once, she didn't see any eyes peering through the crowd after her, no heads ducking away from her gaze—

There. Someone glanced away. Tom Schultz, from her stats class. He didn't even bother suppressing a laugh. He actively pointed at her, acted out writing with an invisible pen on invisible paper, then chortled. One of his friends said something, prompting Tom to unzip his pants and mime urinating on the ground, causing them both to fall into fits of giggles.

Rebekah burned with shame. Why did that little shit, scrawny Tom with his ridiculous hair, not even one of the cool kids, get to treat her like that? Why did he have it out for her suddenly? He used to leave her alone. He had gotten a new fancy car, though. Could he have been the one who'd tracked her and Mike out to the Lee house? If he left the note, then it had to be him. It made sense. He wanted to keep up with the other kids, and as they got crueler, he felt confident amping up his taunts. She would have bet money it was Coralie who'd written the note, but she knew Coralie's handwriting, and that wasn't it. Why would it need to be her, anyway? A lot of people at the school had it out for Rebekah. A lot of them had laughed. A lot of them had latched on to that nickname. And Tom was one of them. And he knew about Veronica's hair. He knew about Rebekah and the Raven. Would he use that knowledge as currency to get in with the other kids? If he was going to go to the police, he wouldn't be taunting her. He'd just do it. No, he wanted to wield his power, make her feel small, keep her in her place.

Just like Coralie.

Rebekah shut her locker and turned to head toward class, then stopped face-to-face with Coralie herself.

Speak of the devil, and she shall appear.

"I saw you with that cop," Coralie said, her penetrating confidence bolstered by something more openly hostile than before. Her laugh pierced Rebekah like knives. "What are you trying to *do* with him? Do you think he actually likes you?"

Veronica and Andrea stood behind her, neither of them participating but neither of them leaving. Veronica consciously adjusted her hat, refusing to look at Rebekah, but Andrea glanced nervously between her and Coralie.

Rebekah tried not to buckle, but then Coralie stepped forward, and Rebekah found herself stumbling back. She hit the locker behind her, and Coralie crept in closer, along with the same dark dread that always accompanied her. She leaned one arm on the lockers beside Rebekah's head, pinning her in place.

"You're worthless, Beka." There was a syrupy condescension to her voice, like Rebekah was a child Coralie had deigned to educate. "You're nothing, just like your drunk mom and your deadbeat dad."

Rebekah said weakly, "Nora isn't—"

"You think that cop doesn't see it? You think he can't smell it on you? You reek of pathetic, and no matter what you do, no matter what you try or where you go, you'll never be able to wash that off."

Coralie straightened, flicking her hair off her shoulder. "I just thought you should know."

She left, and Andrea and Veronica followed her, eyes down. Rebekah couldn't move.

The hallway emptied as passing period came to a close.

Mike had seemed so honest, but she hadn't fully convinced herself he wasn't lying. Why would he have prepped such a perfect date for her after all that time? Why would the house remind him of her when they hadn't been close in years?

After everything she'd done, why could Coralie still get to her?

Rebekah needed to stop circling her, needed to stop daydreaming and dive in for the attack. More than anything, Rebekah needed to see Coralie on her knees in front of the Raven. Maybe it could take a sledgehammer to her legs—no, better yet, scar her pretty face with one of those wicked knives from the cistern. Wound her where it hurt the most. There could be no more waiting for the perfect torture; she'd figure it out later. Rebekah wanted Coralie in the manor immediately.

No, no, Tom had to come first. Tom, who'd somehow found out about Rebekah. She

needed to protect herself—and the Raven—
if she wanted to bring Coralie down and get
away with it.

And damn, did she need to bring Coralie down.

Alice was nowhere to be seen at lunch. Rebekah
glanced around for her but honestly dreaded
finding her anywhere. If she was at one of the
tables, laughing with a group of students, it'd
mean she'd been promoted out of the "social
pariah" group and wouldn't have any reason to
talk to Rebekah again. But if Alice sat alone,
it'd mean she would rather be completely on
her own than sit next to Rebekah, even for the
length of their lunch. But Rebekah couldn't
find her anywhere, which meant there was still
the slimmest chance she was in the library doing homework or staying late in class to talk to
a teacher.

Rebekah did see Tom, warm under the

embrace of a gas-powered lamp, laughing with a group of friends she hardly recognized. Kids cooler than he was. Was he already moving up the social ladder? Normally, he faded into the woodwork, like Rebekah wished she could. Average height, weird hair, bland face. Nothing about him stood out. He was just another boy with well-to-do parents. But he was laughing with kids who weren't on Scotty's level but closer to it than he usually was.

As she observed them, he made a crack, and they all looked over at Rebekah before quickly turning back to each other when they saw her focused on them. They had been caught. And were clearly uncomfortable.

Were they afraid?

A chime indicated a new text from Nora: *Thank you for lunch! It's delicious!* with a stuck-out-tongue emoji. Rebekah had only made a couple of peanut-butter-and-jelly sandwiches for each of them, hardly groundbreaking, and she couldn't even agree they were delicious. But that was just because it was a sunny day. Paint was never a good complement to peanut butter.

Maybe Nora had just wanted to encourage her to make lunch more often. Maybe she would. She hadn't thought that far ahead.

Scotty and his friends were never hard to spot; there was usually a football in the air to catch the eye or laughter so loud that it echoed across the schoolyard. There they were, sitting at a table under a wide-brimmed umbrella. Scotty leaned across the mosaic top to see Eddie's phone, both laughing at some joke. Scotty was officially gauze-free and seemed like he was determined to pretend nothing had ever happened. Hector sat next to him in a long-sleeved shirt, hardly moving . . .

He had his eyes on Rebekah.

He flinched when she met his gaze but didn't look away. He watched her through the shifting crowd of students, a hint of fear in his eyes, but there was something else there, too. Something she couldn't place.

Was he planning something?

Rebekah forced herself to keep his gaze. Whatever he was planning, she had power over him. And Scotty, and Eddie. She knew he knew that, and she pressed it, hardening her eyes until he finally broke and turned away. She won their little contest.

She was winning.

Soon all the shit-brains at Grant High would learn to leave her alone forever—or suffer consequences. And none of them would be able to prove it.

She caught Tom casting looks at her again, either daring or defensive, she couldn't tell. But it didn't matter. He shouldn't have played his hand. It was his turn to suffer.

* * *

That night, Rebekah and Mike went out again, that time to a diner with wide windows where they ordered burgers. She tried to relax, but she couldn't make herself forget Coralie's words, couldn't shake the feeling she'd gotten last night that she couldn't be completely certain Mike meant anything he said, that he liked being around her.

What if he was on to her? What if he'd worn jeans and a fleece jacket today, his curly black hair freed from his uniform cap, specifically to put her at ease? What if he was misrepresenting his investigation to make her think he wasn't looking into her? How could she know for sure?

All she wanted to do was go to sleep and bring Tom in front of the Raven.

"Hector's family is jumping on this, too," Mike complained out of nowhere. He spoke quietly, glancing around to make sure no one heard. "Hector told me straight-out nothing happened to him, but I think all the parents are getting together on this Let's-not-believe-our-kids thing. They just want to have some reason for their kids' sudden change of behavior that isn't their fault, so they're pushing some contrived-accident conspiracy."

"You talked to Hector?" Rebekah asked and only a moment later realized she should have kept her stupid mouth shut.

"I had nothing to talk to him *about* except his parents' unfounded concerns about his mental state. I asked if he'd had any weird accidents or anything else he wanted to report, and he said no." Mike frowned, the expression exaggerated by the stubble that darkened his cheeks. "He said it fast, actually, like he'd already planned on what he was going to say. You'd think he'd want to make something up to sound interesting, but he must understand that these things have real consequences."

They were all lying to Mike because they really experienced what Rebekah put them through in their dreams. Because they didn't want to sound insane.

"Anyway. Sorry to be a bummer; this assignment's driving me up the wall. I doubt I have to remind you about the confidentiality clause on our relationship agreement, do I?"

Rebekah huffed a laugh despite herself. "I don't remember signing anything."

"Me neither." He blushed. It was cute how easily he did that. "But, you know, historically, a kiss used to count as a signature."

"Oh, no, how many goats did I sell you? I'll have to break the news to my mom."

He laughed, louder than Rebekah expected, and buried his response behind a mouthful of fries.

She watched him, his round, friendly face, his kind eyes, and sunshine smile like a fresh outdoor breeze. He couldn't be lying to her, could he? She was lying to him—what if he saw through that? What if he'd seen through it from the beginning?

Mike tilted his head slightly. "What are you thinking about?"

She shook herself out of it. "Sorry. I was just thinking about . . . um, what happened to Eddie."

He covered one of her hands with his, the contact a comforting feeling. "It sucks, what happened to him. Accidents like that are scary; they could happen to anyone."

No, not anyone. Just people like Scotty, and Tom, and Coralie.

"Yeah, I guess it's kind of scary." She pulled her hand free, though it was hard to let him go. "Anyway. You're not finding anything at the school?"

"No." He sat back as their food was delivered then picked up his burger. "Nothing but a rash of bad dreams, apparently."

Rebekah watched him take a big bite and echoed, trying not to sound too interested, "Bad dreams?"

Mike shrugged, taking a moment to swallow. "A few of the students mentioned they had a bad dream the night of the accident. That's not surprising, given what happened to them. Still, it's technically the only thing they have in common." He thought for a second, then grinned. "Maybe I should write that up in my report."

"But it's nothing, right?"

"Yeah, that . . . was a joke, Rebekah."

"Oh." She gave an awkward laugh. "Sorry." She nibbled at her burger but could've been eating cardboard for all she tasted.

Rebekah had been starting to hope that dating Mike would help her avoid suspicion but couldn't help but wonder if it was doing the exact opposite.

Mike added, "If I hint that Freddy Krueger is behind this, I'll never hear the end of it."

Where had the conversation gotten off-track? Why was she feeling so sour if she was sitting across the table from someone who actually liked her? Mike was supposed to be something good about her life. She couldn't—wouldn't—let Coralie ruin that, too.

An idea struck. Something they could do, somewhere they could go, where Coralie couldn't touch them.

Rebekah lowered her burger and said, "Want to go out tonight?"

Mike paused. "Aren't we already out?"

"Yeah, I mean *out* out. Let's go somewhere neither of us have been before."

"Like where? We both grew up here. There's not much left to discover. Maybe a few extra trees."

She leaned forward and lowered her voice. "Have you ever been to the pulp mill?"

Mike half-choked on his burger. "Trespassing?"

he hissed. "You know that's against the law, right?"

"Alice told me it got shut down. Come on, it's super tempting, a factory like that left unguarded. I bet a bunch of teenagers are going to try to break in. Someone should probably check it out and make sure it's clear."

He gave her a searching look, then laughed, loud and carefree. He couldn't be faking that. He couldn't just be doing it for her benefit.

"You're insane, Rebekah, but damn if I don't like it."

"So, you want to go?"

Mike watched her with glittering eyes. Then he nodded. "You know what? Yeah. Yeah. Let's do it."

Rebekah matched his grin. "Let's do it."

15

The pulp mill was bigger than Mike expected: a sprawling, jagged factory that shone in the moonlight against the toothy backdrop of tapered evergreens. A tall chain-link fence surrounded the property, plastered with anti-trespassing signage, but at the corner—not very far from the meager hiking path that had led them around the side of the property—the fence had already been cut and pulled apart.

Rebekah gestured to the rupture and turned triumphantly to Mike. "Probable cause!"

He regarded the factory and said,

half-kidding, "Someone could be seriously hurt in there."

She couldn't conceal a laugh.

Mike held the fence open for her to climb through before following her in. His heart was in his chest, energy at the tips of his fingers, chasing off the chill. He'd literally never broken the law before.

Even then he was second-guessing himself. But Rebekah was like a comet, a fireball, a force of nature. He couldn't help but follow in her wake, get caught up in her orbit, the way the Earth revolved hopelessly around the sun.

The factory lurked silently before them. A series of conveyor belts reached out of the building and up into the starry sky, touching the tops of rain-dampened mountains of pulp. Mike gazed around at a maze of machinery and corridors, tall bare walls and riveted columns, the air thick with salty sawdust.

Rebekah's laugh pierced the silence. She ran

forward, spreading out her arms and twirling as though she were a forest nymph clad in a skirt of leaves rather than a high schooler in jeans and a black hoodie with an old taped-up backpack. Mike jogged after her, caught up in her energy.

The nearest door into the factory was in the back and locked, the handle immobile. But around the corner, Rebekah found a ladder that ran up along the side of the building, leading to one of the stationary conveyor belts. She flashed Mike a reckless look, one he'd never seen on her before, and started climbing.

"Careful," he called up after her, keeping his voice as low as possible, even though he had no reason to think there was anyone within a mile.

"It's a ladder, Mike," she called back, already halfway up.

Regardless of her carefree attitude, he remained poised to catch her in case she fell. But with her sure movements, she was twenty feet up in no time at all. Then she stood on the empty belt and motioned for him to join her.

Gone was the quiet girl he'd lived next door to all those years, sitting in her garden every evening, curled in on herself, bent over her sketchbook, or glancing up through her hair at the stars.

She motioned again, and he followed her up the ladder.

The conveyor belt, easily ten feet across, seemed to grow smaller with each step he took toward it. It was less a massive piece of factory equipment and more a catwalk, angled up toward the sky and devoid of railings. Rebekah had her arms out again by the time he reached her, facing the stars that peeked out from between the clouds.

"Careful." Mike kept purposely toward the middle of the rubbery walkway. "Don't lose your balance."

"Isn't it beautiful? Look."

He followed her gesture: They could barely see the town from there, the view skimming the tops of the trees like a giant field of grass, beyond which, bright as fireflies, the glow of windows and streetlights dotted the darkness. A speckled mirror of the sky above.

"Whoa," Mike breathed.

Rebekah's footsteps tapped against the belt, bringing him back to their escapade. She was, thankfully, walking down instead of up, toward the factory rather than higher into the gusts of winter wind.

The conveyor belt passed through a plastic-curtained tunnel in the wall, over a story from the ground. Heavy strips of plastic only covered half of the opening, so they ducked through and immediately found themselves inside the entrance to the internal workings of a huge piece of machinery, painted green and completely dark. Mike clicked on the flashlight he'd clipped to his belt, but the stark light and stiff shadows couldn't pierce the narrow aperture; although, based on the piles of wooden mulch that those conveyor belts had apparently created, he wouldn't doubt it was a massive chipper. The last thing a human being should voluntarily explore.

To his relief, Rebekah seemed to have come to the same conclusion. She climbed onto the roof of the slightly rounded machine without a second glance inside the shadowed maw. Mike hesitated following her; the path looked precarious at best, and he didn't see another obvious, safe way down. But Rebekah seemed perfectly comfortable walking in the shifting light of his flash, shuddering shadows dancing around them as they moved.

When he tracked Rebekah's motions, however, he saw what she seemed to be aiming for: a little maintenance platform with a railing that nestled up beside an elongated machine a little way down the line. He couldn't tell from that angle if it had a ladder to the ground, but it'd be weird if it didn't.

So he climbed on top of the potential wood-chipper, watching the placement of his feet. If he fell, there'd be no one to catch—

Above him, Rebekah tottered on her step.

Mike raced recklessly forward and caught her hand just as she lost her balance. She gripped his fingers like a vise, even as she found her footing again, then huffed out a breath that echoed through the dark metal cavern.

"Come on," he whispered, and they walked hand-in-hand along the spine of the massive machine. Mike kept his weight low and stepped carefully, but even after her near fall, Rebekah walked upright and unafraid. When they reached the metal platform with its silver railing and grated floor, she jumped down to it with a clang that rebounded from the distant walls.

"Rebekah, you're insane!" he called quietly, with as much tension as awe.

"You don't have to keep your voice down." She said it loudly, standing tall, a presence that could fill the empty factory. "There's no one here."

"I'm not doing it on purpose." He sat and inched down toward the platform. "Besides, you don't know that."

He slipped off of the curved roof of the thing and slid for a moment until his feet hit the grate beside her. She helped him rebalance, leveraging herself on the side of a sawdust-scattered control panel. "Come on. There's a ladder."

Rebekah spun and descended through an opening in the silver rails Mike hadn't seen. He shined his flashlight down so she could see, and her shadow stretched along the cement floor below, shivering and swaying, bridging the space between the green chipper they were on and another blue one running alongside it.

He waited until he heard the clap of her shoes on the concrete floor before following her down, hand over hand again along the cold, dusty metal. The factory hadn't been closed for long, but thick sawdust seemed to cling to every surface, grainy between his fingers and slippery beneath his feet.

"This is so cool." Rebekah turned in place as he reached the bottom of the ladder. "Hey!" She waved him over and opened her phone's camera, framing herself against the dusted machinery.

Mike covered the camera and pushed the phone down with one hand, leaning toward her. "Don't take pictures, Rebekah! We're trespassing!"

"I won't show anyone."

"Maybe not, but it's hard to get rid of that kind of evidence. Let's keep tonight as a memory, okay? To be on the safe side."

Rebekah clucked her tongue and tucked her

phone away. She rested her hand against his hip and covered his flashlight, and leaned up close, met his eyes in the dark. "Whatever you say, officer."

Despite the situation, Mike couldn't resist kissing her, her lips soft and warm beneath his, her heart pounding in time to his own.

When they finally pulled apart, Rebekah took his hand and led him down the long, silent aisle between the giant machines.

The rows of machinery dwarfed them. Great metal contraptions swallowed the pair between them, growing steadily larger as the silent tracks led deeper into the cold dark.

"Have you come here before?" Mike whispered, his voice drifting off into the dust.

"No. I've never done anything like this."

He gave her some side-eye, studying her, not missing the eager edge to her tone. "What made you think of it now?"

She shrugged, her hand still clutching his.

"I heard this place was closed and wanted to check it out. Honestly, I'm . . ." She stopped, as if unsure how to continue.

"What?" he prompted, squeezing her fingers between his. "You can tell me."

There was one of her sad smiles, the one she bore when she thought Mike wasn't looking, but she quickly replaced it with the same bright one she'd worn on the way in there. "I just feel different since going out with you. Like I can do anything."

Mike stopped and turned her to face him, taking her other hand in his. "Me, too."

For a moment, the rest of the world disappeared and there was nothing else but them.

Then Rebekah stepped back and let go of his hand to point beneath the blue chipper, where there were a couple of feet of space between the machinery and the floor. "Do you think I could fit under there?"

Before he could answer, she was on her

hands and knees, peering beneath it; then she was halfway under it, her progress marked by the scraping noise her backpack's zipper made on the underside of the belt.

Mike squatted, concerned. "There might be broken glass."

"Just two giant raccoons."

"What!"

Rebekah yelped and her feet vanished into the space under the chipper.

"Rebekah!"

He threw himself to the ground and searched for her, flashlight in hand, catching glimpses of her giggling face in the uneven light of his torch. She'd tucked her knees into her chest, covering her mouth with her forearm to hold in her giggles, and failing. Mike groaned in relief.

"What, did you think the fake raccoons ate me?"

"I don't know." He took a deep breath, his panic quickly morphing into irritation, mainly at himself for being so gullible. "I wanted to make sure you were all right."

"I'm fine. Come on in. It's roomy under here."

With that, Rebekah crawled through to the other side, navigating between thick metal legs riveted with giant metal bolts to the concrete floor. He only saw that she'd reached her goal when she vanished from his view, lifting onto her knees, then up to her feet. Then she bent down to look back at him underneath it. "I think you'll fit. Ooh, there's a different machine over here. Come on!"

When she disappeared to the side, behind a part of the chipper that touched the floor, she left Mike with no choice but to follow her.

He clipped the flashlight back to his belt, got on his stomach, and army-crawled through the narrow space. He only caught his elbow once on a cold, riveted strut, but he caught his knee twice and inhaled far too much sawdust while he was at it.

When he pushed himself to his feet on the far side, he had to laugh at the dirt and dust that covered his jacket and pants. Rebekah, who'd worn black, wasn't much better off. She sidled down the tight aisle, staring up at the new machine, sawdust coating her from head to toe. It was like they'd rolled around in the dust—which, come to think of it, wasn't far from the truth.

The new machine wasn't self-contained the way the chippers were. It was more of an assembly line, a mess of stations and containers hooked up along a conveyor belt, a little more like what Mike expected to find in a factory. The "belt" itself, a flat snaking line with smooth overlapping metal, was empty. Almost clean compared to everything else there.

Mike's eyes caught on Rebekah's taped-up shoulder bag, as rumpled and mussed with dust as her lovely black hair, and inspiration struck.

"Rebekah?" His tone must have caught her;

she whirled around with the warmth of laughter on her face, wilder and freer than any other time he'd seen her.

"Yes?" She was walking backward beside the snaking surface, as comfortable as if the looming factory was her home.

"Can . . ." He didn't want to put her on the spot. He had no idea whether she enjoyed reading poetry out loud. But if there was one thing Mike's father actually did right, if there was one thing he truly understood, it was the heart of a bookworm. Mike had to trust that.

"Would you read me some Poe?"

Rebekah stopped, surprised. "What, read it out to you?"

He nodded, afraid he looked as awkward as he felt. "Yeah. Someone told me that poetry is best experienced out loud."

She pulled her backpack off her shoulders. "Which one?"

His worry melted away, replaced with a hopeful energy. "I don't know. Your favorite."

"My favorite changes every day."

"Then your favorite for today."

She pulled the book out, dropping the bag to the sawdust floor. Then she beamed—a new, sweet expression, different from the wild grin or the sad smile. Like a fond memory.

The heavy Poe volume fell open at her touch; she flipped through it with a worn-in familiarity, her fingers dancing over the aged papers. Her eyes softened, and she stopped, floating her hand along the page she'd landed on.

One thin beam of moonlight streamed down from a hole in the foggy skylights far above, and Rebekah climbed up on the conveyor belt so it illuminated her in silver as she read from the book.

"Oh! that my young life were a lasting dream!
My spirit not awakening, till the beam
Of an Eternity should bring the morrow."

The words were drier than Mike had expected, but they came to life on Rebekah's tongue. It was a fluttering of the English language, a rhythmic flourishing, an ode to the concept of a dream: the peace and solitude, the potential for happiness captured inside the moments between sleep and wake.

It was like Rebekah sang the concepts in a different language, a melodic experience that conjured inexpressible emotions. Her voice pushed away the sawdust, the slumbering machines, the captured stillness of a place meant to be in motion; intertwined into Poe's words, Mike felt that intangible essence of a dream, felt it slide past his thoughts and strike deep in his heart. Faint scents wafted past, the foul-sweet smell of rot, dry dust, stagnant water. He could almost imagine a ghostly dreamscape: something like the Lee house, but taller and older, with some malevolent air surrounding it.

Bare-limbed trees spread in all directions, a sky without stars.

"Dreams! in their vivid colouring of life
As in that fleeting, shadowy, misty strife
Of semblance with reality which brings
To the delirious eye, more lovely things
Of Paradise and Love—and all our own!
Than young Hope in his sunniest hour
hath known."

Rebekah concluded the poem with a twirl, spreading her arms out to welcome the moonlight that had itself been highlighted in Poe's words.

Mike almost lost his balance when the thick sawdust swept back into him, and a silence that was closer to hibernation than the held-breath stillness of a glaring moon.

Rebekah reverently placed the book at the

edge of the conveyor belt, then held out a hand to Mike. "Come up here."

He approached, doused still in the unearthly air that the poetry had conjured, and climbed up onto a snaking metal track that felt as smooth as a tiled floor. The height wasn't a substantial difference, although a fall from any height there could be dangerous since there were no safeguards in place. But Rebekah's passion swept over him like a tsunami, pulling him down in its undertow, and Mike willingly drowned, hoping the momentum would go on forever.

With the same wild grin from earlier, Rebekah pulled out her phone, swiped through a few settings, and put on a pop song from a decade ago. The audio quality was terrible, but it was loud enough even after she set her phone down.

Then she offered him her hand. "May I have this dance?"

Mike laughed, hesitating at the ridiculousness

of it, then, of course, he accepted. Rebekah pulled him close, her body brushing his as they moved to the music. The beat reverberated off the metal around them, emphasizing the tinny sound, transforming what had once been a pop song into a mess of upbeat chords and nonsensical vocals. Mike relaxed into her, going with her energy, the wild joy of motion, and allowed himself to let his guard down. To divine his own joy, as in a dream.

Her laugh sparkled against the distorted sound, and their footsteps tapped out the rhythm on the disused steel track. There wasn't quite enough room to move much, so they faced each other, taking turns to attempt increasingly awful moves they'd seen online.

Mike had never done anything like that before. He'd never felt so . . . free, like he could do—or be—anything he wanted. The only person there was Rebekah, and she'd never judge him or expect him to be someone he wasn't.

Gone were his erudite parents, judgmental acquaintances, would-be friends, dismissive colleagues, or even strangers. People who only saw a badge when they looked at him, where they might once have seen an innocuous young boy with his head in a book.

Rebekah raised her arms over her head and yelped in surprise when Mike grabbed her around the waist and lifted her into a spin. She stabilized herself on his shoulders and stumbled when he put her down, and then she put her hands on either side of his head and pulled him into a kiss.

They remained there for a while, embracing, listening to the small speaker transition from one garbled pop song to another, leaning from foot to foot in a poor approximation of a slow dance.

Mike wasn't supposed to have gone there; neither of them had. But right then, he didn't want to be anywhere else.

16

Thomas Schultz grasped desperately at dry grass with one hand while being dragged and scratched and ground against rocks and weeds by his other. None of his fingers caught among the dust, nor could they escape the iron grip of his captor. He struggled to keep his senses, to search for any sign of where he was, but the world itself spun and twisted around him, leaving only the impression of sharp scraggly branches against dark sky. Nothing there seemed real—nothing except the cold hand around his.

The dragging finally came to a stop, but the trees continued to spin. He reached out one hand and grabbed something, the edge of a wooden wall, and latched on, struggling to right himself. When he saw a face emerge from the forest, Tom opened his mouth to call to it for help.

Rebekah. The infamous "piss bitch." She stood solid and real, leveling a glare that could ignite coal. The words he'd started to say died at that furious expression.

Strong hands pulled him the rest of the way to his feet, ripping his hand from its grasp on the wall. Tom didn't have the power to fight back; his gaze ripped from Rebekah, and he tried to escape, pulling and shoving and kicking, scuffling in the silent forest, but each punch felt weak and heavy, like he was moving through sludge. All the hallmarks of a dream—but he knew somehow it wasn't a dream. Not exactly. It couldn't be.

Tom couldn't see or make out a single detail about the captor who dragged him into some building—wooden, the harsh smell of oats—and shoved him, hard, and Tom's back collided with a wall. He collapsed to the ground and managed to catch himself on the dry floor strewn with forgotten sprigs of hay. He struggled to catch his breath, scrambling to make sense of what was happening. He was in a corner . . . he was in a narrow room surrounded on three sides by tall wooden walls. The fourth wall was slightly lower, like an oversized stall door, so his captor could peer over it at him.

The captor had no face. Only a shadow with strange white eyes. It wasn't human at all.

"What do you want?" Tom managed to say, trembling in his corner. "Rebekah!" he called out, louder, trying to reach her on the other side of the walls. "Why are you here? Why am I here? What do you want?"

The creature with the gleaming eyes turned away, and there was a sort of scraping noise, together with a soft *fwoosh*. A match lighting.

Louder than it should have been; but that place shouldn't have been at all.

"Tell me what you want!" he yelled, launching himself against the stall door, pushing, shoving, but it wouldn't budge. "I'm sorry I called you a starving artist. You're probably very talented! Rebekah, make him stop, please. I'll never call you—"

There was a sound like a sheet unrolling as the wooden structure ignited with a flickering light, and all the air was sucked out. Tom struggled to see beyond the door, but all he could make out were shifting shadows and arching rafters.

"You know why." Rebekah's voice was too close and too calm, like she was a ghost herself.

"Rebekah!" he called again. "Rebekah, what do you—"

Tom's voice fled in the wake of the memory. Eddie with a broken arm. Veronica with a chunk of missing hair. Hector lost somewhere in the woods, delirious and exhausted, scratches

DANI LAMIA

on his arms. Scotty, who'd pissed in Rebekah's locker, with a tooth missing, claiming it was a football accident but always changing the subject when it came up.

None of them had mentioned the piss bitch thing recently.

Flames licked Tom's shin and he backed into his corner again as fire peered around the edge of the wall, spreading freely on the far side of the door, burning and blackening the spare pieces of straw littering the ground. Smoke crawled against the ceiling, scuttling around the corner. Tom's mouth was dry, introducing pain into his haggard breaths, and then he saw flames fill the empty space over the door, licking toward the smoke.

He was trapped.

Tom went numb for a second; and then he went alive, a freshening panic dancing at the ends of his nerves, details crystalizing and then breaking away: the brilliance of the flames on the floor, the harsh scents of smoke and ash and burning wood, the cool air seeping away behind him as the dry heat of fire pressed into him from the front; and he searched desperately for a place to run, but the wall behind him was solid, wooden planks of stone mortared with cement, their grainy texture ripping his fingernails as he clawed for the slightest weakness.

He swiveled to face the fire that consumed the door and shouted, voice cracking against his dry throat. "Rebekah! Please! Let me out!" He coughed, haggard, and tried to swallow without spit. "Listen! I'm sorry! It was terrible what Scotty did to you, and it was so shit of me to think it was funny! I just wanted them to think I was cool. I'm sorry. I'm sorry!"

The door darkened between the flames then crumpled, breaking down the middle with a crack, and suddenly there was an exit.

Directly into an inferno.

"Let me out, please!" He pressed against the wall, staring into the white-hot flames, rasping, "Please, Rebekah, please, I'm sorry!"

Tom bowed beneath the weight of darkening smoke. His head spun. He couldn't get enough oxygen, couldn't feel his limbs. The smoke had lined his mouth with sandpaper.

Rebekah didn't answer. He had no choice.

With a scream, Tom leapt through the fire-framed doorway.

Mike's phone rang from its little dock suckered to his dashboard, adding a tiny melody to the rhythm of his windshield wipers and the pitter of raindrops that they fought. He tapped the answer button.

It wasn't strictly legal; taking his hands off of the steering wheel to manually answer a phone call was technically a violation of traffic law.

But he didn't have hands-free calling in his car, and it was rare that his father called him, let alone during the workday.

"Hey, Dad," he said, returning his hand to the steering wheel. "Something wrong?"

"No, nothing like that. I just heard you're looking into what's happening to those kids at Grant?"

Mike flinched. "Are you talking about me at work?"

"That wasn't my intention. But Deadra Dioli told me that you talked to her daughter at school, and she asked if I'd heard of it."

Andrea Dioli. On some level, Mike was surprised she'd told her mom about their conversation since she'd seemed determined not to help him.

He avoided the question. "You know I can't discuss investigations with you."

"I know, Mike, and that's a noble position. But there's something about all these accidents that I don't like. Something eerie. I can't put my finger on it exactly." He sighed. "And I know it's your job, but I just . . . I don't know. I just don't like this. I wish you'd stay clear of it."

"That's the thing about being a police officer, Dad. I have to go toward the creepy shit, not away from it."

"Well, can I at least ask you to be careful?"

"I'm always careful, Dad."

"I know, son. I'm only worried about you. I'm your father. That's *my* job." He paused. "Hey—have you had Poe read to you yet?"

Mike grinned. "Yeah, Dad. It was a great idea. Thank you."

"You know it's never too early in the relationship to bring someone by the house."

"That is objectively false."

The radio buzzed. "Romeo four five, divert from previous, code 2. There's another signal four India on Rosewood and Syracuse."

Another one? Whatever was happening to

those students, they could not be called accidents anymore. Six was way too many to be attributed to coincidence.

"I've got to go, Dad," he said.

"All right, I have work of my own. I love you, Mike. Please stay safe. I'll see you tonight."

"Love you, too."

He disconnected and picked up the radio, glancing back at his blind spot. "Four five en route, diverting."

The Schultz family lived a street down from where Mike had been waiting at a red light, so he arrived within minutes, pulling into the half-curved driveway where he found a short, portly man with thinning gray hair and a thick gray mustache fretting beside a classic Mercedes two-seater. Mike checked his watch, noting the time. He'd beaten the ambulance, but only by a few moments, judging by the siren call in the distance.

The man—likely, Mr. Schultz—started forward as Mike got out of the car. "Where's the ambulance?" he demanded as he approached. "Tommy needs medical attention!"

"Don't worry, sir, they're right behind me. Can you tell me what happened?"

"No, no, I'm supposed to show the medics through to where he—oh, thank God!"

As the ambulance turned in through the wrought-iron gate, Mr. Schultz hurried over to meet the EMTs, and after they grabbed their bags from the back of the vehicle, he led them around the side of the house. Mike followed, carrying the notepad he used for the Grant accidents.

The Schultz house was as grand as the others along Rosewood—all clean lines and bright colors, the modern style of the square two-story building complementing the manicured landscaping. They followed a path of paving stones set perfectly into the lawn, passing flower patches, hanging benches, and a pond with its own bridge.

Mr. Schultz led them down a river stone staircase in the backyard where a heavyset woman in a silk bathrobe fretted uselessly over a teenaged boy with blond hair in a stairstep cut, bright burn-red spots singing his bare torso, and black-edged holes in his gray sweatpants. They sat together on the edge of a wide fire pit that played host to a tall pile of charred wood and a pool of water that sat stagnant at the bottom. Neither of them seemed to care about the light rain.

Tom Schultz had a distant look in his eyes, and he didn't notice the EMTs as they carefully assessed and tended to the most dangerous burns.

"Mr. Schultz." Mike gestured for Tom's father

to step aside with him. "Can you tell me what happened?"

Mr. Schultz let out a sharp breath, hands resting on the edges of his rain-dampened sweatpants, but thankfully he didn't rebuff Mike again. "Woke up to the sound of . . ." He cleared his throat. "I think Tommy got too close to the bonfire and managed to light himself up. It was . . . not . . . It's not a sound I ever want to hear again."

"He lit a bonfire alone in the middle of the night?"

The thick gray mustache tilted with Mr. Schultz's frown, a slight pursing of his lips, and he scratched at it as he thought. "Isn't like him," he said, finally. "He's smarter than that. In fact, he's always the one reminding us to keep a pail of water out here. Always had a healthy respect for fire. Anyway, I remember seeing him off to bed."

Mike made notes of everything, organizing them the same as the other cases at Grant High.

Mr. Schultz leaned closer, his voice low. "Are you thinking this is related to those other accidents? Is that possible? What do you think is going on?"

"It's not my job to speculate, sir."

"Yeah, but what do you think? Off the record."

"That's not how it works."

Tom said over his shoulder, "It was nothing."

Mike glanced over. The EMTs appeared to be almost finished with their onsite triage; one of them prepped a stretcher to take him to the ambulance.

Tom winced. "No, I don't know, it was . . . it was nothing, it was just a bad . . ." He seemed to get lost then, a strange apprehension dawning across his expression.

Mike's heart picked up in his chest.

Mrs. Schultz said, "Don't stress yourself, baby. It's okay."

Mike had to know, though. "Tom, were you going to say it was a bad dream?"

The boy met Mike's eyes, a bewildered expression laced with a deep-set fear. Before he could answer, though, his father intervened. "I think that's enough for now. If my son wants to talk more, we'll come into the station later."

Mike nodded, forcing himself to be patient. "Of course, sir. Thank you for your help. We'll be there if you need us."

Leaving them to their recovery, Mike climbed the steps back up to the series of gardens, the flagstone path, doing his best to ignore the creeping sensation dogging him. The burns Tom Schultz had acquired—as part of an accident regarding the fire pit—were extensive. A bad dream alone couldn't do that. It wasn't possible.

Which left . . . what? Some kind of . . . malicious sadist who wanted to torture a bunch of high schoolers? If that was the case, though, how could all of them look so much like accidents? And why did they all mention having bad dreams? Perhaps they'd been given hallucinogens to make them misunderstand what had happened.

Or maybe the culprit had convinced them to share the lie based on the threat of some greater pain.

He needed to get back to the school. He also needed to question Tom, but that could wait until after the kid got treatment since Mike doubted he'd get anything useful out of him at the moment.

Whatever was going on, it was real, not just a throwaway case pawned off on the new guy. There was a connection between the cases, something he couldn't see. But who would believe him? The chief, who barely acknowledged him? Dempsey, who had it out for him specifically? Detective Ash? She would just ask for evidence, and there wasn't any.

He was on his own.

17

Sometimes, the people Rebekah tormented showed up the next day at school. Sometimes they didn't. Her guess was that it had to do with how visible the result of their tortures were; Scotty and Eddie had needed to go to the hospital. Veronica had taken a half-day, like Scotty, but had looked like she'd wanted to take more.

Tom didn't show up the next morning. Rebekah found his friends walking together into the school, but not him. Had he been visibly injured, or was he afraid of her? She hoped it was both.

Good. That was one problem dealt with.

Rebekah leaned back on her planter, crossing her legs and staring up at the sky as it scraped past Grant High's spires. The clouds had come and gone over the course of the week. If they planned to make a return that day, it wouldn't be until later. Right then, the sky was bright and clear, rays of sunlight casting dark shadows through the trees. She took a long, deep breath, closed her eyes, and relaxed in the unseasonably warm morning.

She felt connected to her body, her limbs, the beats of her heart. She focused on her arms, her chest, her legs, filling herself with the glimmering evergreen scent. Fresh dewdrops and sharp pine.

The way Tom had begged her, the way he'd desperately apologized . . . just like Eddie's pleading eyes and Andrea's drowned-out screams. It reminded her of the panic in Scotty's eyes, that very first taste of the same power Coralie wielded every day.

She hadn't felt so calm, so sure of herself in . . . in how long? It was like she was finally free. She could sit back with full confidence that she would be left alone, that nothing would bother her or demand repayment for the indecency of her existence.

Then Rebekah opened her eyes and saw Coralie gesticulating in the parking lot, and her moment of indulgence came to an end. She couldn't relax, not fully. Not until Coralie had met the Raven.

Rebekah was ready. She'd dealt with Coralie's friends; she'd defanged her rich boyfriend and all his friends. It was time to stop circling the queen bee like a rat hugging the edges of the room. Like a vulture over a corpse. She'd thinned the herd enough.

It was time to go in for the kill.

Alice walked quietly toward the doors when the bell rang, a direct route from her squat little Apollo. She didn't spare a glance; she had her hair up in a brand-new braid, hugging a textbook to her chest. Did she still have suspicions? Was that why she wouldn't even make eye contact?

Then she was gone, through the school's automatic doors, and Rebekah was alone again.

Alice had been so quick to turn away. So quick to stop trusting her. Hollowness filled Rebekah's chest. Alice had offered to hang out once in a while, sure, but had she ever actually cared about Rebekah? At her loft, Alice had spent most of the time talking about boys. When they'd gotten ready for the party, she'd been more interested in discussing her new makeup palette than sparing a thought for Rebekah. And Rebekah couldn't remember the last time Alice had texted just to say hi, just to check in on Rebekah and see how she was doing, to see what was up with her.

So her so-called friend had shown her true colors.

Without Alice's innocuous information gathering and social media connections, Rebekah had to linger in the halls and eavesdrop to find out what Tom's story was. It was the first time she felt lucky her school was as small and gossip-heavy as it was; there were so few topics available that what did happen echoed between the narrow walls. She paused at her locker to flip through one of her notebooks and heard a girl with frizzy hair pulled back in a ponytail whisper to her friend as she collected her books.

"All these accidents are wild. It's like there's a ghost haunting the school or something."

"No way, Amara. It's just a bunch of stupid mistakes. You know Scotty and his friends, always pulling stunts."

"But it's not just Scotty, though. Did you hear about Tom Schultz?"

"The guy with the hair? What'd he do?"

Amara leaned in close to her friend, thrilled

to spill the tea. "Apparently, he tried to jump over his own bonfire. But he tripped and fell in."

"Oh, my God. Is he all right?"

"He went to the hospital, so who knows. Lily thinks he's going to come back with half his face melted off."

"I'd run away forever if that happened to me, no joke. Literally, what possessed him to do that?" The girl slammed her locker.

"That's what I'm telling you. This school is haunted." Amara spotted Rebekah and frowned. "Are you listening to us?"

Rebekah stiffened. "No, I—"

"That's an invasion of privacy." With a scowl, she dragged her friend away. They passed tall and slender Principal Bransby, who had his eyes on Rebekah.

He watched her through his glasses unmistakably; he wasn't scanning the crowd or keeping an eye on the students. He was watching *her*, not even pretending to look elsewhere.

Had Veronica told him about her dreams? Scotty?

No. If he had any proof at all, even just the word of his daughter, he would have done something. And he hadn't, which meant he had nothing.

His eyes were cold, though, behind his glasses. It was way more personal than the dispassionate look he gave students in detention. He suspected she was involved, even if he wasn't sure how. That had to be it.

The principal held up a clipboard and marked something on it with a black pen. Then he turned and stalked into the next hall.

Rebekah began to doubt herself. She didn't think she'd left any proof of her involvement in the accidents, other than the injured themselves, but suddenly she wasn't so sure. Yet she did have those souvenirs.

What if it wasn't the Raven doing it, physically

going out and hurting people, throwing Tom through his bonfire. What if it was *her?*

That made more sense than the Raven being some spirit haunting her. It was her imaginary friend, after all, not some stranger inserting itself into her life, right? She was the Raven. Always had been. She crept out of her house under cover of darkness to her targets' homes, kidnapping them and punishing them with greater strength and tenacity than she thought she could ever have. That explained her open window, too.

She should have been frightened by the thought, the idea of acting unconsciously, the line blurring between her and the Raven, but instead . . . she felt excited. Powerful. Energized. The idea that she was capable of acting beyond herself, of taking her life into her own hands, was electrifying.

People like Amara didn't matter. Bransby couldn't get to her. Let him try.

She was so much more than she'd ever thought she could be.

From her lonely perch beneath the art class window, Rebekah watched Coralie.

It wasn't difficult. Coralie was loud and tall and commanding, with perfect makeup and a fashionable knot in her uniform to keep her shirt taut around her slim stomach. She talked and texted at the same time, not seeming to notice that most of the people at her table weren't participating. Even her friends hated her. Maybe she didn't care.

Then again, why would she? So long as they did what she wanted, she had no reason to care.

Rebekah bit her lip, trying to imagine what torture would be best for Coralie. Hadn't she dreamed up all the others on some level? Hadn't she carried them out herself?

She pictured herself grabbing Scotty by the

face and pulling out his tooth with those rust-pocked pliers and felt a vicious thrill. She'd been capable of that. She'd broken Eddie's arm, too . . . how had she managed that one? And what if she got caught in the act?

Through all of it, though, she'd had the strange sensation the Raven was watching out for her. Even knowing it wasn't real, she still felt its comfort, the curious intelligence behind its reflective eyes. She trusted it. Or trusted that side of herself, anyway. The one hiding behind that glossy black cloak.

And if she'd done all that, she could trust herself to come up with the best punishment for Coralie. Something the bitch truly deserved.

"Hey, do you—"

Startled, Rebekah looked up to see Mike standing next to her lunch spot in his police uniform. For a second, she panicked, thinking he was there to arrest her, but no. He was just doing his job, investigating what Amara was convinced was a series of hauntings. She scrambled to hide her panic behind a tight smile.

"Um," Mike looked uncertain, making her worry that maybe she'd read the situation wrong. "If you're busy, it's no big deal."

It must have been painfully obvious how not busy she was, sitting and staring at the tables of students. "Sorry, I was daydreaming. You caught me by surprise."

She'd washed his jacket, and Nora had promised to mend the small hole in the shoulder. She would deliver it to him tomorrow.

Mike held out his hand to help her stand. "Want to go on a walk? We can make it look like I just want to interview you, like everyone else."

"Okay." Rebekah gathered her things and took his hand, trying not to look so eager to talk to a cop.

He opened his mouth to say something else, then frowned. "What's that smell?"

"Paint." She gestured to the window beside them. "It's worse when the sun's out."

Mike blinked. "What?"

"Never mind." Rebekah gave a dismissive wave and started walking, hoping to change the subject. "How's your work going?"

He led her out of the courtyard and onto a more private concrete path between two brick walls. With everyone else at lunch, they had the whole thing to themselves.

Finally, Mike said, "You probably heard about what happened this morning. I went there yesterday, right after it happened, but he wouldn't tell me anything. Just mentioned something about another bad dream." He frowned. "They really do seem like accidents, but . . . I don't know. The longer I work on this, the more I think something more is actually going on. There's so many of them happening so close together, and all in the middle of the night. It's weird. It's got to be more than just coincidence."

Rebekah tried to play it off despite the rising tension inside her. He was getting closer to the truth and didn't even know it. "Weirder stuff has happened." Rebekah bit the inside of her cheek.

"Yeah, you're right. I guess."

Mike's hand found hers. He double-checked that they were alone and held it, walking side by side, fingers intertwined. Rebekah squeezed his hand, and he squeezed back.

"Want to go out again tonight?" he asked, quietly, a corner of his mouth raised in a heart-melting expression.

She wanted to. She really did. But there was Coralie to deal with first. "I'm sorry. I can't. I'm . . . busy tonight."

"Hanging out with Alice?"

"Yeah. Tomorrow, though?"

He nodded. "Tomorrow."

Rebekah liked Mike. More than she'd liked . . . anyone, probably. But she couldn't focus on their relationship until Coralie was dealt with.

Tomorrow, everything would be perfect. Tomorrow, her life would make sense. She might even be able to go a whole day without flat-out lying. To Mike or anyone else. Tomorrow it would all be over.

"Tomorrow."

Rebekah borrowed her necessary textbooks from a librarian who pitied her, which hadn't made her feel any better, but all she could think about was Coralie meeting the Raven that night. So, sitting at her desk in front of a sheet of unsolved formulae, she took out her sketch notebook and started on a new rendition of her imaginary friend.

The Raven was primarily a silhouette, so there

weren't a lot of independent details to cover, but the act of scribbling itself was cathartic.

Dupaw leapt up and sniffed at her art, the silent, smooth motions of a cat wondering if her work would make a good seat. She paused to pet him, scratching behind his ear.

She forced all thoughts of Alice and her avoidance and possible suspicions from her mind. There wasn't anything she could do about it anyway. Instead, she thought about the Raven. The Raven could do something about Alice, but the idea made Rebekah queasy. Alice had some faults, but she didn't deserve the Raven's torture. Neither did Mike, even if he was getting closer to the truth. He wouldn't actually believe that bad dreams could be a connection between the accidents, right? It sounded too ridiculous. Weird, like he'd said, but that's as far as any reasonable person would go.

It didn't matter. Coralie was the last of them; Rebekah would have the Raven in her back pocket if anything else happened, but that should be the end of it. After that night, Mike and Alice would have nothing left to be suspicious about, and everything would be fine.

Finally.

18

When Coralie woke, she was already in chains.

The wood floor pressed cold and unforgiving against her knees. She was wearing what she'd worn to bed, a frilly tank top and fleece pants. Heavy manacles around each wrist held them up in front of her, sharp against the edge of a wooden pedestal, tugging on her shoulders, high enough to keep her from being able to sit comfortably. Kneeling, awkward, her elbows bent. The only light was a candle that flickered blinding-bright, erected on the top of the pedestal, but the flame was too small and hesitant to illuminate the edges of the room.

All she could see was the mottled carpet, wooden walls, and thickly wafting dust motes; all she could hear was her own breath, fast and quiet, and the distant creaking of wood in a strong wind; all she could feel was the rapid heartbeat pounding against her ribcage, her knees, her wrists where they were bound.

"Shit." Coralie's harsh, whispered curse echoed around her as she struggled against the heavy, thick chains, impossible to break on her own. "Shit. Shit."

It was as real as they'd said it would be. Her weight was heavy on the floor, the dust thick in her mouth, her arms straining above her, chilled from poor circulation. It was real; it was all real. But how? Where was she? Had she been kidnapped?

Then footsteps sounded behind her, and Coralie froze. She couldn't turn around, but she already knew who stood there.

"Beka?" Coralie hated the way her voice shook

but couldn't help it. She'd thought she could handle that, *had* to handle it. When there was no answer, she took a deep breath to quell her trembling, fear a deep, primal thing within her, clawing to escape. "Beka, I know it's you. You and that . . . that guy. You—you can't do this to people. It's not—it's not right—"

"Don't call me that."

The words were louder and more confident than Coralie had ever heard from Beka. They filled the room, commanding, vibrant.

"Okay," Coralie said, trying a different tactic. "Okay. Rebekah, right?"

"Yes."

"Okay, Rebekah." She tried again to level out her breathing, but the footsteps kept steadily approaching, and she had no way of guessing what would happen when they reached her. "Okay—please listen to me, I don't know what you're going through, but this can't—"

"You don't know what I'm going through?"

Rebekah's voice turned furious and was much closer than before. "You're what I'm going through. This is all your fault!"

"What?" She couldn't stop herself from scoffing, incredulous. "All this because of a stupid joke?"

"It's not just one stupid joke, Coralie, it's all of them."

Rebekah knelt behind her. Coralie strained to see her over her shoulder but couldn't. All she could make out at the edges of her vision were wisps of black hair against the candlelight. Rebekah's voice grew quiet, her breath brushing against Coralie's ear.

"You're pathetic, Coralie Renner. All you see in people is what you can get out of them. You use them to bolster your own fragile ego. You don't know a single thing about me. You couldn't care less about what I'm going through. You hate me because it's a fun and easy way to feel better about yourself."

"T-that's . . ." Her teeth were chattering so hard it was difficult for Coralie to talk. "T-that's n-not true. It was a j-joke. They were all j-just—"

"If they were all just jokes, you would've pulled them on your followers instead of the poor, fatherless girl with a shit phone and no friends. You pushed me down because you thought I wouldn't fight back. That I couldn't."

A thick piece of fabric came down over Coralie's eyes, yanking her head back and tying taut behind her. A blindfold. She couldn't even see the small flame of the room's candle. She struggled, but the hands bracing her head were as strong and unforgiving as steel.

Rebekah whispered, "You were wrong."

There was a clink of chains above her, and then Coralie's wrists were pulled up, tugging painfully on her shoulders and forcing her to her feet. She stumbled, struggling to keep from tripping and being dragged. The floor changed abruptly from carpeted wood to smooth, slippery stone, and a new cold enveloped her, replacing the slight warmth the candle had afforded.

Veronica and Andrea had warned her, had said it felt real, like an actual place with actual people, but somehow Coralie had still assumed it'd be more like a lucid dream. How else could it be explained? A giant bell tower, a creature with no face, victims with no memory of being kidnapped—it had to be a dream, and even they'd admitted that was possible. But it was real. All too real.

And Coralie really had no idea what they'd do or if she'd survive.

She sensed two people, not just Rebekah. She hadn't gotten a look at either of them, but one person was behind her, and one was leading her by the chains from the front, too fast, tripping her over uneven floors and steps—until they came to a sudden stop. A click and a reverberating clatter meant they'd taken off the chains, and a moment later, she felt one of the manacles come off her wrist.

When she tried to turn, however, she was shoved back into place—and a moment later her arms were re-cuffed behind her. Exposed and alone, fear got the upper hand over her adrenaline. Were they going to stab her? Kill her?

A firm shove forced her to stumble forward. The floor vanished and she fell into what turned out to be a series of steep stone steps—they spun around her, jostling and striking, sharp corners whipping past, pummeling into her from all directions—until she struck a cold brick floor and came to a stop. Distantly, she heard the clang of a metal door being shut somewhere far above.

She was trapped. In what? A dungeon? How long could they keep her there? Veronica had said it had been one extended, frightening event, like a stretched-out moment—but

Andrea had said it felt like it'd been longer than a single night. The place, apparently, warped your sense of time.

It took a while, but Coralie slowly regained her sense of balance and struggled to sit up on the rough, damp floor. Her arms were tied too tightly behind her, and no amount of scraping her head on the nearest step could dislodge the blindfold. She remembered what Andrea had said about the bell and braced herself, waiting for some terrible noise or some other new torture. It could come at any moment; she was so exposed, with no way to tell if anyone or anything approached her. The room was so silent that the ringing in her ears drowned out her thoughts.

"Fuck," she whispered. She'd been so certain she'd be able to withstand whatever Rebekah threw at her. Why had she ignored her friends' warnings? She'd been so certain it wouldn't be that bad, wouldn't be that real. She'd thought it would all be worth it—following Rebekah to the Lee house, working with Scotty to set up the bucket on the roof, digging through her backpack for evidence. Threatening her with that sick little lock of Veronica's hair. Fighting back.

Even though everyone else who'd had those "accidents" had turned up relatively fine in the morning, Coralie couldn't shake the feeling that she might die that night.

Except nothing else happened. No bells reverberated around and through her. No one ripped her hair from her scalp. No one set her on fire or pulled her tooth or broke her arm. Maybe she could survive. Hesitantly, she sat up, trying to listen over her heavy panting, her pounding heartbeat, the high-pitched drone coming from her skull.

A slight breeze brushed against her. And it smelled fresher than she might have expected. She'd thought she was in a dungeon, her imagination painting four close-standing stone walls looming above her, heavy and solid. But maybe there was a window.

Then she heard . . . a crumbling noise. Like loose, falling rocks, pebbles on a cliff, tumbling away to silence.

Coralie searched forward with one foot and found a place where the floor vanished. A leg's length in front of her, the stone rounded off and disappeared into nothing.

Stairs, maybe. Or an endless pit. Or a distant forest, like the backdrop of Andrea's bell tower.

The crumbling noise came again, and under her foot, Coralie felt the edge of the floor give way.

The room was getting smaller.

Coralie scrambled backward, feeling behind her as well as she could with her hands chained together. What if the other side was falling away, too? What if she was on a floating platform, getting smaller by the second—

No, there was the wall. Good. She pressed against it as tightly as possible. She had to get out. She couldn't wait around to see if the floor disappeared and she plummeted to her death. If she could see, it would be easier, but the damned blindfold remained stuck no matter how many times she scratched her face against the wall to get it off. Her cheeks felt wet, whether from tears or dirt, or blood, she wasn't sure. All Coralie knew was that it wasn't a dream. Whatever it was, it *was* real. Eddie's arm *had* been broken; Veronica's hair *had* been ripped from her head. Scotty's tooth *had* been wrenched out. By Rebekah and whoever was with her.

Coralie climbed awkwardly to her feet, using the wall for leverage, and pressed herself as flat as possible against it. She found a corner and pushed back into it, tried again, vainly, to scrape off the blindfold, but it didn't work.

She needed to get out. Find the stairs where she'd fallen and get to the door. That was the only way—

The crumbling noise continued, moving closer and closer. She had no idea where the edge was, how small her platform was getting. The only certain thing was that she was running out of time.

She edged along the wall, feeling her way carefully with her feet. The stairs had to be there somewhere. They had to. She couldn't die. Rebekah hadn't killed anyone yet. She wouldn't kill her, would she?

Her foot found empty air, and her heart seized. She almost lost her balance but managed to stumble back and find her corner again.

It was too fast. The floor was disappearing too quickly. She tried going the other way but ran into the empty air in half the amount of time. Dare she try out from the middle? No, that made no sense.

Coralie panted, listening to the crumbling in the otherwise still silence. Tears pushed out of her eyes, and her throat released a whine; she couldn't move at all, trembling in place, convinced that a step in any direction would be her doom.

"Beka," she said, not knowing if anyone could hear her. "R-Rebekah. Please. Please, you can't—you can't do this—"

Pressing her back into the corner, one foot slipped over the edge of the floor. It was close, too close. She sobbed.

"No, no, no. I'll stop, I'll leave you alone—please, I promise I'll leave you alone—"

The rock shifted under her feet, popping and breaking beneath her toes, and she rocked back on her heels.

"Please, Rebekah, you can't do this!" Coralie screamed. "No— *No!*"

She lost the last of her footing, then slipped and caught her hands on an outcrop of rock as she fell, snapping her shoulders. Her heart in her throat, weightless in the fall, her terror erupted in an involuntary scream as she plummeted into the dark.

19

The clouds were due to come back soon, so Rebekah pulled out her bright red jacket, a gift from someone years ago. She'd never worn it to school, where non-uniform jackets were against the dress code.

She stuffed it in her backpack to put on as soon as her mom's back was turned.

She bounced out into the kitchen and fed Dupaw, humming tunelessly to herself. She felt alive, in touch with herself, acutely aware of the energy coursing through her limbs. Dupaw rubbed his flank on her leg before digging into his food.

Nora came out some minutes later, the bags

under her eyes defined as harshly as her hangover. When she saw Rebekah, she grimaced. "I'm sorry, hon, I couldn't get around to Mike's jacket last night. I'll get it done today, all right?"

"That's fine." Rebekah hugged her fiercely, kissing her on the cheek just to see her owlish look of surprise. "I love you."

Nora melted into emotion. "I love you too, Beka."

She felt invulnerable. Unstoppable. Invincible. Nothing could faze her, no one could touch her, not so long as she had the Raven's power on her side. Coralie's pleas replayed through her mind, the mixture of panic and fear, the desperate futility of knowing Rebekah was the one with complete control over what happened to her. She'd turned the hierarchy of Grant High on its head, sending Coralie plummeting to where she truly belonged.

Everything was different. Everything

was better. It was the first day of Rebekah's brand-new life.

Alice avoided Rebekah again at school, just like everyone else. They met eyes once or twice, but neither made any moves to approach the other. Alice would come around now that Rebekah could put down the Raven. Now that her life was back on track. Now that she'd eliminated the vermin at Grant High.

Not only did Coralie not show up that day, but neither did Andrea. Veronica was there, chatting with a selection of her second-level friends, wearing her special school-brand beanie. She, along with Eddie, Hector, Scotty, Tom—they all actively avoided Rebekah, averting their gazes, skirting her path.

She couldn't wait to see Coralie do the same.

* * *

Rebekah watched Mike tap his fingers against the steering wheel, completely out of time with the Top 40 station playing quietly on his phone through his car's aux connector. He had a frown in his eyes that leaked onto his face, and for a while he drove through soft rain in silence, searching the town's main road for something that he apparently couldn't find.

"Everything okay?" Rebekah asked, fidgeting with the hem of her puffy jacket to avoid reaching for him.

He glanced over as if he'd just then realized she was there. "What? Yeah. No. I don't know. Coralie Rennell broke her leg and dislocated her shoulders last night. Did you hear about that?"

"No." Rebekah did her best to look shocked. Technically, she hadn't known since she hadn't talked to anyone at school that day. "What happened?"

"Fell out of her bedroom window, third floor. She's lucky to be alive."

Coralie's house had *three* stories?

"Another accident?" Rebekah squeezed the arms of her coat.

"Seems like it. The Rennells said she must have fallen while trying to hang fairy lights in her room."

"Must have? What did Coralie say?"

"Her parents wouldn't let me talk to her. It was early this morning, and she was still in the hospital, so they said she'd give me her statement later when she'd had time to rest." He paused, looking disquieted. "Maybe there *is* some connection between them at the school, but if there is, I'm not seeing it. If one person is doing it, then maybe they're picking their victims at Grant High. Could be a drug thing, a seller there. I just don't know."

Rebekah did reach for him then, hoping to get his mind on other things. "Hey, let's not worry about it tonight, okay? Relax and enjoy yourself."

"Sorry. You're right. It's just frustrating, you know. Like I said, I don't have anyone else to tell. But, yeah— Let's have fun tonight. Good call."

Rebekah caught sight of an ill-maintained house, and she lit up with an idea. "Why don't we get takeout?"

"Takeout?"

"And bring it to the Lee house."

A smile grew into a slow grin. "Yeah. Yeah, that's a good idea." His shoulders relaxed. "That's a good idea."

"I've been known to have them," she said, and Mike laughed.

The sun glistened off distant ocean waves, ripples of blue stretching toward the horizon. The beach was never hot there; sometimes it was less cold, sometimes even warm, but the actual beachfront was generally not much more than a series of large, broken boulders under a stiff breeze. Time with the ocean was better spent looking at than experiencing, and the view where Rebekah stood, near the top of the Lee house cliff, was the best of all—choppy waves cutting the water like shading lines in an illustration.

The handles of the takeout bag rustled in Mike's fingers, intermingling with the wind through the trees, bare branches shrouding vibrant evergreens in the distance. "Amazing view, isn't it?"

"Today's a good day." She took his free hand in hers and tugged on his arm, aware of the shadows still lurking in his eyes. "Come on. Let's go inside."

"Yeah."

The Lee house loomed before them, tall and uneven and threatening to come apart, an innocent reflection of the Raven's manor. A safe version of a monstrous thing. A cat with a shadow in the shape of a lion.

Rebekah and Mike entered through the back door again, along the eerily silent hallway. No one else had been there since their first date, so the blanket still laid disturbed on the floor. They swept away some of the dust with the plastic-bristled broom that stood next to the front door, readjusted the blanket, and set up their second picnic. Sandwiches and sodas. A feast for kings.

Rebekah took a long, deep breath of salted-forest musk, feeling out to her toes and the tips of her fingers, because—finally—it was over. She was free. She had destroyed the demons in her path.

"They aren't exactly well-liked," Mike thought aloud, apparently still thinking about his case. "Scotty Trucco, Coralie Rennell. A few students told me in confidence that their popularity is less due to their personality than their . . . well, status. They're not nice, in other words."

"No, I guess not," Rebekah agreed, readjusting herself to lean against him.

"Well, if nothing else, that's something they have in comm—"

She interrupted him with a kiss. When she pulled away, he had an adorable, dazed look on his face, and she laughed despite herself.

"Was that bad?" she asked. "Should I have checked? It was a joke because we'd agreed not to talk about your—"

He cut her off with a kiss of his own, and then they were both laughing, the sandwiches sitting forgotten in their containers. They laid back in one another's arms, focusing on the quiet, dusty ceiling, present in the moment.

Or so she thought.

"I just . . ." Mike sighed and Rebekah resigned herself to more talk about the case. He couldn't seem to drop it. As if sensing her displeasure,

Mike tucked her into his side and kissed the top of her head. "Sorry. I know we agreed not to talk about it, but I can't shake the feeling I'm missing something important, some connection. They all happened in the middle of the night and weren't discovered until morning, and the students chalked it up to a bad dream. Could mean drugs, but the victims were each alone when it happened, and no illicit substances or paraphernalia were found at any of the scenes or in any of the victims' personal possessions, so . . . The only physical connection between them is the school. But I've been all over Grant High already, so if it's there, it has to be something I missed. Something I overlooked."

She pressed closer to him, head on his shoulder. "Mike—"

"I know. I mean, I don't know. I'm sorry."

At that, he trailed into silence again.

Rebekah didn't want to dwell on the past. She wanted the whole thing to be behind them.

It was done. It was over. There was nothing Coralie or Scotty or any of their friends could do to her, to the two of them. She'd scared them away. She'd done it; she, and no one else.

She kissed his cheek.

"Rebekah—"

When he turned his head, she kissed him and ran her hand over his chest. The soft fabric, firm at the buttons; he was still technically wearing his beat-cop uniform, though he'd taken off the badge and belt.

She unfastened a couple of the buttons and slipped her hand through the gap, running her fingers over his warm skin, hoping to take his mind from the case and get him there, with her, into the quiet solitude of an abandoned house on a cliff by the sea.

It was her opportunity to preview the rest of her life. The new normal she'd created for herself. No more hiding. She was Rebekah, she was the Raven, and no one held any power over her anymore. She'd destroyed her own shackles. No one could stand in her way.

She climbed on top of Mike, straddling him. He looked surprised for a moment, but she bent down and kissed him again, feeling his hands on her arms, her shoulders, her cheeks. She unfastened the rest of his shirt buttons and slid her hands over his chest and shoulders, the back of his neck, down his stomach, her fingertips electric with sensation.

She pushed down on him, maximizing their contact, swaying her hips slightly with their breaths. It was a closeness she'd never had, an intimacy she hadn't been sure she would ever feel.

Mike pulled away to take a breath. "Rebekah, wait—"

But she didn't want to wait. Didn't want to stop. She kissed him again, pressing the heat between her legs more firmly against him, needing to know he wanted it as much as she did. It was the perfect night to end the perfect day, and it was all for her.

"Rebekah." He sat up and pushed her away gently, buttoning up his shirt before she could touch him again. "I don't think—"

"Exactly, Mike. Don't think. You've been doing too much of that already." She kissed him again, shoving her fingers into his hair to keep him in place.

Mike pushed her away a bit more roughly. "Tonight's not the night for this, Rebekah. I'm sorry."

"It could be." She placed her hand over the fly of his pants and the obvious bulge there. "Because I think—"

"No!" He shouted, shoving her hand away.

Unbalanced, she fell ungainly onto the blanket, crunching one of their sandwich containers under her hip. Mike sat up and moved back a little, off the blanket and onto the grungy wooden floor, looking flustered. He started buttoning his shirt.

"Sorry." He watched her like he didn't recognize her. "Just . . . I'm all over the place today. I want to relax. No expectations, or . . . or anything."

"I was trying to help you relax."

He finished tucking his shirt into his pants. "I know. Just. Not right now, all right? That's all I mean."

"Okay." She spoke uncertainly, sitting up on the blanket.

She picked up the sandwich container she'd landed on, a black plastic box with a transparent lid, and popped it open to inspect the damage. A flat sandwich, but not inedible.

After a tense moment, Mike took the intact box, and they ate in heavy silence.

20

Rebekah wore the red jacket to school again. Each time she got dress-coded and was forced to take it off, she put it on again at the end of the period. Rinse, repeat. Some of the teachers went easy on her, Mrs. Morell's soft warnings juxtaposed by Ms. Armen's sharp-frowned demerit, so by the end of the school day she'd only racked up three dress code violations.

Alice was, again, nowhere to be seen at lunch. Not even hanging out with a different group. Had she left the school entirely? No, she was still in Rebekah's history class, avoiding all eye contact and focusing all too hard on her notes.

But that was fine. If Alice didn't want to be friends now that it was finally over, that was on her. Coralie still hadn't come to school, and that was its own reward.

Bransby still gave Rebekah sour looks, but no matter what he was thinking, he didn't have anything on her. Expelling or punishing her for no reason would make it look like he was picking on the poorest girl at school. He had no evidence, and if he didn't by that point, he never would.

She met his eyes whenever she saw him, challenging. She'd never taken a teacher to the Raven, and the worst thing Principal Bransby had ever done was raise Veronica. But the knowledge that it was an option filled her heart with pure fire, and when he saw it in her gaze, it seemed to give him pause.

Whether they knew or not, Rebekah had the place under her thumb. No one had any power over her because she'd knocked down every person who had. She could relax in English with the freedom to doodle while she thought, comforted in the whisper-free silence. She could keep her chin up in stats and walk unassailed from the art room.

She spent the day drawing the Raven, sketching herself in its hood with its glaring, reflective eyes. She was no closer to understanding how exactly she could do the things the Raven had done, but she wasn't sure she needed to understand. It had worked. It was like she had a superpower, or some kind of nightmare magic, a shadow she could direct at her enemies.

Rebekah would never have to worry about anyone ever again. For her entire life.

She and the Raven were there to stay.

Nora's car smelled of isolation and faint mold. For the first time in over a week, Rebekah had driven home with her mother instead of Mike, and, of course, the topic of him was not at all politely ignored.

"Slowing down with your new boyfriend?" Nora inquired. "How's that going?"

"Fine," Rebekah answered.

Mike hadn't answered her messages. He'd usually at least send an emoji or two. But there was nothing but the tiny gray read receipt. Like he was purposely avoiding her.

Just like Alice.

"I'll fix his jacket tonight," Nora said. "You can take it over to him, break the ice."

"It's fine," Rebekah repeated, watching the sidewalk disappear through the car window, the uneven grasses pushing into the asphalt to reclaim the land that had once been theirs.

"Wait," said Nora as she turned into their driveway. "What's that?"

She had her gaze locked on their front door. Something was stuck there, at eye level. No, not stuck. Nailed. She cut the engine and they got out of the car together and approached. Their footsteps against the concrete interrupted the still air, brushing against the overgrown garden edging into the front walk.

A dead cat with matted black fur and caked with dried blood was pinned to the door by a long, sharp knife pierced through its chest. Its head lolled to one side, revealing a bloody gash where one eye should have been, and its front left paw dangled stiffly from its body. Nora dropped her bag with a gasp, hands flying to her face.

Dupaw.

Pinned to his chest by the same knife that held him to the door was a crinkled, creased piece of paper. White sketchbook paper. A young man with well-defined muscles tightening his wire noose around the neck of a one-eyed cat. An action shot, flowing lines and forced perspective, focusing on the determination in the cat's eye.

It was the Pluto page that Coralie had stolen.

"Oh, my God!" Nora sobbed. "Who could have done this?" She turned to Rebekah, eyes red and puffy. "That's your drawing, isn't it? Do you know anything about this?"

Rebekah bit her lip to keep from saying Coralie's name out loud. "No," she said instead. Her chest and throat burned, heat on the back of her neck. "No, I . . . I have no idea."

That bitch. Coralie was responsible. But why? How? Hadn't Rebekah and the Raven scared her off well enough? How could anyone spend a night in that nightmare and not come out changed the next morning, warned forever against Rebekah, the acrid fear that still haunted Scotty's eyes?

They both hesitated to touch Dupaw's body. Rebekah glanced next door. Mike wasn't home yet, but maybe Bill would be able to help them.

No. No, she was Rebekah. She was the Raven. She wasn't afraid of a dead cat.

With furious courage, she stepped forward, grasped the knife, and tore it out of the door. Dupaw fell with a heavy *plop*, releasing a cloud of confused insects. Some blood stained the door, droplets reaching down toward the body as if aching to return.

Curiously, she didn't react. If anything, the stench was mildly comforting. It smelled like the Raven and the home the creature had made in her dreams.

Nora, however, gagged, covering her mouth and nose. "Beka, we should've left him up for the police, or at least taken pictures. This is a threat, isn't it?"

Don't worry, Rebekah vowed. *I'll take care of it myself.*

"Sorry," she forced out. "I just hated looking at Dupaw that way. I'll take care of him."

"Beka." Nora placed her hand on Rebekah's shoulder and spoke gently. "Let's put on gloves and bury him properly, okay? Together. He deserves that much. But first, let's get some help."

Without pausing to get Rebekah's opinion on the matter, she shuffled down the porch steps and set off across the uneven grass toward the Wilson house.

Rebekah's heart raced. She didn't want Mike to know what had happened. She didn't want him to think about her in terms of his job. His nose was already so deep in the Raven thing that giving him even a single hint felt wrong.

Dupaw laid unnaturally on the front stoop, limbs stiff.

It was all supposed to be over. She was supposed to have solved it. Why wouldn't Coralie just listen? Why wouldn't she back off?

Nora's knock on the neighbor's door echoed across the yard. Rebekah cursed and chased after her, heavy footfalls in the soft grass, the air thick with promised rain, and right as she arrived, Bill opened the door.

Not great, but at least it wasn't Mike.

Bill's eyes flashed in surprise as he folded up a pair of reading glasses and tucked them into his shirt pocket. "Good afternoon, Nora. It's been a while, hasn't it?"

"Yeah." Nora fidgeted, clearly uncomfortable. She didn't talk to many people besides Rebekah. She went to work, came home, did chores, worked on various home repair projects, and drank. Her only outing was to get groceries, one bag for the house and one clacking with wine bottles. She cleared her throat and motioned toward their overgrown garden. "Is Mike home? He's a police officer, isn't he?"

Bill's thick eyebrows shot up, urgency in the way he straightened his posture. "Are you hurt? What happened?"

Rebekah spoke over the pound of her pulse in her ears. "We don't need to involve the police. I think it's just a prank."

Nora looked at her sharply, exhausted and

exasperated. "They *killed our cat,* Beka! That's miles past what they did to your locker!"

Bill's eyes landed on Rebekah, and she saw the kindest, most patient concern in them, not a hint of pity. It hit her in the chest, a silent wallop. A fresh reminder of what she could have had in another life. What Mike took for granted every single day. A father.

Softly, delicately, he asked, "Who did this, Rebekah?"

Her mouth went dry. She couldn't say "Coralie" out loud. It wasn't Mike's job to fight her battle; she was going to finish it herself. That night. And the less Mike knew about the situation, the better.

Bill offered to Nora, "If you don't want to make an official report, I can pass the message along for you."

Nora started to argue otherwise but saw something in Rebekah's face and relented. "If you would, Bill. Please. Thank you."

"It's no problem at all." He met eyes again with Rebekah, and she saw the same kindness, the same assuredness she saw in Mike's. "Anything I can do to help."

"Thank you so much, Bill." Nora turned to Rebekah. "Let's go bury him, okay?"

They said their goodbyes and went back to their house.

Dupaw was dead. Pluto was dead. Coralie had killed them both. Rebekah would wash her hands, find a pair of gloves, and help her mother bury them both.

Then night would fall, and the Raven would end it.

A blindfold pressed roughly on Coralie's eyelids. Her wrists were outstretched, immobile, to either side, her chest exposed. When she struggled, manacles held her down, binding her ankles together, pinning her to a hard, flat surface. A floor or table, unfinished wood.

She knew exactly where she was from the chill air and the creeping moldy smell. She'd expected to find herself there again. She'd prepared for it. She steeled herself, struggling to ignore the intense vulnerability trembling through her, and recited her speech.

"I'm not afraid of you!" she called into the dark. "You can hurt me, Rebekah, but you can't stop me. I'm not going to let you get away with this—all this—whatever it is! However you're doing it, I won't stop until you give up! You're a monster!"

Nothing answered her but a reverberation of her voice. She listened to her heaving breaths for a few seconds—then there was some other sound, too, another echo. Tiny, crumbling noises bouncing off the smooth stone walls.

Was she going to suddenly plummet into another abyss?

Her leg still throbbed, stiff in her cast. She'd managed to forget how visceral it was, being there, whether it was real or not.

"Can you hear me?" she called, ignoring the blood thudding in her temples. "If you think I'm lying, come take off my blindfold and look in my eyes!"

Her blindfold ripped away moments later, and standing over her was the stranger Andrea and Veronica had told her about. The creature with no face and animal eyes.

When had it approached? She hadn't heard footsteps, and the room—not stone at all, but thick wooden panels, the air as cold as death—was still and silent. Either it had appeared from nowhere, or it had been standing there the whole time, eerily quiet.

Coralie searched the dark recesses of the hood. She thought she glimpsed a face in there, curves of human skin and bone under a stark, unnatural shadow. Whoever it was, it must be a person, not the nightmare creature her friends had talked about.

Up past it, Coralie saw a strange brassy shape tucked against the ceiling. A pillar with some kind of rounded axe at the end, a fixed guillotine that filled half the space up there. Like a swinging trap from an adventure movie, pinned in its starting position against the distant wood.

Her platform was a table in the center of the room. If that thing *was* a swinging axe, it looked lined up to slice through her middle when it was released. She felt a chill, and her heart leapt into her throat. No. Even Rebekah wouldn't go that far. She might cut Coralie up, but she wouldn't kill her. And Coralie could—would—come back for her in the real world. Where she didn't have that place, that demon to fight her battles.

"You," Coralie demanded of the hooded figure, meeting its strange glimmering eyes and ignoring the weapon poised above her. "What are you? What do you get from tormenting a bunch of fucking kids?"

The creature tilted its head and stepped aside. She felt a spear of hope that it would release her restraints. But instead, it undid a knot on the wall.

A thick corded rope slipped free. Something unlatched with a metallic clunk.

The axe swung down toward her.

Coralie screamed, unable to control the sharp panic. The edge of the blade glinted as it passed through a small patch of light. She braced herself, trying to press into the table.

The axe swung toward her—

—passing an inch or so above her bare stomach.

With the sound of a gear turning, the massive axe reached the top of its arc and slowed to a weightless stop.

Then it swung down again on its own weight.

She felt a soft breeze as it passed her by.

It was a pendulum, swinging endlessly back

and forth, and her stomach was less than a hand's width beneath the lowest point of its arc.

Coralie panted, sweat cooling on her exposed skin. She tucked her tummy, core engaged, although if she arched her back, it looked like the axe would only nick her.

Girding herself against the table, she tore her eyes from the bronze blade long enough to find the strange, hooded figure. It was still in the room, standing somewhat behind her, far enough that she had to strain her neck to avoid raising her stomach.

A soft puff of wind, the low *whooom* of something heavy moving through the stagnant air.

"You can stop this." Coralie tried to reason with the thing, trying—failing—not to dissolve into begging. "I don't know why you're helping her—you don't have to. I know you don't have to. Can't you see this is wrong? Can't you see—"

The axe drew her attention as it swung past again. A fraction closer to her stomach. She looked up desperately at the base of it, where the rounded end of the pillar rotated in place. There was some space between it and the distant rotting mess of wood acting as a ceiling.

When the axe reached its apex, the base lowered a fraction more—and the razor-sharp blade swung down again, heavy and unstoppable, maybe half an inch above her. Every swing lower than before.

"Please," she entreated, looking back at the lurking shadow. "Please. This is too far—you know this is too far, don't you? You—please—please, whoever you are, you have to know this is too—"

A sharp pinch of pain. She'd leaned too far back, and the axe had nicked her stomach. She laid flat again, hyperventilating, struggling against her restraints in the narrow time she had left—

A sharp red line oozed atop her stomach, agony shooting through her entire body.

The axe swung up again, its massive weight relentless.

Coralie screamed. "No! Please! Please, I'll leave off. I mean it this time, I'll leave off. I'm sorry I killed your cat. It wasn't worth it! No—"

It came back down, a tiny bit deeper, light streaks of red on its blade. The pain burst through the numbing force of her adrenaline, and her begging broke into incoherent screaming, mindless struggling—she pulled too sharply against the restraints as the unstoppable pendulum dug into her gut. White-hot misery seared her throat, and her wailing was animal.

Everything was beyond her control. The pain, her own desperate yanking on her restraints, the screams filling the wooden room, the bronze axe smeared with dripping blood, all of it happened to her, despite her. She was a prisoner, swept up in the tide of forces that beat down on her—and the axe sliced through her again, burning deeper—she hadn't thought the pain could get any worse—

"Rebekah!" she cried, a ragged scream, her vision clouding to white. "Rebekah! Please! *Please!*"

The sharp, curved blade sliced again, and the pool of her blood reached her shoulder and poured from the table, a dark river flowing from her veins. She screamed and cried, choking, desperate, strength and resolve fading. Still, the blade kept swinging, piercing, digging, tormenting, ignorant of her pleas, indifferent to her terror, an inferno of anguish, until sensation blurred into a dark, numb, thoughtless, bleeding haze. She tried to scream, tried to breathe, but exhaustion pulled her under.

Within minutes, her blood had poured out on the wooden floor, and she'd stopped making any noise at all.

Her spine let out a mournful crack when the axe shuddered through it.

21

Rebekah shot up from her bed, panting, her darkened room floating uncertainly in her vision, one hand pressed over her mouth, an odd pocket of clammy warmth among the winter cold.

"No," she moaned. "No. No, no, no, no."

She hadn't meant to kill anyone. The Raven wasn't supposed to kill anyone. Her stomach revolted and she pushed herself off her bed, stumbling across the hall into the bathroom where she slammed the door shut behind her. She barely had time to raise the cracked toilet seat against the ceramic tank before she vomited into the stagnant water.

No. It hadn't happened. It couldn't. That's—it was too much. The Raven was just supposed to scare Coralie, not actually—

But everything she'd dreamed about before had come true. Every injury she'd caused had become real. There was no reason to think it would stop.

Coralie was dead. And the Raven was Rebekah.

She stood and rinsed out her mouth, then splashed her face, salty with tears and sweat. She sank onto the tile and curled up against the wall, breathing hard, feeling hot and cold and numb all at once.

Coralie was dead. Rebekah had killed her. She'd done it with her own hands, that night, running wild from her bedroom window, possessed by the mad demon from her dreams.

No, no, no, it couldn't be real. She couldn't have done that. She didn't have any blood on her hands, her arms, her legs—she couldn't have—

Even the Raven hadn't gotten any blood

on its glossy cloak. It had stepped back from the spreading pool on the floor, content to watch from a distance, Rebekah standing silent behind it.

Unable to move. Unable to help. Or had she just been unwilling?

Coralie limp beneath the wicked pendulum, looking like a macabre version of a magician's trick, guts and blood trailing out of her two halves.

Rebekah scrambled back to the toilet and heaved again, trembling.

The blood had been so thick and so abundant. Pouring on the floor, pooling on the table, spreading lazily to meet Coralie's restrained, motionless fingers.

It was her fault. It was Rebekah's fault.

She sat there, shocked and shivering, until sunlight glinted weakly through the narrow window.

* * *

At some point, Rebekah got up, got dressed, and started portioning Dupaw's food on auto-pilot. She didn't feel anything, and didn't think at all, letting herself go through the various motions of morning work.

Coralie was dead. And even after the terror of last night's dream, some small, sick part of Rebekah felt a little relieved about that.

Was that part the Raven, too?

An otherworldly groan made Rebekah jump and drop the cat's spoon, only to discover that it was the hinges of her mom's bedroom door. She hid her trembling by turning away to grab the spoon from the tile—but when she stood up, she remembered there was no Dupaw to feed. She stood, focusing on the bowl against the black countertop, frozen, her chest tight with terror. That she'd be caught.

"Morning." Nora shuffled into the kitchen

as though everything was precisely the same as it'd been yesterday. As though it was a perfectly normal day.

"Morning." Rebekah forced the word out, though it felt like nothing would ever be normal again.

There was a pause in the conversation, an unnatural stillness, and Rebekah knew Nora was looking at the bowl of food. She turned just in time for Nora to cloak her in a hug.

"Hey, honey," Nora said quietly. "I miss him, too. They'll find out who did it, and they'll protect us, all right?"

Nora kissed her on the head, and Rebekah clutched her in return. For a moment, it was like she could hide in her mother's arms forever, hide from Dupaw, from Coralie, from her dreams.

"Come on, Beka. Let's go to school."

School. Where Coralie wouldn't be because

she'd been gutted—because Rebekah had cut her apart, had even cleaned the blood off her hands before she'd had a chance to wake up.

Rebekah nodded, not trusting herself to say anything.

The clouds softened the light, blanketed the world in quiet. Nora vanished to her office, leaving Rebekah alone on a deserted campus. Her footsteps echoed from the stone walls as she walked down the concrete path, from the parking lot, across the empty lawn, along the planters lining the school's ostentatious brick wall. She stopped and looked at her usual seat, the piece of cement surrounding the bare bark of a deciduous shrub, as dim and gray as the rest of the morning.

Should she tell Mike?

No. No, that was a bad idea. That was a terrible idea.

It must have been a mistake. She was the Raven, and she regretted it. Which meant the Raven regretted it, which meant killing Coralie was a mistake. She'd gone too far by accident; she'd gotten wrapped up in her emotions and committed a crime of passion.

She shouldn't have done it. It shouldn't have happened. But then again, if Coralie hadn't killed her cat, Rebekah wouldn't have gotten incensed enough to do it. She probably wouldn't have called anyone back to the Raven's manor a second time, not even Coralie herself.

It was Coralie's fault. Even then, everything was still Coralie's fault.

Rebekah sank into her seat, feeling empty.

Mike didn't show up at the school at all, not from what Rebekah could see. No sign of him anywhere or anyone being called out of class for interviews. No one approached her at her spot in the morning or acknowledged her in the halls.

She was completely alone. Ignored. Allowed to do whatever she wanted without Coralie and her posse breathing down her neck. It was everything she'd ever asked for. And yet, instead of triumphant, she felt hollow and dazed.

Through her classroom window, as she tuned out Ms. Armen's staccato lesson about early American literature, Rebekah saw a woman with a messy brown ponytail and a badge on her belt talking to Mr. Ellison, whose deep red hair made him easy to identify. They stood in the parking lot, deep in some serious discussion, the woman taking notes on a pad in her hand, a closed umbrella hanging from one of her arms. Mr. Ellison kept his hands behind his back, even though he wasn't teaching.

They'd taken Mike off the case and replaced him with a real detective. Her. Rebekah instinctively understood. What was she going to do?

Principal Bransby emerged from the main entrance and physically inserted himself into their conversation, shouldering in front of the art teacher. Rebekah's survival instincts clawed inside her, adrenaline burning through her veins.

Bransby had always suspected her but hadn't wanted to act, with so much to lose and so little to gain. But suddenly it was different. What was he telling the detective? She needed to know, needed to find out if the principal was finally making his move against her.

Rebekah had thought herself untouchable because what had caused the injuries was some magical thing in her dreams. But it wasn't, was it? It was her, climbing out of her window, using pliers, and stealing locks of hair. And if it was her, then she might be trackable.

Shit.

The bell tolled the end of class, and Rebekah stuffed her notebook in beside the Poe book.

She'd thrown it in her backpack mechanically, and when she saw it there she'd thought it would make her sick all over again. But the tome, with its embossed raven, was still comforting, an unchanging weight from her childhood.

She slipped her backpack over her shoulder and followed the crowd out into the hall. There had to be something she could do, some way she could—

Something slammed into Rebekah's head. Something hard, like a rock.

She bashed into the polished wood floor, and it took a moment to get her bearings, lights and windows twirling above. The patch of skull above one of her ears flared with pain, and there was a rousing commotion surrounding her in the hall. People gasped and shouted, laughing, taking out their phones.

Scotty stood over her, wild rage in his eyes, his hands balled in fists. He didn't say a word.

The muscles of his tight jaw were outlined against his cheek.

Coralie was dead. And he knew who had killed her.

A security officer shouted and pulled Scotty away, giving Rebekah the space to find her feet again.

What if he told the detective what Rebekah had done?

No. No, she could fix it all. She could still fix it. It wasn't too late.

Rebekah lingered outside her house that afternoon. She had what passed as her sketchbook sitting on the porch, next to the carefully folded fabric of Mike's stitched-up jacket, but she was too anxious to draw the Raven—and wouldn't be able to draw anything else—so she actually wound up weeding the garden while she watched the narrow street for blue sedans.

She couldn't feel the cold, could barely feel the stalks between her fingers.

She needed to talk to Mike. She needed to know what was happening. And . . . she needed to apologize.

Maybe not in that order.

When she did see his car, she didn't give him a chance to avoid her. She dropped the weeds, grabbed the jacket, and rushed across to his driveway to ambush him. She worried he might drive on past, but he slowed and pulled into the driveway; she reached the driver's side of his car just as he turned off the engine.

His expression was distant through the window, though, and guarded when he stood from the car, his hand lingering on the door. He wore his crisp police uniform, a notebook-sized metal box under one arm.

"They took you off the school, didn't they?" asked Rebekah, trying to sound calm. "I didn't see you there."

Mike only nodded. Her pulse kicked a notch higher.

"Uh, listen." Her fingers tensed on the folded jacket she held. "I'm sorry about the other day. I went too far—"

"It was Coralie Rennell, wasn't it?"

She stopped. "What?"

"She was the one who broke into my car and set up the bucket at the Lee house. She's—she *was*—after you a lot, wasn't she."

It wasn't a question, his eyes boring through her. Her body tightened, squeezing the breath from her lungs.

"I don't know." A half-truth. "I don't know who did that."

"But she was after you a lot. And it was Scotty Trucco who—who vandalized your locker. And Veronica, who made that party video."

Of course Mike found out about the piss bitch stuff. In all his student interviews, someone would have told him eventually.

"Mike, I don't know what you're—"

"It's a murder investigation now, Rebekah," he said coldly. Pain flashed in his gaze before he hid it away. "Out of my hands. And I can't risk getting involved at this point. More than I already have, anyway," he added darkly.

"Mike . . . you don't—you don't think—"

"No, I don't. I'm not supposed to. The chief made that perfectly clear." Finally, he focused his eyes on her. "I shouldn't have . . . no matter how much I've always liked you, I shouldn't have. Not right now. I didn't take it seriously enough, and now someone's dead. Someone I might have been able to save if I hadn't—" He cursed under his breath and looked away. "It's my fault it got this far. If I'd kept my mind on the job instead of getting distracted, I would've seen there was a clear connection between them. I would've seen what was right in front of my face."

Rebekah was stunned, gutted. And terrified.

He hung his head, defeated. "Doesn't matter. I've been taken off the case because it isn't some high-society joke anymore. It's in the hands of Detective Ash now. A real cop. All I'm supposed to do is stay out of it. And—I'm sorry, Rebekah. But I'm staying out of it."

He walked away without sparing her a glance.

Who did she have left? Nora? Alice? The Raven?

None of them knew her. She wondered if any of them even considered her a person in her own right rather than just a means to their ends. Nora mostly overlooked her, overwhelmed by her daily tasks. Alice had treated Rebekah more like some fictional friend she wished she had than a real person, back when she'd treated her like anything at all. And the Raven . . .

Rebekah didn't know what it was. Not anymore. Not at all.

She was completely alone.

Rebekah placed the folded-up jacket on the Wilsons' porch and turned for home, avoiding any glimpse through the wide window of the reading room, and hoping she didn't look as cold and lost as she felt.

22

The book sat prominently on Rebekah's nightstand, where she'd placed it every night since Scotty had pissed in her locker. It had brought her immediate relief, the long-familiar words of Edgar Allan Poe, a reignited piece of her childhood. Memories of splashing devilishly in the shallows of a dark pool of emotion, playing at the compounding grief and guilt and pain Poe had striven to encapsulate in his words.

That had been before she'd known what being alive meant. It'd been before she'd known not having a father was weird. Before anyone had outwardly shown her any ill will. Sadness and anger and pain had been fake playthings, dolls in a decrepit house she toyed with in her dreams and vivid imagination, only to drop to the floor when her mother called her for dinner.

Holding the book then, flipping through its carefully preserved pages, reverently pausing over the signature on the title page, brought its own unique mixture of feelings. Comfort, left-over from those long nights as a kid. A shivering sort of mystery at the way it had disappeared and reappeared in her life, manifesting when she'd needed it the most. A deep-sought gra-tuity at the words themselves, the through-to-her-bones honesty Poe's stories wrought with-in her. And a seeping dread, wondering at her connection to the entity she'd long ago dubbed the Raven, wondering what it meant that she still longed to be in its company.

It might have gone too far with Coralie—*she* might have gone too far—but still, the Raven only wanted to protect her. It was her creature, and she knew it would never hurt her. It only wanted the best for her.

She didn't want to dream about it that night. If she did, she felt she'd have to make a decision. She didn't want to yet, not while she could still imagine she had at least one friend in her life— even if that friend was one she'd made up.

The first waft of dust and cloying rot brought such a rush of comforting power and effervescent energy that Rebekah spent a long, perfect moment simply existing in the manor—drifting toward the basement, her feet light on the creaking boards—before she remembered she hadn't intended to go there at all. She didn't want to face the Raven. She didn't want to face what had happened.

But it was too late.

She padded down a twisting staircase, which itself was off-putting in its familiarity. The

dream mansion had never repeated itself before. The bottom of the steps hosted an empty
stone room, an open archway at the other end;
beyond that, an underground, man-made lake.

It was the cistern. The same place where she'd
tortured Scotty Trucco.

Rebekah walked slowly through the arch
into the high-vaulted room with its indirect
light, the perfectly round platform in the middle of a perfectly still pool of water. Last time,
the water had been a dark, murky green, but
time had stained it red.

The room hung heavy with the scents of mold
and mottled blood. The racks of torture implements had vanished from their posts around
the edges of the pedestal. Instead, there were
only two shapes illuminated by the ghastly yellow light from above.

The Raven, standing tall and stoic. And beside it, a long wooden box bound in chains. It
stuck half-out from the floor so that it balanced

over the calm, deep, bloody water, ready to fall at a breath.

Scotty Trucco was inside that box.

Rebekah couldn't see or hear him except for a muffled thud now and then, but the knowledge was certain. It was clear and obvious, a fact, as sure as if she'd put him there herself.

She had, hadn't she? She must have. Because of what he'd done at school.

"No," she heard herself say. "No. We can't— it's too far now. Not this."

The Raven cocked its head and strode toward her. Even after what had happened, she wasn't frightened. She couldn't imagine the creature laying a hand on her. The Raven was nothing but her own dark servant.

It slowed to meet her, standing over her on the narrow strip of stone between the basement and the slimy, cleared-off pedestal. Fixing her with those reflective, animal eyes from deep within its shadow.

It reached forward and took her by the forearm. It was a gentle motion. Careful not to hurt her. Its fingers—supple leather gloves decorated with glittering red filigree—slid down to her hand and calmly gripped it, lifting it between them. For a crazy second, Rebekah half-wondered if it was going to kiss her knuckles, but it stopped, covering her hand with its other.

Then it spoke. A soft, rational voice.

"He will talk," it breathed.

A chill went up Rebekah's spine because she knew the Raven was right. Scotty had already threatened to do it. He knew she had done it. All of them did. And since Coralie had actually died, they might be less inclined to stick with their old stories. They might decide to take the risk and tell the truth, even if it sounded insane. After all, they had the same story to tell, and suddenly there was a "real cop" on the scene.

"But . . ." she floundered. "But there has to be a different . . ."

But there wasn't a different way to guarantee Scotty's silence. Killing him was the only way to protect herself, to cover her tracks. The threat at school had been public; she needed to retaliate immediately. Show them what would happen if they revealed her. Then there would be no way to track it to her. Nothing but a series of unfortunate accidents.

Images of the blood-smeared blade of the swinging axe and how Coralie's screams had died to whimpers, her whimpers to choking twitches, filled Rebekah's brain.

The Raven whispered, "They don't care about you."

The truth bit deep. Scotty, Eddie, Andrea—they had no reason not to turn on her. No reason to think of her as a full person.

It stood before her, as kind and patient as ever. As kind and patient a friend as she'd ever had.

Still, she needed to be sure.

Rebekah walked around the Raven, heedless

of the slippery edge of the narrow stone path, and approached the wooden box. Without moving it from its precarious position—and without bothering to undo the chains—she opened the lid, which came apart with an easy tug.

Scotty jumped at the sudden motion, causing the box to tilt dangerously toward the pool. Rebekah stood on the near edge of the box to anchor it in place. It was far heavier than it looked: thick, solid wood reinforced with bands of iron, the center of gravity placed precisely on the lip of the stone island.

Scotty's head was on the far end, teetering over the water. He wore the same pajamas as last time, red sweatpants without a shirt, and he'd been bound by a series of small chains with his arms crossed over his chest. Surrounding him, stuffing the empty spaces like packing peanuts, were heavy iron cannonballs. No gag or muzzle over his mouth that time.

"Rebekah. You killed Cory. Didn't you? You fucking killed her, you Carrie-ass bitch!"

Fury burned hot in his eyes, but there was something else there, too. Terror. He struggled against the small sets of shackles, gritting his teeth, his skin marked red along the chain that ran across his broad shoulders, but there was no way he could get out.

Rebekah found she couldn't answer him. She had killed Coralie, but she hadn't wanted to. At least, she hadn't meant to.

Instead, she asked, "Why did you do it?"

Scotty blinked furiously. "I'm—what? Do what?"

They watched one another warily. She'd meant to ask something else, demand he admit whether or not he'd been planning to report her to the police, insane story or no. But when she opened her mouth, that question came out instead. Something that, in all that time, she'd never actually asked.

Reckless power rolled through her. She was the one in charge there, not Scotty. To prove it, she jostled the coffin box to remind him and couldn't help grinning at how panic drained the color from his face. "Why did you piss in my fucking locker, Scotty?"

His eyes flashed in recognition, and his struggles intensified as he flinched away from her glare. "It—it was just a joke. You're—you know, you're the weird girl, and that thing at the party, and Eddie said—look, it wasn't like I tortured or *killed* anyone, so what's the big deal? Is that why you're doing all this? It was just a fucking joke!"

"A joke?" Electric vengeance jolted her, urging her on. She leaned forward to whisper, "Then I bet you'll find this hilarious."

Rebekah kicked his coffin and Scotty's terror broke through like sun from behind a cloud.

The weight of the cannonballs splashed

Scotty and his chains into the still surface of the bloody water. He opened his mouth to scream, but murky blood-stained water flooded in to shroud his face. Panicked spurting as he tried to breathe, a final glimpse of frenzied terror in his eyes, then he disappeared into the dark depths.

He'd called it a joke. Right up until the last minute, he'd called it a joke.

Scotty was dead.

Rebekah stared at the disturbed surface, and her need for retribution slowly filtered away. A single moment of passionate fury, and she'd killed him.

A soft weight landed on her shoulder, and Rebekah looked up to see the Raven. Its thumb massaged her lightly, its eerie white eyes fixed on her, calm comfort in their depths. The freeing sensation that she'd done the right thing.

Without a moment's thought, Rebekah

pulled the Raven close and embraced it. For a moment, it seemed surprised, stiff with its arms hovering in place, but it soon returned the gesture, bowing its head to press reassuringly against the top of hers.

The Raven felt warm. She thought she detected the shape and weight of a person beneath that glossy cloak, a neck, torso, legs. Pressing her ear against its chest, she even heard the soft thumps of a heartbeat, soft and slow. Reassuring.

Was the Raven real?

It didn't matter. Whether or not she'd killed Coralie, whether or not she'd meant to kill Coralie, she'd killed Scotty with her own hands.

Rebekah woke early the next morning, shivering beside the open window, and quietly wondered why she wasn't damp with bloody water, why her fingers hadn't pruned overnight. She'd killed Scotty. She'd spent all day yesterday reeling over Coralie's death, only to commit the same crime with Scotty. That time with the certainty of knowing she'd done it herself.

She wanted to hug Dupaw, but he was gone, too.

She managed to pretend to be a normal person in front of her mom, making toast, wrapping a school-approved scarf around her neck, accepting the hug that had become a part of the routine since their cat's murder. The charade lasted all the way into Grant High. Rebekah even managed to rustle up a few genuine smiles during the car ride, and if Nora noticed she avoided all questions about Mike, she seemed to put it down to normal teenage behavior. Hopefully, she would figure out from context that they'd broken up or something and that Rebekah wasn't keen on talking about it.

Which, in some way, was exactly what had happened.

* * *

Normally, Rebekah stuck to her well-trodden paths and places, which was probably how Alice had managed to avoid her so completely up until then. She always sat at the same planter before school, the same spot of concrete at lunch, haunting the same wood-paneled hallways between classes. But that day, Rebekah was determined to track Alice down.

Sure, Alice might not randomly text Rebekah asking what's up, but she had used to at least give her the time of day. And right then, Rebekah needed her friend back. She needed someone other than the Raven on her side.

And she needed to make sure no one had told the new detective about her, or failing that, at least to know when it happened. Alice was a lot better at surveillance. She was invisible, rather than outright derided, and unlike Rebekah, hadn't been blocked on social media by most of the student body.

To find Alice, though, meant Rebekah had to do things differently—steering clear of the planter and the art classroom window, the piss locker, keeping an eye out for intricate strawberry-blond braids. Trying to avoid running into her own ghost.

Yes, it meant that she didn't have the time to get to her locker before or between classes. No, she didn't care.

She did find Alice, eventually: she found her taking a circuitous route along a hall on the other end of campus, nose buried in her phone. Far away from any of her classes.

"Alice," Rebekah said, and the head of fancy braids jerked up. They stopped together, standing in a slanted beam of sunlight next to a display case filled with football trophies. Rebekah stood with her back to the case to avoid the pictures of Scotty Trucco interspersed among the brassy awards. So far, she hadn't heard any reports of his death, but that didn't mean they weren't coming—or that what had happened to Scotty wouldn't be a deterrent for the others.

Alice blushed, the redness that came so easily to her, taking root in her neck and blossoming into her cheeks. "Hey." She glanced down the hallway like an animal searching for escape. It was the end of passing period, meaning they'd be late for class, but also that the hall was basically empty. A sparse moment of privacy.

"Hey. Look, I'm sorry," Rebekah said. "About how things have been, and how I snapped at you that one time. I . . . miss you."

Alice relaxed visibly, her expression shifting from anxious to hesitantly hopeful. "I miss you, too. But things have just been so weird lately, and I had to focus on school—"

"I know, I get it. I totally get it, no problem." Rebekah chewed on her bottom lip. "Listen. I get that . . . I get why you thought that, okay?

And, yeah, it was kind of nuts how all those people were targeted. But I didn't . . . I wouldn't have . . ."

Alice tensed again, concern nestling in her brows, but she didn't respond.

Damn it. Lying was hard and she didn't want to push Alice further away, so Rebekah tried a different course.

"I'm . . . I'm worried, Alice." Her fingers danced on her backpack strap. "Um. Did you hear about Coralie?"

"Yeah. Of course."

"There's . . . there are cops looking into it, and I'm really worried, Alice. Because you had some really good points before. About the others. And me. And how they picked on me. And . . . what if the cops make the same connection? But they don't know me, so they wouldn't understand. What if they arrest me? What would happen to me if they did? What would happen to Nora?"

Alice's eyes softened.

"I'm just . . ." Rebekah tried to look sympathetic, real fear seeping into her tone. "I don't know what to do. I need your help. I need my friend back."

"Rebekah . . ."

At the hesitancy in her friend's tone, Rebekah knew she'd have to lie again to get what she wanted. Knew it had to be the best lie she'd ever told. Softly, confidently, she said, "I didn't do it, Alice."

A few taut seconds ticked by before, finally, Alice nodded. "I . . . I know, Rebekah. I know. I'm sorry. But I'm here for you now, okay?" She opened her arms for a hug.

Rebekah accepted, feeling sick and lonelier than she had before she'd sought out her friend in the first place.

From behind them, a man's voice asked, "Shouldn't you girls be in class?"

Rebekah jerked, startled. Principal Bransby

stood straight-backed at the next intersecting hall, peering at them through thick glasses. He met her eyes. Unrelenting. Unmoving.

Alice bowed her head and apologized before scurrying off to her class. Rebekah tried to copy her, but the moment they were alone, Bransby spoke again.

"Have you been staying safe, Rebekah?" His voice was impassive, his eyes piercing.

"Yes, Mr. Bransby. I've been fine."

"No dangerous activities? It's been particularly unsafe at night."

That was a threat, wasn't it?

She squared her shoulders, refusing to let him scare her. "Nothing I can't handle."

"Children are the worst judges of what they can handle."

"I'm not a child."

"My apologies, Rebekah. You're right. You're eighteen, aren't you?"

He put a weight on the number, tightening

his eyes. Eighteen—old enough to be tried as an adult.

His efforts to scare her meant nothing, though. Nothing scared her anymore. That was the rule. She'd won, gotten what she wanted. No one could threaten her because hers were the sharpest teeth. She straightened her posture.

"Yeah, I'm eighteen. And I'm smart enough not to do anything too dangerous, like go mountain biking in the middle of the night by myself."

He flinched at the reminder of Veronica's accident. Rebekah felt a little triumph at the sight of it.

"So, thanks for the concern, but I don't think anything's going to happen to me."

Voice clipped, Bransby said, "I'm only trying to look out for my students. It's a trait that I share with the school nurse. How *is* your mother doing?"

Rebekah's chest constricted. "She's fine."

"Good. She's fortunate the school board and I are understanding of her situation. If something were to happen to her position here at Grant High, I'm not sure what she would do."

Threatening Nora was a step too far. Rebekah wondered how confident Bransby would be inside the Raven's manor.

The image shattered her strength, replacing it with the spreading pool of Coralie's blood, with the silent way Scotty had slipped into the water.

Bransby leaned closer, saying quietly, "If you've done anything that might compromise your mother's job, I promise it won't have any effect on her standing if you come forward."

He wanted her to confess. He believed it was her, but he wanted her to turn herself in so he wouldn't have to explain *why* he thought it was her. Because he had no proof.

She said, as genuinely as she could manage, "It means a lot that you'd reach out to me when you already have so much to worry about. I mean, with everything going on, it makes you wonder about the safety of everyone else in school."

"Rebekah," Bransby started, an edge of affront beneath the cool outer shell of his voice—

"Thank you, Principal, but I'm late for class."

Rebekah walked away, her cool, confident exterior at odds with the scalding panic rising inside her.

Unfortunately, her worry hadn't been baseless, the fear hitting Rebekah hard again whenever she saw the flick of the new detective's brown ponytail. Detective Ash, Alice reported, had been making her rounds across campus, asking questions and taking notes. And there she was, looming over the lunch crowd, a haunting catastrophe.

As Rebekah watched through the misty rain, Tom artfully escaped a conversation with the detective, but Rebekah caught a look from Eddie, sitting still at a mosaic-topped table. Puffy red eyes no one around him acknowledged, cast still clamped around his arm.

Rebekah unraveled again, pressed into her lunch spot, staring into Eddie's eyes through the crosshatched branches of a shrub. Rebekah had killed Scotty. She could call Coralie's death an accident all she wanted or blame the Raven—if that even meant anything—but *she* had killed Scotty.

She'd pushed him into the water, in a fit of hot anger, like fire roaring through her. She'd killed him herself. There was no taking that back.

For the first time since taking out Scotty's tooth, Rebekah was the first one to glance away. She ate mechanically, tasting nothing.

He'd called it a joke. He had looked into her eyes and called it a fucking joke.

She gazed at her peanut butter and jelly sandwich and felt outrage and guilt swirl inside her.

Alice sat down silently at some point; Rebekah didn't notice until she asked softly, "What happened with you and Mike?"

Something else Rebekah didn't want to talk about.

Alice took Rebekah's hand, apparently misreading her silence. "Hey. It's all right. They'll find whoever did this. They'll find out the truth, okay? You have to trust the cops. They know what they're doing. They won't get their information from gossiping teenagers, right?"

Rebekah nodded numbly, and Alice continued, "Did I tell you I've been looking into it myself, and I think I'm onto something?"

Rebekah stiffened, shocked out of her stupor. "What? What do you mean?"

"Don't worry, I'm being careful. I'm not stupid. I just . . ." She looked around them before dropping her voice. "I wanted to know . . . whether or not it really was you. So I've been looking into it. And, honestly, it can't be you. I knew that. I think I knew that all along, I was just taking my time, because . . . I mean, I was kind of jealous of you and Mike. But my point is, some of the stuff that's happened is just way too intense for you to have physically done it."

Wait a minute. If Alice knew all the details of what happened with each accident, then did she also know about the dreams, about the Raven? Bile burned hot in the back of Rebekah's throat, her temples throbbing. If the Raven knew Alice had been investigating, he might come after her and . . . Oh, God. "You stopped, right? When Coralie . . . ? You stopped."

"I told you, I'm being careful."

Rebekah squeezed her friend's hand. "Please, Alice, listen to me. Stop. I want you to be safe. I just . . . I have a bad feeling. Please, trust me."

Alice opened her mouth, then closed it. Then nodded. "Okay. I'll stop."

"Thank you." Rebekah took a deep breath.

Alice nudged her shoulder with one of her own. "Don't worry, Rebekah. I trust you."

Just then Detective Ash glanced toward them from where she stood speaking to Eddie. Exhaustion lines framed the detective's sharp eyes, as gray as her namesake and unforgivingly present. The look was fleeting, but still, it drilled into Rebekah, a piercing cold right down to her middle, making her suspect Eddie had said something, implicated her somehow. Ash would head their way next. It was in her body language. Rebekah couldn't bear talking to a detective. She couldn't threaten her like she could Bransby. She couldn't lie to her like she could to Alice. She had to get away.

"I have to piss," she said abruptly. As she headed toward the exit, moving as casually as possible, she felt every set of eyes on her, burning into her back.

23

Rebekah was determined not to dream about the Raven that night. In fact, she tried not to sleep at all. Armed with the excuse that it was Friday, she brewed up a batch of coffee and sat at her desk in the cold of a wide-open window, rain splashing on the sill, lights on, music playing through her phone, trying to draw a Pluto comic.

The familiar lines of the one-eyed cat felt hollow as she forced herself to scribble them. Insincere. It reminded her too much of Coralie, of Dupaw, of the snickering laughter in English class. But it was something to do, something to focus on, something to occupy her time. Anything other than falling asleep.

Standing in one of the house's hollow halls, surrounded by the skitter of insects, the long shadows creeping in, Rebekah's heart sank.

She'd fallen asleep, but she didn't know how, couldn't remember even feeling tired. All her work, her focus, her dedication, and she'd been dragged there anyway.

Hopeless, she padded through the house, footsteps softened by the gritty dust between her bare toes, in part because she knew exactly where the Raven was. Which meant she knew exactly who it had kidnapped.

The study. Where Eddie's arm had been broken.

There was a dull roar in her ears. The hall leading to the narrow bookless study stretched before her, darkness behind her, dusty windows along one wall, letting in shafts of piercing moonlight. She felt exposed. Watched. Anxiety prickled her skin.

She didn't want Eddie to die. But she'd thought she didn't want Scotty to die. She'd thought she didn't want Coralie to die, her guts spilling out like lifeless snakes onto the floor.

But if Rebekah didn't meet the Raven, if she left Eddie alone with it, he might die anyway. She couldn't see or feel beyond the shifting walls of the mansion, the skulking miasma of rotting flesh that permeated the howling wind. If her body was up, moving, acting in the real world, there could be no way for her to know if he'd die by her hand or not.

The shadows that had once offered her safety occluded secrets of their own. The hideaway tunnels that had once provided salvation hosted watchful eyes, staring out at her, waiting for her to betray herself again.

No. She didn't want to kill Eddie. She didn't

want to kill anyone else. She reached the door to the study and pushed it open.

Eddie was strapped to a table, the chair nowhere to be seen. Like the cistern, the study matched Rebekah's memories, full of sooty shelves and a faceless stone bust, vaulted windows that let in the rain.

The Raven stood over Eddie's restrained body, its eyes fixed only on Rebekah. Waiting for her. Expecting her.

Eddie made no noise, but the irregular, muffled thud of his pulse filled the room, speeding up and slowing down, amplified by a gramophone sitting in the corner. The machine wasn't connected to him, from what Rebekah could tell, but she knew it was Eddie's heartbeat just the same. He wore the same leather muzzle as before, and he stared at the ceiling with tears streaming from his face.

He knew he was going to die.

Rebekah stood tall. The Raven was her creature. Part of her. It would listen to her.

"Thank you," she said, her voice shaking as she tried to meet the Raven's eyes. "Thank you for helping me. But . . . not . . . not this, anymore. Okay? I . . ."

Eddie's eyes flicked to her with a mad hope, his projected heartbeat stuttering. The Raven rounded the table, shifting silently over the groaning wooden floor, and approached Rebekah just as it had with Scotty.

She swallowed. "Let him go. That's—that's what I want. That's how you can help me."

The Raven's head cocked to the side. "He will talk," it breathed, a perfectly calm fact.

Fear rolled through Rebekah, a cold panic, because it was right. Because she'd killed people, and if Detective Ash uncovered the truth, then it must be—had to be—Rebekah at the end of the line. Eddie's heartbeats grew louder, filling the room, thumping against the windows, against the doorway, against her skin.

Her stomach twisted, heavy and sick. "I . . . I just wanted to be as free as them. I wanted to take their power away. That's it. That's all I wanted. I didn't want this."

"He doesn't care about you," the Raven said gently. "He will destroy you without hesitation."

Eddie made noises against his muzzle as if trying to argue against the Raven's assumptions. But with his life so clearly on the line, there'd be no way to know if he was telling the truth. After all, Coralie had promised to back off the first time, too.

Coralie had promised to back off both times, but it'd be impossible to know if she would have kept her promise the second time.

"I'm . . . I'm sorry," Rebekah whispered, wincing against the pummeling bass of Eddie's heartbeat. "Not this time. We'll—I'll—come up with something else, something real. Okay?"

"This is real."

"Yes, exactly, that's the problem."

Its head tilted the other way, eyes reflecting the moonlight as it regarded her. Featureless and black as shadow. Then it ducked its head into a shallow bow.

Rebekah let out a breath, and so did Eddie, although his came through in a muffled sob, reflected in the muffled beats through the gramophone.

"I will protect you, Beka." The Raven glanced up, its gaze unknowable but piercing in the dim light. "Even if you refuse to protect yourself."

It pulled a gleaming dagger from within its glossy cloak and turned around, quiet as a wraith. Rebekah's heart constricted, and she dove forward to grab it, but the muscles beneath the smooth black cloak were whipcord-tight, far too strong; she never would have been able to pull it away.

The knife went into Eddie's chest with the same smooth silence as all of the Raven's movements, as though it were slipping the blade into its sheath.

The heartbeat stopped. Eddie hadn't even had the time to scream.

The Raven stepped back, disappearing from Rebekah's grasp as she fumbled to remove the knife. As if that action could undo what'd been done. But the dagger had impaled Eddie's heart with exacting precision. Silence wrapped around them with an oppressive chill.

Eddie was dead. The Raven had killed him.

Against Rebekah's explicit request.

She turned around, shaking. Her creature stood unruffled as it always had.

"Why?" she begged, and only then became aware of the tears on her face. "Why? I didn't want this. I told you not to!"

"He laughed," the Raven answered, its soft voice stark against the silence. "He mocked you and treated you like nothing. He would have led to your downfall."

"Then—then I would have dealt with that somehow!" Her voice trembled. "Done something, thought of something, Or maybe I wouldn't. I don't know, okay, I don't know. I just don't get to have what they have. I'm not allowed to."

She hadn't meant to say that out loud, but the truth of it struck something dark and true. Even after three people had died, she still felt bitter and resentful that they'd been better off than her all along.

"You *can* have what they had." The Raven swept toward her, its voice firm with resolute confidence. "This is what you deserve, what you've fought for, what you've earned. This is your story, Beka. This is your soul."

"What are you?" she demanded. "I thought

you were me, but if you're me, then why can't I—" She choked on the words, on her own tears. "Why can't I—"

"I am yours," the Raven answered, then bowed and vanished into the dark shadows.

Rebekah woke up crying.

Her window was still open. She swallowed a sob, searching through blurry eyes for a knife or a splatter of blood somewhere in the darkened room. But there was nothing.

She grabbed the Poe book off the nightstand and leaned over it, hugging it as tight as she could, fingernails digging into the leather.

After a moment, she pulled back and looked down at the book's cover, taking in the sanguine embossing gleam in the imperfect moonlight, just like the filigree on the back of the Raven's gloves.

Rebekah pushed the book back onto the

nightstand. On a whim, she crossed to the closet and grabbed one of the stuffed animals she'd unearthed in her hunt for a new backpack: a lumpy frog, luminous green fuzz puffing out from it like a wispy halo. Its smile was as disingenuous as it was unrealistic.

She didn't care. She drew herself up against the cold wall beside her bed, held it against her, and pretended it was Dupaw. She pulled her blanket over her head and sat in the dark, trying to hide from everyone and everything.

Trying to hide from the alluring glare of the Poe book and the raven on its cover.

Rebekah drew that next day, nonstop, bowing toward her notebook like it might swallow her whole. It was Saturday, so no school, no one to avoid. Her plans of keeping Alice on her side, of keeping an eye on the detective while somehow avoiding her, they felt thin. Transparent. Useless.

If she couldn't even control the Raven, then what could she control? It was the only thing in her life that had seemed to give her any amount of agency, and that had been pulled away from her.

Three people dead. They had to have found Eddie in the morning when the sun had first peeked through the damningly open window. It was late again; Rebekah had wasted hours doing nothing, scribbling like some madwoman, empty bags of hastily snatched snacks shoved to the side like the piles of laundry that littered the thin carpet.

She didn't know where Eddie was in the real world or what had happened to him, but still, it was her fault that he'd died.

No.

Not that time. She'd told the Raven to stop.

But if *she* was the Raven, then why had it

ignored her? Had she, on a deep level, wanted to kill Eddie? Was she a murderer, all the way down to the core?

After all, she'd killed Scotty herself.

Exhaustion pulled at her, threatening to pull her under. She couldn't remember the last time she'd had a good night's sleep. Before the murders, certainly. Before the tortures. Before the Raven had invaded her dreams, which had become nightmares . . .

She shook that off and continued drawing, obsessed. Obsessed with finding peace, with finding rest, with finding anything other than the numb resignation that nothing mattered anymore.

The cop, Alice, all the other people at Grant High who might tell on her, none of them mattered. What happened to Rebekah after all that, it didn't matter either.

Rebekah turned the page and drew the Raven again. She'd drawn them holding hands before, and she drew it again, the familiar pen marks against the page. But that one came across more as if the creature was pulling her along, yanking on her arm, threatening to tear it out of its socket. Its grip cool and firm on her wrist, the faint outline of a human nose under that dark hood.

Mike knew the truth. Or at least, he could. He had all the pieces. If he believed in the impossible, he'd be able to put it together. He knew the dreams were related, knew Rebekah was involved somehow. He knew . . .

Sitting in the chilled stillness of her bedroom, between her sketchbook and a pile of crumpled chip bags, elbows sore where they'd pressed against her desk for hours on end, Rebekah realized that the slight flicker in her chest was a tiny beacon of hope.

Mike was already close to the answer. He might understand, might even—more than anyone else—have a *chance* at understanding what was going on.

If there was a way to stop it all, to stop the Raven, then maybe it would be with Mike's help.

Rebekah had never actually snuck out of the house before—at least, not as herself. She must have done it as the Raven, but she had no memories of it. So she kissed her mom goodnight, waited until she was certain she was sound asleep, and finally made use of the open window for the first conscious time.

Vaulting the windowsill was unsteady and imperfect, and she made more of a ruckus than she meant to when she half-fell into the shrub that ended precisely where the window began—but then she was out. She closed the window again and backed up, staring at the house, waiting for Nora to call for her.

Nothing happened.

She shouldn't have been so worried. After a certain hour, Nora was all but guaranteed to be dead asleep, whether from her own exhaustion or having passed out from drinking. Given that it was the weekend, Rebekah would have bet on the latter.

Okay. Rebekah turned around to face Mike's house. A stretch of grass and a couple of shrubs stood sentry to their individual gated backyards. Nervous in her stomach, out to her fingertips, compounding the wintry cold. But she had to try. She couldn't let the Raven win.

Refusing to sleep hadn't worked. Telling Mike the truth, though, that might work; he might be able to stay up, keep an eye on her, stop her.

She needed to push through the anxiety that welled in her throat, that buzzy feeling in her head like she was making a terrible mistake. Going to prison would be better than killing everyone at Grant High. Killing Detective Ash.

She repeated that to herself. She knew it would only be a matter of time until it got that far. She'd already entertained the thought, although it made her feel sick to acknowledge it.

If she didn't act then, the Raven would come for the detective, someone who had never lifted a finger against Rebekah, who had never even met her personally. Someone who was only doing her best to protect high schoolers.

No. She needed to tell Mike. Needed him to help her stop it. He'd know what to do.

Energy building in her legs, hot in her chest, she sprinted across to Mike's front door—

—where she saw someone moving in the front room, the reading room, and stopped in her tracks. A tall man in a jacket perusing his library. Bill. He'd probably make her go home if he saw her.

Shit. Maybe she could climb up to Mike's window, if she could figure out which one was his, or . . .

Duh, just call him.

She ducked back between the two houses to keep Bill from spotting her, found Mike's contact in her phone, and dialed. He didn't answer, so she kept calling over and over until he realized it was important.

He realized it on the fifth call.

"What is it, Rebekah?" he said instead of hello. He sounded half-asleep. She'd probably woken him up.

"You're right," she said. "You're right, and I need to tell you everything. Please. Can I come up to your room?"

"My room? Wait, right about what? Rebekah, it's almost midnight."

"Please. I need you to keep me awake tonight. If I—if you don't, someone else is going to die. I just know it."

"Wait, Rebekah, are you serious? What are you talking about?"

"It's me." Tears pushed out of her eyes again

and she felt vibrant and dizzy, sick to her stomach. She was making a mistake. A terrible mistake—but the words were already out.

She swallowed. Silence on the line.

"It's me," she repeated. "I need to tell you the truth, Mike. Right now. Please."

"Um. Yeah. Yeah. Okay, I'll let you in."

"Not the front door. Your dad's still up. I don't want him to see me."

"Oh, he's always up late. Um, there's a shed in the backyard. Go in through the gate. I'll meet you there."

"A shed?" She'd imagined that conversation taking place on Mike's bed, not a drafty wooden room. Then again, maybe the cold would make it easier.

"Yeah. My dad got it for woodworking but never actually did anything with it. It should be unlocked; I'll meet you there."

"I—" she started, but Mike ended the call

with a beep. She blinked at the phone for a moment, then looked back at the gate.

Okay. It was better than nothing.

She approached the Wilsons' wooden gate and, heedless of spiderwebs, groped for the latch on the other side. One benefit of calling a nightmare manor "home" for weeks on end was an underdeveloped fear of the macabre.

She thought of Nora's reaction to her treatment of Dupaw's body and wondered if it was a benefit after all. Just another thing that pinpointed her as different from everyone around her.

Rebekah pushed the gate open then closed it as silently as she could behind her.

Like her backyard, Mike's was primarily grass and mud with a concrete porch offering poor shelter from the elements. It wasn't raining that night, but the heavy odor of last night's storm implied it could at any moment.

The half-dried mud cracked under her footsteps between wisps of grass.

The shed had been painted black, crouching in the corner of the yard like a shivering dog. There was a latch on it, but as Mike had said, it wasn't locked.

Rebekah glanced back at the sliding door that glowed with a distant light. The lamp from the front room, maybe. Or Mike coming down the stairs. Or maybe his mom was awake, too, a family of night owls.

She lifted the latch slowly, wincing at the expectation of a rusty groan, but it made no sound as she pulled the bolt back and swung the door open.

A dark toolroom with an unlit bulb hanging in the middle, still and silent. In the dim moonlight, a glimmer of blades, saws, screwdrivers, and drill bits reminded her of that first night in the cistern, the array of tools the Raven had prepared surrounding Scotty. As if the creature itself hadn't yet decided exactly what to do with him.

But then she blinked, and it turned back into a perfectly normal toolshed. Blades, saws, yes—but also tape, pencils, markers, rubber bands. Rebekah took a moment to calm herself, stepped inside, and pulled the door mostly shut behind her.

The space was small and smelled like dust, but it was comfortable. A safe place, maybe. Somewhere no one would look.

Somewhere she could be locked inside.

24

Mike took the stairs as quickly and quietly as he could. He didn't know what to make of Rebekah's call. Honestly, he didn't know what to make of Rebekah, period. He'd accused her of having something to do with the murders, and she was saying he'd been right.

He thought of their slow dance in the pulp factory. It almost didn't seem real anymore. She could be in danger, as she'd implied, or she could be lying to get him out of the way. He had no way of knowing.

When he reached the bottom of the stairs, Mike hesitated, listening. He saw the glow of the doorway to the reading room, and after a few moments, he heard the shuffle of a page turning. His father was obsessed with reading, with "experiencing the soul of art," even at—Mike checked his watch—roughly midnight. Mike's dad became famously unobservant when he was lost in a book, but still, Mike didn't know how well he could rely on that right then.

Part of him wondered if maybe he should tell his dad what was going on, maybe have him serve as a kind of backup. But, no. His bookish professor father didn't know the first thing about self-defense, and explaining the situation to him might generate enough noise to wake up his mom, which would kickstart its own avalanche of problems. Besides, Rebekah wasn't a threat, not to Mike.

Was she?

Tense, Mike snuck to the back door, avoiding the spots of floor that would groan under his weight, and stepped into his yard boots before heading out. In accordance with years of muscle memory, he quickly slid the door open and swept it closed behind him, stopping just short of the jamb. He listened for a long moment, and when he heard no searching footsteps, he inched it shut. Crisis avoided, he trekked across the muddy backyard, breath frosting in the chilly night air.

Inside the shed, he found Rebekah standing in the corner, shivering in the dark like a skittish animal. She hugged herself, exhaustion heavy in her eyes, limp curls of hair framing her face.

Despite everything, he felt the urge to wrap his arms around her.

He shut the door behind him then flicked on the solitary bulb to illuminate the windowless space with a bald yellow light. Rebekah flinched and squinted but didn't say anything, her jaw tensed shut.

He stood between her and the door. "What do you want to tell me?"

Her gaze never darted to the door behind him, so either she didn't notice he'd trapped her, or she didn't care.

"Please hear me out," she said, finally, a slight crack to her voice, arms clutched a little tighter around herself. "Just—just listen to what I have to say first. Okay?"

Mike swallowed. "Rebekah . . . listen, if this is a confession, I need to take you to the station to do it right. You won't be hurt or put in any danger. I promise."

Rebekah bit her bottom lip, he noticed, the way she always did when she was nervous. "It . . ." She paused, as if to actually consider the idea. "No, it isn't a confession. Sort of. I—please, Mike, just listen."

The fear in her eyes was real. Whatever was going on, she was in danger, or at least believed herself to be. Mike stepped forward instinctively to comfort her but stopped himself.

"Okay," he said instead, dread trickling down his back. "I'll listen."

She nodded and took a moment to gather herself, pressed against the tools along the back wall of the shed. Any one of them could be used as a weapon, all of them within her arm's reach. He shouldn't have suggested that location.

"There's a . . . a creature in my dreams. Sort of like an imaginary friend, but way too . . . real. I call it the Raven."

Mike listened to her story, each new statement wilder and less believable than the last. She said this "Raven" had killed the kids at school who had tormented her, transporting them to nightmare dreams to do its work. She tearfully admitted she'd been on board with most of it, that she'd gotten high on the power it had given her.

Dreams. Mike felt a chill.

And the fact she'd enjoyed watching those accidents come to pass?

"I killed Scotty," she admitted, lines of tears on her cheeks. "I think we both killed Coralie, but I killed Scotty. And—and the Raven killed Eddie. I told it not to, but it did anyway. I didn't want to. I don't think I wanted to. But I don't trust myself anymore, or the Raven, if we're two different things, so I need to stay awake tonight."

She obviously believed everything she said. Mike could see it in her trembling fear, the way she clutched at her clothes and wiped away her tears with the back of a shaky hand.

He stepped forward and spoke softly. "They're nightmares, Rebekah. That's all. I know it feels bad, but it doesn't mean you're at fault here."

"No, it does," she insisted with confidence. "Because I dreamed about these things before— maybe *as* they were happening. Don't you see that? The Raven pulled Scotty's tooth out before I heard anything about that stupid football accident. I haven't talked to anyone today about

Eddie, but I know he's dead. He was stabbed. He was stabbed, wasn't he?" Her voice shook, her knuckles white she clenched her hands so tight. "Through the heart. Dead instantly."

That froze Mike in his tracks. Eddie's body had been found that morning, every bit as much an "accident" as Coralie Renner running her car point-blank into a brick wall and slicing herself open with her seatbelt. Eddie had apparently slipped while trying to make a midnight snack in the kitchen and fallen face-first onto his knife. Just as Rebekah said, unerringly through the heart.

But no one knew any of that. Detective Ash had insisted the precinct not divulge any information about Eddie's death and had even sworn his parents to secrecy. Mike had personally kept watch over social media and the local news outlets to catch any leaks. There was no way Rebekah should have known how Eddie had died.

Rebekah continued, "No one told me what happened to Scotty, but I bet he drowned. No one told me what happened to Coralie, but I bet—" Her face screwed up, like she was half disgusted, half desperately sorry. "I bet she was—was sliced open across the stomach—"

"Hey." Mike did pull her close then, couldn't help it, wrapping one arm around her and placing his other hand on the back of her head, his fingers threading through her cold, straggly hair. At first, she didn't do anything, just stood there against him. Then she broke down completely, hanging on for dear life as she sobbed into his chest. He shouldn't have done it, realizing too late that he'd left himself vulnerable to attack, but damn it. His mind was still racing over the fact she knew about Eddie's death. That had to mean she was involved somehow. Otherwise, how would she know . . .

But if she was involved, why tell Mike any of

it—why make up that story about the creature in her dreams?

"I need to stay awake tonight," she whispered. "If I do, no one will get killed. I promise."

"That's not how it works. This isn't *Elm Street*."

"I promise."

Her arms tensed around him. Well . . . he could play along, for her sake. He could stay up one night. If she remained at his side, and someone died, he'd know she was innocent. They both would. He nodded, still holding her, not wanting to let her go.

"Okay," he said. "Let's stay awake. You and me, okay? Everything's going to be all right."

"I . . . I really hope so."

She tightened her grip, and they stood like that for a little while.

They spent a few hours watching videos on Mike's phone, chatting about inconsequential topics, not wanting to leave the toolshed for fear of running into Mike's parents. They wound up sitting in the corner, their knees brushing against each other as they did their best to stay awake.

Mike woke to a sore back and the dusty scent of a rain-soaked attic. He was seated on something hard, leaning against a wooden wall. Tools hung above him, a clawed hammer, a selection of wrenches in order from large to small, several handsaws of various lengths. On the underside of a table, he saw the pale outlines of spiderwebs in the sparse morning light. Quiet. Peaceful, almost.

His muscles were cold and his stiff joints cracked as he stretched then pushed uncertainly to his feet. He checked his watch: a little later in the morning than he usually got up.

The toolshed was empty. He'd fallen asleep, with Rebekah, after promising he wouldn't.

With a jolt of alarm, he realized she wasn't with him.

Mike searched the tiny space as though she could possibly have been hiding in some shadowy corner, but there was no sign of her. It didn't seem like she'd sneak out on him after everything she'd said, but then maybe she'd told him that crazy story to distract him. But if that was the case, then why hadn't she taken the opportunity to . . . well, do whatever it was she'd created the opportunity to do?

Frustrated and confused, Mike pulled out his phone and found several missed calls. He opened his voicemail and paced, listening to Officer Dempsey's annoyed tone in the message.

"Where the hell are you, Mike? There's been another one. Ash wants you here."

Another death. Mike's chest tightened as he lowered the phone.

Rebekah had disappeared, and then there was another murder.

The house wasn't as glamorous as some of the others scattered throughout the moderate forest, but it had its own picturesque beauty, standing two stories tall at the crest of a hill. On any other day, it'd be a lovely sight, the way it sat framed by evergreens and overlooking the valley, even in the sprinkling rain that sparked little flashes of cold against his skin; but death had a unique way of casting a pall over the most idyllic view.

Mike brought his posse box into the house, his entire collection of notes. The front door stood open, and Dempsey and Mitchell loitered near it, pointedly glancing away from him when he arrived. Dempsey was the one who'd forced Mike into documenting the weird accidents, but he resented the way Ash had requested to use Mike as a kind of impromptu assistant. Mike had been right to give up on befriending Dempsey; he'd never really had a chance.

He followed the sound of voices past a sunny kitchen, up a narrow set of stairs, and toward a loft with a slanted window where two middle-aged men cradled one another, both outfitted with matching sets of baby-blue pajamas. The chief, sitting politely beside them, motioned for Mike to cross the open doorway.

Detective Ash stood in a small bedroom, taking notes on the narrow pad she always seemed to have on her. She stood out in her bright police jacket against the muted browns and pinks of the room, and a small gas mask sat disused around her neck. She looked wrong against the teen-girl background, out of place, an intrusion into someone else's life.

She looked up when Mike entered. "Wilson.

Good. Don't worry, the gas has dissipated. I want your opinion on this."

Mike stiffened. Ash had never asked for his opinion before, only his notes, for what he assumed was simply a head start on the investigation. "You . . . do?"

To that, she only nodded and motioned toward the open door on the other side of the room. He peered into the narrow bathroom.

Tan-painted walls with pink accents: picture frames, a matching set of soap dispensers, fluffy hand towels. A pink toothbrush beside a half-crumpled tube of toothpaste. A makeup box, bright gold-yellow with silver highlights, with a smiling sun in the center.

And a dead girl on the floor.

She was on her side, twisted awkwardly, like she'd collapsed and knocked herself against the bathroom counter. She wore a set of baby-blue pajamas that matched her fathers', her hands wore pink rubber gloves, and a sponge lay discarded on the tile next to her.

Behind him, Ash said, "Alice Bedloe. Eighteen, senior at Grant High School. Chloramine gas. She closed herself in and mixed bleach and ammonia in the sink."

"An accident?" he asked without thinking.

"What do you think, Wilson?"

Mike tore his focus away from the scene and turned to Ash, who watched him intensely. For a split second, he was convinced she knew about Rebekah, knew he'd tried to stay up all night watching her. Knew he'd failed. That she'd disappeared, and . . .

Could Rebekah have done that to her friend? How?

Mike swallowed. "They . . . all look like accidents, on the surface, but . . . why was Alice cleaning her bathroom in the middle of the night? Why didn't she try to escape the chloramine gas? Doesn't it have a smell? How could

Eddie have landed on his knife like that? And Coralie, right into a wall—there weren't any skid marks, she hadn't been drunk . . ."

Ash motioned back around the room. "There's no sign of a break-in here, no sign of a struggle."

She didn't agree with him. He deflated. "Yeah, I know."

"You misunderstand me, Wilson." His eyes flicked to her again. "I agree with you, but there's something else going on here. I've read your notes and investigated the high school myself. Most of the kids were friends, except for Alice here."

Rebekah. That's what connected them. Mike's mouth went dry as he peered into the bathroom, the girl's strawberry-blond hair in a messy braid. It ate at him that he wasn't leaping to suggest it.

He hadn't put Rebekah in his notes. In fact, he'd actively avoided it. The only person who

could have outlined a solid connection between them all and Rebekah, outside of the rumor mill, was . . .

. . . Alice.

And Mike.

"What is it?" the detective asked, maybe seeing something in his eyes. He'd never been very
good at poker.

If he told her about Rebekah, they'd bring
her in and question her, put her under observation. If the killings stopped, then . . .

Well, then no one else would die.
That'd be good.

But it would also mean Rebekah really
was guilty.

"Officer Wilson?"

Mike needed to tell her. If he wanted to be
a police officer of any caliber, he needed to do
the right thing and tell Ash about Rebekah.

"Nothing. Sorry. Got lost in thought."

She gazed at him as if reading those very

thoughts. But then she turned away and kept talking, pointing out various pieces of the scene. Mike didn't hear any of it.

He couldn't do it. He couldn't do the obviously right thing. Because of Rebekah. Because she'd come to his house in tears last night, and because he still had feelings for her, despite everything.

Mike wasn't a police officer. He was a coward.

25

Rebekah couldn't feel her limbs.

She'd curled up in the corner of her bed some time ago—back against the wall, heels tucked under her, knees pressed up against her forehead, arms tense, hands curling around her shins—and she hadn't moved from that spot. Her awareness of her muscles had long faded, leaving only the darkness, the cold winter's breath from the window buffeting against the hot pressure inside her, and the feeling of her kneecaps digging into her hairline.

Whenever she closed her eyes, she saw the dilapidated chapel, the rows and columns of lit candles coating the floor and tables like a harnessed housefire, all surrounding a chair in the middle. Alice, strapped in, blindfolded, calling out for help.

Rebekah tried to keep her eyes open, but the scene swam in her vision, superimposing itself on her thighs. The candle flames flickering with an unsettling peace, releasing poisonous gas as they burned. The Raven's hands on Rebekah's wrists, its voice in her ear, as calm as the candles, explaining how Alice had been set to betray her. Explaining, in a deliberate, soothing manner, that it was only looking out for Rebekah's safety, even while its fingers tightened like iron cords.

It hadn't worked. Waiting until the morning hadn't been enough. Getting Mike to watch over her hadn't been enough. She should have locked herself up, turned herself in to the precinct like he'd asked. Anything.

Did Mike know Alice was dead?

She didn't remember leaving the toolshed, wasn't sure if he'd watched her walk out or if she'd overpowered him. Wasn't sure what had happened to him at all.

Next thing Rebekah had known, she'd appeared in the woods, outside of a shack made of buckled wood and gnarled roots, overgrown and sinking into the soft forest floor. The Raven had emerged from the shanty, a sweeping shadow, dark black with piercing white eyes; it had caught her and pulled her into an embrace, using its otherworldly strength against her.

She'd tried to force it to stop, begged and demanded that it listen to her, but it had only fixed her with those animal eyes and whispered four words, perfectly reasonable, like the kind clucking of a parent.

"You are still afraid."

It had said the words gently, as though it understood something far deeper and more complicated than she did.

"You don't need to be afraid any longer."

"I'm not afraid!" Rebekah had tried to say,

but the words passed insubstantially through the creature before her. "You're not listening to me—"

"I'm not listening to your words, Beka, but I am listening to your heart. Come. Let us go home."

It had snatched her in its arms then, bridal-style, and sprinted through the trees with such speed that she'd been forced to clutch it around the neck to keep from falling. Sharp, leafless branches had shot by on either side, reaching out for her, threatening to scrape and claw her skin.

She'd never been afraid of those trees before. She'd never been afraid of the Raven before. But braced in its arms, she had felt the human shape of it more than ever; its strong arms and hands, the soft silent huffs of its breath, the angle of the nose and chin shrouded in its hood. The chest and abdomen that normally remained shrouded under its cloaked silhouette.

Whatever the Raven was, it was more human than she'd first thought. It was a twisted part of her, or maybe some evil spirit that'd latched onto her, but she remembered thinking, just then, staring into the dim, shrouded shapes of its cheeks and neck, that it might actually be a person. Somehow.

It had carried her through one of the manor's broken windows, its cloak slipping around the jagged shards like a tongue lapping between teeth, and set her down in front of Alice, who'd been strapped to a chair. Blindfolded.

Rebekah couldn't explain how she'd known the candles were poison. She couldn't explain why she hadn't been able to rush forward and free her only friend, why she'd barely managed to struggle against the Raven's firm grip, why she'd listened to its whispers as Alice had gasped and gagged in the toxic air.

"This is how life works for them," it had said, a deep and confident kindness in its soft voice.

"Those without art, without soul. They can take whatever they want. They can do or be whatever they want. Why shouldn't you have the same thing? You, creator of art, bearer of soul, who are so much more than they. Why should you be denied the privilege to which they had been born?"

A familiar rawness ached in her chest as she curled up on her bed, tightening her grip on her legs, pressing back against the wall. The Raven had been right, of course. It was right, and that was the worst part.

The nausea that rolled through Rebekah's stomach was a familiar one, although it'd never been that strong before, piercing through her numbness like mud sloughing over a corpse. She needed to vanish; she needed the disappearing act her mind performed when she drew, melting into her art. A ghost couldn't feel sick to its stomach. A creative spirit couldn't feel guilt, or anxiety, or terror. At least, that's how it'd always worked before.

But when Rebekah finally looked up from her hollow brace, her joints and muscles protesting as she unfolded, she didn't see her sketchbook on the nightstand. Or the bed. Or the floor next to the bed, or the desk, or in her backpack, or in the crack between the mattress and the wall. She did find the frog stuffed in there again and reached in to rescue him, staring into his empty, too-bright eyes.

Her sketchbook was gone. Maybe the Raven had stolen it, or maybe she'd done something with it when she'd climbed through her window last night.

She tried to sit and disappear again into her thoughts, but the only company there was a foggy replay of her nightmare. The Raven's hands tight around her wrists, its soft voice in her ear, Alice's desperate calls for help, the bright flicker of the flames against her blindfold.

Alice was dead.

Rebekah couldn't breathe.

She searched her room again for the sketch-book, then opened the door to check in the living room, instinctively wedging her foot against the frame to prevent Dupaw from rock-eting past her and hiding under the bed, but of course, he wasn't there.

In the narrow hall, nothing greeted her but the quiet hum of the heater.

On a Sunday, Nora would normally be working on one of the multitude of projects she had going in her bedroom, or maybe meal-prepping for the week or fixing some part of the house. She didn't seem to have any recre-ational hobbies and never did things just for fun. Whenever she wasn't working, sewing some hole, fixing the sink, or spending time with Rebekah, she was staring into space with a glass of wine in her hands until she caught herself and went to find something to work on.

When Rebekah got to the main room, however, she saw Nora sitting at the dining table between the front door and the couch. Pale and staring, without the comfort of a drink. The only item on the table's surface was Rebekah's black-bound, repurposed note-sketchbook.

Nora had opened it to one of the pictures of the Raven. The shadow creature standing at the side of a laughing girl.

The sight of it clenched Rebekah's stomach, a rotting feeling at the back of her throat. She remembered having difficulty drawing the creature at first, thinking it was too tied up in hazy dream logic to make any sense, but the depiction on the table was uncomfortably accurate.

She'd drawn the thing so often over those—what, two weeks? Was that all?—that she'd gotten good at it. The Raven was almost as natural a subject at that point as Pluto, who she'd been drawing for years.

Nora's eyes were red.

"Mom?" Rebekah broke the silence.

Nora registered her for the first time. When she blinked, she released a few pent-up tears. Rebekah stood waiting, tense, unsure. The heater shut off automatically, casting an oppressive quiet over the house. Nora's gaze slipped down to the sketchbook again, something hollow and terrible in her eyes.

"I know I've never told you," Nora said, her voice quiet and trembling. "Even when I was drunk, I never told you. It's the only thing I've ever been certain of. Beka . . . Beka, where did you . . . how did you . . ."

She closed her eyes on a chorus of tears, and Rebekah scooched past the corner of the sofa to sit next to her, careful not to hit the bookshelf as she pulled a chair out from the table. She sat and twined her arm with Nora's; she'd used to do it a lot as a kid, but she hadn't done it for a long time.

Nora badly suppressed a sob and squeezed

Rebekah's other arm with her other hand, but when she opened her eyes, she looked at the sketchbook instead of her daughter.

She asked, "Did you see him?"

Rebekah didn't really know how to answer. She hadn't ever seen the Raven, not when she was awake anyway.

Wait, "him"?

Instead of answering, Rebekah asked, "Why? Who is that?"

Nora covered her mouth to suppress emotion that clearly threatened to overtake her. Rebekah offered as much comfort as she could, intuition telling her she was about to learn something that could never be taken back. As much as she wanted, needed, to know, she felt the urge to run.

Nora knew who the Raven was.

"Beka . . . ," Nora whispered. "That's your father."

Rebekah froze. Quiet cold filled her up, the silent panic prickling on her shoulders.

The Raven. A nightmare creature with no face, a soft voice, and gentle motions. A creature that had killed four people. She tried to reconcile it with the images she'd invented in her head, a lonely girl with hope in her heart: her father, a tall man in a polo shirt, a short man in a suit, a shadow waving goodbye, not knowing he wouldn't return.

She'd always known those men had never existed. Her real father was worse than her musings. But—to be the Raven? A literal nightmare?

No. It wasn't possible. Couldn't be possible. The Raven would have told her.

"You're old enough to know now, Beka. I . . . your father didn't walk out on us when you were a baby. The truth is, I don't know who your father is. I don't know his name."

Rebekah opened her mouth, but nothing came out. She tried to imagine the Raven and

Nora in the same room, but they were from two completely different worlds. The Raven wasn't real. It couldn't be.

"I was only a little older than you are now. I was walking alone, in the dark. Taking a short-cut along a hiking path through the woods. I was stupid, but . . . but that's no excuse for what he did."

The chill gripped Rebekah, colder and tighter, a hollow terror that blanked her mind. She thought she knew what Nora was about to say, but every cell in her body hoped she was wrong.

"He was stronger than me." Nora gazed at the sketchbook, into the round, white eyes of the Raven. "He was faster than me. He was . . . wearing all black, black boots, black gloves . . . sometimes I can still feel the leather fingers gripping my jaw. I tried to memorize his face, but it was all shadow, a black raincoat with the hood up hiding him. The only thing I saw was . . . was the way the light reflected from his glasses."

The sob finally tore from her mother's throat as she relived the past trauma. Rebekah tightened her grip.

Stagnant air weighed heavily in the messy room, the numb silence of lost breath. Sharp pain spiked out from Rebekah's hollow center, grasping her memories of the Raven—of her father—of Nora—and staining them all with a lightless terror.

She tried not to, but she imagined a young Nora walking alone on a dirt path, the Raven emerging from the shadows behind her, more creature than man. But it was a human thing that it did to her—that he did to her, forcing her to the ground—her mother screaming—

"Hey."

Rebekah blinked through what she realized were tears. Nora's eyes were red and puffy but filled with selflessness, the same selflessness that had always driven her.

Nora was a better person than Rebekah could ever be.

Rebekah had been absorbed in self-pity for years. Yeah, things were bad at school, but Nora had been *raped.* Her mother was the most hard-working, selfless person Rebekah had ever met. Rebekah got bullied and started killing people. Nora deserved so much better than that.

Nora hadn't even wanted her. Worse than a simple mistake, Rebekah had been born from violence. She'd been forced onto Nora, upending her whole life, forcing her to work every second of the day just to keep them both fed and off the streets.

"I'm sorry." Rebekah tightened her grip. She didn't know what else she could say. "I'm sorry. I'm sorry, Mom."

"Oh, Beka. Oh, honey, none of this is your fault." She kissed the top of Rebekah's head, Nora's tone fierce as she rocked her from side to side. "I love you, Beka. I love you so much."

"But how? If—"

"You don't ask me how I can love you, Beka." The admonishment was softened by the crack in her voice, a slight squeeze. "You're my daughter. I love you more than the whole world. Never ever doubt that."

"Never ever," Rebekah repeated, feeling five years old.

They held each other for several long, quiet moments, punctuated by sniffles, the comforting thud of a heartbeat under Rebekah's ear pressed against Nora's chest.

Eventually, Nora pulled back to look at her, cheeks starting to dry. A serious expression. "But how did you see him?" she whispered. "Where? Please, Beka."

Warm, steely arms. A soft voice whispered in her ear, fingers tight on her wrists. Alice begging for freedom.

Rebekah's voice stuck in her throat, hands tightening on her mother's arms. She couldn't explain. Nora would never believe her. But there was nothing Rebekah could say other than the truth.

What was the truth, anyway? Her father hadn't run out on them like Nora had told her. She'd been trying to protect Rebekah from the knowledge that her real father was a rapist. An evil, cruel stranger. A criminal, but far worse than that word implied.

That was the Raven. Not some creature of Rebekah's invention, a shadow she'd nicknamed herself. He was a person, a terrible person, or at least a shadow of one.

What if it was a demon all along? One she'd inherited somehow. Or . . .

No. She remembered its arms, the shape of its nose. The way its chest had puffed with breath while it carried her. The Raven was a real person.

"Beka?" her mom whispered. "You need to tell me if you saw him. Please."

Rebekah couldn't. She couldn't let Nora know her daughter, the only thing left in the world she truly loved, had become a murderer. She deserved so much better.

"No," she answered. "Not . . . um. Not physically. He was in a few of my dreams."

Nora let out a little gasp, and Rebekah flinched, only then realizing how it sounded. Gesturing to the sketchbook, she stammered, "I swear I . . . I didn't know—I thought I made it up—"

Nora pulled Rebekah close and wrapped her arms around her again, kissing her hair, leaning their heads together. "Beka, it's okay."

They rocked there together, holding one another, comforting one another. But Rebekah knew it wouldn't be okay until she figured out a real way to stop the Raven.

To stop her father.

26

Rebekah told Nora she was going out to tend the garden, despite the unrelenting, dense rain brought by the thick rolling clouds. Nora shouldn't have believed her. Or maybe she didn't believe her and just trusted that Rebekah needed to be alone.

After their conversation, Nora went for the wine. Rebekah knew—deep in her soul—that she shouldn't have left, that she should have insisted they stay together. But she didn't have time. The Raven needed to be stopped.

She grabbed her bag and started toward Mike's house, only to find his car missing from the driveway. His working on a Sunday was unusual, but maybe he'd gone off somewhere else, too. Maybe he was upset about waking up in the toolshed alone. She couldn't remember if he'd tried to stop her from leaving, but she'd basically confessed to him. Maybe he thought she was a killer and that she'd lied about everything.

Her steps faltered.

Or maybe the Raven had done something to him . . .

With a cold, fresh spike of fear, Rebekah fumbled for her phone and dialed Mike's number, standing in the middle of her lawn under the battering weight of the rainfall. The Raven had killed Alice—it had *killed Alice*—over the mere idea that she'd gotten close to the truth. Mike could report what she'd said to the police, and the Raven might see that as a threat.

Voicemail. She left a halting message, so devoid of information it sounded like a Mad Lib, and hung up. A moment later, she couldn't even remember if she'd left her name. It didn't matter. It wasn't like he didn't know who she was.

Mike was fine. She knew that, didn't she? She knew that for certain. The Raven had carried her over to the rotting chapel, carried her to her room, knowing she wouldn't go willingly. Maybe that meant that it—*he*—needed her presence in order to go through with its plans. Maybe he needed her to be in her bedroom, specifically. Which meant she'd know if Mike was one of his targets. Okay. That made sense. As much as anything did at that point.

So if Mike was at work, she could find him there. But—did she really want to walk into a police station with everything she'd done? She wouldn't be surprised if they could smell her guilt.

She should turn herself in. She knew she should. The certainty clawed at her, the darkness, the acrid pain. Images of her sprinting down the street, running from a perceived mob, screaming at the top of her lungs in a mad fever filled her mind. If she walked into a police station, she'd wind up tearing down the brick walls, ripping the heart out of the floorboards.

She wished she could see Alice, that she was still alive. She wanted to sit in the hot tub and talk about nothing, listen to her ramble about boys. The pain of her friend's loss struck hot and sharp, bright against the pelting rain, and her hand rushed to her mouth to suppress a fresh sob.

If the Raven needed Rebekah to be near her bedroom to do its work, then she needed to be as far away from it as possible.

Rebekah never biked for its own sake, but whenever she did pedal across the town, she found the steady movement comforting, similar to what she felt diving into her art. As she rode up the mountain, everything from the outside world melted away, leaving nothing but her, the bike, the rain, the road. The sounds of the chains, the clunky gearshift, the steady back-and-forth motion of her legs. Trees flew by, tall and varied, the fullness of evergreen interrupted by gray-limbed deciduous patches, branches gathering drops of rain into bunches before plunking them unsteadily on the dusty forest floor. The work of pedaling filled her up and pushed away the wordless grief settling heavily around her like a shroud.

The Lee house weathered the rain as well as it did the sun, its boards soaking up the drizzling water, transforming from old tan to deep brown in a cobbled-together approximation of what it might once have looked like. The ocean rolled darkly behind it, distant colorless waves chopping in the wind, framed by bowing cliffside trees.

And, in front of the house, resting on the

gravel driveway with the comfort of an old friend, sat a blue sedan.

Rebekah stopped, gaping at it, breathing hard after the long uphill ride. Mike was there. Alone, maybe. He'd ignored her call not because he was busy, but because he expressly didn't want to talk to her.

Should she leave?

Leaving was an option, but she'd already done that once. If he was there because of what she'd done, then leaving again would only make things worse.

And she was tired of running.

So she walked her bike around to the back door and hesitated. The moment she opened it, Mike would know she was there. As completely as the house muffled exterior sounds, the interior ones echoed, trapped in their decrepit shell.

She stood at the back door, in the shadows, droplets of rain snaking down her neck, and her mother's words struck her again. The Raven, a real person in a raincoat and glasses, attacking young Nora in the middle of the night. Nausea rolled through her in quivering waves, because it was the same Raven she'd embraced, played with as a child in the dreamlike house they'd invented together, that had taken her hand and promised her everything would be all right.

She'd trusted him.

Rebekah sank to the muddy ground, her back against the soggy wood of the Lee house's ragged back door, her strength gone. She'd put her life into the hands of a person she barely knew, never thinking he'd betray her. She should have seen it coming. Should have known the Raven wasn't an "it" but a creature of her own creation. Should never have insisted he was a part of her and could therefore do nothing wrong.

But he'd approached her when she was most vulnerable and taken advantage of her anger. He'd used her to get his fucking kicks, to torture and murder teenagers for—for what? Bullying?

She should have seen that. No matter what she was going through, she should have seen that.

Even knowing the Raven was a real person, someone using her for his own cruel ends, a part of her still wanted to trust him. He'd been so kind, so gentle, so caring—but he'd lied to her. He'd killed people. He'd *raped Nora.*

The door opened behind Rebekah, and she caught herself on the uneven wooden floor. She looked up, feeling heavy and sore, and shouldn't have been surprised to see Mike standing there in his half uniform. Staring at her. He was wearing his washed and repaired windbreaker. He looked as tired as she felt, hair messy from the rain and stubble on his jaw.

She couldn't read his expression from that angle, but it wasn't welcoming.

"Rebekah?" His voice rose above the roar of the rain. She was numb and drenched, sitting against the muddy ground and unforgiving wood.

Mike narrowed his gaze on her. "Where did you go last night? Why did you leave the shed alone?"

"Because what I told you is true." Her tired words were no match for the rainfall, but she thought he heard her. "Alice is dead, isn't she?" Her voice cracked sharply, bringing back the hollow pain that'd embraced her for hours that morning.

Mike stumbled back, paling, the boards beneath him groaning under his weight. "How did you know that?"

Rebekah climbed to her feet, soaked to the bone, leaning on her bike rather than the splintering wall of the Lee house. She met his eyes and saw a trace of fear there, sinking any hopes that things could go back to the way they had been.

"I know who it is," she said, ducking her head. "No—no, I don't know who it is. But I found out it isn't me. I . . . I really thought it was, for a while, and I don't know what that says about me, but . . . but the Raven isn't me. It's . . ."

The word caught in her throat. Mike stood there, silent, waiting for her to continue, looking frozen himself. She had to say it.

"It's my father." She swallowed, her mouth sandpaper dry. How could it be so dry when she was soaked to the bone? "The problem is, my mom and I don't know who that is."

"You don't know who your father is?" Mike's flat tone rang off the walls of the muted hall he'd stepped back into, disbelief etched into his features. "That doesn't make any sense, Rebekah. And if it—if it isn't you—how'd you know someone died last night? How'd you know it was Alice? No one knows yet except the family and the precinct."

Rebekah pulled her bike inside and shut the door. The wood croaked as Mike stepped back again, one hand at his empty hip as though reaching for his weapon.

She couldn't blame him under the circumstances.

"The . . . dream house I told you about," she said as calmly as she could, shivering in the drafty hall, "the Raven . . . it—he—brought me to where he had Alice tied up. I tried to make him stop, but he . . . he won't listen to me anymore. I don't know if he ever did or if our plans were just the same . . . in the beginning."

"Then—why did you come here? Were you looking for me?"

"No. I mean . . ." She wrung out her hair, droplets painting circles on the sagging wood. Mike stopped retreating, standing at the far end of the hall by the mostly dry foyer. "Well, yes, I tried to find you at your house, and then you didn't answer your phone, so I thought you were at work. I came here because I . . . I didn't want to be around anyone."

He huffed a dry laugh. "Then we have that in common."

She took a tentative step toward him. "Mike—"

Mike retreated farther into the foyer, one hand held up in warning. "Stop, Rebekah. What do you want from me? What are you looking for? An alibi? Are you going to turn yourself in?"

She took off her sodden jacket and draped it atop the bike. His words hurt, but she had no one to blame but herself. Of course he thought she did it. She'd thought the same thing.

And even if everything else could be written off, she *had* killed Scotty.

She stayed in place and tried again. "I'm trying to find out who the Raven is. Who my father is. Maybe then we can stop him. But we have no way of knowing his identity."

"Wait. Do you—I mean, if you believe this dream thing—if you want my help, I need some kind of proof. Because right now, Rebekah, you look guilty as hell. I want to believe you. I do. But what else can I think? You practically confessed last night. And there's no way you should know what happened to Alice or Eddie. Unless you were there."

"I know it sounds insane," she admitted, inching toward him. "But it really was all a dream. I don't know where Alice was found or what the real scene looked like or how poison gas can be made to look like an accident. I didn't know Scotty lost his tooth playing football either. I just knew he lost his tooth."

"Because you saw it in a dream?"

"Yes."

His voice was firm, desperate. "Proof, Rebekah. Tell me you have proof."

Rebekah paused, partway into the foyer. From there, she saw the mussed blanket, the wooden floor swept free of the dust where they'd had their picnics.

Did she have proof?

She blinked. "I . . . I don't know. Not exactly. All I know is everything's connected to this book somehow." She dug the Poe tome out of her backpack, her movements haphazard and half frantic. The book itself was wet from the rain soaking through the bag, but it was still legible. It hadn't been smart to take it with her, but she hadn't felt like she had a choice.

"More Poe?" Mike eyed the cover. "'The Raven.' You're kidding, right?"

She shook her head. "No. Look."

Rebekah strode toward him, startling him, but instead of heading to Mike, she crossed the foyer and sank down onto one of the fluffy blankets, pretending the fact he'd afforded her such a wide berth didn't bother her at all.

She opened the pages to somewhere in the middle because it didn't matter which story they read, exactly. It only mattered that they read from the book. She didn't know how she knew that, but she did.

The Raven had given her that book all those years ago. The only thing in her life that had seemed to come directly from the dreams, like Rebekah had dragged it with her into the real world, clutched in the arms of a young girl who didn't know any better.

"Come here." She didn't look up at him. "Please."

Mike hesitated. All around them the silence of the house echoed, drowning out all outside sound. Nothing but their breaths and the leak that dripped by the front door, staining an almost-perfectly-round shape into the wood, remained.

Then his footsteps creaked as he approached and sat, somewhat beside her, settling into the place where they'd once shared an improperly packaged cake, his body radiating a comforting warmth even at that distance.

She'd never done anything like that, but the knowledge, the certainty it would work, came from somewhere deep within her. Maybe the same place where she knew what the dreams were. Who the Raven was. What she did each night, whether she climbed out from her window, how she'd gotten her hands on the pliers and Veronica's hair.

Hands on the book, her intention sharp and clear, Rebekah felt a tendril of dreamy power. Reminiscent of the Raven's aura, it felt dark and empty, yet full of weight and possibilities, like ink poised above the surface of a blank page, a million-billion nothings aching for the chance to exist.

"Here." Rebekah stopped at the page labeled *The Fall of the House of Usher.* She read out loud, knowing Mike read the words with her over her shoulder, and the words glimmered with power, the calm purchase of art, of creation, filling her up, pushing the outside world away.

"'Shaking off from my spirit what must have been a dream, I scanned more narrowly the real aspect of the building. Its principal feature seemed to be that of an excessive antiquity. The discoloration of ages had been great. Minute fungi overspread the whole exterior, hanging in a fine tangled web-work from the eaves. Yet all this was apart from any extraordinary dilapidation . . .'"

27

The manor itself looked to be in perfect shape—perfectly intact, anyway—even while each stone crumbled and wooden plank rotted. As though the house had been left to age perfectly undisturbed by sun or wind, a drying-out sandcastle in a child's backyard. To see the whole of it was to sense a steadfast strength, a fortress still promising to endure centuries to come.

The sky crept above, a cleaner dark than Mike had ever seen. No clouds, no stars, nothing but a glaring moon and an endless black. In each direction stood an eternity of dry dirt and leafless trees, the suffocating muffles of a vindictive quiet. And the building that loomed over him . . . decaying and impenetrable, ramshackle and steadfast. Looking at it produced a twisting sensation that promised it both was and wasn't merely a dream.

Wait, hadn't he seen that place before?

Something tightened on his hand. He pulled away fast, startled—but it was Rebekah. She'd been trying to hold his hand. Nothing more.

He said her name, but his voice sounded distant, even to himself. Like he was standing in the middle of an empty plain. "Where the hell . . . what the . . . ?"

"This is the place I was talking about," she said quietly.

She looked . . . different. Like she belonged there. A ghost that flitted between the dead trees, a face that peered out from the windows. A second ago, in the Lee house—it felt so far away in Mike's memory, something he had to piece together to recall—she'd been drenched in the rain, muddy from her bike's backsplash. But there, in the dream, she was dry and clean, her hair loose around her face, and something empty in her eyes.

She reached out again, but he stumbled away. Hurt flashed across her face.

"What the hell," Mike repeated, as he tried to orient himself. But there was no orientation. He couldn't be convinced there was an up or down, let alone cause or effect. Even his watch had changed, its analog face blank.

He knew with complete certainty that that place didn't exist—and yet he was there.

"Mike." She spread her arms, placating. "Mike, I told you. This place . . . it gets under your skin. I need you to calm down—"

"Calm? How the hell can I be calm? You—you—you brought me here—I don't even know how I know—"

A creak split the air, cutting through the

silence like an axe through wood. It was the heavy front door swinging open.

Rebekah clutched Mike's hand and turned on her heel, yanking him into a sprint.

He stumbled after her as they slipped on the dust, running around a corner of the house where the gnarled forest broke for a dead garden—dry, scratching weeds grouped in sections and crumpled around one another. She pulled him down a path, away from the looming manor, toward an overgrown iron archway that only led into darker trees.

"Why are we running?" Mike called, but he thought he already knew the answer.

"The Raven," she answered, confirming his wild thoughts. "I didn't think—I should have realized—he might think I brought you here to kill you."

"Can't you tell him you didn't?"

"He won't listen to me!"

The moment the garden disappeared behind

them, Mike knew he was lost. The trees blocked the view of the dry weeds and the sagging manor with its gables pointing to a starless sky. Within moments, he was convinced that the empty husk of a forest stretched forever in every direction.

He could see himself running through those trees, lost and alone, chased down by the silence, by sourceless footsteps, searching desperately for some way to know his location, some method for finding north or south. Knowing even while he marked the trees as he passed that the effort was futile.

Mike felt—knew, somewhere deep in his stomach—that it would happen, that he would be lost forever if he didn't have Rebekah leading the way. She knew exactly where she was going because she was a part of that place. Just as much as the Raven was.

Rebekah pulled Mike around a bushel of limbs that reached straight out from a twisted trunk as though straining to wrap their wooden fingers around his arm. In less than a moment, the manor shuddered into his sight again. Had it suddenly struck upward from the dirt, or had it been waiting there all along, perfectly shielded by the nightmarish trees? Was there a difference?

He didn't know anything anymore. Couldn't rely on what he'd once known about the world, about what he saw. All he could do was hold on to Rebekah's hand and run.

They passed through a side entrance and their footsteps thundered over a threadbare rug. The heavy scent of dust smacked into them, mingling with that enduring whiff of rot that seemed to permeate the entirety of that strange world.

Rebekah stopped halfway down the hall, and Mike almost tripped over himself to keep from running into her. A curtain, rather than a door, covered the doorway she stared into. She pulled it open and nodded him through, glancing behind them. Mike ducked in without hesitation.

The room beyond could not possibly be inside a mansion. The wooden floor had a smooth concavity and it shifted beneath his feet as though the room's foundation had been replaced with a roiling, swelling sea. Lanterns hung from the curved ceiling, sweeping to and fro with the motion.

Rebekah shut the curtain behind them and pulled Mike stumbling after her, through a narrow doorway and into a closet-like room within a room that might have served as some kind of bunk on a ship. The only furniture was a hammock that swung, stained and limp, from one wall to the other, and a pile of upright barrels; and set into the wall opposite the doorway was a round porthole that made Mike freeze.

Beyond it was the sea. Gray in the moonlight, stretching inevitably to blend into the darkness long before reaching the horizon. No mansion or forest in sight.

"Hey," said Rebekah, among the creaks and groans of an entire ship. "You okay?"

"Am I okay?" he echoed, his voice a dry shadow of itself. "I—I don't know what the hell is happening. It's a dream, but—but it can't be a dream. But it can't be a real place either. I want to say it's a nightmare, but I know you're real. I know you're you, anyway—how the hell can I know that? What did you do to me?"

A mix of shock and hurt passed over her features before she covered it with a sad smile. Wrong. It was all wrong. Rebekah, a ghost in her own right, dressed in black, who seemed to belong to the walls of the mansion—the ship?— holding his hand. He looked down then, his skin flushed compared to hers, his blue police uniform vibrant against the muted tones of the world around them. She belonged there, and he didn't.

But . . . did she belong there, or had she simply been there so long that she'd allowed it to change her?

Footsteps creaked on the floor of the shifting room beyond. The sound made Rebekah tense, and she pulled Mike behind the pile of barrels. They crouched there together, and she kept his hand tight in hers.

Despite what she'd told him, her fear of the Raven seemed deep and sharp. The Raven—her *father*—was the true killer, not her. Maybe he'd roped her into believing in his grotesque crusade for a while, but the blood poured from his hands, not hers.

The Raven, perhaps knowing they were trapped in that corner or perhaps toying with them, glided slowly, soundlessly, from the doorway to the piled barrels. He rounded the corner and stood in their only exit, highlighted by the swinging lanterns and what moonlight leaked in from the porthole. Light glinted from his black hooded cloak—reflected white from inhuman eyes. Fresh adrenaline galvanized Mike's resolve, burned through his veins.

Real. It was all real. That place. That creature. All of it.

He believed her story. Every word.

Without a thought, he pushed himself in front of Rebekah and stood tall, his hand instinctively going for the empty holster on his belt as if he could rely on the phantom weapon there.

"No!" Rebekah shouted. "Not him. He's done nothing wrong."

The Raven tilted his head, and Mike felt an iron-hot fear because it made him look even less human than he already had. But it was Rebekah's father, wasn't it? It was a real person. A normal person. With a beating heart, like anyone else.

The Raven stepped forward, smooth and graceful, pinning them farther into their corner.

A faint stiffness forced itself around Mike, a

sudden chill, like standing bare in the heavy rain—and, like the invisible tugs of a spider-web, the nightmare tore away.

Mike and Rebekah woke up, gaping at one another, hands clasped tight, on the blanket in the uneven foyer of the Lee house.

Rebekah didn't know how she'd forced them awake, exactly. She hadn't done anything like it before, at least not when it came to the semi-real world of the Raven and its manor. Honestly, she wouldn't have been sure it was possible, at least not while the Raven was present.

But she'd used that power, the one allowing her to take Mike into the dream. She didn't feel it anymore, that ephemeral creative spirit. She'd only borrowed it from its true master.

If she'd used that power before, though, could she have stopped what had happened?

No, Mike and Rebekah were still in the

Lee house. They hadn't moved. Maybe she'd never actually snuck away from her house to begin with—but then, why was the window always open?

After all that time, she still had no idea.

Mike pulled his hand slowly out of hers. Pale, he scrambled to his feet and paced the length of the room without speaking a word.

Rebekah let him be, knowing what had happened was . . . insane to someone like him who hadn't grown up with it.

Her phone lit up with a notification. She opened it, then winced at the list of missed calls there, all from Nora. Seven in total, each with a voicemail waiting for review. She stuffed the phone in her pocket, leaving them unheard.

"Okay," Mike sighed eventually, his voice shaking. "Okay. That was . . . real, but . . . but it couldn't have been. There's no way it . . . No, it couldn't possibly be real. It was just a dream."

"We're awake now, Aren't we? You believe this is real."

His chuckle sounded harsh, incredulous. "Yeah. Yeah, I can tell we're awake now, but I feel like I shouldn't trust even that. Shit, Rebekah."

"I have some proof, then. I know what you dreamed about. We were together at the mansion. We ran through the forest, then I took you into a room like a ship on the ocean. Or . . . maybe it *was* on a ship on the ocean."

"Oh. Shit." Mike stopped in his tracks and blinked at her. "Yeah. Okay. That means . . . that means there's no way it couldn't be real. You know exactly what I dreamed about because you were there, too, weren't you? There's no other way you could know that." He nodded and his eyes tracked off into nowhere again. His voice was tight and breathless. "That helps. Thank you."

"No, thank you, Mike. Really."

He checked his watch and squinted at its

face. "We need to figure out who the Raven is. Who your father is."

"But that's impossible. My mom was the only witness, and she didn't see anything. There's no way to know."

"If we can track down where and when this happened . . ."

"It was eighteen years ago, Mike. How are we going to figure out who took a walk on a path in the middle of the night eighteen years ago?"

He started pacing again and ran one hand through his hair. "Damn it, there has to be a way. We can't let him get away with this."

Silence settled again as they thought.

The Raven was her biological father. Desperately, her brain put the Raven's silhouette into one of her dream images of her imaginary father, but it didn't fit. Even in her imagination, his eyes—his glasses—glinted white from the shadow of the cowl. The Raven couldn't look innocent. It was a murderer, a rapist, and even in her own rosy imaginings, it was a creature of nightmares.

He. He, he, he. A real, physical person. A human being who wasn't Rebekah.

A *fallible* human being.

She snapped out of her thoughts, not realizing how cold she was until she shifted and the cloud of warmth beneath her rain-damp blanket puffed away into the decrepit house. She met Mike's eyes and said, "If he's doing these things in person, he has to be somewhere in town."

Mike let out a harried breath. "Honestly, can we be sure he is doing these things in person, given the situation?"

"He must be. This book appeared in my room from nowhere. My window was left open; the pliers and Veronica's hair wound up in my bag. I thought I was doing it myself, but . . . I don't know anymore. We ran a long way just now. If we acted that out, shouldn't we both be off in the middle of the woods somewhere?"

"He chased us," Mike countered. "If he's doing this stuff in person, shouldn't he be in the room with us now?"

They both went quiet again, listening for fading footsteps or a third huff of breath. Would they have heard a car pulling away from the gravel driveway through their collective panic, through the weirdly soundproof makeup of the Lee house? Would they have heard footsteps on the noisy floorboards? But if there was some insane magic, if it wasn't physical at all, they couldn't stop it. Not from there. Not from reality.

Rebekah knew what she needed to do. An eerie calm flooded through her.

"There's only one other person who knows who the Raven is."

"Who?" Then it landed. "No. No, that's not a good idea."

"I've gotten it—him, to talk to me before. Despite all this, I think he still just wants to protect me. He likes me, in his twisted way. If he thinks I admire what he's doing for me, I think I can get him to talk."

"No." He closed the distance between them and clutched her arms. "Rebekah, it's too dangerous. We need to figure out how to stop him without you going to sleep again."

"How is that possible? If you can think of some way to do it, then please tell me. Because so far, I've got nothing. Neither do the police, or they'd have found him already."

The resignation on Mike's face was close enough to an answer. She took both his hands and moved a fraction closer so that their body heat warmed the space between them.

"I'm the only person who can figure this out."

"Rebekah, I know I'm not an experienced cop, but the one thing I know is that you can't trust a killer. If someone's gone deep enough to torture and murder even one person, then you can't understand their mind anymore. They've become something completely different than you or me. You can't predict what they'll do or whether they have a moral compass, let alone what's on it."

A sharp blade of regret bit into Rebekah's chest as she remembered how she'd felt standing over Scotty's coffin. Leaning her weight on the corner, watching him squirm in his chains, the weird power and vindication that had flooded through her when she'd kicked him into the water.

The Raven had killed Coralie, Eddie, and Alice, but Rebekah had killed Scotty.

She pulled away from Mike, replacing his warmth with stagnant rain-scented air between the walls.

"I can do it." She didn't meet his eyes for fear of what he'd see there. "I'm going to do it. This is . . . this is my mistake. My responsibility. I decide how to fix it."

Breathless, Rebekah hazarded a glance up at

him and found Mike watching her like she was some strange animal.

Like maybe he knew why she'd pulled away.

"Okay," he said at last. A release of breath as much as it was a word. "You're right. I . . . can't think of a better way. But I wish I could. You shouldn't have to put yourself in any more danger."

"Honestly, I don't think he'll hurt me. But he might hurt you. You're a cop, and you know the truth now. He killed . . ." Her voice stopped working. Rebekah shivered, hugged herself, and forced herself to finish. "He killed Alice for less."

Mike's eyes danced over her, his jaw tense like there was something he wanted to say. Maybe something he wanted to do. But he paced away instead, rubbing the back of his neck. When he turned to face her again, it was with a determined expression. "I'm staying with you. Not in the dream world, but here, by your side. I'll stay up to watch over you, to make sure you don't wander off and no one sneaks up while you're sleeping. Okay?"

She wasn't sure that would work or if it would keep him safe. None of the other targets had needed to be "read into" the dream the way she'd somehow done for Mike, but what if the Raven dragged him in anyway?

All the same, she couldn't bring herself to tell him no.

"Fine. But we should get back to my house," she said. "He wants me to be in my room. If he thinks I'm cooperating, he might let his guard down and come in through the window like he must have been doing all along."

"What, now you want to be bait?"

"If you ambush him from there, then we're done. We've got him."

Mike let out a long, wavering breath. "Shit. Okay. Let's do it. I just need to grab my belt first. Fuck. This is . . . this is insane, Rebekah. This is completely insane."

"I know."

He gave a tired chuckle. "I guess this is *Elm Street* after all."

28

The front room of Mike's house was, thankfully, dark when they arrived. Bill wasn't in the reading room for once. Mike parked in his driveway, and they stole across the lawn together through the sodden downpour, carefully watching the shadows through the front window for movement.

It wasn't too late, but Rebekah thought there was a chance Nora might be asleep already. Then again, would she have been able to sleep after blowing up Rebekah's phone like that? If she was worried about all the weird accidents and deaths, if she was worried about how Rebekah might take that horrible truth?

She started to call for Nora when they walked in because she wasn't in the living room, or sitting at the small round table, or occupying the square foot of the wraparound kitchen, but stopped herself. She might as well show Mike to her room before Nora saw them. Better to ask forgiveness than permission.

Oh, shit, her bedroom. Rebekah hadn't cleaned it in . . . a long time. Dirty clothes on the floor. Books and notepads askew.

Whatever. Too late. Besides, they had more important things going on.

She led Mike silently into the narrow off-white corridor and paused at her bedroom door, watching the other end of the hall where Nora's stood ajar.

She motioned into her own room and whispered, "Wait in there for me."

"Why?" he asked, matching her volume.

"I need to check on my mom. I'll be back in a sec."

He cast his own glance down the hall with a concerned look, like the Raven might be waiting in ambush. "If you need me, just shout."

Rebekah nodded, and he disappeared into her room.

She crept to Nora's door and pushed it open just wide enough to poke her head through.

Nora was asleep on top of the blankets and comforter, fully clothed, laying a touch too close to one side of the double bed.

Rebekah considered leaving but stepped through and pushed the door closed behind her, approaching the side of the bed Nora faced and kneeling.

Her mother was dead to the world, mouth hanging open, hair half-mussed and catching on her tear-stained cheeks. One of her hands drooped over the edge of her mattress, pointing clumsily to an empty bottle of wine on the floor.

"Mom," Rebekah whispered.

Only snores in response. Rebekah reached out—hesitated—shook her shoulder.

"Mom."

Nora blinked awake, taking a few moments to focus her eyes. When she did, she reached out and pulled Rebekah into a hug.

"I'm sorry, Mom. I didn't mean to make you worry."

"Shh, it's okay. It's okay. I'm glad you're safe, honey."

"I love you, Mom."

Nora held her a little tighter. "I love you so much, Beka."

Rebekah pulled away, but not before Nora stole a kiss from her cheek.

"If I don't . . ." Rebekah started.

Nora watched her, patient, half asleep, her runny mascara softened by her smile.

Rebekah squeezed her hand. "Nothing, Mom. Never mind. I love you."

"I love you, too, honey."

Rebekah stood again, and Nora was back asleep within moments. She didn't need to warn her mom about anything. It was going to be fine.

It had to work.

She slipped from the room and carefully shut the door, silent in the space of the hall. She entered her room and Mike stood from the desk chair, hands pressed flat against his hips, his feet planted on either side of a stack of scratch paper.

She winced. "Sorry about the room."

"No, you're fine. Mine's been worse."

Overtaken by an uncertain silence, Rebekah navigated to the bed and sat on the unmade sheets. She needed to fall asleep; that was the whole point in going there. But she was too awake, too nervous, leaning her chin on her hands, bouncing one leg on the floor.

"Hey." Mike crouched in front of her, meeting

her eyes. "You don't have to do this. We can find some other way."

"No, we can't. It's okay. I can do it." She took a long, deep breath then lay on her sheets and blankets without even taking off her shoes. Like mother like daughter, she thought wanly.

Rebekah stared at the ceiling and made herself relax, focusing on her breath, her shoulders, her face. She'd always loved her bedroom. That night was the first time she'd ever been, on some level, afraid to sleep there.

Without looking at him, Rebekah asked, "Why did you say you're not an experienced cop?"

A slight pause. "Rebekah, I don't think now's the best time—"

"I won't be able to fall asleep like this. I need to think about something else."

"Right. All right." When he sat, there was the familiar and annoying creak of her desk chair. It was reassuring. "Well . . . I graduated from the academy and everything, but I've only been on the force a year, and I don't really get along with anyone at the precinct, so I mainly get stuck doing all the crap jobs . . . I don't know. Even the other new guys look down on me."

She glanced over at him fiddling with one of the vibrant green erasers that had long ago been shaped like animals but had been worn away until they were just lumpy pebbles smeared with pencil lead.

Mike continued. "I don't know exactly why I can't really relate to anyone else there. People tend to specialize, you know. They're worse at stakeouts but better at paperwork, worse at taking statements but better at observation, that kind of thing. Up until I started working on this Grant High case, I didn't think I had anything I was better or worse at. Just average at it all. I want to get better, and I will, but it'll take time, you know? And it's just frustrating not being there yet. Like getting a C at everything I do."

"What's wrong with that? C is passing."

He let out a scoff. "Yeah. Passing. But I want to be A+." He picked up a torn piece of paper sitting amongst the mess at the table, studying it. "Is this a doodle?"

"What is it?"

He showed it to her: a sketch of Pluto stretching from months ago. She'd completely forgotten about it.

Rebekah shrugged. "Just practicing cat stretches. It doesn't really count."

"It's good. You're good at art, Rebekah. This is just a practice sketch, but it's better than anything I can do," he admitted with a sigh. He replaced the paper meticulously like it belonged there. "I'm sick of being middling, I guess."

"But like you said, you'll get better. Just be patient."

He paused, rolling a pebble that had once

been an alligator between his fingers. "Patience isn't my strong suit."

Rebekah realized she could lie there talking to him for hours. She felt more comfortable with him than she had with . . . maybe anyone. He cared about her, and he'd known enough about her to take her to the Lee house on the first date. He knew everything about her—everything that mattered—and he was still there, being vulnerable with her. Being genuine with her.

"Hey." She yawned, drawing his gaze.

"Yeah?"

"I'm sorry I lied. This was all happening before we . . . well, reconnected. I knew what you were doing at my school when we first talked, and I pretended I didn't. I lied to you. I should have told you then. I should have trusted you."

He gave a soft, sad look, a shift of the stubbly beard he hadn't had time to shave. "Maybe.

Maybe not. If you'd told me the truth, I might've just brought you into the precinct."

"That might've been the right thing to do."

Their gazes met again, held for a slight moment before hers drifted shut. His expression lingered in her memory: his uncertain look, the turned-down corners of his mouth.

Yeah. It might've been the right thing to do.

Rebekah's first location on the property of the nightmare manor was rarely the same twice, except when she and the Raven had revisited the cistern and the study. Those had been repetitions: the same hallway, the same torture chamber.

That night, she was in the garden again. The dry, sharp weeds, the iron gate that looked out upon an endless, twisting forest. Just like last time, the Raven had Veronica on her knees, her hands bound behind her, hand clenched in her luscious hair. Without her beanie, Rebekah could see the bandage affixed to Veronica's scalp, the wound still healing. The silver moonlight washed out the green of her flannel pajamas as though threatened by the vibrant promise of life the color implied.

Still, calm, as though nothing had changed between them, the Raven hovered beside Veronica, its gleaming eyes locked onto Rebekah. Waiting for her permission.

Those weren't reflective animal eyes, she realized. They were eyeglasses caught in a glare. The Raven wasn't an unknowable creature. He was her birth father, a rapist. An evil man.

How did she know he wouldn't kill her? Had she made that up all along, desperate wishful thinking?

He proffered a knife, silently, the way he did before. Not *to* her, merely asking for permission.

Veronica gasped, her eyes squeezed shut, then let out a weak sob as she shook in her restraints.

Rebekah hadn't come up with a plan. She hadn't even thought to. "Dream about the Raven again and get him to identify himself," that'd been the start and end of it. How the hell had she thought she'd manage that?

She walked toward him and held her hand out for the knife.

The Raven tilted his head, maybe in surprise or confusion; with his features completely hidden, there was no way to know. But he did give her the blade.

When her fingers closed on the black handle, she had a wild thought: What if she attacked him? What if she killed him?

But he was faster and stronger than she was. He'd kept up with Hector, had overpowered Scotty. There was no way she'd manage to land any blows unless she surprised him from behind, and she doubted even that was possible, not inside the dream.

Rebekah lowered the knife to her side and looked up into the Raven's featureless white eyes.

She tried to say it calmly, or as calmly as she could, knowing what she did then—how he'd traumatized Nora. But she wanted the answer for herself, for her mom.

"Who are you?" she asked.

He didn't answer. He stood, waiting, holding Veronica in place, knowing he had the advantage of time. If there was such a thing in that place.

Rebekah took a step back, closed her eyes, and took a deep breath. That place belonged to her. She used to think the Raven himself belonged to her, too. After all, he needed her for his schemes, didn't he? Needed her in her bedroom, needed her presence. Maybe her power over that place was stronger than his. She tightened her grip on the knife and opened her eyes again, steeling herself.

The Raven tilted his head the other way.

"I'm not asking." She forced her uneasiness aside. She needed full confidence, whether real or fake. "Tell me who you are."

Veronica opened her eyes and glanced between them, wary. She didn't wear a muzzle, but she didn't dare speak.

The Raven took a slow step forward, but Rebekah held her ground. Proximity was meaningless, anyway. If Hector's chase through the woods was any indication, physics and physical prowess meant nothing there. That place was a dream, and confidence should be the ultimate power.

Right?

"I am not a person," said the Raven in his calm voice.

"You're lying. I know you're my father." Her voice cracked on the last word. Then she set her jaw and stared into those inhuman eyes, telling herself it was only a mask that he wore in the dream. He was real somewhere, as real as she was.

The Raven tilted his head again and whispered, "Then why the anger? I'm looking out for you, Beka. That is what fathers do."

His acknowledgment shot through her, churning in her stomach. She'd had a faint remaining hope that Nora was mistaken or that the Raven was a nightmare creature created by the two of them, but that last hope vanished on his cold breath.

"You're not a real father. You never cared about me." Her words came out on a wave of truth, driven by the cold tendrils in her chest squeezing her gut. "Whatever magic this is, it only works because of me. You're just using me because you have some sick drive to murder people."

His voice drifted on that same calm, unfettered whisper. "I didn't murder Scotty Trucco."

Rebekah's breath caught. The sheer quiet of the garden broke for the scuffle of dust as she stumbled back, catching herself on numb legs.

The Raven stood in judgment, a black statue made of shadow and glimmering light.

He breathed. Rebekah knew that he breathed, had felt it when he'd carried her from the tool-shed. He wanted to convince her that he was an immutable, inhuman spirit, but he was far from that. He was alive somewhere. He was fallible. He had to be.

She heard a distant splash and saw the shape of Scotty's coffin disappearing into the water. Legs trembling and throat constricted, she dropped the knife.

Scotty was dead because of her.

The Raven bent and picked up the blade.

"No!"

Energized by desperation, Rebekah hurled herself at the Raven, knocking them both to the ground. She tore the knife from his hand

and threw it, and it vanished into the forest, disappearing on the whistling winds. Then the Raven clutched her and rolled her underneath him, pinning her to the dirt.

He was stronger. Damn it. She'd known that.

"You can't kill anyone else." She stared defiantly into his inhuman eyes that bore into her. She tried to see past them to his face, knowing they were only dream-influenced eyeglasses, but whatever glare shone from them never seemed to subside.

"I can't?" he asked in his eerie calm voice.

"No. I won't let you. I know you need me."

"You think you know what's best, Beka, but you're only a child. When you grow older, you'll see I'm protecting you."

"I don't want you to protect me. Not if this is how you do it!"

"Beka—"

"And stop calling me that, you slimy fucking rapist!"

The Raven stilled, the wind stilling with him as the whistles subsided to silence. Veronica had pushed herself away from them, back toward the cold iron gate, but she stilled, too.

"I can see you won't cooperate." For the first time, she heard anger in his voice, sharp vitriol biting through the false calm. He leaned in, his hold on her arms tightening. "You'll see, Beka. Once this story reaches its conclusion, you'll see I'm doing it for you."

He stood in a flash, pulling her sharply up and after him with a vise-like grip, leading her away from Veronica with long, swift steps toward a barred door that hadn't been there before and the manor beyond.

"No!" She struggled, stumbling, trying to dig her heels into the scratching weeds. "Damn it! At least tell me who you are!"

The hall beyond the door opened into some basement level, cold and dark with a smell of mold and stagnant water. Like the cistern. For a moment all she could see was Scotty in his box, struggling against his chains as she kicked him into the water.

If she'd once felt embraced by the dilapidated walls, she currently felt compressed, as if the manor was a great throat clenching to swallow her. Her once-play-place turned hostile. She'd been wrong all that time; it wasn't her dreamscape, it was the Raven's.

Rebekah stumbled and fell, skidding her knees against cobblestone, but the Raven dragged her to her feet again and tossed her forward into a dark-black nook in the wall.

She slipped and caught herself on the damp floor of a dim recess, surrounded on three sides with dark stone brick coated in some sort of mucus. It must have been a type of mold, but it put Rebekah in mind of a stomach, the wet, acidic walls holding a distant, dwindling light.

The opening he'd shoved her through was

smaller than before. When her eyes finally adjusted to the dark, she saw the movements: bricks, mortared quickly but carefully atop one another, the movements of black-gloved hands entrapping her in the narrow nook.

"Wait!" She scrambled to her feet, slipping on the mystery substance that dripped from the walls onto the floor, thrusting her hand through the opening. "Wait, please! Don't you need me?"

The Raven shoved her back. She hit the wall behind her, launched forward, and pressed against the new wall, but it was as though it had already been in place for years. Solid, dusty, and slowly moistening until she couldn't differentiate between it and the other walls except for one horizontal opening.

"Don't kill Veronica!" she shouted. "Please! Leave her alone! If you don't care about her, at least think about her father, what it would do to him!"

The Raven hesitated before sliding the final brick in place. Rebekah felt a pinprick of hope. He peered in at her, one reflective eye, like she was a specimen in an aquarium searching for a way up the sheer glass walls.

"Embrace this," he said in his smooth voice. "And you will be free."

"What?"

He placed the final brick, and the light winked out.

"No!" Rebekah slammed her fists against the wall, shoved at it with her shoulder, but it may as well have been a slab of granite. Everything was perfect darkness; sheer silence but for her panting breath, her racing heart, in a space not nearly wide enough to stretch her arms.

Her panic fizzled, caught in her throat. Veronica. The Raven would kill her. But didn't he need Rebekah to do it? Or had he always just wanted her there?

He didn't need her, and that place didn't belong to her. She'd only been a guest all along. The Raven had never been her creature, and that dreamscape had never been her nightmare.

It was nothing but a trap.

Veronica. There had to be a way to save Veronica. Rebekah had saved Mike. She'd saved him by waking up.

Rebekah shut her eyes—as though it made any difference—and tried to wake up. But she didn't have the same power as before; she groped for it, searched for it, tried to recreate it. She pushed herself with as much confidence as she could muster; pinching herself; slapping herself; visualizing her bedroom; but when she opened her eyes, she saw only darkness.

She couldn't wake up.

No. No, that couldn't be how—that wasn't— no, no, that could not be how she—

Rebekah, hiccoughing in her trembling panic, pressed and pounded against the heavy bricks. But every wall was as old and set-in as every other wall; with a single turn-about she'd forgotten which one was new. They were all identical, perfectly square, a pitch-black arched rectangle with one worthless soul trapped inside.

She screamed, scratching at the moistened bricks, the mortar between them. "Come back! Leave Veronica alone! Please! Please, I—I didn't—she didn't do anything to me! She just laughed, she—okay, she took the videos, but that's all! And it doesn't matter! Please! Come back!"

Pain stabbed through her shredded fingertips. She snatched them away from the wall; she couldn't see it but felt a crack in one fingernail. She put it in her mouth, tasting blood. She cursed and pulled back from the wall she'd been wailing against, bumping against the other wall behind her.

No. There had to be some way out. There needed to be.

"Nora!" she called out. "Mom! Mike, you're supposed to be watching me! Mike! Can you hear me? Please!"

But her words reverberated off the cold brick and nothing more.

She sank to the floor, holding her injured finger close to her chest. There was no way to control the Raven. She'd been stupid for thinking there might be. Mike had told her it'd be dangerous, but she hadn't believed him. The Raven would never hurt her. He was a disgusting excuse for a human being, but he wouldn't hurt her. Everything he did, he did for her, right? She should be able to waltz up to him and demand that he stop, and he'd respect that. Right?

What a fucking idiot.

"Not like this," she muttered, shutting her eyes against the impenetrable darkness, squeezing herself against the cold. Why couldn't she wake up?

She couldn't see, couldn't move. Was that what it had been like for Scotty, wrapped in those chains? Eddie, strapped to that heavy table, the rain thundering beyond the narrow window? Coralie, watching the axe swing down toward her?

That was the Raven's world, and he'd consigned her to die in its walls.

No. No, that wasn't quite true. He'd said she'd be able to get out, eventually. Even in his cruel insanity, he wouldn't kill her. Was there a way to use that? Could she play against that?

The questions felt weak when she spoke them to herself. Trying to play against what she understood the Raven to be had gotten her there. Mike was right; there was no reasoning with whatever he was.

Even if she was one herself.

Maybe it was better that she be left there, in the small dark. Like the Raven had said, she'd earned it. It was what she deserved.

29

Mike should have brought something to do—literally anything—but he hadn't, and Rebekah was dead asleep. *Asleep. Just say asleep.*

He still sat at her desk, surrounded by scattered pencils and sheets of scratch paper, so he grabbed some and started doodling. The pictures were crap, of course, especially compared to the lifelike studies of stretching cats that littered the desk like castoff diamonds, but it was something to do with his hands. In a moment of inspiration, he grabbed one of her sketches and tried to trace it in the moonlight.

Mike fell into a trance, following her lines

with the pencil. Simple, repetitive motions, shapes and smooth textures that helped take away some of the tension. The moonlight was softer there than in Rebekah's nightmare, more like a comforting hand on the shoulder than descending blades. The darkness was kinder, too: familiar shadows that bowed to dim light.

How long was she supposed to take?

When Rebekah and Mike had woken from her insane dreamland together, he'd checked his watch immediately. What had felt like ten or fifteen panic-filled minutes in Rebekah's manor had turned out to be two hours.

But did that mean that everything went by slowly in that dream world? Or did time simply have no meaning at all?

He'd know if something happened to her. He would. If something happened to Rebekah, it would *happen* to her. Someone would break in, or she'd sleepwalk out of the room, or something.

So, her still being asleep was good.

Wasn't it?

Mike doodled some more, apprehensively checking his watch all too often. Watching the minutes tick by into hours.

That couldn't be right. She was supposed to confront her father and get information out of him, then wake up. That was her part of the plan. Unless they were sitting down together to go over a detailed list of incriminating information, something must have gone wrong.

Shit. She shouldn't have gone in alone. Even knowing she had power over or understanding of that hellish place, Mike should have gone with her.

He thought about the empty forest, stretching out forever, but trying to picture the trees themselves got him nowhere—the memory wafted away, like the impossible geometries of any dream. He remembered the terror, though, the absolute certainty he would have died out there if not for Rebekah's guidance.

Mike would be more than useless there. His gun might not work. He didn't even know if taking cover, as a concept, would function. He wouldn't be surprised if Rebekah's father could see through the walls.

Still. Damn it. There had to be something he could do.

There wasn't.

Dawn rose behind torrential cloud cover. Eventually, Mike realized the world itself had brightened enough to count as daylight. And Rebekah was still asleep.

He had refused to sleep. He'd almost dozed off once, but the idea of waking to find her gone again had terrified him awake. He'd instead spent the night thinking in circles, making lists of plans and ideas that didn't go anywhere, occasionally pacing through the obstacle course across the carpet. Once he'd even considered cleaning her room for her but worried she'd take it as an insult. It was just something to do with his hands, his time, anything other than worrying himself sick.

He had also berated himself for hours: for agreeing to the plan, for being unable to help, for not being able to think of anything better. His only solace was that the window had remained closed. Rebekah had said her window was open each morning the deaths or accidents had occurred. No one had come in while Mike's back was turned, and Rebekah herself was still there.

And somehow it was the next day, and she still wasn't awake.

A sharp and blaring three-note tone erupted from Mike's pocket and he leapt to his feet in anticipation—of what, who knew, really—but it was just his phone.

A call. Not Dempsey, but Detective Ash herself.

No. No, if Ash was calling, then—but Rebekah hadn't moved. Her window hadn't opened. No one could have died. He would have known if they had, right?

He answered the phone to cut off its repetitive tune, and only when he held it up to his ear did he recognize that it was probably a mistake.

"Hello?" he asked, eyes on Rebekah.

"Wilson. Veronica Bransby has been killed."

"Oh, God, no."

He hadn't meant to say that out loud.

Ash paused. "Officer Wilson, I understand that you're still relatively green, and I wouldn't normally put you in this position. But you're the only one who knows this case as well as I do, and we're flat out of time. Meet me at the hospital."

"That's not possible," he said, feeling airy and dazed. "She couldn't have—"

"I know you can handle this, Wilson." Her tone was kind but stern. "I'm guessing this situation is the worst thing you've ever dealt with firsthand. Maybe worse than anything you ever imagined encountering as a small-town cop. But you want to do the right thing, I know you do. You're smarter than half the people in this town. Snap out of it and meet me at the hospital before another kid gets killed."

He couldn't leave Rebekah. He'd promised.

It was past time for her to wake up anyway.

"Okay. Okay, I'm on my way."

"Thank you."

When he heard his phone's beep herald the end of the call, he tucked it away and crouched beside where Rebekah lay on her side, relaxed into what seemed like a peaceful slumber.

"Rebekah. Rebekah, wake up."

She didn't move.

He shook her shoulder. "Rebekah."

Nothing.

He jostled her harder. "Rebekah. Rebekah!"

He turned her onto her back, and her head rolled on her pillow. No response at all.

She couldn't wake up.

Shit. What could he do? He couldn't shoot that enemy, couldn't grapple dreams, punch nightmares in the face. His hands tensed on her shoulders, and he shook her hard enough to rattle her teeth. "Rebekah! Rebekah! Wake up!"

The door opened, and Mike spun to see Nora, mussed hair and smeared makeup, her eyes wide as she took stock of the room.

Mike stood and said, "I can explain—"

Nora raced to Rebekah's side and took her wrist, checking her pulse with one hand while patting her cheek with the other. She felt her forehead, snatched a dirty spoon from the floor, wiping it off on her shirt before holding it in front of her daughter's parted lips to make sure she was breathing.

"Beka?" she called, patting her cheek a bit harder. "Beka!"

Still no response.

Nora rounded on Mike. She was shorter than he, but she loomed over him and demanded, "What did you do? Did you drug her?"

"No! I didn't do anything!"

"What are you doing here?"

"Nothing! I—Rebekah asked me to—" To *what? He* couldn't tell her the truth. She'd never believe it. Hell, *he'd* never believe it—if he hadn't experienced it firsthand.

Nora's expression soured as she gave him a quick once-over, her gaze fiercely protective. "I'm calling an ambulance. Now. And you best get out of here, Michael Wilson, if you value your career as a cop at all."

His stomach twisted. "I know how this

looks, but I swear I didn't—" It wasn't a battle he'd win. Not then, anyway. "Look, I'm on my way to the hospital to meet Detective Ash right now anyway. I can drive you both—"

Nora slapped him, the bright smack loud as thunder in the quiet room, and it sent him reeling and tripping over dirty clothes and stuffed animals. Furious, Nora pointed to the door, placing herself directly between him and a still unresponsive Rebekah. "Get the fuck out of my house!"

He couldn't stay. He had a duty to his department and to Rebekah. Her mother was there. She was a nurse. She'd take care of her daughter. He went to the door, then stopped and looked back. "Please, whatever you do, don't let her out of your sight."

Then he ran for his car.

The hospital looked older than it was, with stone brick walls and a steep roofline. It could almost be mistaken for Grant High or for the mansion of a rich eccentric. Rows of austere windows were the only clue to the orderly layout inside, while the wooden doors, decorative steps, and attic gables struck a picturesque portrait against the ashy deciduous forest that surrounded it.

Detective Ash stood under the awning outside the main entrance, between the doors and the wheelchair ramp that had been installed like an afterthought at the edge of the front steps. Then she saw Mike approach at a half-jog through the rain, and she pushed away from where she leaned against the wall, her gaze expectant.

"Where is everyone?" he asked when he reached her, slightly out of breath.

"The other officers, you mean?" Ash led him inside the hospital. "They're at the crime scene."

"Then why aren't we—"

She cut him off, holding up her notepad and pen in one hand. "There has been a death or accident every single night for the past week and a half. And we're going to solve this case before sundown to stop any more from happening."

Lines etched the corner of her mouth and dark smudges marred the skin beneath her eyes, a testament to her exhaustion. Mike doubted she'd slept any better than he had since the horror had started. "You and me?"

"Yes. You have good instincts and you're thorough, Wilson. I gave you a list of questions for the students, and you went above and beyond. You're new, but you've got the makings of a fine detective one day." She sighed and glanced sideways at him as they walked. "That, and there's almost nobody else. So, today's your big break. Come on, Officer. The victim and her family are inside."

His heart fluttered with hope. A big break

was what he'd hoped for since graduating from the academy, just not that way. His smile was rueful as he followed her down the corridor toward the ER.

Principal Bransby looked hollow, narrow, and spindly, like his vigor had been drained out of him. He slouched in a plastic bucket seat in the ER lobby like a spider trying to hide in the corner of a cup, legs and arms splayed in awkward directions. At first, Mike couldn't see his eyes through the glare of his glasses, but when Ash said his name, Bransby moved slightly to reveal a gaze as lifeless as the trees outside.

"My wife can answer your questions," he mumbled, gesturing weakly to a nearby hall.

"Of course, sir," Ash said, full of decorum, as she turned and led Mike in the direction of the morgue.

When Mike moved to follow, however,

Bransby belatedly recognized him. He clutched his arm to stop him, increasing threefold in height as he straightened, his body reviving with some new emotion.

"Officer Mike Wilson," he said, eyes unwavering, full of intent.

"Yes?"

"You—you were with her. You're dating her, aren't you?"

Ice froze Mike's bloodstream, and he jerked his arm from the man's grip, doing his best to ignore Detective Ash's intent stare burning a hole through the back of his head.

"Mr. Bransby, I don't think—"

"Where is she?" Bransby persisted, his voice growing louder. "Right now, where is she?"

"Sir, please calm down."

The automatic emergency doors whooshed opened with a blast of cold air, along with a stretcher—with Rebekah's familiar sleeping face. Mike couldn't help but watch her pass by, his heart in his throat.

Bransby pushed past him then, but Nora—who raced alongside her daughter's stretcher with the EMTs—warded the man off with a glance. Whatever the man saw in her face stopped him cold.

Mike raised his hands defensively until they passed.

Bransby watched after Rebekah, devastated, his face devoid of color.

Ash stepped forward then as Rebekah and her mother disappeared into the busy ER. "Mr. Bransby. Can you please clarify your questions to Officer Wilson?"

"Veronica told me everything," he mumbled, tears sliding down his colorless cheeks. "She shook me awake in the middle of the night and told me that Rebekah had saved her life. She was speaking nonsense, of course, and I was afraid for her mental state."

Ash asked, notebook in hand, "Do you re-member exactly what she said?"

"She told me about the nightmares. That Rebekah was behind them—and that struck true for me, true enough that I kept listening—but then she said Rebekah was trying to stop it now."

Mike blinked, taking that in. "What do you mean, Rebekah saved her life?"

Bransby met his eyes, his anger replaced with grief and resignation. "Veronica said Rebekah had attacked the dream creature who threat-ened to kill her. She said the thing dragged Rebekah away. She said Rebekah was sure to be killed next."

Ash continued scribbling on her notepad while Mike's world rocked on its axis.

"I didn't believe her," Bransby choked out. "Of course I didn't, not for a moment. But she begged me not to leave her alone for the rest of the night. She's too old to make those demands, but—but this was different. It—" The man's voice grew small, as if he still didn't believe what he was saying. "Like the world itself bowed around Veronica as she described what had happened to her. I thought it was exhaustion— it felt like exhaustion. It felt like falling asleep reading, the way the characters and images mix up in your head. The man who—" He clenched his eyes shut. "The man who killed my daughter isn't real. He killed her. I felt him kill her. I—I felt him snap her neck." His voice cracked. "That moment will haunt me for the rest of my life. But when I opened my eyes, he was gone. They were both gone. She had fallen from our balcony—two rooms away—without me noticing at all. He has Rebekah. She tried to save my daughter, and now he has her. Don't let him kill her, too! Don't let him kill any more of our children!"

"I won't, Mr. Bransby."

He shook Mike with a steely grip. "Promise me!"

"I swear. I'll find Rebekah."

"Before nightfall!"

"Before nightfall."

Bransby dropped his arms like they'd developed leaden weights. The intensity of his gaze gave way to a grave exhaustion once more. "Thank you. Thank you. I'm sorry. I need to be with my wife now."

He trod away, leaving Mike with Ash, who crossed her arms, looking puzzled.

"Do you believe him?" she asked.

If he told her the truth, he knew he could be fired, but the Raven had Rebekah. Nothing else mattered. If he could convince Ash of the truth, they could work together to find her.

"I . . . to tell you the truth, Detective, I already understood it to be something like that. So, yes, I believe him."

She gave him a speculative look. "Do you have any proof?"

"No physical evidence. The only proof I have is that it happened to me, too. I experienced it myself."

She lifted her chin. "Explain."

Ash was shockingly open to the idea of magical Poe dreams. She gave no indication whatsoever that she believed him, but after they moved to a private patch of plastic chairs and he told her everything he knew, her frank acceptance of the situation made him feel comfortable enough to tell her the things that really *should* get him fired: his relationship with Rebekah, and how he'd omitted her from his reports.

"I know that already," Ash said when he'd finished, surprising him again.

Mike froze. "I, uh—what?"

"Rebekah was a very obvious hole in your

notes, and anyone could see she had motive. But I had personally verified that it was physically impossible for her to be the culprit, so I wrote it off."

"It—you wrote off me falsifying my reports?"

An emotion he couldn't place flickered through her gaze. Understanding, maybe, or acceptance. Whatever it was, it made him feel a tad better about everything. "For the time being, yes. You didn't want anyone to know you were dating a suspect. She wasn't a suspect, so I didn't consider the relationship important to the case."

"But she *was* a suspect. She's literally the culprit—technically. At least the gateway."

"If what you say is true."

"You're the one who said we need to move as fast as possible!" He gestured vaguely toward where they'd taken Rebekah. "If you don't believe me, why are you taking the time to ask me all these questions?"

Unfazed by his outburst, she said, "More information is always better. Whether or not that information is true is important, but not always paramount."

So she didn't believe him.

"Look, I'm going to find out who the Raven is," he told her, fist clenched against the arm of the uncomfortable seat. "I'm going to stop him, and no one else is going to die. You can help if you want."

"Slow down, Wilson." For the first time, she seemed to feel the exhaustion manifest in her eyes. "I've been over the facts a dozen times. These deaths *are* accidents. Even the accidents were accidents. Only one of them was a lie: Scotty Trucco didn't lose his tooth playing football with Hector, he'd lost it by walking into a door. Hector agreed to . . ."

Her voice faded, along with the bright lights of the hospital and the feeling of his weight in the chair. Mike nodded sharply awake, blinking.

"... and will predictably continue to happen until something changes." Ash peered at him. "You need a coffee?"

"No." Weakness rolled through him. Exhaustion, but not exactly. More like a comfortable, warm blanket, almost like ... like falling asleep to a book. Shit.

"I'll get you a coffee," said Ash. "I need one myself."

He grasped her arm, stopping her as she turned away.

"No, it's not that. It's the Raven." His pulse stuttered. He wasn't sure how he knew, but he did. It was the middle of the day, not the middle of the night, but Mike knew in his soul he was right. "I need you to go to Rebekah now, Detective Ash. Please—it's impossible for us to find the Raven without ... her ..."

Then reality dissolved as darkness pooled around him, the promise of comfort, of weightlessness. Sleep, pressing in where it wasn't wanted. Vaguely, he registered Detective Ash shaking him as he slumped in his seat.

"Officer Wilson," she said with genuine concern. "Mike?"

"If we can find out who . . . the Raven . . ." he managed to mumble before the darkness pulled him under completely.

30

The pitch blackness was a still and silent creature itself, crouching, watching, salivating with puffs of stale breath, too large and formless to capture with the eye. It was a predator that chased and captured its prey between immemorial claws, impossible to keep at bay except with its equally amorphous opposite. But light could only be conjured and didn't live naturally in the deep places that darkness called its home.

Rebekah felt crushed under its weightless enormity, suspending time and life in equal measure. Her only touchstone was the cold, moist brick of her narrow enclosure, the two walls pressing in from the corner into which she'd pushed herself.

That was her punishment. For killing Scotty. For mutilating Veronica and Eddie, for torturing Hector and Andrea. For thinking that anything those kids had ever done could justify what she'd done to them in return.

She'd been angry. Frustrated. Jealous. Everything in her life had been truncated just because of her mother's unfortunate situation, just because her father had walked out . . . had been a rapist.

It was he who had started it all. It was because of him that Nora spent her nights with a drink in her hand. It was because of him that Rebekah knew the twisting manor, that Scotty's tooth had been ripped out of his skull, that Coralie had been cut in half, that Veronica's hair had been torn from her scalp.

Whatever the Raven was—whatever fucked-up human being had attacked Nora eighteen years ago—nothing would change him. He wouldn't apologize, and she wouldn't believe him if he did.

She needed to stop her father.

Rebekah shut her eyes and felt the walls with some greater sense, the part of her that knew intimately into what shape the manor had twisted itself. The place would not respond to her, would not bend to her requests, but she could feel the dimensions of her enclosure and the sprawling impossibilities of the dreamscape beyond.

Her father was . . . nowhere. At least, she couldn't sense the familiar presence of the Raven anywhere within the shifting nightmare. Was she unable to know where he was? Or had he . . . woken up?

Leaving her there alone?

She hadn't known that was possible. It couldn't be possible. She tried to will herself awake again, but her eyes opened to the same darkness, the heavy scent of rot, wet dust, tinged with distant sulfur.

She'd done it before. She knew how that power felt. The ready energy of creation, the spark of artistic passion. She had to bring what she wanted to life. That's how the Raven worked. She'd bet on it. He considered himself an artist, bringing to life the reality he envisioned. She reached out, straining, searching for that power again.

The last time she'd conjured it, Rebekah had held the book in her hands. She'd been preparing to dream, to bring Mike in with her.

It clicked. She knew exactly where to find it. The power sparkled, invisible in her hands, like bated breath. She couldn't use it to wake up, but she could bring someone else in with her. That felt intimately familiar; she'd used it before. *She* had used it, more than once, to direct the Raven to her latest target. Without even realizing it.

Now her target was the Raven himself.

Rebekah threw the power out of the dream, out into the world. She needed the one person who could understand, the person who could help her defeat the Raven.

She reached past the walls, beyond herself, straining desperately beyond the confines of her tomb, and called Mike's name with her mind.

Darkness. Twisting, pulling, tugging at his arms, creeping at his back. It wasn't the pleasant, languid shadows of Rebekah's bedroom. No. It was the vicious dark of the Raven's nightmare, knowing, volatile, black claws swiping at Mike's feet.

When he opened his eyes again, he stood in an intersection of two hallways, four identical paths stretching out from him. He turned to examine them, but even in a set of four, they blurred in his vision, exchanging places. They weren't all identical—one hall was bare, groaning wood; another flashed with ornate decor, golden filigree shimmering in the thick rug; the third was lit by a torch, or lantern, or moonlight; and the last stretched into darkness. But whenever he turned from one to another, they danced before him, swapping places.

He was standing still, and already he was lost.

Where was the Raven? Hadn't he pulled Mike in, ready to sweep every threat off the table? Was he sitting somewhere nearby, or somewhere far above, laughing at an already-checkmated game of cat and mouse?

But Rebekah was there, too. Somewhere.

"Rebekah!" he called. Could she hear him? He needed her to, because he couldn't take a single step without her guidance. "Rebekah!"

He prickled with a fear that his call would be heard by the wrong person. But what else could he do?

Then he heard something, an echo of an echo, but it faded sharply.

"Rebekah!" he repeated, listening.

The flicker of a torch. The groan of the manor against a distant gale as though it struggled to keep itself in one piece. A quiet moan that could have been planks of wood bowing beneath a footstep.

And a voice. Distant and muffled.

"Mike!"

His name floated toward him along the ornate passage. He blinked and the hall bared itself, the light flashing from flickering fire to smooth moonlight. Was it a trick? Was that still the right direction?

"Mike!"

It was a ghost's voice, a soulful call. But, yes, it came from that direction. Before he could rethink himself, Mike sprinted toward it.

Shadows nipped at his heels, the moonlight extinguishing as he passed. He began to wonder whether the darkness itself chased him, and what it might do if it caught up.

"Rebekah!"

The dust throttled his voice, pulling back on it like reins on a misbehaving horse. But she was still calling out for him regardless. So perhaps she could still hear him . . .

"Mike!"

It was louder. Closer.

He sped up, following the voice blindly around turns, down a flight of unnatural stairs suspended in an endless darkness, and plunged into a stony cold basement, the sulfur scent swept away by that of acrid algae.

"Mike!"

Yes. It was her voice that time rather than a haunting memory. Muffled still. He followed it, and the lamplights flickered after him, shapes twisting against the wall in a battle of light and shadow.

"Mike, are you there?"

He stopped, cocking his head. The voice was clearer than before but still muffled.

"Rebekah?"

"I'm trapped!"

It was so close it sounded like it was coming from within his head.

"I can't find you!"

"I'm bricked in!"

He didn't know what that meant. "Bricked in?"

Then it hit him. There. Beside him. An archway that had been closed in.

"Rebekah!" He rushed to the wall, pushing against it, testing its strength. "What happened? Are you hurt?"

"Mike! Thank God, it worked!"

"What worked?"

"I'll explain in a second—just push!"

The wall was solid stone. He needed more than muscle to bring it down. Mike searched for some tool he could use to break through, but the basement was nothing but empty stone and rotting wood, a corpseless catacomb. A waiting tomb. Besides, whatever the place was, it wasn't real. He couldn't be sure a sledgehammer would even work there, no matter how he wielded it.

"Damn it. I need tools."

"Just push!" she called again. "We can do it. We can break it together."

"How the hell can you know that?"

"This place works on confidence—just do it! Trust that it'll work, and it'll work!"

Trust was difficult with her after everything that had happened, but he was out of options. So, despite it all, he did.

Mike shoved against the wall, straining, putting everything he had into dislodging the mortared brick. He imagined Rebekah doing the same, both pushing uselessly from opposite directions, propping up the wall if nothing else—but, no, it had to work.

It could work. It *would* work.

Suddenly, the bricks shifted under his hand, mortar started grinding to dust.

They doubled down on their efforts, panting, sweating, and then there was a moment of renewed vigor, and in a moment, the wall collapsed, bricks falling away like the flaring of a dancer's skirt. Tumbling stone crashed to the cold, wet floor, echoing distantly down the smooth walls. If the Raven hadn't known Mike was there before, he would then.

Rebekah stood inside a small alcove, the interior of it gleaming with sweat and slime, an exhausted smile on her lips.

He pulled her into a hug.

"Thank you so much," she whispered, wrapping her arms around him tighter. "Thank you for finding me. I know you didn't want to come here."

"I wasn't going to leave you here." He pulled away, searching her somber green eyes. "But why did you need me? If it's all about confidence, you could have done this yourself."

She tilted her head slightly. "No, I couldn't. I needed you to bolster me. I knew that. I don't know how. I just did. Part of me understands how this place works; I just have to listen to it."

"Then do you know how to stop him?"

Rebekah braced, chewing the inside of her cheek, searching her mind, her hands tense on his arms. "This is his place. He has the power here. But that means this place is a part of him. It's modeled after Poe stories, but it has parts of him, too. There will be a clue here, I know it. We just have to find it. Right now."

"No way. He brought me here. He could be anywhere. Fuck, he could be watching us right now, Rebekah. You can get us out, can't you?"

She finally pulled away from him with a sheepish grin that looked ghoulish on her dreamlike pallor. "Um, I'm the one who pulled you in."

"Wait—*what?* You can do that?"

"I think I've been doing it the whole time." She winced. "At least part of the time. But what matters right now is we're alone. He's awake. We need to act now, before he brings someone else in."

"That sounds really dangerous. What if he comes back?"

Rebekah met his eyes and straightened her spine. There was a certainty shining through her, more brilliant than anything he'd seen from her before, and again he found himself caught up in her orbit. In that moment, she was strong, vibrant, and true—inspiring in her ferocity.

Deep in his heart, Mike knew then that their slow dance in the pulp factory hadn't been fake. Their relationship hadn't been meaningless. What he felt for Rebekah was real, thrumming through him, aching in his chest.

There was no one else like her.

"We can do it," she said, fire illuminated in her eyes. "We will stop him. We have to."

If the nightmare bowed to confidence, then Rebekah could be its queen.

"We will," he said, and felt the heat of her fire in his veins.

Rebekah led Mike on a journey through the unnerving corridors: some long and narrow, some tall and bright with malevolent moonlight. She ducked through doorways and careened around corners with the grace of a cat who knew the ins and outs of its home; she didn't have Mike by the hand then, so he did his best to keep pace, feeling like an awkward dog with lumbering feet. He moved as much to catch and keep up with her as to stay at the fore of those clawing shadows that nipped at his heels.

It was like Rebekah was a spotlight that

chased away the shadows, and he needed desperately to stay inside her aura.

They explored the mansion with a pattern that felt too random to be thorough, but on the other hand, it might not be possible to explore a nothing-place like that with any sort of logical system. So they searched dry, dusty attics, forgotten bedrooms, and moldy kitchens. The macabre details blurred in Mike's head, blending into a complexity of geometries that would set Escher reeling.

Hallways broke into rooms that branched off into more hallways, windows with crooked views of the endless forest opened to reveal plain walls behind them. The impossibilities canceled each other, created each other, and Mike began to despair that there was anything to be found at all aside from shadows and dust.

Rebekah finally stopped in her tracks beside a wide grand staircase and inspected the panel of a wall, tracing her finger over a small knot in the wood and, with expert motions, cracked open a secret door to reveal a low, narrow tunnel.

He shouldn't have been surprised, given the sprawling manor around him, but all the same, in all their searching—had it been hours? Days? Minutes?—they hadn't yet encountered anything similar.

Rebekah crept into the crawlspace and held out her hand to him. Mike hesitated, his chest tight from memories of fake raccoons in his father's library. He tried to make a joke of it but stopped himself. For all he knew, talking about them would conjure something far worse.

"Where are we going?" he asked instead, stooping to follow her into the passage.

The door slammed behind them and he jumped, knocking his head on the ceiling. He'd explored every nook of that nightmare, but still, a fresh rush of terror raced through him.

"I've been here before," Rebekah said, seemingly to reassure him. "I mean—I know that doesn't make any sense in this place, but—follow me."

The passageway grew smaller as she crawled on hands and knees into the dark, Mike right behind her, doing his best to ignore the hot bile burning the back of his throat. She seemed unaware of the groaning wood beneath them, the distant whistling of the wind through a hollow, the skittering of insects churning inside the walls, an invisible swarm tracking their progress.

Finally, the passage opened into what once must have been an office—covered floor to ceiling in sullen faces with glimmering eyes and grimacing teeth. Taxidermy animals filled every corner of the space, prey mounted on the walls, predators laid out as rugs on the floor. The nearest lamp glowed from within the grasp of a stuffed serpent, bearing its fangs in an expression as much of sorrow as pain.

"Here," said Rebekah, with a note of surprise. "It's this way. Follow me."

She led him, not through the sole doorway, but into the disused fireplace. She pushed aside a few bricks and crawled through yet another passage, narrower than the first, and he followed, clinging to her aura.

Mike wasn't claustrophobic. At least he never had been before, but the Raven's nightmare world could change all that. As he slithered through the suffocating space, he had the insane feeling that Rebekah was a ghost, as natural to that place as the Raven himself, and that Mike was the only thing there with a beating heart. Instead of superior or alive or thankful, it only made him feel vulnerable.

Rebekah found a hole in the wall, broken planks of rotting wood reaching from each direction with jagged claws as if about to close again. She snapped a few off to widen the opening, climbed through to the other side, bedraggled and streaked with spots of ash and dust, and then offered her hand to help Mike.

Once he was on his feet, he looked around the space. The ironwork crosshatches of a glass dome sliced into the sheer moonlight. Motes of dust suspended in the breathless air. A decaying painting hung over a fireplace that looked like it hadn't seen a blaze in epochs. A few armchairs faced a window. And one thick desk centered on one wall, ornate with cloven feet, its top empty. Rebekah's hand lingered over a rectangular spot on its surface, free of dust or age.

"It's exactly how I remember it," she whispered.

"What is this place?" Mike asked, his voice low as he processed everything.

More than any other room in the impossible nightmare—more than the endless forest, with roots and branches that twisted around limbs; more than the cold, dark basement, like a waiting tomb; more than the brittle garden with sharp, dry weeds jutting like spears from a rotting battleground; more than any of the dozens or hundreds of haunting rooms he'd scoured that night, fearing the Raven might turn his eye on them at any moment—that empty library got under his skin.

There was something deeply wrong there.

"This is where I found the Poe book," she told him. "And . . . I think this room reflects him the most. Maybe that's why I never see him here. Because if I ever saw him in this room, I'd be able to see his face under his hood."

Mike faced the desk, bathed in icy moonlight. He glanced at the window, which stretched across one wall, looking out on the dying grass, the desperate trees, the empty bookshelves stretching wall to wall. Three armchairs, each a different type.

Sickening pressure built in his chest, weighted in his gut. He couldn't move, but he needed to see the rest.

Slowly, he forced himself to turn around.

The marble-brick fireplace, cold and empty

from disuse. The mounted head of a coyote, gaping with sharpened jaws.

He stumbled back, dizzy, lightheaded. Time stopped, and he gasped, choking on the thick air, the knowledge of the truth. The library felt wrong because that manor was foreign, a nightmare place, but that room had been intimately familiar from the very first.

"What is it?" Rebekah stepped close, apprehension in her eyes.

"It's . . . It's the reading room." His voice was little more than an echo, and it felt like someone else was speaking, like he was haunting himself. "It's my . . . It's *our* reading room, in my house, but bigger and without any of the books. That's my chair." He pointed a shaking finger at one armchair, taller than one of the others but the same shape. "And that's my mom's. And that . . ."

The final one had something resting on its

moonlit cushion. A skull, on its side, like it'd been tossed there.

Rebekah gazed around herself then, placing it. Unable to move, he watched her land on the conclusion.

"Oh, my God, Mike. The Raven—" She hesitated. "My father. He's . . ."

Mike's voice broke. "He's my dad."

31

Rebekah wished there was some way to disprove it, some clue that would point wildly in another direction, but instinctively she knew Mike was right.

The Raven was Mike's father, Bill. He'd been next door all the time, stalking her mother, keeping tabs on her, all while raising another family.

All while raising Mike.

She suddenly saw Mike in an entirely different way, his black hair, the shape of his jaw half-hidden by his beard. She remembered kissing him there, at the corner, below his ear. He looked like her.

"You're my brother." She hadn't even been aware she was going to speak.

Helockedstunnedeyesonhers."Half-brother."

They hung there, maybe thinking the same thing, a lingering static moment.

"No," Mike said, breathless, unable to accept the truth. "I'm wrong. It's not possible. The Raven can't be my dad."

"Mike." She reached out for him, but he pulled away. "Mike, someone will die tonight if we don't stop him."

"My dad—*my dad?* He can't do anything! He's got tenure, but he barely works, he never contributes to the house, he flat-out ignores everything my mom says—all he does is read and read and read! He's kind, he's book-smart, he's incompetent, he's just not capable of—of whatever the fuck this is!"

Rebekah felt a pinch of his pain, remembering the compassionate way Mr. Wilson had treated her when Dupaw had been killed. How he'd seemed to see her for who she was. The only adult to make her feel like she was understood.

Coralie had died that night.

The manor shuddered to life around them. Its shadows deepened, its windows glared, its ivy gripped the walls with desperate purchase. A moment previous, the manor had been creeping and dark, but quiet, like a half-open eye; that eye had opened, and it loomed with every bit of its familiar intensity.

"He's here," Rebekah said.

The terror was stark in Mike's eyes. "It can't be time already."

Rebekah listened to the manor, feeling it. Since she'd experienced the difference, it was obvious. The Raven breathed some kind of life into that place. It wasn't life, exactly, but it was vigor, and it responded naturally to his presence.

"He brought someone with him. I don't know who, but he's going to kill them, I know he is."

Mike nodded, still not looking at her.

"Someone's going to die." He shook his head like panic was something he could just banish the way a dog shook off water. "Fuck. Okay. How do we find him?"

Instinct and certainty. No time for second-guessing. Rebekah held out her hand and Mike took it, grounding himself with a long, shaky breath.

"He has a gravity here," Rebekah explained. "That's how I was always able to find him when I dreamed about this place, back when I thought . . . Never mind. Just close your eyes and try to feel for him, like you're leaning downslope."

"I—I doubt it'll work for me, Rebekah. You're a part of this place, but I'm a stranger here. I'm nobody."

"It'll work." She met his gaze, squeezing his hand. "You can do it. Say it."

He hesitated, blinking at her, seeing something in her, but she had no idea what.

"Okay," he said at last. "I can do it."

She nodded. "Come on. We can still get there in time."

Of course she didn't know that. There was no way she could know that. But she needed it to be true.

He shut his eyes, and so did she.

As familiar as it was, that place was—at its core—a nightmare. An alien brush along the spine, a haunting feeling of being watched, studied, followed. The monster peering out from the darkness, the ghost reaching in from the doorway. It was familiar places with unfamiliar meanings, the warmth of comfort tainted by the cool touch of despair.

It was into that lingering panic that Mike and Rebekah immersed themselves, reaching into the fog of unknown places, their eyes shut and their senses expanding. That place was impossible. And so were they.

The calls and moans and rattles of the aged house, the innumerable scratches of insect legs against the surface of stone and rotting wood, swirled together into a thick mucus of sound. It clung to the walls, smoothing the corners, shrouding the dim light, drifting, making rivulets as it slipped along the floor.

Moving as much by thought as by form, they followed the river of shadows out of the great manor, sunk their feet into the muddy embankment of the dead garden, where fallow weeds bent to their own weight. Even the moonlight seemed to refract from some distant point, out in the endless forest; slivers of white cut through the trees and illuminated stark paths between trunks and tangling branches. One of them shimmered brighter than the rest; they followed the beam.

The light came not from the sky but from inside a small cabin, shining vibrantly through boxy windows. It was a dark place, forgotten, cobwebbed—but they knew who was inside.

Rebekah tugged on Mike's hand, and they opened their eyes. They'd moved from the library to the forest, but the brilliant beam of stolen moonlight was gone, lost to the swirling shadows of the impossible river. If they were in a dream, then what had that been?

"He's in there," Mike whispered, watching the unassuming little room.

The shack. Alone in the woods, a narrow wooden door, like an outpost sinking into the soft earth. Rebekah had been carried away from there, the memory warped by a terrible guilt; when she and Mike had tried to stay awake, had failed at preventing Alice's death, the Raven had carried her away from that isolated shack.

She gazed ahead at the door. "Your toolshed."

Mike turned to her. "What?"

"Your toolshed. That's where he is."

"Are you kidding me? That's not possible. I'd have known if he—"

"That's where he is, Mike. I'm certain of it. You need to go find him."

"But—wait—wait, wait, this is my *dad* we're talking about." His breaths quickened, eyes wild. "Sure, he's in love with Poe, I guess—but *this?* He's just a professor, Rebekah! Most of his thoughts revolve around literary theory! He can't be—he—he can't be—" He stumbled back from the tiny cabin, hand grasping a tree trunk, bark crumbling to the ground. "No. No, no, no."

"People have died!"

Rebekah hadn't meant to shout. Mike was in shock. He needed a soft hand, one of Nora's enveloping hugs. But every moment they wasted was another moment the Raven might add a fresh body to his pile.

She tried again, quieter. "There's a killer on

the loose, and we're the only people who can stop him. You're a police officer. This is what you're trained to do, Mike."

He froze.

"I'm sorry your dad is a murderer and a rapist. Mine is, too. But if we go right now, we can stop him before he does anything else. You have to go out into the real world and find him. Stop him. I'm useless out there, but if I stay here, I can distract him and buy you some time. It's the only way."

Mike breathed for a moment, looking from her to the shack. "What if it's empty?"

"It isn't. He's there, Mike."

He ran both hands through his hair and stood for a long moment. When he turned back to Rebekah, his eyes were dark with primal fear, but his voice was steady. "Okay. Okay, I . . . okay. Be careful, Rebekah. Please."

"You, too."

They hesitated, a protracted moment where gazes locked, knowing something else should be said but neither certain of the words.

Then Mike woke up.

Rebekah stood alone in the silent forest, accompanied neither by the shuffles of animals in the underbrush nor by the ruffles of wind through leaves. It was the still, dry air of a crypt, traced through with a floating scent of rot, as though the land itself had one foot in its grave.

She whispered, "I know you're there, Mr. Wilson."

The silence bowed toward her as she stepped forward, feet sinking into the plush soil. The doorknob turned unevenly, catching on rust and age.

Then the door swung open to release a flood of glittering light.

32

The shack door released a burst of laughter, music, and the clinking of glasses; the room beyond glimmered with dazzling light and brilliant color, paneled with wood painted blue.

Far bigger than the shack in the woods that encompassed it, the space was decorated with brightly clothed guests with vibrant masks and small tables covered in colorful cloths, laden with multi-hued candles. Thick, tied-back curtains framed a wide archway at the end of the room. Backlit stained glass cast disjointed azure light across the mass of faceless people who mingled and laughed and murmured to one another over the music, all dressed in impossibly extravagant gowns and suits, unmarred by the limitations of physics, with masks that spiked and curled and flared out from their faces.

Had Mr. Wilson hidden in there on purpose?

Rebekah shut the door behind her and knew without looking back that it vanished into the wall. A stage stretched along the edge of the room where faceless musicians whose upbeat notes mingled discordantly with those leaking in from elsewhere; she climbed it for a vantage point from which she could see what she'd already come to expect.

Beyond the archway at the end of the room was a similarly extravagant chamber displayed in vibrant purple, and on the far side of that room stood a forest green archway, and behind that, bright orange—the rooms linked in a long chain, each one bedecked floor-to-ceiling in their respective colors, like a rainbow displayed in layered depth.

The last room, barely visible at the end of the chain, would be empty and black, its backlit stained-glass windows dripping scarlet on the velvet floor and monochrome tapestries.

That was where the Raven would be.

Rebekah leapt from the stage and tried to rush down the long, multicolored center but found herself abruptly lost among the small tables, the folds of cloth, the convoluted masks betraying eyeless faces. The partiers all stood taller than Rebekah, laughing and babbling, and their flamboyant, spectacular costumes crowded around her until the only way she could discern the room she was in was through a glimpse of the intricate mural on the ceiling.

Damn. Her plan wasn't going to work. She needed to reach the Raven quickly—despite what she'd told Mike, before it was too late for his new victim. She had no idea how long the kill would take. They could already be dead, or it could be within moments. The only way to be sure was to get there as quickly as possible, which couldn't include swimming against the convoluted current of flaring skirts and corded shoulders.

She felt the eyeless gazes of the guests closest to her, featureless faces given form by the colorful and individual masks. They observed her, the nearest ones taking notice before the rest, a rippling of fabric and ghostly visages swirling out from Rebekah's epicenter, spreading a hush that allowed the music to sweep in full: a rapid heartbeat of a rhythm that sent electronic thumps through her chest.

Then they laughed.

Their masks glared with the lights of mechanical eyes, and the growing laughter replaced the music; it rose into a chant, two words long, roared in a language that didn't exist. But it wasn't hard to guess what they were saying.

Piss Bitch.

The chorus speared through Rebekah all

over again. She couldn't move; made of something other than herself, she stood fast, held in
place by the weight of their stares. Their words
haunted her, attacked her—the stench, the hot
energy of sprinting down endless sidewalks—

Mike's kind worry, the way he'd reached out
for her, pulled her into a hug when she was
drenched in urine. Mike. Her half-brother. Oh,
God—oh, God, the way she'd treated him—

Confidence. Rebekah needed confidence.
That was how the nightmare worked. She needed to *know* they didn't care about her—*know*
she could make it there in time—*know* the
guests would part before her like fish avoiding a shark.

Their bodies shook with their laughter. Some
pointed. Some swirled their drinks. Some held
up little colorful boxes, facsimiles of smart-
phones with glaring cameras.

The place wasn't real. It was a dream, and they
were only ideas of people, puppets at best. But

they were everywhere, standing tall, pressing in around her. Laughing like pointed attacks, tearing with hooked knives at her heart.

People had died. Another life was on the line right then.

Let them laugh.

Rebekah pushed the tension off of her. A weight clawed for purchase as it fell, descending as she straightened. The crowd, pairs of hollow eyes, chanting "piss bitch" in their made-up language—but when Rebekah walked forward, they parted for her.

Their laughter quieted as they edged out of her way, the chanting dying off like wisps of disturbed smoke. The music that had used to fill the multicolored hall gave way to a dead silence, emphasized by the voiceless stares of the crowd. The sight of it gave her a creeping, unnameable feeling, their eyes, their deference; something sweet but crusted with sharp guilt.

It was that then-familiar sensation of power. The ambrosia of being feared.

Rebekah embraced it, knowing it would feed off of itself in that nightmare, knowing that the more powerful she felt, the more power she'd have.

She sliced through the crowd like a knife through whipped cream, then ran, then sprinted, her eyes on the single patch of shadow standing at the end of the parade of light. She'd run in that nightmare world before, fleeing the Raven, whether as a game of catch or as prey, but then, the colors swimming and parting around her, she was, herself, the shadow.

The hunter descending.

Mike woke slowly, sluggishly, his eyes adjusting to the glare of incandescent lights.

". . . sense," said a voice said over the scratching of a pen. "Not at any of the locations."

He blinked around him. He was in a hospital bed, a plastic chair at his side, Detective Ash talking to herself as she sorted pages of notes on her lap.

His dad wasn't there.

"I've eliminated every slight possibility that I've been able to think of, even the ones that aren't possible in the first place. I keep feeling like I'm on the verge of comprehending some perfect answer, but then it just vanishes like—"

He caught her eye, and she froze, then leapt to her feet. "Officer Wilson!"

"Where's my father?" he croaked, his throat parched. "He's at home, isn't he?"

"Are you feeling all right? Should I call a nurse? Let me call a nurse." She pushed a button by his bed.

Mike spotted his clothes in a neat little stack nearby and started to sit up. "I have to go."

"No. You should at least stay long enough for the—"

"I know who it is." Mike fumbled out of bed, his movements wobbly, and slid into his pants. He tugged off his hospital gown and put on his shirt, leaving it half unbuttoned for the time being, snatched his windbreaker, slipped into his shoes, and made for the door. He only paused long enough to look at Ash and say, "The Raven is my father."

Before she could react, he ducked around an approaching nurse and sprinted for the exit.

Forest green gave way to bright orange. Orange gave way to pristine white. White gave way to deep indigo, indigo to inky black.

Rebekah stopped in the archway, a shadow against the room of shadows. The room was empty but for two countenances, one contorted in fear and one unreadable but for the glimmer of two white eyes, both shapes illuminated by shattered red light.

Andrea, the last of Coralie's trio, strained against her leather gag. She looked exhausted, a haunting hollowness in her gaze that lit up into a fresh fear when she saw Rebekah, her shirt taut across her shoulders, her arms tied behind her. The tip of a long, narrow sword rested against her chest.

The Raven stood beside her, one arm out between them, his fist extending the hilt of the sword toward Rebekah. He held it still, watching her. He'd been waiting for her.

It was the Raven, as it always had been. Even though she knew the truth, it was difficult to see kindly Mr. Wilson beneath that wraithlike shape. A hood with no face, an enveloping cloak that glimmered red in the light.

A grandfather clock loomed behind them both, ticking quietly.

"Let her go," said Rebekah, pushing that feeling of power ahead of her, the one she'd collected from the stares and bowed heads.

Andrea blinked in surprise. She turned her gaze to the Raven with a new, fervent hope.

"Take the sword," the Raven said in his calm voice, and for the first time, she recognized him from her childhood. From an eyebrow raised over reading glasses, a careless hand gesturing from across the lawn. "It's time to finish what you started."

No. He couldn't get to her anymore.

She accepted the sword. Andrea squeezed her eyes shut, but Rebekah held the weapon by her side. "I didn't start this. You did. You have no right to put it on me."

"This is of you. For you. Because of you. You can't fight this, Rebekah. You've already embraced it."

She thought of Scotty sinking below the water, but the Raven gestured grandly past her, behind her. Holding tightly to the sword, Rebekah looked over her shoulder.

Every room of the rainbow lined up behind

her, but they shared a floor of blood. The partiers in their extravagant gowns and elaborate masks all lay dead in her wake, slashed and slaughtered, slices of glittering fabric twisting through the scarlet floor like organs embroidered in a gruesome tapestry: no movement, no sound, only the ticks of a grandfather clock that stood behind Andrea.

The sword in Rebekah's hand, once clean, dripped with congealing blood. She dropped it, stumbling back; although the floor was plush velvet, there was a clatter like steel on wood.

"No. No, it wasn't me. I never wanted—"

"Don't lie to yourself, Beka," whispered the Raven. "Don't lie to me. To say you never wanted this? You are my daughter. You are of me. I know what you want."

"That doesn't mean anything. It doesn't mean anything."

"What is your plan? You're going to let them

get away with it? You're going to let them get away with all they've done?"

That was what had always hurt her the most, that they could get away with it. With everything.

That *he* could get away with everything.

Rebekah met his eyes, glimmering pinpricks of white light, knowing it was only a dream's twisted reimagining of round glasses.

She knew him. He wasn't some imaginary friend, or a demon, or an unknown piece of her heart. He was Mr. Wilson. Bill. Her neighbor, a professor who spent his time reading. Just a man. An acquaintance, a near-stranger who kept his true nature hidden from his family.

The white light dimmed from his eyes as she stared him down. The shadows bled away from his face, dark red light finding purchase on his cheeks and round nose, thick eyebrows and black-gray stubble.

He lowered his hood, and there he was. Bill Wilson. The monster who'd raped Nora.

The dark of night blinded Mike when he got outside, disorienting him, but he didn't have time. He sprinted through a downpour for his car, struggling to find his keys in the pocket of his windbreaker.

"I'll drive!" called Detective Ash, practically from beside him. She impatiently indicated a sleek muscle car. "You just woke up from a ten-hour coma. I'm not letting you drive anywhere, especially not in this rain."

"I need to get to my house as soon as possible. If you don't believe me—"

"Get in the car, Wilson. Don't worry, I know where you live."

They slid inside the vehicle and the car came to life with a roar.

* * *

"Bill Wilson," said Rebekah, and she saw his eyes behind those reading glasses, a flash of surprise. "You're lying. You don't care about me. You just know that if I blame myself for these murders, you'll be the one getting away with it." She took a few steps to the side, putting distance between them without leaving the too-quiet, velvet-draped room. Closer to where the sword had fallen. "If you really want me to find my own justice, you should know you're at the top of the list."

He tilted his head. It sent a wave of chills down her spine. She could see his face, but he was still the Raven. He moved the same way, like a shadow; the same strength gathered behind him. He still owned those walls, still ruled over that dream world.

But he wasn't omnipotent.

Mr. Wilson turned toward the wall behind

him, and Rebekah took the opportunity to pick up her sword again—holding it out before her, the bloody blade between them as he turned back and raised his own weapon.

Another sword, exactly as long and sharp as hers. Clean but stained red in the tainted light. He stood still and tall, chin raised in challenge, his blade poised beside hers.

In the Raven's quiet voice, he said, "I know your soul, Beka. It's the same as mine."

"Take my name out of your mouth!"

She clashed his blade away, flecks of dried blood from her sword speckling the black walls. She'd never held a sword in her life, but she swung the sharp point toward him, pressing her weight behind it. He blocked, parried, moving impossibly fast. She slashed at him again and again, each time earning only a clash of steel on steel, a spattering of dried red flakes.

Panting, Rebekah paused, and so did Mr.

Wilson, with the same calm expression he'd always held.

She felt hot beads of power, a numbing fury that focused her gaze. If that place worked off of confidence, then she would become a fireball, torching it to the ground. And there was nothing the Raven—her father—*that rapist* could do to hurt her.

With a scream, she attacked once more. He brought his sword up to defend again, but the power of her blow knocked it from his fingers. It flew toward Andrea, who braced for impact, but it impotently struck the side of the grandfather clock.

Rebekah shoved her father against the night-black wall, her bloody blade against his neck. His hood had slipped off, but his eyes were determined where they locked on hers.

She could do it. Kill him. There was more of that creative power rolling through her, stronger than before, piercing through to the heart of the nightmare, and she knew—like the inevitable conclusion to a story—that if she killed him there, then he would die.

An accident. Working in his toolshed in the middle of the night, beneath an ill-hung blade, glancing up to the rafters. She could see a round sawblade wiggling loose, glancing off the wooden supports and falling at an angle, directly toward his neck. She could almost sketch the lines of the accident, paint the boundaries of the death onto a blank page.

Beneath the red light, the blood along her blade pretended to be a pristine silver.

"Take it," Mr. Wilson urged in his own voice, a kind voice, the voice of her neighbor. The voice of a person. "It's your birthright, Beka. You're already a natural—you took someone into the dream all the way from wakefulness! I've never been able to do the like. Take it, and you'll be more powerful than I've ever been. I know you will. Nothing will stop you. No one will ever stand in your way."

Take it. The reins of the story, the power of the Raven. That was the power she felt around her, the dream itself pulsing like distilled music. If she killed him, she would become the Raven.

Powerful. Magical. Able to reach into people's dreams and manipulate them, control them, maim or kill whomever she wanted.

"Take it," he repeated, louder. "Take what's rightfully yours."

She refused to move. Shaking. Tears in her eyes.

"This is the end of the tale," he explained gently, watching her. "You have to decide whose blood will paint the epilogue. Stop her and come with me—or stop me and take the power for yourself. I love you either way, Rebekah. This is your story. Make the choice."

The sword against his throat, the round blade dangling from the toolshed wall. Andrea behind her, whose only crime had been laughter. Poetry ebbed through Rebekah like ocean waves, aching to crash to shore.

"No." She pulled away and lowered the sword. "No. You don't get this. You can't have me."

"This is all for you."

"No, this is all for you!" She trembled, his image swimming in her tears. "I was just a lonely girl desperate for someone to understand what she was going through. You manipulated me. You took advantage of my anger and my vulnerability, and you tried to turn me into you. You used me to validate yourself, to prop yourself up, to give yourself power. But now I know what you are, and I know exactly how to avoid it. I can see you, Bill Wilson. And you disgust me."

Rebekah dropped the sword again with a heavy exhalation. "But that's not my problem, is it? You're the one who has to live with yourself. I get to walk away and move on. I get to leave you behind and replace you with better things. I get to learn from this and become better. You have to go on knowing you're a monster, that both of your children despise you."

Anger flared in his eyes, deeper and wilder than she would have expected. He watched her for a moment, unmoving, his mouth twisted into an ugly sneer. "Michael has nothing to do with—"

Rebekah mustered every ounce of power she had left and launched at him again.

Mike sprinted from Ash's car and around the back of his house, through the rain, through the garden fence, slipping in the muddy yard but regaining his balance. The toolshed didn't look very much like the one in the forest, but nothing looked right in that nightmare, not even Rebekah.

The light was off. What if Rebekah was wrong? What if—

Mike tried to open the door, but it was locked. If his dad was in there, then he heard him. But at the same time, if he was in there, then there wasn't any other way out. He was trapped. Mike pounded on the door, shoved his weight on the handle, shouldered into it, but the lock remained sturdy.

"Open up!" he shouted. "Police!"

Ash shattered the door open with a single well-placed kick. He hadn't even heard her follow him.

And there he was. The Raven stood alone inside, wearing a black raincoat and black gloves, facing away from the door. No, not alone. There was something else in there, too. Something Mike couldn't see. A cloud of dampening thought. With a chill, he placed the feeling: it was the way he'd felt listening to Rebekah's reading in the pulp mill, lingering between dream and reality, an echo of the Raven's nightmare trying to emerge.

Blades of various tools gleamed from the ceiling in the uneven moonlight. They shone red, as if from an odd reflection; they hung silent, radiating malice, the stillness of a crouching predator. The dream itself came alive there, haunting the toolshed, the weapons, the Raven himself.

Mike stood powerless in the doorway, pelted by rain, beholding the eerie silence of the two shapes in front of him. He knew for a fact—how could he be so certain?—that even taking the Raven into custody would not prevent bloodshed. He'd walked in on whatever magic it was that caused those accidents to happen, but he wasn't magic himself. He was just a guy with handcuffs and a gun. Nothing he could do would divert the dream magic from twisting reality into itself.

"What the hell," Ash breathed, her gun drawn and pointed at his father.

Bill raised his arms, covered by his shiny raincoat and leather gloves; Rebekah grabbed them and yanked him away from the wall, twisted one arm behind him with a supernatural speed, and kicked off the wall to shove him face-first to the floor. She reached out with the Raven's power, out toward the real world—

—but so did he, dreams and darkness weaving around them like spineless tendrils, tying them to a point that didn't exist, a dream anchored in its own nothingness. Like a vampire, he sucked her power away, the control over reality that allowed the Raven to create accidents, to drag strangers into that null place as they slept. She felt it draining away like water through a sieve.

"You can't fight me, Rebekah," he said against

the black velvet floor. "You can't fight me without killing me."

"Maybe not by myself."

She flung her final handful of the Raven's power out into the real-world toolshed she sensed was there. A single tendril piercing through the veil between dream and wake, death and life; a leap of faith, an arm reaching out of a yawning chasm.

Mike caught it. She felt him tug as if on a cord.

"Go to hell, asshole!" she screamed, and shoved Bill out of the dream and into the toolshed, the force of it toppling her, rolling her flat onto her back.

He was gone.

Rebekah gaped at the velvet-shrouded ceiling. The dark tapestries, illuminated dimly by fragmented scarlet light. The swords lying on the floor, both bloody in the reddishness. The silence broken by the ticking clock and . . .

Andrea, gagged, bound at her wrists and ankles.

Rebekah scrambled to her feet and rushed to her side. There weren't any ties or bindings on the back of the muzzle, no locks on the chain around Andrea's arms and legs. Rebekah inhaled, closed her eyes, and pulled the gag free, breaking the shackles with no difficulty at all. When the other girl was free, she crouched before her and took her hands. "Andrea, I'm—I'm sorry—"

Andrea wrapped her arms around her, trembling. Rebekah held her tight, and they sat there for a few silent moments, finding comfort in their shared warmth.

With a sniffle, Andrea pulled back, searching Rebekah's face through her own tears. "Get me out of here. Please. Please help me! Before the clock strikes midnight!"

Rebekah glanced up at the clock, where the minute hand was steadily approaching the hour.

She nodded, held onto Andrea, and focused on waking up.

Mike stood unmoving. The Raven's back to him, Ash beside him. Rain thumping on the toolshed's roof.

The dream reached out for him.

Mike flinched by instinct. He knew he wasn't asleep, he knew he was awake, that he was in the real world. But the dream reached out, searching for him anyway, like the encompassing memory of a story. He nearly turned and ran, refusing to fall under the power of the Raven again—until he realized it was Rebekah on the other end.

Not for the first time, Mike put his life into her hands.

He caught the power she tossed him, held on to it like the end of a rope, and he pulled on it, not hesitating to wonder why or how, because

Rebekah had said the dreams worked on confidence, and Mike refused to fail.

There was a *crack,* inaudible but sharp, and with a gust of cold wind, the dreamlike power vanished entirely. He blinked, came alive like he was shaking off a daydream, and in the stark awareness of reality, the man in the black raincoat stumbled, off-balance.

Mike seized on the moment of vulnerability, attacking from behind, tackling his father to the wooden floor smeared with mud. He focused on getting the handcuffs on before letting himself glance up at the face.

That was his father's chin, pressed sideways against the floor. His stomach churned, a rolling nausea threatening to spill out.

"Michael."

The sound punched him in the chest. It was too familiar. Too many kindly reprimands came to mind, too many book suggestions, help with homework. Good-natured lectures about art, about poetry, about the soul of literature, a piercing moment of familiarity amidst the chaos—as though Mike had only interrupted a good book, not a murder scene. His hands started to sweat where they held onto the slick raincoat.

"Shut up," Mike demanded. "You're under arrest."

"This is ridiculous, Michael. I'm your father."

He said it so simply, so easily. Mike hauled him to his feet, cold with rainwater, hot with nerves.

Ash lowered her weapon and took quick stock of the situation before holstering her gun and stepping forward to read Bill Wilson his Miranda rights. "You have the right to remain silent. Everything you say can and will be used against you in a court of law."

Mike dragged his father out into the slippery mud, into the pelting rain.

"What exactly is it you think I've done?" his father asked.

"Kidnapping, assault, murder, rape, take your fucking pick." Mike couldn't stand to look at him anymore. He let go and let Ash took him from there.

The detective continued as if his father hadn't spoken. "You have the right to an attorney—"

"I've done nothing but what's best for your sister!" his father yelled over his shoulder. He twisted in Ash's grip to try and see Mike, but the detective shoved him forward, around the side of the house and toward the driveway, a firm hand on his shoulder. At least if Mike stayed there he wouldn't have to see his father's face again. He could keep tricking himself into thinking—just moments at a time, just long enough to stay functional—that it was only the mysterious Raven, and not his flesh and blood.

But then the Raven shouted back in his father's voice, "I know you love her as much as I do! Even before you knew she was family, you cared for her, and I know you love her more now that you know the truth."

"Shut up," he growled to himself. Enough. Then, before he knew what he was doing, Mike raced around the house to Ash's car. The back door was open, and his dad looked up as he ducked his head into the vehicle, meeting Mike's gaze.

Not the Raven. His dad's face. Kind eyes, reading glasses, thick eyebrows, round nose. Mike felt clammy, hot and sick, mouth running dry in the soaking rain.

"She's family, Michael," his father said, as smoothly and passionately as if he was giving a lecture. "There is no line too far to cross when it comes to the safety of your family. If I have the ability to help her, how could I hesitate to use it? If I have the ability to teach her, to provide her with a better life, how could I—"

"You fucking raped her mother!" Mike

screamed, unable to control his rage any longer. "You raped Nora. Then you moved in *next door* to her, and now you're murdering a bunch of fucking kids! Who the fuck are you?"

"I'm your father, Michael. I always have been, and I always will be."

Despite how the evening had gone, despite the handcuffs binding his wrists behind him, Bill Wilson seemed taller, bigger, more confident and certain than he ever had, staring at Mike over the top of his reading glasses with conceited patience.

He still thought he was right. He still thought he was blameless.

Ash finished shoving his father into the backseat and slammed the door, though Mike and his father continued to stare at each other through the window, illuminated by the dim reflection of a streetlight. Ash didn't say a word, just walked around her car and got behind the wheel. As she started the engine, Mike tried to wrap his head around what he finally understood to be truth: Professor Bill Wilson, a murderer, a rapist, the nightmare Raven. Not a demon, not a lie, not a story. Just one terrible person.

He turned and walked away, not looking back as Ash's car pulled onto the street.

33

A toolbox from the shed was logged into evidence. It was painted black with a red raven on it. It contained a wealth of odds and ends, some normal tools, some more questionable, and, most importantly, a few of them organic—including a lock of red hair and a lone canine tooth. The most damning evidence found for a case everyone was desperate to solve.

Rebekah forced herself to burn the Poe book. It was probably worth a fortune, and, regardless of everything, it felt like an integral piece of her life, something that defined her even more intimately than her art. But she needed to destroy it. She needed to know it wouldn't be able to hurt anyone else, either through her, the Raven, or anyone else he might be able to rope into his nightmare.

Rebekah tried to tell Nora the truth, but the words wouldn't come out, not yet. She thought maybe Nora understood anyway or had an inkling of an idea because she followed Bill Wilson's trial with a disgusted but dutiful regularity.

And, all of a sudden—just like that—life tried to go back to normal. The school hosted a memorial, and Bransby resigned from his position, but otherwise, it went on. They were supposed to get right back to it, like nothing had happened at all.

Mike and Rebekah met at the Lee house again. Not on purpose. They hadn't had much time to talk, what with him embroiled so deeply in his—their—father's case. All Rebekah knew was that one moment, she was leaning on her bicycle's handlebar, wondering why she'd gone out there, and the next, his car was rolling loudly into the overgrown gravel drive.

She gazed at the house as he got out, listening to the thud of his door closing and the crunch of his footsteps on the gravel. The Lee house was framed on either side by the vibrant forest, overhead by the blue sky. The clouds had opened up again, at least.

"Hey." Mike's voice.

"Hey."

There was a series of crunches as he rounded the hood of his car and leaned against it.

Rebekah glanced over at him then, noticing the bags under his eyes, the tightness of his crossed arms. Since they'd found out they were siblings, all the romance between them had evaporated like a breath on glass. Even thinking about the kisses they'd shared gave her a queasy feeling. It obviously wasn't a biological thing, or they wouldn't have been . . . attracted . . . in the first place; but it was real, whatever it was.

"Is it his fault?" Mike asked suddenly. "That we like this place?"

The Lee house, old planks and boarded-up windows, the overgrowth that crept up to the sagging front stoop. Its similarity to the Raven's manor was imperfect but still eerie.

"I don't know," Rebekah answered. "Maybe."

Mike smacked his hand against the hood of the car, an echoing bash that startled a murder of crows into flight from the trees nearby, before pacing across the shaggy, brown weeds.

"This isn't right," he growled. "We can only pin him for one murder. He doesn't have motive, and too many of them look like accidents. All he lacks is an alibi, but there's no evidence placing him at any of the scenes. He'll go to jail for twenty years tops, and then he'll be released on the world like nothing happened.

Fuck. What he did deserves life, without parole. I can't believe he's going to get away with this." He reached his car again and kicked a tire in frustration.

"Mike."

He turned toward her. "No. There has to be something we can do. Some way to connect him to the other murders. Or some other way to punish him ourselves. There has to be."

She placed one hand on his arm to get his attention.

He opened his mouth but paused when he saw her expression. "What?"

"That's exactly how I sounded when all this started." The words came out more quietly than she meant; they came out more truthfully than she meant. "That's what started all this. I couldn't let them get away with it. It wasn't fair. There had to be some way to punish them myself."

He shook his head. "No. This is different—"

"It isn't."

"He *murdered* people, Rebekah. He raped your mother. And they're going to let him. He lied to me, to my mom—he completely ruined your mom's life!"

"Hey," she snapped. "Don't say that. What he did was unforgivable, but my mom loves me."

Mike blanched. "I'm sorry, I didn't mean—"

"You need to let it go. You need to let *him* go. You're not going to change him, but if you hold on to that anger, you're going to let him change you. Trust me."

"Rebekah, I don't—"

"Trust me."

He slumped against his car. "I'll . . . I'll try. It'll take a while, but I'll try."

"Thank you." She nudged his shoulder with hers. "Hey. You can call me Beka if you want."

"I thought you hated that name."

"It's personal, that's all. I feel like it should only be used by people who actually know me."

He smiled, then winced. "Um, you know, about what happened between us—"

Rebekah tensed. "I was hoping you wouldn't mention that."

"Yeah, I—look, it's . . . weird, and I don't want to leave that as the bedrock for how we know each other. So, is it all right if we start over? Get to know each other again, as friends?"

"As siblings," she corrected him with an awkward laugh.

"Yeah. Siblings." He chuckled, too, and suddenly it was like a weight had been lifted. Like some barrier had been broken. They'd addressed it, laughed at it, and passed over it together, and ideally they could put it behind them.

"Yeah," she said. "I'd like that."

The moment broke with a chime from Rebekah's phone, and she checked her message, surprised.

She had thought Andrea would hate her,

blame her for everything, disappear from her life altogether, maybe move away to some town that wasn't full of terrible memories, like Hector had. But instead, she'd asked for Rebekah's number.

Her text just read,

hey, what's up?

Rebekah felt a small crack in her chest, and what flooded through her was something like relief, something she'd been holding back. For the first time, she felt like she could let go of everything. No more secrets, no more pretending, no more curling up inside herself.

It might be harder for her than some others, but Rebekah could do anything she wanted. She had a friend, a brother, a mom who cared about her. She could just be . . . herself, with them. She could just be herself without them, too, if she wanted to.

"Hey, you okay?" Mike asked.

Rebekah realized she was crying, hot tears cooling on her cheeks in the soft breeze. "Yeah. Yeah, sorry. It's nothing. I'm just . . ." She laughed. "I got a text."

Mike raised his eyebrows, confused, but when she opened her mouth to explain, she found herself saying, "Want to come hang out with me and Andrea?"

Mike blinked, then a surprised expression spread on his face. "Yeah. Sure. Want to put your bike in my car?"

"No, I'll meet you there." She mounted the bike and raised the kickstand. "I bet you can't beat me."

He didn't have time to respond before Rebekah spun around and set off down the grassy hill at full speed.

"Hey! No fair!" He called after her, but the trees were already whizzing by.

There, in the security of the lush green, she called out her laughter to the woods.

She was finally free.

EPILOGUE

Bill lay awake in the middle of the night.

His prison wasn't the romantic stone dungeon that ran rampant in literature. It was a sorry mess of metal and drywall, unhappy guards and pent-up prisoners, food that tasted like grease and spit.

At night, however, when there were no sounds but the snores and mutterings of distant murderers, no light but a shielded one in the corridor their night-vision cameras needed to work—and, occasionally, a sliver of moonlight that filtered through the grimy window— he almost felt free.

Without the book, it was more difficult to

find the place of his dreams, but not impossible. Without the book, it was more difficult to spy into the dreams of others, but not impossible. In the middle of the night, in the humid huffs of the inefficient air conditioning, anguish and frustration and horror roaming the corridors like a pack of wild dogs, he could reclaim the power they had tried to strip away from him.

He lay awake in the middle of the night, the power of the Raven at his feet, and dreamed about his children.

Other books by
DANI LAMIA

Scavenger Hunt
In a world of wealth and power, siblings
feuding over the estate of their recently
deceased father are sent on a scavenger hunt
with the family fortune as the prize. But
things turn deadly as long-buried secrets are
revealed and it becomes clear that only the
winner will survive.

666 Gable Way
When a young woman who has always
suppressed her disturbing psychic powers
finds herself faced with a hostile witches'
coven, she must embrace her power in order
to save her life.

Stay up to date
Follow Dani on Amazon & Goodreads

https://www.amazon.com/author/danilamia